UNDER EGYPT

A Novel of the Future

by

Douglas Menville

AND

Rae Odell

The Borgo Press
An Imprint of Wildside Press

MMVII

To all those who helped and encouraged us along the way.

Copyright © 2007 by Douglas Menville and Rae Odell

Grateful acknowledgment is made to the following publishers and organizations for permission to reprint copyrighted material:

Association for Research and Enlightenment (A.R.E.): The epigraph at the beginning of the book and other excerpts from the readings of Edgar Cayce quoted in the text are Copyright © 1971, 2007 by the Edgar Cayce Foundation.

Alfred A. Knopf, Inc.: Excerpt from "The Stones," by Sylvia Plath, from *The Colossus and Other Poems*. Copyright © 1960 by the Estate of Sylvia Plath. Copyright © 1981, 2007 by the Estate of Ted Hughes. Used by permission of the publisher.

Library of Congress Cataloging in Publication Data:

Menville, Douglas Alver.
    Under Egypt : a novel of the future / by Douglas Menville and Rae Odell.
    p. cm.
    ISBN 0-89370-838-0 (cloth). — ISBN 0-89370-938-7 (pbk.)
    I. Odell, Rae. II. Title.
PS3563.E58U6 2007
813'.54—dc 19
88-34592
CIP

FIRST EDITION

CONTENTS

PART ONE: THE PENTAD

PART TWO: THE MISSION

PART THREE: THE WEAPON

ACKNOWLEDGMENTS

This novel took more than twenty years to gestate, from its first nebulous concepts to final manuscript revision. During that time, which often seemed like a prison sentence, many people offered sorely needed encouragement, advice, assistance and inspiration. Some of them, sadly, are no longer with us; most, thankfully, still are. We would like to express our most sincere thanks to all who have given of their time, their wisdom and their kindness.

Once the novel was finished, many more years passed in an attempt to find it a home between covers. At long last, through the graciousness of Robert Reginald of Borgo Press and John Gregory Betancourt of Wildside Press, it has found that home.

Space prohibits a complete list of those who have helped us along the way, but the following people gave a full measure and often more: Judi Strom; the late Anita Diamant, the late Humphrey Evans III and Robert Withers, who as agents first said yes; Kenneth Skidmore and other kind members of the Association for Research and Enlightenment in Virginia Beach; the ever-present spirit of Edgar Cayce, whose psychic readings provided the inspiration for this story; Ron and Eve Honthaner, staunch friends for many decades; Jim and Alex Stinson; Ray Bradbury, for enduring friendship and encouragement; Nik Grant; Gene Hardy; Mike Ashley; Rosalie Copeland, my beloved wife; Brenda and Johnny Altieri, who suggested the not-yet-used pseudonym "Daniel Mudville"; Betsy Ashton; Eli Goodman; Ken Thies, for valuable aeronautical information; the late Mr. and Mrs. Raoul Louis Menville Jr., for great love and encouragement; Michael Haworth, who stayed up all night reading the manuscript; Barry Levin; and William Fix, for valuable criticism. Our gratitude to you all!

This in position lies,
as the sun rises from the waters,
the line of the shadow (or light)
falls between the paws of the Sphinx,
that was later set as the sentinel or guard,
and which may not be entered from the
connecting chambers from the Sphinx's paw
until the time has been fulfilled
when the changes must be active in
this sphere of man's experience.
Between, then, the Sphinx and the river.

—*Edgar Cayce Reading 378-16*
October 29, 1933

PART ONE

THE PENTAD

...somewhere in sands of the desert
A shape with lion body and the head of a man,
A gaze blank and pitiless as the sun,
Is moving its slow thighs...
　　　　—W. B. Yeats, "THE SECOND COMING"

CHAPTER ONE

THE SPHINX AND THE FLAME

GIZA PLATEAU: 30 OCTOBER 2020. 2:00 A.M.

The cool, arid air of the Egyptian night whistled softly past the sleek silver fuselage of the solar-powered *Dawn Wing* as it spiraled slowly down toward the Giza Plateau. The tiny plane circled silent as a dream on the desert wind, its small but powerful hydrogen-plasma engine emitting a faint blue glow against the moonlit sky.

Inside the cockpit, the pilot, Eris Campbell, glanced over at her companion and smiled softly at his strong, handsome profile, limned in the emerald glow of the instrument panel, as he carefully scanned the moonsilvered sands below. She was very glad to have him with her this night.

Unwilling to waste the half hour to forty-five minutes it would have taken to get to the Giza Plateau by taxi, Eris had wakened Chris out of a sound sleep and had dragged him, growling and complaining, with her to the nearby Cairo airport, where the *Dawn Wing* was hangared. Now, five minutes later, they were circling above the ancient geometry of the Giza necropolis, its excavations and causeways, ruins of tombs and temples, and great scattered heaps of stone a fascinating jumble of lines and angles from the air. Dominating this intricate study in ebony and alabaster were the three great squares of the Pyramids.

But Eris' sharp eyes were drawn to the smaller figure of the Sphinx, to the east. Here was the great stone guardian of centuries, now appearing tiny and helpless from the air, that had *called out to her* with vivid silent need in the ominous dream that had awakened her sweating and gasping and sent her out into the night. The memory of that dream was still clear and terrible as she anxiously scanned the desert below for any sign of trouble.

But although she could see nothing except the timeless city of the dead, apparently undisturbed and dreaming in moonlight, the feeling of something very wrong refused to leave her. It tugged and worried her psychic senses like a dark wind.

Eris wondered whether this baleful nightmare was a premonitory dream; she had never had one before, but she knew many fellow psychics who had them regularly. This one had not been realistic, as most prophetic dreams were, but symbolic, a cry for help from the Sphinx itself, yet it had the disturbing urgency of a prophetic dream. Could it have anything to do with the recent series of terrorist bombings in Cairo, she wondered? Tourism was one of the last resources left to an almost economically bankrupt Egypt, groaning under the weight of ninety million people on the edge of starvation. But tourists no longer felt safe here—the bombings had become too frequent and too dangerous a risk.

In desperation, Egypt's President Saoud Ed-Din Fahey had appealed directly to his friend, United States President Thomas Warren, and Warren had sent Chris and her, two of his top psychic agents, to investigate the bombings and help the Egyptian government bring the terrorists to justice.

So far, Eris reminded herself grimly, they had had no luck at all. During the six weeks they had been in Egypt there had been several bombings but no suspects, no leads. The most puzzling thing about this tragic reign of injury and death was that unlike most terrorist organizations, this one made no proud proclamations of responsibility for the bombings, as usually occurred with political groups. In fact, the bombings didn't seem to be politically motivated at all! Instead of the usual terrorist targets—embassies, government buildings, important political figures—these attacks seemed

10

directed only against civilians: airports, night clubs, hotels, restaurants, cinemas. It was as if the terrorists were deliberately trying to scare tourists away from Egypt. If so, they were succeeding. But why? And who were they?

"Everything looks quiet to me, Eris," Chris said, the noise of his voice in the small cockpit startling her out of her ruminations.

Eris shook her head. "Can't tell from up here, Chris. The feeling of trouble I had isn't going away. I'm going to take her down so we can check it out on foot."

Chris nodded glumly. "I thought you'd say that. Looks like a good place to land over there south of the Pyramids."

Eris' large aqua eyes flashed warmth at Chris as she banked the little craft to begin her descent. Christopher Troy understood her as few people did; she knew he respected her psychic intuition and "hunches." He was a strong, comforting companion in times of trouble; and right now it felt to her as if this might be one of those times.

The engine's blue glow died away, and as the two agents stepped out of the plane onto the silver sands, the immense silence of the desert night seemed to press down upon them with the weight of centuries. A chill wind rose, biting through Eris' khaki blouse and slacks and whipping her thick honey-gold hair into tawny froth. She zipped up her leather jacket and looked around, breathing deeply of the pure, cold air. The faint odors of cinnamon, myrrh and resin seemed to ride the wind like fragile birds for a moment, then blew away into the darkness.

God, it was beautiful out here, she thought as she and Chris started off over the argent terrain. It seemed almost unthinkable that anything human could disturb the timeless tranquility of the ancient stone sentinels that loomed before her in moonwashed splendor. Yet that nagging feeling of danger, of *wrongness*, still plagued her, like the sharp twinge of an aching nerve.

Perhaps she was overreacting, she thought, suddenly unsure of her feelings for the first time. What if this were nothing more than a plain old nightmare? After all, it didn't make any sense at all that anyone would want to bomb the Sphinx! No tourists out here this time of night. What if—

Eris' boot thunked into an object on the sand that felt at once soft and heavy. She looked down.

It was the body of a man.

"Oh, my God," she exclaimed softly; then, quickly kneeling beside the body, turned it over.

Shock-widened eyes stared sightlessly at the moon. The man's throat had been cut, thoroughly and professionally. A large patch of blood, black and ugly in the moonlight, was slowly seeping into the sand beneath him.

Chris whistled softly. "He's a government guard, Eris. They still keep a few on duty out here at night to prevent stray tourists from climbing all over the Pyramids and killing themselves. Looks like he hasn't been dead long."

"There's his weapon," Eris said, pointing to a dark object half buried in the sand a few feet away.

Chris walked over and picked it up, brushing the sand from the stock and barrel. It was a Russian-made Kalashnikov AKM-2 automatic assault rifle, sleek, deadly and efficient.

Chris smiled grimly at Eris, who was just getting to her feet. "Well, you were right. Something sure as hell *is* wrong out here tonight."

Eris put a slim sun-browned hand on his arm. "Chris, I knew that dream was too vivid to be just another nightmare. I *felt* it too strongly. And somehow it has to do with the Sphinx. It was *calling* to me for help. I know that sounds crazy, but—"

Chris put his hand on hers and smiled. "Not as crazy as you might think. You know the large red granite stela between the Sphinx's paws? It tells the story of how, around 1400 B.C., the young prince Tuthmosis IV was hunting in the desert one day and decided to rest in the shadow of the Sphinx. He fell asleep and dreamed that the Sphinx called out to him for help, promising him the Double Crown of Egypt if he would clear away the sand which had nearly covered its body. He agreed, and shortly after became king. During the first year of his reign, he kept his promise and cleaned off the sand."

Eris flashed him a radiant smile. "So I'm in royal company, huh? Well, the Sphinx didn't promise me a reward, but

12

its message was terribly urgent...I got the feeling of a far worse danger than just sand this time."

Chris nodded, his face grim and wary now. Together, their eyes on the brooding, moonsilvered monolith ahead, they resumed trudging through the sand toward it.

As they approached the south side of the Sphinx, standing guard over the crumbling remnants of the temples before it, Eris thought that from the side it looked strangely vulnerable, almost childlike. Quite a different impression from the frontal view, where it appeared always stern and enigmatic in its timeless, battered beauty.

As they rounded the enormous mound of masonry that was the right paw of the Sphinx, they froze. There, back between the great paws and fully illumined by the moon, they saw a group of men working busily at something, surrounded by boxes and bundles of different sizes. Directly behind them, the timeworn stela of Tuthmosis IV thrust upward like a great gate to an unknown chamber, stark and cold in the moon's rays.

A huge black man, well over six feet tall, his hairless skull gleaming like polished obsidian in the moonlight, was directing the men around him. Although Chris and Eris were watching in absolute silence, some inner sense seemed to alert the big man to their presence. He turned slowly and faced them. For a moment his eyes seemed to catch the moon's rays and flash green fire, like a cat's eyes.

In a voice like frozen stone he said quietly, "Kill them." Immediately the four Arabs behind him dropped what they were doing and began to run toward Chris and Eris. As their dark *galabias* swirled out behind them, they looked like huge black bats skimming over the sand. Chris could see the moonlight striking white sparks from wicked curved blades being withdrawn from their robes as they ran.

"Hold it!" Chris shouted in a commanding voice, raising the assault rifle toward them. They came on as if they hadn't heard, or noticed the weapon. Chris could see that he might as well have shouted at the wind, so he fired a quick burst from the rifle, stitching the sand at their feet into white plumes. The noise was thunderous, staccato echoes rolling away over the sand in invisible tumbleweeds of sound.

Still the men came on, not faltering an instant. Chris could see their faces now, dark beneath the darker turbans that covered their heads. They looked mean as hell.

His adrenalin began to pump as he realized that he and Eris were going to have to take these babies out by hand—he couldn't just mow them down in cold blood. Besides, they needed captives, information, not more dead bodies.

Throwing the weapon aside in disgust, Chris yelled to his partner, "Watch yourself, Eris—I think they're high on something!"

She nodded; then as the first man reached her, grinning nastily at the thought of an easy kill, she deftly pirouetted ninety degrees to her left, graceful as a ballerina, and whipped a piledriver boot into his midsection with dazzling speed and precision. The results were devastating. The Arab's breath left his body in a sudden *whoof* as he went spinning back to slam into the Sphinx's right paw with incredible force. He went down and didn't move.

Chris grinned to himself. God, he loved to watch her in action!

Hearing the sound of a sandal scuff alarmingly near him, Chris whipped around to see one of the ugliest human faces he had ever beheld leering at him with a mouthful of rotten teeth under a great hooked beak that looked as if it had been broken more times than its owner could count. Two burning, glassy eyes confirmed Chris' suspicion that these men were indeed drugged to the gills.

His timing a second off, Chris suddenly felt a fiery pain blossom in his left side, saw a curved knife, partly streaked with his own blood, flash up before him. *Damn*, he thought, relieved to see that the blade wasn't buried in him but angry with himself for his carelessness, the bastard almost took me out!

But his attacker had been just a little too eager, and before he could strike again, Chris grabbed his knife hand and slammed it down on his own upthrust right knee with a satisfying crack. Surprised by the rapid recovery of what he thought would be a quick kill, the man yelped and the knife

14

went spinning out of his hand. In the same movement, Chris swiveled to his right, grabbing the man's upper arm with his left hand, and bending forward, flipped the thug over his back in one smooth motion. The wind went out of the astonished Arab as he landed heavily on the sand. Before he could recover, Chris stepped forward and decked him with a quick, short kick to the jaw. Hoping he hadn't broken the man's neck, Chris whirled around just in time to block the second man's descending knife and deliver a crushing elbow to his mouth. Chris felt some bad teeth suddenly get a lot worse as dark blood sprayed his arm.

"*Ya Allah!*" the Arab screeched as he reeled backward, still clutching the knife. Eyes blazing with pain and fury, he launched himself again at Chris, only to find himself suddenly disarmed by a quick high kick to the wrist. Before he could react to the pain of snapped bones, Chris chopped him down with a hard right. A smaller man than the first, he hit the sand like a sack of meat and lay still.

As Chris stepped back, rubbing his knuckles and feeling considerable pain now from the knife wound in his side, he heard an ominous metallic *clack-click* behind him. He whirled instantly, to see the first Arab standing a bit unsteadily, but with the discarded AKM-2 pointing directly at him.

The Arab was in no hurry now. He hurt, and the man who had hurt him was now at his mercy. He chose to savor the moment, grinning and cursing Chris and the majority of his ancestors in Arabic, describing how he was going to chop him into camel food very slowly, starting with his legs and working leisurely upward in short bursts, leaving the heart and head for last.

Chris started to say something to the man in Arabic, anything to buy a few seconds of time, when suddenly a golden-khaki thunderbolt hurtled across the sands and smashed into the astonished Arab with the force of a fullback for the San Francisco Rams. Before he could scramble to his feet, a slim fist whipped into the air and down again with a solid *chunk*, and the man relaxed into oblivion for the second time that evening, his much-broken nose broken once more.

As Eris got to her feet gracefully, brushing the sand off her clothes, she grinned broadly at Chris.

15

"Thanks," he said gratefully. "That's one I owe you."

She walked over to him and gave him a warm hug. As she pulled him close, she felt him wince. She stepped back quickly and seeing the dark blood on his shirt, exclaimed, "Chris! You're hurt! What happened?"

"One of 'em nicked me. Nothing serious, but it hurts like hell." He saw the concern in her eyes and suddenly felt that that look was well worth the pain.

Turning back to the Sphinx, they saw that the area between the paws was now empty. The huge leader had fled during the fighting.

"Dammit," Chris swore, "the big one got away while we were screwing around with these whacked-out thugs."

Eris scanned the moonglowing sands for any trace of movement. "They can't have gotten too far—"

A whisper of sound made them suddenly turn, to see a dark shape rapidly scudding away over the sand like a wounded crow.

"One of our playmates making a break for it," Chris exclaimed. "I'll catch him! Watch the others, Eris. Take the rifle."

Eris stretched out an imploring hand to him, even as he was off in a spray of sand, running after the fleeing Arab.

"Chris, no! You're hurt! We don't need him! We've got the other three—"

But Chris was already out of earshot, running easily and determined not to let this one get away. He wanted to bring in all four of the Arabs for questioning; the more prisoners, the more chance they might get some desperately needed information out of them about the bombings, for he felt that somehow this bunch was connected to them.

Chris could now see that the running man was the second Arab who had attacked him, the smaller one with the broken wrist, which didn't seem to be slowing him down any. He was skimming over the uneven terrain of rock and sand like a scared jackal, taking a diagonal course away from the Sphinx toward the Great Pyramid, which loomed about 500 feet to the northwest.

As he ran, Chris breathed in great sucking gulps of the cold arid air, holding it in his lungs, feeling it warm into his

16

body, then expelling it in long sighs. He was glad he had kept up his running while they had been on assignment in Cairo; he and Eris ran and performed yoga and Tai-Chi exercises together early each morning before breakfast. It felt good to run, to release the tension of the moments before when he had come close to never running again.

His side wound began to pain him now, as sweat ran down into it; he was shocked to see how much blood had spread across the front of his shirt. Keeping a small part of his consciousness focused on the man he was pursuing and on the physical act of running itself, he began to perform some of the mental disciplines he had learned during his training periods, separating his mind from its seeming center in his body, lifting it out and "above." He told himself that he was not a body, but a being of mind and spirit, able to control absolutely the puppet he had created in order to live in this physical dimension; that as he was responsible for all his body's pain and sickness, so he could remove this pain and heal that body. He began to visualize bursts of white light flowing from his hovering mind/spirit down and into the knife wound in the body's side. Gradually he could feel the pain diminish, the bleeding stop, until finally the slash no longer troubled him. Then he returned his consciousness to his physical vehicle, for he knew he would need it soon.

Now Chris' boots pounded loudly on the asphalt of the road that wound around and between the two largest Pyramids; he could hear the frantic *slapslap* of the man's sandals ahead. Chris was gaining, and the man knew it; several times he cast anxious glances back over his shoulder.

Looks like the little creep is heading for the Pyramid, thought Chris. I wonder if he thinks he can shake me by climbing it? Well, he's got a surprise coming—I've been up and down that rock pile a few times myself. Although not in the middle of the night with a hole in my side, trying to catch an Arab hit man!

Chris' surmise was correct: a few minutes later, he saw the fugitive reach the base of the Pyramid and bound up the side, agile as a monkey, apparently unhampered by his broken wrist.

Chris had to give the little fuck points for guts—it couldn't be easy for him. Each of the more than two million crumbling limestone blocks weighed at least two and a half tons and was half the height of a man. The moon gave lots of light, but moonlight can be tricky—sometimes you see things that aren't there—and one wrong step can send you plunging almost 450 feet down to some very hard-packed sand.

Pausing a second to catch his breath at the foot of the Pyramid, Chris was overcome briefly, as he always was in this spot, by the sheer immensity of the monument, stark and beautiful in its geometric simplicity.

As he began the arduous ascent, he saw that the Arab was indeed a skillful climber; he was already about one-third of the way to the top. Climbing among the huge stones carefully but with as much speed as possible, Chris recalled a trick taught him several years ago by an Arab guide named Youssef Hazim, who used to dazzle the tourists by climbing to the top and back down again in the incredible time of seven minutes and twenty seconds! Hazim had told Chris, "The trick is to climb zigzag, not in a straight line. Balance is extremely important, and you must concentrate wholly on the climb. You must let nothing distract you."

As Chris began to follow a wide zigzag path up the side, he noticed with satisfaction that his adversary apparently didn't know this trick; he was climbing in a straight line, although quite rapidly, but Chris soon began to gain on him.

The Arab scrambled over the top when Chris was still about fifty feet behind him. Chris saw his head pop over the edge once, note Chris' position, then disappear again. He would probably be waiting to ambush him when he got to the top, Chris surmised, with a kick or a quick push that could send him hurtling down the stony mass to his death.

As carefully and quietly as possible, Chris began to edge over toward the corner to his right and transferred himself onto the eastern face of the Pyramid. Then he quickly completed the climb, crawling over the top silently, approximately ninety degrees to the left of the Arab, who was crouched down watching the south side like a cat at a mouse hole.

18

As he stood up atop the thirty-three-foot-square apex, his boot crunched on some loose rock and the man spun around, a look of surprise and anger on his dark face.

Chris smiled and walked toward him confidently. "Okay, pal, it's all over," he said in Arabic. "Thanks for the exercise, but now we need you to answer a few questions for us."

But instead of shrinking back, the Arab began to walk toward Chris, saying nothing. An ugly gap-toothed grin split his face and his good hand dived beneath his dark robes.

It came out holding another knife, curved blade glittering ice in the moonlight.

Chris stopped. "Hot damn," he said aloud to himself in English. "This just isn't my night...."

* * * * * * *

From their respective vantage points, neither Eris nor Chris had time to notice a strange shimmer in the night sky, hovering some distance away like a heat wave distorting the stars behind it. It was all that could be seen of an odd, crescent-shaped craft about fifty feet in diameter, protected from human observation by an invisibility field that warped light rays around it.

Inside, the huge black man who had been at the Sphinx peered down at Chris' pursuit of the last Arab thug. The Arab was just pulling himself up onto the Pyramid's flat top. Another few minutes and Chris would join him.

The black man watched intently, his strange feral eyes glowing with anger. Beside him crouched a grotesque and misshapen figure, a dwarf whose large head was completely covered by a dark ski mask. Like the larger man, he too was dressed entirely in black.

"I think we better use the box, Furca," the big man rumbled in a voice like distant thunder. "He might capture Hamid...and we can't allow that to happen."

The dwarf's eyes flashed bright malice behind his mask. "You're right, Reaper. *She* doesn't like loose ends. Here."

The little man handed the one called Reaper a small black box with four tiny green lights on it. All but one were dark. Beneath each light was a red button.

Reaper put his thumb on the button beneath the last light, its small viridescent glow like a firefly in the darkness of the cabin. He looked down again at the two men atop the Great Pyramid. Hamid had drawn his knife and was slowly circling around Chris.

"Wait, Reaper," said the dwarf. "The man is unarmed. Perhaps Hamid will—"

"Can't take the chance, Furca. She said *nobody gets captured*. That means *nobody*. I don't know who these two are, but they're not just tourists out for a moonlit stroll. They're professionals. Probably Americans, from the look of 'em. I don't want any American agents trying to make our birdies sing, get me, little man?"

The dwarf's eyes grew dark with anger, but only momentarily. He was used to insults from this ebony giant, but even with his impressive knowledge of occult and arcane lore, Furca didn't relish a confrontation with him. Instead, he focused his attention on the man atop the Great Pyramid, and under the mask licked dry lips in anticipation of what was soon to occur.

Turning to the third occupant of the craft, a being not human but resembling a humanoid goat in appearance, Reaper issued a curt order: "Take us home."

The goat-man's eerie slit-pupiled eyes flickered acknowledgment and his gloved hands began to manipulate a bank of glowing controls before him.

The invisible craft began to rise slowly, a noiseless shimmer against the darkness. Inside, Reaper's thumb jammed home the fourth red button on the small black box. For a second, he felt the box grow warm in his hand; it seemed to pulse faintly, like a human heartbeat, then grow silent.

The green light went out.

* * * * * * *

The Arab was closing in on Chris now, backing him toward the precarious edge behind him, still grinning confidently. He was keeping a wary eye on Chris' feet and hands this time; he wouldn't be caught off guard so easily again. His broken right wrist dangled uselessly beside him as a painful reminder and a spur to avenge himself on this American dog who had dared defend himself from attack. Chris could see dried blood spotting his chin.

Chris felt his exertions catch up with him in a rush. He was still breathing hard from the grueling climb, and his side was beginning to pain him again. His knees felt like they were made of Jell-O. Keeping his eyes on the gleaming knife, he prepared to grapple with his grinning adversary. But suddenly, the man stopped.

He began to wave his arms in the air as if clutching at something unseen. The knife dropped from fingers suddenly gone nerveless, clanged on stone. His eyes jerked open in horror and surprise and his mouth gaped wide for a scream that never came. Instead, a horrid whistling wail issued from his throat as a blast of superheated air exploded from lungs already beginning to shrivel like tissue paper in a fireplace. Chris was reminded absurdly of steam hissing out of a teakettle. Even several feet away, he could feel great heat beginning to radiate from the Arab's body.

Now the man's body began to jerk like a puppet, and Chris saw with horror that smoke was beginning to curl out of his still-gaping mouth, his nose and ears.

Instinctively, Chris stepped back in alarm just as a brilliant blue flame hissed out of the man's mouth. Split seconds later, patches of blue fire burst forth all over his writhing body, igniting his robes, until he became an incandescent torch, totally enveloped in a brilliant cobalt flame as hot as a welder's arc.

All this occurred in an eerie silence except for the hissing of the flame and the mad scuffling of the Arab's sandals on stone. An overpowering stench of burning flesh stabbed Chris's nostrils like a knife. The heat was so intense that he could feel his own hair begin to curl and singe and his face felt as though he were facing an open hearth furnace.

21

As he put up his arm to shield his face and moved back farther, he saw the man's eyeballs explode outward from the pressure as the fluids in them turned to steam.

Then the flaming figure reeled backward, a hissing blue torch, and was gone over the side, plunging down the rocky north face of the Pyramid like a human firework, a cerulean pinwheel scattering a trail of flickering blue fire after it.

Chris rushed to the edge and peered down in time to see the flaming horror still bounding from tier to tier, a mad will-o'-the-wisp that finally winked out as it hit the desert sands far below. He shuddered and closed his eyes, the fiery figure still burning on his retinas in a yellow-orange afterimage. His skin tingled as though sunburned and his shirt felt uncomfortably warm. The nauseating odor began to disperse in the cold desert wind.

What in the name of God happened to him? Chris wondered, still in shock. Trying to strengthen his wobbly knees, he began to climb down the great stone blocks to where he could see Eris waiting for him on the road at the base of the Pyramid.

About forty-five minutes later, Chris staggered down the last tier of crumbling stone into Eris' arms. He held her close for a few long moments, catching his breath. He seized the chance to use her concern for him as an excuse to press her to him, enjoying the comfort of her warmth against the chill desert air and relishing the pounding of his heart against her soft breasts.

I wish I knew what she was feeling right now, he thought. I know what *I'm* feeling. What will it take to unfreeze this woman? How can she be so warm and so cold at the same time...?

As if reading his thoughts, Eris stepped back, her beryl eyes full and anxious as she searched his face in the moonlight. "I was afraid you might be in trouble, Chris, so I ran over here after I tied up the Arabs and checked out what those goons were doing at the Sphinx. On my way over, I saw a blue flash on top of the Pyramid and I didn't know *what* to think! What was it, Chris? And what happened to the Arab?"

"Wish I knew. One minute he was about to carve me up into shishkabob and the next he went up like a torch in a burst of *very* hot blue flame! Hell, you'd have to have heat of over 2,000 degrees Fahrenheit to totally incinerate a human body like that! There's nothing left of him but ashes!" Chris pointed to a few blackish smudges on the sand.

Eris shuddered, then shook her head as they turned to trudge the distance back to the Sphinx. "It's weird, Chris—I can't understand it. I mean, I've heard of spontaneous human combustion, of course—that's exactly what this sounds like—but it's extremely rare. It seems to strike at random, and nobody really knows what causes it."

"Yeah," said Chris, "but this was just too convenient to be a million-to-one incident." He shrugged. "Well, maybe one of those other weirdos you tied up can shed some light on all this."

But once more in the shadow of the colossal stone beast, an even greater shock awaited them.

"My God, Eris—look!"

Eris' eyes widened as she gasped in horror. Where she had left the three Arab thugs bound and unconscious were now only three faintly smoking piles of greasy black ash.

"It happened to them, too, Chris! Just like the one on the Pyramid!"

Chris shook his head, his mouth tight. "This definitely takes it out of the realm of coincidence, Eris. Somebody *did* this to them. All of them—probably so they wouldn't talk."

"But that's horrible, Chris—inhuman! And *how* in God's name could anyone do this by remote control? And if they *can*, why them? Why not you?"

"I don't know, Eris, but I think we're dealing with a lot more than mere terrorists here. Say—what *were* they doing over here, anyway? You started to tell me back there."

Taking his hand, Eris led Chris past the small Roman altar between the Sphinx's paws and over to the towering masonry of the statue's right paw, almost up to the great stela. There he saw several bundles of dynamite piled against the stone, with coils of wire and a detonator device on the ground nearby.

23

"Jesus K. Christ, Eris—they were about to blow up the whole goddamn Sphinx! They must be terrorists after all!"

"Look closer," Eris said, pointing to the heaped-up explosives. "There's not enough dynamite here to destroy the whole statue. The paw, Chris—only the paw !"

The great Sphinx stretched in the depths of solitude,
Who seems to drowse in a dream without end.
　　　　　—Charles Baudelaire, "LES CHATS"

CHAPTER TWO

ANCIENT WARNINGS

CAIRO: 31 OCTOBER 2020. 8:30 A.M.

Colonel Habib Zaid leaned back in his black leather chair and smiled, white teeth dazzling in his dark, handsome face.

"I'm afraid I would be forced to consider your story incredible, my friends," he said, taking a draw on his ill-smelling Russian Sobranie, "were it not for one fact which we have kept secret for several months."

Eris and Chris leaned forward, alert and interested. Even Chris' weariness seemed to drop away like a discarded garment.

"As you know, since you have been working with us there have been a number of bombings in Cairo, but we have not been able to capture any suspects. However, a few months before you arrived, we did arrest one suspect, a notorious criminal wanted by the police on several charges, including murder. His name was Tamil Naguib. He was put into a cell with another man awaiting trial for stealing mangoes from a fruit stand in the Khan el Khalili. The next morning, when we came to remove Naguib for questioning, he was not there. Only a small pile of black, greasy ash was left on Naguib's bunk. Oddly, the covers and sheets of the bunk were only slightly charred. His cellmate was found gibbering to himself in one corner of the cell, muttering that

25

Naguib had suddenly burned up in a burst of blue flame. Naturally, we thought the thief was lying, that somehow he had managed to set Naguib on fire as he slept, but our doctors soon advised us that there was no possible way for the man to create a fire hot enough to completely incinerate a human body. Then we learned of spontaneous human combustion and had no choice but to assume that this was one of those rare and mysterious occurrences."

"Yes," agreed Chris, "that's what we thought, too—until we saw the other three."

"Now, by combining our information, we have put together two more pieces of this bizarre puzzle," Zaid said. "We now know that the burning deaths are no accident—although how they are accomplished is beyond my comprehension—and we have definitely linked them to the terrorist bombings. But as you have stated, we are dealing with much more than the usual terrorist group here."

Eris tossed her honey-gold hair back and asked, "Colonel, do you have any idea why this group would try to blow up the *right paw* of the Sphinx in the middle of the night? It goes against the modus operandi of the previous bombings, in which only locations crowded with tourists were chosen. The only reason they tried to kill us is because we tried to stop them."

Colonel Zaid shook his head. "Frankly, no, Eris. I could see mutilating a national monument as a gesture of protest, I suppose...but somehow I feel a deeper mystery behind this incident. It puzzles me as much as it does you...."

Finishing their cups of cinnamon tea, Eris and Chris rose to go. The Colonel thanked them once again for being alert enough to save the Sphinx from disfigurement. He liked and respected these two young Americans and enjoyed working with them. He felt that if anyone could get to the bottom of these strange events they could, and he had *carte blanche* from President Fahey to give them anything they needed. As he ushered them cordially out of his office, he promised to post a heavy guard around the Giza Plateau every night from now on to prevent a repetition of last night's incident.

Back at the hotel, as Chris drifted away into much-needed sleep, a blissful smile smoothed out the lines of exhaustion on his face. Eris stood beside the bed, her aqua eyes deep with feeling for this man she had come so close to losing.... Black memories began to roil up within her at this thought, but she forced them back, willing her focus on the present, on *this* man.... For a few moments her gaze traced the fine laugh lines that webbed the corners of his eyes, wandered across the fine-boned face, bronzed by the hot sun of Egypt. She leaned over and kissed him gently on the mouth.

Then, silent as smoke, she was gone.

GIZA PLATEAU: 31 OCTOBER 2020. 11:30 A.M.

She stood under the burning sun and the intensely blue sky, once more confronting the infinite gaze of the colossal Sphinx. She felt an inexpressible sense of relief and pride, a fierce joy that she had been able to answer the psychic call to save this mighty monument from further disfigurement.

As she stood there, gazing at its battered visage like any awestruck tourist, Eris began to feel something, way in the back of her mind, a whisper of awareness.... She stilled herself, drew herself within as much as possible, closing her eyes to the harsh desert glare, her ears to the distant cries of camel drivers and vendors haranguing their scrawny animals and the few hardy tourists who ventured out here now.

Eris recalled her vivid dream, the silent call for help and the dangerous reality it had portended. Is the Sphinx trying to speak to me again, she wondered, here in broad daylight?

She could feel a fine sheen of perspiration glossing the hollows of her neck, beading her forehead, trickling between her breasts, as she concentrated, clearing her mind of all thought as if meditating, *listening* with her inner senses....

And then she seemed to be suspended, floating in a time out of time, waiting....

Distantly it came, then, a whisper at first, impossibly far away yet pressing into her consciousness with an urgency impossible to ignore. It was a voice, yet not a voice, it was the sound and feel of sand shifting over rock, ageless as the desert....

Then there were words, soundless and intense, bursting like bright bubbles of color in her mind:

Hail! Beloved of Isis and of Osiris thou art. For I have called once again into the world of men and thou hast answered. For this, grateful am I to thee.

Eris realized with a shock that the voice was speaking Old Egyptian, but that she could understand it perfectly!

Who are you? she asked, knowing the answer.

I am that I am. was the reply.

Men have known me as a reflection of their vanities, gods have into me their essence poured; Arq-ur, Ra-Harakhte, Khufu, Father of Terror, Asriaio, many names, many faces have I had since carved was I from the living rock. Not does it matter. I am the Guardian.

Floodtide, summer, autumn, all to me are one, even as all the years are one, and all the ages. But now must I break my silence to warn thee of an evil that comes swiftly, as comes the vengeance of Horus upon the unwary. Beware the star that blinks; beware the Daughter of Set, She-Who-Is-To-Be-Feared; beware the Shaker of Worlds....

Eris felt the words trail off and away then, as though the speaker were fading back through nameless dimensions whence it came.

Wait! she called silently, frantically. *Please! What is this evil? Who is the "Daughter of Set"? Please....*

But it was no use. The presence was gone. Eris opened her eyes, dazzled for a few moments by the brilliance of the day around her. Her mind whirled with the impact of the message she had just received. The Sphinx! Speaking to her to warn her...of what? Did it have to do with last night?

Above her, the great calm face brooded distant as ever, peering toward the Nile and beyond the world. The Daughter of Set? The Shaker of Worlds? Damn, thought Eris, the Sphinx sure believes in preserving its reputation for riddles!

In the heat of a desert noon, Eris felt a chill ripple through her body as she turned back toward Cairo.

A woman in the shape of a monster
a monster in the shape of a woman
the skies are full of them.
    —Adrienne Rich, "PLANETARIUM"

CHAPTER THREE

WOLFE ISLAND

EASTERN CANADA: 31 OCTOBER 2020. 10:25 P.M.

Each year now, November swept down upon Eastern Canada like a great mad bear. Howling like harpies, the winter winds furiously battered the provinces of Quebec and Ontario, bringing with them frigid curtains of snow and sleet and reducing the picturesque St. Lawrence Seaway to a slush-choked spew of gray ice and water black and cold as a demon's soul. At the narrow mouth of the St. Lawrence, where it spilled outward from the glacial expanse of Lake Ontario, were many small islands, forming a shining wonderland of blue and green in the spring and summer that once lured millions of vacationers to frolic and marvel among its beauties. But now, in the icy clutch of winter claws, the Thousand Islands along this inland archipelago were a frigid hell in which the wind-chill factor brought the temperature down to eighty degrees below zero day after frozen day.

A few miles to the southeast of Point Frederick, just off the coast of New York, lay eighteen-mile-long Wolfe Island, once the largest of the tourist-swarming islands, but now a fortress surrounded by a high stone wall that ringed it down to the shoreline. It had been purchased as a private estate fifteen years ago and since then had been closed to all tourists. Its land had been allowed to grow wild and beautiful, but

30

now the chill white shroud that covered the surrounding patchwork of land and water enveloped Wolfe Island as well.

Near the center of the island, its massive gray chimneys and crenelated walls thrusting up out of the white drifts, lay the sprawling, fifty-room Bane Mansion, a fascinating architectural mixture of Art Nouveau towers and cupolas and the rugged, traditional lines of a Scottish baronial manor house.

Inside this massive residence, the great luxuriously furnished rooms were heated to almost tropical intensity. The howlings of winter were ignored; summer bloomed among elegant antiques, large lush carpets and somber paintings in great gold frames.

And in her sybaritic bathroom of onyx and gold and black marble, Lady Nicasia Bane, mistress of the manor, luxuriated in the steaming fragrance of her bath, the water caressing her small perfect breasts and long white thighs like a lover. It was perfumed with sandalwood and musk and almost hot enough to boil an egg.

Opening eyes amber and hypnotic as a tiger's, Nicasia stared across the humid room at what looked like a large black fire hose thrown carelessly in one corner. She duplicated this image in her mind and spoke a name without speaking: *Typhon.*

Instantly, there was a dry rustle and the fire hose began to move, slowly, sinuously uncoiling itself, moisture glinting on squamous black surfaces. An ebon head as large as a ham lifted from the center of the coiling and two large slit-pupiled eyes, green and cold as Arctic ice, glared from either side. A black forked tongue flickered like negative sparks around the blunt snout, testing the steamy air.

Misstresss...? The word...*uncoiled* itself in Nicasia's mind, and she smiled again. Languorously, she raised a white swansneck arm out of her bath and motioned to the jet-black, twenty-two-foot African python to come forward. With an effortless ripple of its powerful muscles, the creature slid over the gleaming tiles like tar spilling across glass, until its heavy head rested in the air only inches from Nicasia's heat-flushed face. A *frisson* not of fear, but more of admiration, danced down her spine as she locked the reptilian eyes with her own. This magnificent and unique serpent had been

31

specially created for her by genetic engineering, its intelligence far greater that that of an ordinary python. It was capable of limited telepathic communication, using and understanding simple words and images. Nicasia knew that despite Typhon's apparent emotionlessness, he was totally devoted to her, perhaps sensing an affinity beyond his ability to comprehend.

Gently, she stroked the midnight head, crooning softly to this monster who could swallow her whole if he chose. The black forked tongue danced.

Mentally, Nicasia told the snake, *Go find Reaper, Typhon, and tell him I'll meet him in the east wing bedroom in half an hour.*

Yesss, Misstresss, came the cold response in her mind.

As the great ebon reptile turned and slithered noiselessly away on its errand, reluctant to leave the humid atmosphere, Nicasia once more closed her eyes and thought about what tonight would mean to her and to her mission. They cannot refuse me after this, she gloated. After tonight, they *must* give me what I want...the heart of Egypt will be mine.

Forty-five minutes later, Lady Bane was pacing the deep white pile rug in the east wing bedroom with long, graceful strides. Swirling shoulder-length hair, black as a raven's dream, framed a face of striking beauty, and a skintight gold pantsuit displayed her slender figure dramatically. Her bare white feet, delicate as doves, sank deeply into the lush pile at each step, like snow meeting snow, and her golden eyes snapped fire.

The room, mirrored on two sides, was filled with a crackling primitive energy, making the heavy antique furniture and ornate king-size bed seem somehow too civilized. The entire north face was a window; Nicasia watched herself mirrored in dark glass as she paced back and forth, oblivious to the storm raging in the blackness outside.

The man with the feral green eyes watched her too. Seated on a couch facing her, at well over six feet in height and with over 250 well-distributed pounds to play with, his was an awesome figure. Due to the warmth, he had stripped down to a pair of white cords which accentuated the rich dark chocolate of his massive chest. His large, perfectly shaped bald head gleamed softly in the muted glow of the indirect lighting; a small solid gold earring glittered in his right ear.

A chuckle rumbled deep within his chest like the sound of an approaching thunderstorm. Raising an almost empty glass of Chivas Regal, he asked, "How about a drink, Lady? Good for jumpy nerves...."

Abruptly, Nicasia halted her pacing. She padded lithely over to Reaper, took the glass from his hand and set it down on the black marble coffee table. Then, placing her slender hands on his broad shoulders, she looked at him with hypnotic intensity. Her large eyes were enigmatic furnaces of citrine flame, unsettling even to this man who was seldom unsettled by anything. Her hands on his shoulders were cool and dry, smooth as the petals of flowers. Mentally, Reaper corrected himself: Whoa! Only jumpy nerves in this room are mine! This one's a fuckin' ice cube. Just walkin' off the time, I guess.... He wanted to say something flippant to break the disquieting electricity between them, but he kept silent. He wished she would say something.

After a long moment, Nicasia broke her almost serpentine scrutiny to glance at the solid gold holochron on her wrist. She touched a button and numerals glowed in the air above her arm: 11:35. A smile as cold as a glacial wind brushed her blood-red lips. When she returned her glance to his, Reaper could see anticipation and excitement now blazing within those sulfuric pools.

At last she spoke, almost whispering the words. "It's time, Reaper. You wait here while I go open the lift. I'll buzz you."

"Sure, Lady," he growled, annoyed by this secret she refused to share with him. But he reminded himself that she had promised to share a much larger secret tonight, very soon now....

As Nicasia left the room, Reaper let out a breath he didn't know he'd been holding in a hiss of disgust. Nicasia Bane was not like any other woman he'd ever known...and he'd known plenty. There was a...*strangeness* about her, something that at times almost chilled him, but it was nothing he could put his finger on. Sometimes it bothered him, as

33

it did now, for she was the only person who had ever made him feel that flickering flame of fear, although he had often caused that flame to blaze high in others.

He muttered an obscenity and stabbed a button on the couch arm; one of the mirrored walls began to swirl with colors and an image swam into focus on the wall-sized 3-D television screen. Reaper poured himself another glass of Chivas and sat back.

Ignoring the babble and jitter of the electronic wall, he smiled to himself, enjoying the rich mellow burn of the scotch. After tonight, Nicasia would reveal more of her secrets to him, and he was eager to learn them. Thanks to her, he'd come a helluva long way in a very short time. Not bad for a poor, raggedy-ass kid from Jamaica. Yeah, he'd had a rotten fucking background, all right, he recalled, as he rubbed the broad, lumpy nose which still pained him occasionally after all these years, a nose broken by a crazed PCP addict with a brick when Reaper had been only eighteen. He still remembered the pleasure that shook his body as a lion shakes its prey while he slowly choked the life out of his assailant, tasting his own blood in the steamy Jamaican night. It was his first kill. It was not his last.

Reaper Drum had been born in Savannah-la-Mar, near Kingston, Jamaica, the son of a notorious voodoo priestess, Ursulie Drum, who had been run out of Haiti for including human sacrifices in her ceremonies. Not that this was anything new to the centuries-old tradition of *Petro*, or black magic voodoo, which flourished alongside the harmless *Legba* ceremonies, but Maman Ursulie's excesses were so severe as to shock even the repressive government of Haiti.

In Kingston she quickly established herself as a power to be feared among the blacks, and soon the smell of blood and burning flesh mixed with the wild throbbing of the voodoo drums and the eerie chanting of the frenzied celebrants under the swollen crimson moon of Jamaica.

Before he was seven, Reaper had witnessed sights that would have whitened the hair of Caligula; by the time he was twelve, he was a full participant in the rituals, the *papaloi* chosen by the spirits to rule with *mamaloi* Ursulie.

But Reaper was born with a measure of intelligence as well as great size and strength, and his mother's indulgent and debauched ceremonies soon began to bore him. Just after his fifteenth birthday, surfeited and restless, Reaper Drum struck out on his own.

After his mother's death a few years later, Reaper found that she had left him little money, as power and self-gratification had been her goals, not financial gain. He had no education, so he could not find a job in Kingston except as a heavy laborer, and this he disdained.

Finally he was forced to take a job as a dock hand, where he had the altercation with the man who broke his nose. He escaped prosecution for the killing with a plea of self-defense, but from then on, he vowed to find an easier way to support himself. He left Jamaica for the United States, working his way up the Atlantic Coast at a variety of illegal activities, including smuggling arms and drugs.

After another "necessary killing" on the job, Reaper felt a resurgence of that same fierce exultation that had swept over him before. He came to realize that killing was a profession that promised not only emotional satisfaction, but substantial financial rewards as well.

In New York he became personal bodyguard to a Mafia hit man by disposing of the one he already had, and spent several years apprenticing the trade. He soon became a master of his bloody craft and spent several lucrative years practicing it. The name Reaper, bestowed by a mother with apparently prophetic insight, became ominously appropriate. His fame spread quickly among the underworld; to the law, he was a deadly shadow who could not be caught.

But then he made his first mistake: after blowing away the wrong man one night, he was arrested, convicted, sentenced to prison and then deported to his own country. He arrived back in Savannah-la-Mar broke and full of rage on his thirty-fifth birthday.

The same week, while attending a voodoo ceremony, he'd met Nicasia Bane. She was the most beautiful fox he'd ever seen as she stood there in the ceremonial firelight watching the writhing, moaning shapes of the half-nude dancers. She had money written all over her. He had willed

35

her to notice him, and after several minutes she had walked over to him.

"Are you good?" she asked as she measured his huge frame with molten sulfur eyes.

"I'm the best," he had replied without smiling.

"How would you like to go to Canada?"

He pretended he hadn't heard her.

"I'm offering you a chance to get out of here. Take it."

"You can't afford me," he said at last, looking her up and down insolently.

She smiled, a dazzle of white in the fireshot gloom. "I can afford anybody I want. But I want you." Then she reached into her purse and brought out two thousand dollars in one-hundred-dollar bills. She handed the money to him along with a card that said "Bane Enterprises" on it. "Be at the airport at seven o'clock sharp tomorrow morning. Don't be late."

Then she was gone, and Reaper, who had been down to his last three dollars a moment before, now had a small fortune clasped in his hand. Way to go, baby! He congratulated himself, permitting himself one of his rare smiles. I think you just got a hit from Lady Luck herself!

The next morning they were in a sleek private jet flying to Wolfe Island. She had given him an easy smile when he asked her, "What if I hadn't showed? Just took your snaps and split?"

She shrugged. "Then I would have known you weren't the man I was looking for. Two thousand dollars is a small price to pay for that knowledge. But it was a safe bet. I'm seldom wrong about men...."

So a new partnership had begun. Reaper had soon proved himself more valuable to her than even she had anticipated, and she quickly gave him more and more responsibility, until he had become her right-hand man, second in command of her strange and numerous minions and answerable only to her.

She had educated him up to a high-school level with her DLI (Direct Learning Input) system, in which informational audio and video are fed directly into the learning centers of the brain via electrodes. Then she had put him in charge of

36

the six-month bombing campaign to terrorize Egypt, and that had gone off without a hitch, except for the last job, when those two agents had interfered. Too bad, he mused, he might have been able to find what Nicasia was looking for if he had been able to blow up the Sphinx's paw, but she wasn't angry about his failure. "I'll find it, don't worry," she had told him. "When it's all mine, I can search for it at my leisure."

But she had remained maddeningly secretive about what "it" was. So far, she had adamantly refused to tell him any more than necessary for a particular assignment; what her long-term goals were remained a mystery to him. But he knew it was something big ... *real* big!

A particularly obnoxious commercial at a substantially higher volume than the rest intruded on his thoughts, so he punched a button to turn off the sound. Slouching back in the couch's soft embrace, he took another sip of his drink and waited for Nicasia to summon him down to her own custom-tailored version of hell.

Therefore I will shake the heavens, and the earth shall remove out of her place...and the heart of Egypt shall melt in the midst of it.

—Isaiah 13:13, 19:1

CHAPTER FOUR

CATACLYSM

CAIRO: 1 NOVEMBER 2020. 6:30 A.M.

Eris pressed her cheek tightly against the smooth iridium-silicon surface of the *Dawn Wing*, enjoying the cold burn of the fuselage on her exhaustion-flushed skin. Running her hand over the sleek craft like a lover caressing her mate, she watched the sun begin to streak the gray distance with smears of rose and lavender.

She was looking forward to today's excursion: Chris' knife wound had healed nicely, so she had proposed that the two of them take a day off and fly up to Luxor, have a picnic and poke around among the ruins they both loved so much.

Chris had readily agreed, and now as he came toward her across the dawnflushed concrete of the runway, she could plainly see the concern on his face. Exhaustion and worry had marked her, she knew, and she was touched by the feeling she saw in his eyes this morning.

"Hey, you okay, Eris?" he asked. "We don't have to go if—"

"No, no, I'm fine," she replied with a wan smile. "Just a little beat after last night. I'll be okay."

"Sure—we both need to get out of here and just goof off for a while."

38

Eris tossed her tawny hair, now sparking copper high-
lights as the blazing sun-god climbed above the horizon,
washing the eastern skies with flame.

"Come on, partner," she said, her smile widening. "Let's
mount up."

Chris grinned assent, and they had soon buckled themselves securely into the small cockpit.

As Eris busied herself with the routine preflight check of
all instruments and systems, she began to feel a little better.
She could almost feel the plane tremble with joy at the
thought of flight...or was it her trembling? The little craft's
slim delta wings were fully extended to expose the maximum
surface area of their silicon solar cells to the sun's light; they
would be partially retracted for flight configuration. The solar power absorbed by day was stored in a compact system of
lightweight batteries behind the cockpit, ready to be utilized
for overcast days or night flights.

Completing her preflight check, Eris inserted her key-
card into the ignition slot and the plane whispered into life.
The instrument panel glowed emerald as digital readouts
skittered on. Fans swept air into the two forward scoops, to
be converted into water, then cracked electrically into hydrogen and oxygen. The oxygen would be stored in tanks for
high-altitude flight and the excess vented; the hydrogen,
through an ingenious combination of donut-shaped magnetic
coils, laser blasts and high-voltage current, would be superheated to the unbelievable temperature of 200 million degrees Fahrenheit. Then, as ionized plasma, hotter than the
center of the sun, it would be thrust out of the rear propulsion chamber, ready to hurl the little craft across the sky at
almost five times the speed of sound! This plane was indeed
a triumph of aeronautical genius, developed under the aus-
pices of the super-secret Psychic Intelligence Agency, of
which Eris and Chris were members. Recent important
breakthroughs in lightweight heat shielding, hydrogen fusion
technology and other related areas had enabled PIA scientists
and engineers to produce an airplane that needed no fuel
tanks. It literally ran on air!

Eris had nearly exploded with pride when President
Warren had asked her to test this plane on the mission to

Egypt. Sure, she was a world-renowned test pilot and stunt flyer, but this—Wow! It had been love at first sight, and she had christened the ship *Dawn Wing*, having an artist friend paint an Egyptian winged solar disk on either side of the fuselage for her. She could think of no more appropriate insignia for a solar-powered aircraft.

Eris was as at home in the cockpit of this aeronautical marvel as a cowboy on his horse. She gave Chris a thumbs-up gesture and a smile, then switched on the radio.

"Cairo Ground Control, this is *Dawn Wing* eight niner seven Charlie, ready to taxi, VFR to Luxor, over."

The response came back quickly, in heavily accented English: "*Dawn Wing* eight niner seven Charlie, you are clear for runway one five. Taxi to warm-up area, over."

"Roger, Ground," Eris replied and noting the flashing green light from the control tower, released the brakes. The plane began to taxi down the runway. As happy as she was to be at the controls of her baby once more, she couldn't shake a growing feeling of uneasiness that seemed to enshroud her like a dank fog. It was a repetition of last night's feeling, and it made her nervous as hell. Her skin began to itch and tingle. She glanced out of the cockpit toward the west and was startled to see a sickly yellow glow in the sky. Her consciousness suddenly seemed to want to leave her body and go out flying on its own. She shook her head, clearing her senses. Shape up, Campbell, she told herself firmly. You're tired and you've got the jumps. Knock it off—you've got a flight to make.

She glanced at the digichron on the instrument panel. It read 0700:00.

WOLFE ISLAND: 31 OCTOBER 2020. 11:40 P.M.

Leaving Reaper Drum to his musings and his scotch, Nicasia Bane hurried to the nearby library, a vast room dim and musty with the smell of old books. The high dark-paneled walls and floor-to-ceiling walnut bookshelves crammed with thousands of volumes reminded her vividly of her late husband, Lord Harcourt Bane. She experienced almost a twinge of regret that he was no longer around; she

40

recalled this room as his refuge. He had spent many hours here with his aromatic pipe, away from the hectic concerns of business, reading and writing and longing for his native Scotland. She recalled how her beauty and intelligence had *blitzkrieged* him into marriage sixteen years ago, when he had been lonely and vulnerable. He had been exactly what she had been searching for, and together they had built his already considerable wealth into a vast financial empire. Fortunately for him, Harcourt had never discovered who—and what—Nicasia really was. His death had left her in sole command of billions, the ideal position to carry out her plan, an important phase of which was imminent this night.

She smiled wryly in the gloom as the thought came to her that as a matter of fact, her dear, departed husband was *still* quite useful at times....

Nicasia moved through shadows and silences to the fourth shelf center on the south wall. She removed a fat leather-bound volume of Robert Burns' poetry, exposing a small panel with numbered pushbuttons and a small, round silver-rimmed hole beneath them. Glancing at the time (11:45), she punched the buttons in a certain sequence, then inserted her right index finger into the hole, holding it steady for a moment. There was an electronic beep and a section of the bookshelf slid noiselessly out of place, exposing a metal door. She pressed her right palm against a small rectangular panel on the door; the panel lit up and the door slid back, revealing an elevator.

Walking in, she felt the metal floor icy against her bare feet as she picked up the elevator phone and called Reaper. "I'm in the library. Come now."

Seconds later, Reaper was standing beside her in the elevator. She pushed an unmarked button and the cage began to descend with a distant hum. She wet her lips as they passed the second and first floors. The elevator stopped at the basement and opened.

They stepped out into darkness—an immense unheated chamber far below the mansion. The cold steel floor burned Nicasia's feet like fire, but she was oblivious to the pain—it only spurred her on.

41

She touched a wall switch and strong lights glared into life, searing their eyes at first. The large room was lined with banks of sophisticated computers; one entire wall was an electronic map projection of the world, with colored lights indicating all major cities. At this moment none was lit. Another switch and power thrummed through the complex, a tinge of ozone coloring the smell of cold metal as lights glittered and danced on the silent computer banks.

Reaper whistled softly, impressed despite his desire not to be. He shook his head. He had suspected Nicasia had some kind of underground lab, but not a goddamn Pentagon war-room!

"What's all this shit for, anyway?" he asked her.

Nicasia looked at him, amused by his reaction. "You'll see, darling," she purred.

Going over to a master control console, she glanced up at a large digital clock over the board. 11:58:04.

Suddenly her mouth felt as dry as sandpaper. "Two more minutes," she said, licking her lush red lips. She glanced up at the domed ceiling, where a large star map portrayed the heavens with the accuracy of a planetarium. Certain star clusters were linked by glowing lines of various colors. The bright white star Algol, over one million miles in diameter, three times the size of our sun, was the point from which the lines extended, an incandescent spider crouching at the center of a glittering web.

As Nicasia gazed at the glowing representation of Algol, she seemed to drink in energy, strength, purpose; she could almost feel invisible waves pulsing through the awful deeps of space toward her, levering her to an almost unbearable pitch. These last few moments seemed to drag by with agonizing slowness, but this operation had to be performed with precise timing. This planet's astrological forces were coming to a perfect alignment: at precisely midnight, Lilith and Pluto would lock into a baleful conjunction, adding powerful destructive energies to those she would generate here. Add to this the channeling and focusing of negative thought forms generated by the black witchcraft covens celebrating Allhallow's Eve, and you had a potent brew indeed!

42

11:59:30. Nicasia turned to a black pyramid-shaped communicator, thought it on, and spoke into it: "Kalon 22, this is your Queen speaking. I am ready for energy beam transmission to initiate Cairo Operation. Are you ready to receive? Over."

One thousand miles above the earth, hidden from visual and electronic detection by an energy screen, a gigantic alien spaceship locked into geosynchronous orbit over Cairo was preparing for its part in the night's event. In response to Nicasia's inquiry, a bleating voice answered, "Yes, Queen Tiamat. Computer ready to initiate destruct sequence. Transmit at will."

Nicasia nodded in apparent satisfaction, then took a small silver key out of a pocket in her gold pantsuit. With it, she unlocked a red lever; next, she punched up a set of coordinates on a nearby keyboard. A VDT screen lit up with:

LATITUDE   30N03
LONGITUDE 31E15
MAGNITUDE R7.9

TARGET SITE: CAIRO, EGYPT
CONDITION YELLOW

READY FOR TRANSMISSION.

She glanced up at the wall map as a small yellow light winked on at Cairo. Placing her hand firmly on the red lever, she wet her lips once more and fixed her eyes on the large red-glowing numerals relentlessly flicking away seconds.

12:00:00. Closing her eyes, Nicasia pulled the lever down, quickly.

The computer banks suddenly sprang fully awake, lights dancing, relays chittering. A pulsing hum, like some enormous insect caught in a giant web, filled the chamber. Words raced brightly across the display screen:

DESTRUCT SEQUENCE INITIATED.

TRANSMISSION TO KALON 22 UNDERWAY.

005...004...003...002...001...
TRANSMISSION COMPLETE.

FIVE SECONDS TO CONDITION RED.

Nicasia's golden eyes bored into the glowing screen as the seconds ticked off.

High above earth's atmosphere, Kalon 22's computer was performing several functions simultaneously in nano-seconds. The energy beam transmitted by Nicasia's machine was being received, electronically augmented, and focused for transmission back to earth. A sensor beam lanced out, probing the density and composition of the rock substrata beneath Cairo, analyzing molecular structures, stress conditions, fault locations and other pertinent information, then feeding these data back to the alien computer, where they were utilized in the generation of a terrible energy beam that built and built...and then hurtled down through the skies, an invisible lance of death.

...003...002...001...
CONDITION RED
MAGNITUDE R7.9.

The yellow light on the wall map turned crimson.

Her eyes bright and feral, Nicasia swung around to face the puzzled Reaper. "It's done," she said softly.

Reaper still had no clear idea of what had happened. He knew it had something to do with Cairo, and he had a feeling it was something he sure as shit wouldn't want to be there to see. But his puzzlement was building into irritation now.

"*What's* done"? he growled. "How 'bout lettin' me in on it?"

Nicasia laughed. Instead of answering him she turned away, her face suddenly tight, as if searching for something in the electronic hummings of the large room around her. She spied a handmirror lying on a nearby table, walked over and picked it up. The ornate glass was studded with amber diamonds (to match your eyes, her husband had told her long ago when he'd given it to her), and she gazed deeply into it, noticing the diminished intensity in the cat-agate orbs that stared back at her, trying to probe past the weak human façade that masked the real being inside. For a moment she felt drained, unable to make contact with herself, unable to touch the alien urgency for the terrible deed she had just done. A brief flick of panic danced in her mind; she could hear the wind between the worlds blowing darkly; she was trapped, betrayed by the weakness of this small human female body, by the emotions that struggled to soften her adamantine will. She felt mired in alien flesh, drifting in emptiness, alone, alone....

Cursing, she broke the hypnotic spell, hurling the mirror away from her. The sound of glass shattering brought her focus back to the present, back to Reaper Drum, standing next to her, his face a thundercloud of irritation and impatience.

Nicasia laughed again, a bit shrilly this time. She was beginning to feel the cold now, as if all her body heat had pumped away out into that devastating beam. She realized she had kept Reaper in suspense long enough.

"It's cold," she said. "Let's go upstairs. I'll explain it all to you, darling, when we're warm and cozy again."

Yeah, he thought. Warm and cozy. The chill of the room was beginning to get to him too. He wanted a drink.

Nicasia shut down the computer room, then she and Reaper returned to the upstairs bedroom, Nicasia sending him on before her as she closed the secret elevator door alone.

CAIRO: 1 NOVEMBER 2020. 7:01 A.M.

As Eris rolled the *Dawn Wing* down the runway, picking up speed for liftoff, she suddenly began to hear a distant rumbling, like a storm gathering. Strange, she thought, the tower hadn't advised her of any storm conditions nearby. She could barely hear it over the whine of the engine and the wind whistling past the fuselage, but *it didn't seem to be stopping!* She looked over at Chris to see if he heard it too, but before she could ask she felt a sharp vibration throughout

45

the plane, as though the landing gear were bumping over rough terrain.

Chris glanced at her quizzically as the shuddering continued, increasing, but said nothing.

Eris decided she had better abort the takeoff and find out what was wrong. Maybe this was a major structural deficiency just now making itself felt. She didn't want the plane to shake itself apart while she was doing (she glanced at the airspeed indicator) 130 knots!

As she reached for the throttle to cut the engine, she saw with horror a 150-foot metal tower with a huge radar dish atop it swaying like a sapling in a hurricane! It was only a few yards off the runway to the left and a few hundred feet ahead of them; it began to topple slowly, like a felled tree, right across their path.

Then it all crystallized in her mind in one terrible instant: impossibly, a major earthquake was causing the shuddering and rumbling and was toppling this radar tower!

As they hurtled toward it at just over 160 miles an hour, Chris and Eris saw the massive steel skeleton smash into the tarmac, ripping up great chunks of runway surfacing. The huge dish's leading edge crumpled like a dixie cup when it hit the ground.

Split-second options raced through Eris' brain: they were going too fast to stop, but not fast enough for liftoff! Even if she yanked the stick all the way aft and goosed the engine full throttle, the slim delta wings just couldn't provide the lift without the airspeed. Her only chance was to risk a hard turn to the right, although it might damage the nose-wheel and the main landing gear. It might also rip the plane apart! And if that plasma engine got loose, God help this airport! The PIA engineers had told her that the engine could never explode, but she wasn't so sure. If it did, it might go up like a miniature H-bomb, leaving Cairo a smoking hole in the desert!

Yelling at Chris to hang on, Eris spun the nosewheel and slammed on the right brake, slewing the little craft sharply to the right. If she could make a complete U-turn before smashing into the tower, she could cut power and coast to a stop back the way they had come. If not, they had bought the farm!

The craft responded instantly, dipping sharply to the right as the wheels screeched terribly in protest. The plane groaned at the awful stress, but it wheeled around, left wing tip just missing the tower with less than a foot to spare. The turn seemed to take forever, but they made it. They had missed the tower and were safe for—

"Omigod!" Eris yelped as she looked up to see the enormous needlenosed bulk of a Boeing 797 hypersonic ramjet liner bearing down on them like an avalanche!

Cairo Tower had cleared them for immediate takeoff, she recalled in a flash, and they meant *immediate!* For this mechanical behemoth was also in the process of taking off right behind them and moving much too fast to stop!

Immediately she whipped the plane around in another sharp turn, this time to the left, as she hit the throttle. "Hold on, Chris," she yelled, "this is gonna be worse than before!"

The angle of the turn carried them off the edge of the runway and onto the uneven sandy ground beyond. There was a sharp bump and glass tinkled as one wheel smashed into a runway landing light. Then they were around the fallen tower in a wide arc and back on the runway, where they could continue the takeoff.

There was a tremendous roaring crash behind them that seemed to fill the world. Chris and Eris watched in horror in the rear-view mirrors as the giant jetliner, unable to stop in time, plowed into the fallen tower. It seemed to come apart like a tinkertoy: the looming circular edge of the dish ripped into the cockpit like a hot knife into butter, killing the flight crew instantly. A moment later, the crumbling aircraft dissolved in a ball of white-hot flame as the hydrogen fuel tanks ignited.

The shock wave from the explosion seemed to kick the *Dawn Wing* into the air as Eris wrenched the stick back and zoomed up in a steep climb, quickly leveling out to gain more speed, then sending the airplane high into the morning sky, away from the mushrooming cloud of smoke and flame that pillared up from the runway like an erupting volcano.

Stunned by their near brush with death, Chris and Eris could only stare open-mouthed, appalled at the fiery horror beneath them. Then, recalling the cause of all this, the earthquake that had hit Cairo with no warning, Eris banked the airplane toward the west to inspect the damage to the city.

Chris put his arm around Eris' shoulders admiringly. "Lady, that was some kinda flying! If you hadn't been the most skillful pilot on this entire planet today, we'd have ended up like...that, down there."

Eris managed a weak smile, still shaken by the flaming destruction below, and thankful to have Chris with her now.

As they flew west, they could see tall plumes of black smoke billowing up in many places, most of them from fires caused by broken gas mains. Although there was considerable structural damage throughout the city (their hotel, the venerable Continental Savoy, was still standing), the worst damage seemed to be confined to the west bank of the Nile: the districts from Imbaba to El Giza were almost uniformly decimated, as though flattened by some tremendous cosmic hammer.

They circled low over the city, noticing that the once-proud 590-foot Cairo Tower on Gezira Island was down and that most of the island's elegant parkland was under water. Just south of there, the smaller island of Roda had almost completely disappeared! It looked like all the bridges crossing the Nile were down, which would make it extremely difficult to get aid across to the stricken West Bank; only a portion of the 26 July Bridge looked undamaged. They could see throngs of people and animals, like colorful insects, milling about in terror and despair, jamming the streets and blocking the access of ambulances and rescue vehicles.

Choking back scalding tears of horror and pity, Eris turned the slightly battered but intact *Dawn Wing* back toward Cairo International Airport, where rescue crews and fire wagons were battling to extinguish the fiery carcass of the great hypersonic jetliner that had become a flaming tomb for 356 people, the most serious air disaster in Egyptian history.

WOLFE ISLAND: 1 NOVEMBER 2020. 12:30 A.M.

Back in the hot white bedroom once more, Reaper Drum drained a hefty glass of scotch, enjoying the cool clack of the ice cubes against his teeth.

Nicasia turned off the wall TV, from which a stunned newscaster had just confirmed her operation in Cairo a success.

"Well, darling, aren't you going to congratulate me?" she asked, hands on slim hips, tiger eyes blazing with triumph. "After all, it's not every day you meet someone who can level a city at the flick of a switch."

"Sure—congratulations," Reaper rumbled, lifting his glass in a grudging salute. "So you trashed Cairo with an earthquake. Terrific. Wanta tell me how you did it?" He grinned broadly at her. "Sure you do."

"Well, I think I'm entitled to brag a little, don't you? What you saw downstairs is the most advanced electrosonic weather control device ever constructed. It was installed especially for my mission here."

Reaper's eyebrows lifted slightly. "Weather control? How the hell can you control the goddamn weather? You God in disguise?"

She laughed, enjoying her triumph and his confusion. "Not quite, darling. But it's fun to pretend now and then. Actually, weather control's old stuff by now—the Americans and the Russians have been playing around with it for years. But not like this—my machine's a thousand times more powerful and precise than theirs. One hundred per cent controllable. What happens is that my equipment generates and transmits a beam of electrosonic energy up to another machine on board a starship orbiting above the target city. That machine amplifies and relays the signal in a tightly controlled pulsar modulation frequency to the exact latitude and longitude of any target site I choose. Because of the range of magnitude and the focusing capability, the radius of destruction can be extremely precise. For example, tonight, only that portion of Cairo I wanted to destroy went down. You'll see as more details come in on the news. Our headquarters at Zeinhom was practically untouched, as it's on the other side of the Nile, well away from the epicenter."

49

Reaper knocked back another slug of Chivas. "Okay, I'm impressed. Now you can tell me *why* all this death and destruction."

Nicasia's face hardened. "This was a warning to the Egyptian government, Reaper. They've been stonewalling me long enough. If they don't give me what I want now, the rest of Cairo will suffer the same fate—and I may have to sacrifice Zeinhom then. But I think this should be enough to do the trick—the last economic straw, after the droughts, the famines and the bombings."

"So that's it," said Reaper, beginning to put it all together. "That's why you've had Furca and me and the 'extra crispy brigade' over there blowing up tourists."

"Right! I've been playing hell with the weather in Egypt for several years now, gradually softening them up. That was Phase One. You were Phase Two, and quite successful, overall. Tonight was Phase Three. Egypt is on the verge of total economic collapse now. After tonight, they'll *have* to accept my offer. Their American and European friends won't be able to bail them out this time, so when I waltz in with my package of...ah, foreign aid...they'll no longer be able to refuse me."

Reaper poured himself the last few ounces of scotch left in the bottle. "So what is it you want'em to sell you? What's so important you're willing to wipe out half a city for it?"

Nicasia sank down onto the couch beside him and brought her glowing yellow eyes close to his. "Why, the Giza Plateau, darling. I'm going to buy the entire Giza Plateau."

Being a President is like riding a tiger. A man has to keep on riding or be swallowed.

—*Harry S Truman*

CHAPTER FIVE

THE PRESIDENT

WASHINGTON, D.C.: 31 OCTOBER 2020. 11:55 P.M.

President Thomas Fairfield Warren, an incorrigible nightowl, sat alone in the White House screening room watching a CIA briefing film on the latest UFO landings in Peru. Pouring himself another cup of lukewarm coffee and lacing it with a shot of Old Bushmill's to keep his deep Irish fires burning, the President smiled to himself as he recalled the acute embarrassment of the scientists and the military when they could no longer deny the existence of UFOs, due to the fact that one had finally landed in an Iowa cornfield, discharged its extraterrestrial occupants and remained there until the authorities and the press arrived to make it official at last: the first authenticated contact between man and beings from another world! It was tremendously exciting, that May morning in 2017, and he could still recall his own delight, amazement and gratitude that it had happened during his administration. He liked to think they had been waiting for someone friendly to the idea of extraterrestrial contact to be elected President, but that was just a little private conceit of his.

They were humanoid in appearance, highly intelligent and peaceful. They communicated by telepathy but also understood human speech and were willing to share many of their highly advanced technological secrets with us in return for being allowed to observe our people and culture at close range. They had been observing us from a distance for centuries and monitoring our radio and television broadcasts since 1945, as many people had believed, and at last they felt that the time had come to risk contact in order to be able to narrow down their fields of study. So they had decided to land in a remote area and reveal themselves and their mission to us at last. It was as simple as that.

Of course, the panic and paranoid public reactions so long predicted by the military did not occur. Thoroughly prepared for the eventual coming of space visitors by radio, films, television and other aspects of popular culture, people welcomed the aliens cordially. Although awed by their technology, the public was charmed by their novelty and lack of hostility. The most interesting effects occurred among the top echelons of the Air Force and the astronomical community, which had worked so hard for so many years at suppressing and discrediting all UFO sightings. Their credibility with the public was severely damaged. They couldn't explain away this one as swamp gas or a weather balloon, not with the aliens standing in front of their ship and being interviewed by the press on international television.

The President's musings were suddenly interrupted by the soft buzz of the screening-room phone. Startled, he picked up the receiver to hear the familiar Southern drawl of his secretary, Rowena Percal, vibrant with excitement and alarm: "Tom, you won't believe what's just happened..."

"Try me, Row—what is it?"

"There's been a tremendous earthquake in Cairo! Half the city's been destroyed! We're waiting for the casualty report now!"

"What? That's impossible!"

"Yes, sir, but it happened."

"Get Harry for me right away, then come on over here, will you?"

"Yes, sir."

Just as Rowena hung up, the other three lines lit up. The second line was Vice-President Harold Acedorian, not only the President's trusted second in command, but an old and valued friend from their days together in the Senate.

"Harry, I just heard about the quake!" Tom snapped angrily. "What the hell's going on? Why wasn't there any warning?"

"I don't know, Tom. Maybe QEWPIE is down—"

"I don't think so," Tom said. "We're linked into a fool-proof computerized quake prediction network with forty-four nations, including Egypt. As soon as they had any warning, we'd have known about it too. Unless somebody in Seismic Central didn't get the word to us immediately, in which case, heads are gonna roll!"

"I'll call them right now, Tom, and find out if they picked up anything beforehand."

"Good, then call me right back, Harry—no, better yet, come on over here as soon as you can."

"Right." Harry hung up and Tom quickly disposed of the other two calls, both close advisors. Neither had any new information.

Tom poured himself another Irish coffee and gulped half of it down before he realized what he was doing. He knew he was going to need a clear mind for whatever was coming down the pike. He shook his head, unable to believe that the multibillion-dollar earthquake prediction system had failed.

After the eruption of Mount Shasta and the second eruption of Mount St. Helens, and the West Coast quakes that followed, a highly sophisticated earthquake prediction network had finally been perfected. QEWPIE (Quake Early Warning Prediction Information Exchange) was the product of decades of research by seismologists and other scientists all over the world, designed to prevent as much further loss of life and property as possible. Through a complex computerized system of satellite sensors and seismic probes covering the fault systems of forty-four participating nations, QEWPIE was able to measure minute changes in electromagnetic radiation, planetary alignment, radon gas levels, pre-quake microtremors, magnetic changes in rock strata, animal behavior and many other factors, coordinate and analyze these data and produce predictions of earthquakes up to three days in advance. Its accuracy had increased to 99.75 percent during the last two years, and QEWPIE now could predict not only exactly where and when a quake would

53

strike, to the hour, but also its duration and magnitude. It had saved uncounted thousands of lives in Claifornia alone and all over the world, simply by giving people time to prepare themselves and, to a certain degree, their possessions and property.

How the hell could it have failed to warn Cairo? Tom wondered. He would have to find out—fast! He couldn't afford to let the influential West Coast voters feel they were once again at the mercy of unannounced temblors.

Rowena Percal entered the screening room, wearing her wrist-vid recorder, bright blue eyes shining with excitement. A Virginian, Rowena was a sincere, mature woman in her late fifties with a kind, round race set off by stylish blonde hair cut short. She was small, attractive, and energetic, and totally devoted to the President.

Motioning her to have a seat, Tom reached one corner of the room in two long strides, where he picked up a small white phone with no buttons. There was one like it in the Oval Office, and in many other rooms in the White House. (Unlike most of the other White House phones, the instruments in the screening room had no video units.) Tom spoke a code word into the receiver; there was a small humming tone, a click, then a soft feminine voice said,

"I know, Tom, I just saw a bulletin on TV."

"I'll be there as soon as I can get away, Tom said. "I have to get rid of the Press first.... I haven't even seen my staff yet. Shine up your crystal, Jaca, I'll need you to read for me tonight."

"All right, Tom. I' ll be waiting."

Hanging up the white phone, Tom turned back to his waiting secretary and gave her a big smile. "Row—you're always here when I need you. Just stick real close to me and record everything that happens, okay?"

Rowena nodded and returned the smile, activating her wrist video unit as Harold Acedorian burst in to the room, out of breath, his full head of gray hair mussed and uncombed.

Nodding to Rowena, he said, "Tom, I talked to Seismic Central. They're in a panic over there, don't know what the hell happened. They picked up nothing at all—not a twitch—

54

until the quake hit, at exactly midnight our time. Then everything lit up like the Fourth of July!"

"Do they know how big it was?"

"Not exactly, yet, but it was a whopper—at least a seven. The epicenter was directly under the western section of Cairo, on the west bank of the Nile. They're estimating casualties in the thousands and tens of millions in property damage."

"Dammit, Harry!" Tom slammed his fist on the arm of his chair. "You know what this means, then. Somebody created this quake deliberately! And nobody has the ability to create man-made quakes except us and Russia."

The Vice-President managed a grim smile. "As far as we know, Tom. But weather control is like nuclear weapons—the secret's bound to get out sooner or later. It's one of the things we've always feared—that maybe North Korea or terrorists would start experimenting with a weather machine of some kind. We know the Russians sold the technology years ago."

Tom rubbed his chin nervously, feeling the late-hour bristles which fortunately didn't show.

"But it just doesn't make sense, Harry. I mean, why Egypt? If it was one of the Islamic countries, you'd think they'd hit Israel first, wouldn't you?"

"I just don't know. But we're gonna have to have to tell the Press something tomorrow. Their number one question's going to be, How could a major quake strike one of our allies without prior warning? Is the QEWPIE system proving unreliable?"

"You're right, Harry. QEWPIE's going to have to take the heat. We're going to have to tell them that the system screwed up, but we don't know how or why yet, and we're checking it out. We'll have to stall as long as we can. The truth is an unknown at this point, and our suspicions could cause a real panic. We sure as hell don't want another Gulf War.

Harry nodded. "Sometimes it's best to admit you don't know a damn thing, and this is one of those times. But now we've got to find out what's really going on—fast! It won't take Seismic Central long to check out QEWPIE and discover it's still functioning perfectly, which fact they will rapidly and loudly announce to the world. We'll have to have something ready to cover that."

Tom closed his eyes, trying to slow down the churning turmoil in his mind. "Okay, Harry, that's your job—damage control. Work out a story—something about a freak circuit malfunction due to a sudden sunspot bombardment or whatever. Talk to Kirkman over at Cosmodyne—he's a computer whiz, he'll help you out, give you some language. He's a friend, and he owes me—"

The executive phone chirped, cutting him off. Harry picked up and when he heard who was calling, his eyes widened in concern. He held the receiver out to Tom.

"It's President Fahey of Egypt."

"Saoud!" exclaimed Warren, grabbing the phone. "Thank God! I'm relieved you called. I was afraid you might have been.... Yes, yes, we know all about it—it's terrible!" There was a long pause, during which Tom's face changed, became ashen with concern and shock. "Oh, no...that bad? My God.... And you had no warning at all?...No, neither did we.... Listen, Saoud, I need some time. We're assessing your situation right now via satellite and we'll be sending you food and medical supplies as soon as possible.... Yes, tomorrow at the latest.... How about the Aswan Dam? Is it holding?.... Good, good.... What? Russia? Hell, I don't think so...it doesn't make sense.... That's right....Well, I'm going to do my damnedest to find out. Look, I've got to go now, but I'm relieved that you and your family are all right. I'll keep you posted, and if you find out anything over there, let me know, will you? Right.... Yes, you too. Goodbye."

Harry's legs suddenly felt like Jell-O. He hadn't liked the look on Tom's face during the conversation and he liked it even less now.

"How bad?" he asked.

"Pretty bad," Tom replied. "The western half of Cairo is leveled, thousands dead, thousands more injured. Oddly enough, though, very little damage on the east bank, thank God. Their seismographs registered the quake at 7.9...."

"Christ," breathed the Vice President.

56

Tom picked up his jacket. "Harry, get on that computer thing for me right away, will you? If you have to wake people up, wake 'em up. If Fahey calls back with anything, you take it. Try to keep him calm. I have to get over to Jaca's— she's our one hope of unraveling this thing fast. If she can get a reading on what's going on, maybe we can figure out how to deal with it. I'll be back in a couple of hours and we'll go over whatever we've got."

He turned to Rowena, grinned and said, "Row, I want you to do a "Nixon" on what you've been taping. Cut out any reference to the weather-war business. Keep the rest and file it for me, okay?"

"Gotcha, Chief," she replied.

The President was out the door and into the cold Washington night so fast the Secret Service men in the corridor were left yards behind and had to scramble to catch up.

It is the business of the future to be dangerous.
—Alfred North Whitehead

CHAPTER SIX

THE PRESIDENT'S READER

WASHINGTON, D.C.: 1 NOVEMBER 2020. 12:15 A.M.

It was still snowing lightly, but the main fury of the storm had spent itself and the great dark cloud masses were beginning to roll away down the black November sky, allowing a star or two to gleam through like the eyes of hopeful children. The President was oblivious to the weather as he entered the waiting black Cadillac Elecdorado, the first presidential limousine ever powered solely by electricity. Two Secret Service men piled into the plush interior with him as he told the driver, "The Ciencé house—fast."

As the big car moved quickly and silently, like a prowling black panther, through the dark, slush-choked streets of the Capitol, Tom settled back and closed eyes burning with fatigue.

Could it really be Russia or North Korea? he wondered. Why, for God's sake? What can they hope to gain by destroying Cairo? They can't foist it off as a natural quake—they know we have QEWPIE. It just doesn't make sense. With all the internal strife they have to deal with, why would they blow it all like this?

Tom's mind flashed back over the delicate situation that had existed back in the 1970s and '80s, when Russian scientists had developed a machine, based partially on some secret experiments by the strange genius Nikola Tesla, which was able to selectively control conditions in the ionosphere and

58

troposphere, causing freak weather incidents and disasters almost at will anywhere on Earth. They had begun experimenting in the United States and other western countries, creating unusually severe storms, droughts and floods. U.S. Intelligence had quickly discovered what was going on, although the news was carefully withheld from the public, and the government had immediately begun its own weather war experimentation in an effort to catch up with the Russians. It was Sputnik *redux*.

A top-secret project was set up in Fairbanks, Alaska, under the code name "Operation Plowshare." Development had been rapid, particularly since the U.S. had access to the notes and plans that had been seized from Tesla's laboratory by the FBI immediately after his death. Soon the U.S. weather device was returning droughts, blizzards and tornadoes in kind.

Then came the fall of Russian communism in 1989 and the splitting off of the former Soviet Union into many smaller independent states. A weakened Russia agreed to halt further experiments in the spirit of the uneasy accord that was created between that country and ours.

U.S. scientists were aware that earthquakes could also be caused by a Tesla-invented mechanism that could interfere with the Russian device, but fortunately, Soviet scientists hadn't attempted this. The quakes that had occurred during recent years were all natural in origin.

So where does that leave us? Tom wondered. We still don't know a damned thing. If it weren't the Russians or another country, then it was a natural disaster. But if so, why didn't the warning system work?

A few minutes later, the presidential limo arrived at the private entrance to a large estate. An elegant snow-covered sign over a high iron gate read: CIENCÉ PARK. The driver pushed a red button on the dashboard and a few seconds later, the gate rolled back. The big car moved noiselessly through spacious grounds beautifully landscaped and covered with a great white blanket of snow, past tall dark skeletons of trees dreaming of spring, until it reached a large English Tudor-style house. A light burned over the carven oak front door, transforming the drifting flakes into chips that glittered like diamonds.

"Let me go in alone," Warren told the Secret Service men, as he got out of the car. The front door opened as he reached it, his shoes crunching in the wet snow, and Jaca Ciencé, dressed in a white Grecian robe that bared one alabaster shoulder, was waiting just inside, like a goddess welcoming him to the Mysteries. She stood a foot shorter than Warren, with soft shoulder-length hair the color of honey and apricots and striking gray-green eyes that changed color according to her mood. She greeted him with a warm smile and a long, sweet kiss, her face radiating an almost ethereal beauty.

After a long moment, Tom held her at arm's length, gazing into the mysterious depths of the eyes, now green as emeralds, that captivated him anew each time he saw her. They had no need of words—each basked in the warmth of the other's inner sun. Tom reminded himself for the hundredth time how incredibly lucky he was to have this woman at his side when he needed help, with her fathomless reserves of love and spiritual strength.

"Follow me, Tom," she said, after he removed his overcoat and wet shoes. The house was warm as a summer's day as he put on a white silk robe with a purple tassel and slipped his feet into white ermine slippers like hers.

As he followed Jaca out of the large elegant living room which glowed darkly with the rich, warm wood of antique furnishings. Tom remembered their first meeting, years ago, when he had been a junior senator. She was a world acclaimed psychic, medium and crystallographer, reading for the rich and famous, and he had come to her for political advice, but skeptical of the occult. She had seen deep and true into his inner self and told him that what he really wanted to do would be right for him—to run for President. Her uncanny sensitivity to every nuance of his character and aspirations had completely captivated him, and she gave him the final ounce of courage and determination he needed to take the giant step. He had believed her when she said he could win—and he had won.

After the election, Tom had wanted to show his appreciation in some way. Jaca had explained to him why only pure quartz crystal and not glass must be used in scrying, or crystal-gazing, as it is commonly known.

"Crystal oscillates at its own natural frequency until you touch it," she had told him. "Then it begins to feed on the electricity that surrounds your living cells. It vibrates in sympathy with you and acts as an amplifier for your psychic receptors."

So he had begun searching for a really fine crystal for her, but had had difficulty in locating one. However, a few months later, the Chinese Ambassador was able to purchase for him what was considered to be the largest and finest pure quartz crystal in the world. It measured an incredible 24 and 7/8 inches in diameter and weighed 106 and 3/4 pounds, hand-crafted from flawless Burmese Quartz. Jaca had been ecstatic when Tom presented it to her and from then on had insisted on reading for him whenever he wished, at any hour of the day or night. She had been of immense help to Warren, providing both spiritual and mundane guidance in times of need, and they had become very close.

Until he had met her, Tom had felt sad and depressed after the death of his wife. Then Jaca Ciencé had entered his world, and although the opportunities for them to be together had been agonizingly few, Tom felt that a great emptiness he had too long ignored was now filled with a special light. For her, he found that he was willing to take chances that had seemed unthinkable before.

Taking Tom's hand, Jaca led him upstairs and into a round high-ceilinged tower room with a large Indian mandala made from precious gems set into the floor. Here the only light was from a large beeswax taper, striking an aureate glow from the solid gold Sanscrit symbols for the ancient word-sound "OM" set into twelve separate seat locations around the periphery of the multicolored mandala, one for each sign of the Zodiac.

Each taking a small pillow, Tom and Jaca sat in the lotus position, facing each other in silence across the glittering gem-flower. Closing her eyes, Jaca concentrated, slim fingertips pressed to her temples, and from out of the darkness

61

above, her great crystal ball slowly began to descend between them, gently cradled in a net of small golden chains. There was no audible hum of machinery as the brilliant sphere descended until it hung suspended at eye level. Tom was reminded of a crystal womb, waiting to be filled with the light of life.

Then the golden chains supporting the ball fell away, forming a glittering web across the surface of the mandala, *but the crystal remained in place, apparently suspended in mid-air!* This was always the spookiest part to Tom: he conjectured psychokinesis, but doubtfully, because this would take too much of Jaca's concentration and energy—or would it? What else? Hidden wires? Microwave suspension? Antigravity? He would love to know, but he felt certain that Jaca would only smile and say, "Sorry, Tom, trade secrets, you know!"

A voice like a mountain spring, far away but very clear, seemed to speak silently to him:

> *Still your mind now. Become receptive.*
> *The how is not important to you...listen to the*
> *what, the where and the when....*

Then, light streamed up from beneath the jeweled mandala, shooting beams of rainbow radiance into the deep dark of the room, bathing Tom and Jaca in vibrant tones of ruby, gold, amethyst, green and blue. With the light came a soothing warmth that seemed to penetrate deep into Tom's body, showering every cell with tingling, polychromatic energy. Yet the great crystal remained clear and waiting. A delicate scent of jasmine caressed his nostrils as he eagerly watched the beautiful quiet face across from him.

Jaca's eyes were now closed and she had relaxed into a light trance, linking her consciousness with the crystal's vibrations. In a soft, low voice, she asked, "What questions do you have? The teachers are with us now."

Tom felt tides of power beating through the room like waves on a shore and felt the spiritual warmth of many presences clustered around them, unseen and waiting.

"The Egyptian earthquake earlier tonight—was it natural or man-made?" he asked.

Jaca's eyes snapped open and the crystal suddenly became alive with vivid colors and symbols visible to her inner vision only. Tom saw nothing different, although he stared deeply into the pellucid depths, as if trying to see what Jaca saw.

Peering intently into the mysterious sphere, Jaca spoke: "The cataclysm was not a natural one. There is nothing wrong with the warning system. The earthquake was caused by a machine."

"Damn!" Tom snapped. "I knew it! Was it the Russians?"

Jaca shook her head. "No. They're as perplexed about it as you are."

"Who, then? North Korea? I don't understand."

"The picture is cloudy, very dark.... I see the face of a woman with eyes like a tiger's...she's very beautiful, but she's not human...."

"Not human? What—?"

"Please...let me continue.... She comes from a dark, evil planet in this galaxy.... I'm being shown a strange symbol...it's the magical seal of her sun.... It's the seal of...Algol, the Demon Star."

Tom felt an icy wind sweep suddenly down his spine. "The Demon Star? Oh, come on..."

"This star is well named. It is a malefic influence, giving off waves of dark psychic radiation that affect all the worlds of the galaxy to varying degrees, but especially the planets in its own solar system. They've become hellish worlds inhabited by worshippers of the Dark Power of the universe—the same power we call Satan or Lucifer. The eighth planet—Caput Algol—is the homeworld from which this woman has come."

Tom shuddered. no longer warmed by the rainbow light. "But who is she? You say she's an extraterrestrial but looks human?"

"Yes...through the use of vile scientific and sorcerous techniques, she has been physically transformed from her nonhuman alien shape into that of an earth woman in order to work undetected here. She is actually the Queen of the Algolians, and her sacrifice was a great and agonizing one. It has fueled her hatred of the earth and its people and spurs her on toward her terrible goal."

"How did she come here? We've had no reports of unfriendly spacecraft."

"There is an Algolian starship secretly in orbit around the earth at this time. I'm getting a name...K-A-L-O-N...and then a number that translates to...Kalon 22...this is the Algolian ship, which is hidden from radar or visual detection by an energy screen. There's a lot of advanced equipment aboard, including part of the weather machine used to create the earthquake in Cairo."

Tom groaned, grinding his teeth in horror. "Oh, Christ...this is much worse than I feared...." His mind spun like a cyclone. A malevolent planet with a fully perfected weather weapon, apparently using it to create strife and suspicion between nations. It was truly diabolical...but why?

"What the devil...what does she want?" Tom asked. "Is she trying to start World War III?"

"She wants to bring the nations of the world to their knees, worn out economically and spiritually from the cumulative effects of many apparently 'natural' disasters. She has been responsible for much of the destructive weather and many of the climactic catastrophes that have plagued the United States and other countries recently. Her eventual goal is nothing less than total control of the planet—absolute submission to the hordes of Algolians who are looking for a new world to inhabit and plunder as they have Caput Algol, now sterile and overcrowded."

"Holy Mother of God," Tom murmured. "But what about the people of earth? With eight billion population, we're overcrowded, too. What could they possibly want with eight billion slaves?"

"The Algolians possess sophisticated methods of mass extermination. They will destroy most of the world's population and keep the rest for slaves. Their Queen is utterly ruthless and will stop at nothing to achieve her plan. She is also very powerful financially and can utilize black magic in her cause as well as the advanced scientific devices developed on her home planet. She has hundreds of followers, both human and nonhuman, strategically placed around the world. They too worship the one they call the Dark Father. They draw strength from negativity and evil and will do anything she commands."

"Well, who *is* she, for God's sake, and *where* is she—?"

"She's not far away, yet I can't see clearly just where she is right now.... It's not in this country.... I believe there are...barriers, yes, psychic barriers preventing the information from coming through clearly.... She's very powerful...."

Impatiently, Tom asked, "Can't you tell who she is? Her name?"

There was silence for a moment, while Warren forgot to breathe.

"The name...just won't...come through now. Perhaps later on."

Tom fought back disappointment and frustration bitter as bile in his throat. "Is there anything else you can tell me about her, whoever she is?"

Silence for a moment, as Jaca's inner vision again probed deeply into the crystal, then: "Yes...there is one other thing, which may help you identify her. It's not completely clear, but it appears that within the next few weeks she'll be negotiating to buy some property...I see pyramids...ah, it's the Giza Plateau. She's trying to purchase the Giza Plateau from the Egyptian government."

Tom was dumbrounded. "The Giza Plateau? That's insane! The Egyptians would never sell the Pyramids, the Sphinx, their most precious national treasures...."

"They may be forced to. The destruction of a large portion of Cairo will prove a disastrous blow to the Egyptian economy. In order to keep the country from going bankrupt, they may have to accede to her demands. It will all be done in secret, so that the Egyptian people and other governments won't find out until too late."

Tom rubbed his chin nervously. "Yes, I can see how Fahey might buckle under to the economic pressure and ram this deal through the Egyptian parliament, but I still don't know *why* this woman wants the plateau. Can you see anything more?"

Jaca's eyes grew more distant, like a gray-misted lake at dawn. "Let me see.... I'm getting something very strange...but very important.... A buried city...a pyramid...a machine of some kind...."

Suddenly Jaca's voice changed, her intonation became slower, more formal and controlled. Tom received an overwhelming impression of great power and peace as he realized that a spiritual teacher from the inner planes was taking over and speaking directly through Jaca, using her as a medium. It was still her voice Tom heard, but deeper, more resonant; the consciousness behind it was of a higher spiritual nature than that of earthbound souls.

"I give you greeting, Thomas Warren," the presence said. "My name is Klorian. I have been assigned to instruct and guide you in the difficult task facing you during the days and months to come. Because of the extreme importance of the information I must impart, I have decided to speak directly to you through this channel—with her permission, of course."

Tom was amazed and impressed. He had never witnessed Jaca's mediumistic abilities before, although she had told him about them. Her body leaned forward slightly, hands clasped, and a piercing intelligence gleamed in her now-emerald eyes.

"There is much you must know," continued the spiritual teacher. "A great effort must be made against the dark forces which now threaten your world. I can help you, as will those who work with me and those who are my teachers, but the ultimate fate of your people and your planet rests with you and those who work with you.

"Your first task will be to mount a secret expedition to Egypt as soon as possible. There is a buried city there, under the sands of the Giza Plateau. In that city, which was constructed thousands of years ago, is a ruby pyramid. Inside this beautiful structure is a machine called the Immobilizer, also constructed ages ago and left there by an advanced race from the stars."

"So that's it," said Tom, as light began to dawn. "A super-powerful machine...and the Algolians know it's there? That's why this woman wants to buy the plateau?"

66

"Yes...her black divinations have revealed to her the existence of this machine, and she is desperate to possess it.... This Immobilizer could speed the completion of her plan by many years, for with it she could render the entire planet virtually defenseless against the Algolian hordes. This is why you must find it before she does. With it, you can neutralize her weather machine and the other scientific devices the Algolians have given her. But you must work rapidly, before she can block your access to the plateau."

Tom's mind spun frantically, a vortex of anxiety that threatened to swallow him up. He realized that he was soaked with sweat, the white robe sticking to his back. Taking a deep breath, he steadied himself, then said, "Okay, Klorian, thanks...that clears up part of the mystery, puts it in game terms we can all understand. Madame Algol wants the Immobilizer to stop the world, and we want the Immobilizer to stop her. What's the best way to go about beating her to the punch?"

"The symbol I see is a five-pointed star—a pentagram—with a separate, smaller star beside it. There are five people who are to combine their talents and courage for this mission. They will be led by a young woman, whose strong positive nature will help to balance the negativity of your female adversary. They will form a Pentad, a very powerful occult force, for five is a potent number, strong against evil. It represents justice and victory; the upright pentagram is also the symbol of humankind."

"Who are these five people, Klorian?"

"They are five of your agents in the Psychic Intelligence Agency. Their extrasensory gifts will prove very helpful in the coming struggle. They will have spiritual help and guidance on this endeavor, but their way will be long and difficult."

Hardly daring to, Tom couldn't stop himself from asking, "Can you see the outcome? Will we get the machine before the other side...?"

"At this time, I cannot tell for certain. There are many choices to be made on both sides, and the alternate realities shift and eddy like a network of mists, probabilities which will become real to you only as you choose them. Remember always that there is free will, Thomas Warren. It is up to you and your agents to choose correctly."

"Then let's worry about the present right now. Who are the five Psi-Spies? And what about that small star you saw next to the big one? What does that mean?"

"The small star represents a young Gemini woman with a sweet face and a lovely, unspoiled soul. Her eyes have extremely sensitive retinas which enable her to see the auras of hidden minerals and water deep underground. You have already used her successfully in other assignments, although she is new to your organization."

"That's Gabrielle Bane."

"Her fate is not an easy one, I'm afraid," said Klorian. "She must become a sacrificial lamb for the advancement of the others on the side of Light. She must undergo terrible hardships, both mental and physical, but she will have spiritual help."

Tom felt dread clutch his heart with a leaden glove. "What sort of hardships? Can she handle them?"

"Her soul has accepted this responsibility," replied the spiritual teacher. "Do not grieve for her. Her courage and goodness can see her through the ordeal, even when it seems to all of you—and especially to her—that all is lost, but success will require careful planning and preparation and great spiritual strength from the rest of you. Her consciousness at the physical level is unaware of what must be done. You and the others must guide her. But you will know what to do when the time comes, if you are strong and do not give in to despair."

Tom nodded soberly. "All right. Who's next? Who are the main five?"

"Next I see a male, young, laughing, vigorous. Gray eyes, black hair, tall and strong with an open, friendly nature and a creative imagination. His psychic talent is clairaudience and he is very knowledgeable concerning ancient Egypt. This comes from experiencing many lives in that land. He will be a very valuable member of the team. I see a lion basking in the warmth of the sun—he is a Leo."

"That would be Christopher Troy. He's—" Suddenly a terrible thought smashed him like a fist. "Klorian! Troy and

68

Eris Campbell were on a mission for me in Egypt when the quake hit! My God, I'd forgotten until now.... Are they all right? Can you see them?"

A moment, then Klorian answered, "Yes, they are both unharmed, although they have come through great peril. They are at present helping the injured in Cairo."

Tom heaved a great sigh of relief. "Thank God...."

"It will also interest you to know that the bombings in Cairo which you sent these two to investigate were also part of the Algolian woman's campaign of terror, to force the sale of the Giza Plateau for her purposes."

"Yes...it makes sense, ties in to the whole picture. Can we—who's next? Sorry for the interruption."

"There is no need to apologize, Thomas Warren. A leader who is not concerned about those he leads does not deserve to lead. I see cameras and photographs around the next man. He is sensitive, impulsive, also tall, but fair-haired, with brown eyes. He was born in Paris, but educated in England and America. His psychic talent is clairvoyance, his symbol a centaur. He is a Sagittarian, in some ways similar to you."

"That's André Renard—he's also on assignment for me now, with Gabrielle. A good man. Who else do you see?"

"This next man is dark and intense, bearded, a Scorpio and very stubborn, but with a good heart. The son of an Israeli mother and a Japanese father, he has surrounded himself with mathematical symbols. He works with both the physical and psychic sciences, seeking ways to combine them and make each enhance the other. He has a great deal of ambition and has already made remarkable contributions to your sciences. I see him accepting a prize of some sort."

Warren grinned. "Avram Sumi. He was awarded the Nobel Prize in Physics this year."

"Yes...he has developed a machine which will be of particular value to your expedition. He has also trained himself to perform feats of psychokinesis, a psychic talent well worth utilizing in the coming trial."

"Number four? asked Tom, feeling more at ease now.

"The fourth man is black, with lively brown eyes and a most energetic temperament. He is an electronics and computer expert, with several degrees in advanced engineering and metallurgy, and is also one of the few living adepts at the ancient art of alchemy. An Aries, his alchemical work has enabled him to transmute much of his naturally impulsive nature onto a higher spiritual plane. He has a fine sense of humor and will be a loyal companion. His psychic talent is psychometry.

"With this man I see a peculiar cat, a very special creature. It is not alive, yet seems astonishingly so. A remarkable creation indeed, produced by this man's daringly innovative genius."

"That's Raymond Gaunt—terrific!" Tom exclaimed. "Now, who's going to lead this team? Didn't you say it would be a woman?"

"Yes...she is young and beautiful, with long blonde hair and blue-green eyes. She has the gift of retrocognition—she can astrally visit the past."

Tom smiled. "Eris, of course. But she's so young—why should she be the leader? Why not somebody with more experience?"

Klorian smiled with Jaca's lovely mouth. "She is a Capricorn...they are natural organizers. And besides, she is so charming and well-liked that the men will not mind taking orders from her. It also has to do with certain karmic responsibilities she has undertaken in this life."

Tom nodded, pleased with the choices. "Fine, Klorian. These are my top agents. Now, what about this buried city they're supposed to find? Where is it?"

"The Sphinx appears...the Temple of Records. Your people will discover this city far below the sands of the Giza Plateau. Inside the Ruby Pyramid are the records and treasures of the past...the history of your civilizations, both known and unknown to you, the true history of your world and its peoples, stretching back millions of years. The time has at last arrived when this information must be brought forth. And with it, the Immobilizer. I must leave you now. I have other business of a pressing nature, and besides, I do not wish to tire my lovely hostess."

Jaca's eyes closed, then opened, clear and focused on the present. Her spirit, temporarily and voluntarily dispos-

70

sessed, had returned to her body. Coming out of her trance, she asked sleepily, "Well, does that do it for you?"

Tom grinned at her, his head still whirling from the incredible information he had absorbed. "I'll say—your man in Nirvana took over and really laid it on! Do you know what he told me?"

"No. I was off somewhere else, but I don't quite remember it now. Somewhere nice and restful...."

"How do you feel?"

Jaca stretched luxuriously, reaching above herself into the multicolored beams that still radiated upward from the crystalline mandala. "I feel great! My teachers always leave me with a big shot of energy, although my throat still feels a little funny. I must have done a lot of talking."

Tom nodded, still feeling as if he'd been kicked in the head. "You sure did, lady, you sure did."

As they got to their feet, the rainbow radiance died away and the glittering golden chains mysteriously moved upward and reformed themselves around the darkened crystal, cradling and lifting it slowly back up into the darkness.

Shaking his head, Tom moved over to Jaca, held her close to him. "Someday, you've gotta tell me how you do that, sweetheart," he murmured.

Her answering laugh was like muted wind chimes. "Can you stay?" she asked softly.

"Mmmm...don't I wish! But I have to get back and brief Row and Harry on this thing. They'll be waiting up for me."

"Is it very bad, Tom?"

"Worse than I thought, love. I'll talk to you about it in the morning." Jaca pressed her slim body to his tightly, as if trying to pass some of her energy to him. "Don't worry, darling. Whatever it is, we'll have lots of help from the inner planes. We'll do whatever has to be done. Come...I'll walk you to the door."

Reluctantly he released her sweet warmth and they left the tower room, hand in hand.

At the front door, once more attired in his street clothes, Tom again embraced Jaca, kissed her long and deeply. "I love you, sweet sorceress." he said.

She smiled up at him, radiant as dawn, with eyes of molten emerald. "And I love you, Mr. President.... Call me."

Tom squeezed her hand and was out the door into the frosty night. He cast an adoring glance back over his shoulder as she whispered after him, "God go with you, Tom...."

The snow had stopped falling and the night was rapidly clearing into crystalline coldness. His breath steaming like a radiator, Tom looked up at the star-littered blackness, wondering which one was Algol....

"Drive me around for awhile," he told the driver as he got into the waiting limousine. He wanted to do some thinking, sort out the incredible information he had received, before conferring with his staff back at the White House.

Over the moon we could hear
the voice of the president,
clear as a church bell,
simple as ether.
　　　—*Jerome Rothenberg, "A POEM FOR THE WEATHER"*

CHAPTER SEVEN

THE SUMMONING

WASHINGTON, D.C.: 2 NOVEMBER 2020

The next morning, after three hours of deep and dream-less sleep, President Warren was in the Oval Office early, talking once again with the President of Egypt. After some difficulty at the Egyptian end, the com line had been cleared of static and put on Top Secret Scramble. On the video screen, President Fahey's normally light-chocolate complex-ion looked ash-gray, his face tired and haggard, hls eyes red from looking at too much destruction and death.

"Saoud, how are you?.... Fine...we received your dam-age report this morning.... Yes, it's terrible, but it could have been worse. At least most of Cairo is undamaged.... Yes, I'm afraid you're right...that casualty figure will probably go much higher as they find more bodies in the rubble.... No, it *wasn't* Russia.... Yes, I'm relieved too, but we're up against something else, maybe a lot worse.... Saoud, I'm sorry, but I can't talk about it yet...no, not even to you.... Because I need verification, proof. Look, I'm going to send some of my best agents over to check this out in detail. They're specially qualified for this kind of operation, but I'll need your full cooperation, okay?...Great, I knew I could count on you. There'll be five of them...when? Around the middle of November, I'd say.... Well, they need two weeks to prepare, that's why. This has got to be absolutely top secret—I don't want *anybody* to know what their real mission is except you.... Right. I'll let you know as soon as I have proof. I'm asking you to trust me on this, Saoud.... In the meantime, we'll keep sending you all the food, clothing and medical supplies we can scrape together....

"Now listen, there's something else I have to ask you...it's very important.... Have you been approached by anyone lately wanting to purchase the Giza Plateau?"

There was a long, shocked silence from the Egyptian President. His face seemed to turn even grayer. He looked like he was going to throw up. Finally he said, "Yes, but how could you have known about it? We have kept this top secret!"

"Don't worry about a security leak, Saoud. Just call it an educated guess, based on some preliminary facts we've uncovered here.... Now *who* is it that's trying to buy the Plateau? Is it a woman?"

Fahey replied that the identity of the actual person or organization was unknown; they wished to remain anonymous. Several months ago, a man claiming to represent a powerful monied interest approached the Minister of Finance, Serabi Khadiz, and made the offer. Because of the terrible economic situation in Egypt, Khadiz had been pressuring the government ever since to accept the offer, but Fahey had been opposed to it. He didn't like dealing with anonymous parties, and he didn't like the idea of selling Egypt's most famous piece of real estate to some foreign interest. It would be like selling part of the history and culture of Egypt, betraying the very birthright of the Egyptian people.

"How much did the man offer you?" asked Warren.

Fahey told him. Tom whistled through his teeth. "That kind of money means we're not just dealing with some eccentric Howard Hughes type with a whim to own his own pyramid. This has to be a *giant* multinational conglomerate of some kind—a real dinosaur! Well, Saoud, I know that kind of a deal must seem very tempting right now, but it's extremely important that you stick to your guns and keep opposing this sale!...Yes, more important that you can possibly imagine.... No, I can't tell you any more than that now... you've *got* to trust me on this.... I promise I'll let you know what's going on the minute I'm certain. You've got to do all you can to rally support in parliament against Khadiz. If you can't defeat the sale, at least do everything you can to stall as long as possible. We need time right now—as much as we can get!.... Okay? .... Good man! I knew I could count on you. Keep me posted, will you?...Yes, you too...our prayers are with you, Saoud. *Salaam aleikum.*"

Tom closed his eyes for a few seconds, resting his head in his hands. His eyelids felt hot and gritty and a vague feeling of uneasiness drifted through his mind like a gray wind. God, he thought, I can't believe all this is really happening....

But it was, he knew with grim certainty, and his next move was to locate the five agents who would be brought back here for briefing and training at PSI-QUARK. Shaking off the hazy fog of fatigue and apprehension, he poured himself a cup of black coffee from the carafe on his desk and slugged it down. He felt better as soon as the caffeine began to assault his nervous system.

Pressing a button on his desk, he watched a 6"x9" section of the gleaming polished oak transmute itself into a glass screen. The video display terminal of the President's private microcomputer glowed with the words, READY FOR ACCESS.

Pressing another button to activate the voice-response program, the President asked the computer to display the locations of the six Psi-Spies he wished to contact. In seconds, the following information spilled across the screen in lines of emerald light:

BANE, GABRIELLE, PIA # 6, NEW ORLEANS
CAMPBELL, ERIS, PIA # 12, CAIRO
GAUNT, RAYMOND E, PIA # 5, IBIZA, SPAIN
RENARD, ANDRÉ C, PIA # 8, NEW ORLEANS
SUMI, AVRAM, PIA # 14, GENEVA
TROY, CHRISTOPHER D, PIA # 17, CAIRO

After memorizing the numbers and locations of the agents, Warren switched off the computer and the small screen became a wooden desktop once again. He buzzed Rowena and told her to hold all incoming calls for half an hour, then settled back in the plush presidential chair. Closing his eyes, he began a special series of mental exercises to enable him to still his mind, tune out his immediate surroundings and concentrate.

After a few moments, he felt himself reach alpha, felt his pulse and heartbeat steady out, and began to concentrate on the round, quarter-sized medallion he wore next to his heart chakra. He marveled at the power and precision of this almost miraculous device, developed through the superb interaction of scientists and psychics at last working together, instead of at odds as they had for so long. The Psychic Intelligence Agency, under the able leadership of Dr. Gideon Stack and the President's close supervision, had created a special environment in which this cooperation was bearing incredible fruit: the fusion engine and the solar-powered plane; the toxic-waste-eating Pseudomonas IX, mutated descendant of the original artificial oil-eating microorganism developed years ago to clean up petroleum spills; and amazing breakthroughs in the control and manipulation of psychic and paranormal phenomena.

And of course, the medallion, composed of a special alloy of gold and copper according to the ancient formula for the fabled Atlantean metal called *orichalcum*. It was the development of this device, along with Jaca's eerie talents, which had finally made the somewhat skeptical President a firm believer in the incredible potential of ESP as a force for the advancement of mankind—and a powerful weapon against aggression.

The President recalled almost with awe how, deep in the subterranean laboratories of PSI-QUARK (the code name for PIA headquarters), Eris Campbell had reached back with her mind through millennia of time, through countless mist-shrouded former lifetimes, into a time before recorded time, into the minds and crucibles of Atlantean priest-scientists, to bring forward the long-forgotten formula for *orichalcum*, the sacred metal of the Lost Continent. Then Raymond Gaunt's

76

amazing skills in the ancient art of alchemy, working with the psychic enhancement devices of Nobel Prize-winning Avram Sumi and other brilliant scientists, and incorporating the latest advances in nanochip circuitry, had produced the "Mentacom Medallion," ("MM" for short) now worn by the President and each Psi-Spy in the PIA.

Utilizing the naturally high energy fields surrounding the Psi-Spies, each agent's medallion was attuned to a special occult number assigned to him or her. Once the individual vibratory rate of that number was contacted and brought into that agent's consciousness, strong mental concentration resulted in two-way telepathic communication, enhanced, amplified, transmitted and received by the medallion. The MMs were attached to each agent's chest, near the heart chakra, with a non-irritating organic adhesive which could only be removed with a special solvent. The only other way for an agent to lose the medallion was to have it torn off, taking the skin with it.

By linking himself telepathically with all his agents, the President had at his command a totally secret communications network (called PSINET) through which he could contact any or all of them almost instantly, at any time, in any spot on Earth.

Now the President was concentrating on Agent 14, Avram Sumi, busy with experiments at his lab in Geneva. At the moment, Sumi was deeply involved in a mathematical equation and didn't feel the round disk begin to grow warm against his skin, the way in which each agent knew when mental contact was desired.

Receiving no response, Tom again sent out his thoughts:

PSINET 21 CALLING 14. ACKNOWLEDGE! URGENT!

Slowly, Sumi began to become aware of a mental call intruding on his lofty calculations. The pure, rarified world of higher mathematics was like another universe to him, far removed from the mundane duties and irritations of everyday reality. Coming down out of it was almost like coming down off a massive drug dose; the diamond-bright euphoria of intellectual concentration quickly faded away, to be replaced

77

by a gray depression. Instead of the crystalline perfection of numbers and abstract formulae, there were now imperfect *people* to deal with. And they always wanted something.

So now it was the President, Sumi realized, as the number 21 vibrated in his consciousness. Well, at least he usually has something interesting to say. Let's see what it is.

PSINET 14 HERE, BOSS. OKAY, WHAT'S SO URGENT? YOU SLIPPING IN THE POPULARITY POLLS ALREADY?

Tom smiled despite his seriousness, visualizing Avram Sumi's dark, saturnine visage far away in Switzerland, mischief twinkling in his midnight eyes.

SORRY TO DISAPPOINT YOU, BUT THEY STILL LOVE ME OUT THERE IN GRASSROOTS LAND. I NEED YOU RIGHT AWAY. IMPORTANT AS-SIGNMENT. REPORT TO PSI-QUARK IMMEDIATELY FOR INTENSIVE TWO-WEEK TRAINING. I'LL GIVE YOU ALL THE DETAILS WHEN YOU ARRIVE.

NO FAIR. YOU PROMISED ME A VACATION. BESIDES, YOU DON'T PAY ENOUGH TO LURE ME AWAY FROM WINE, WOMEN AND PARAPHYSICS.

YOU CAN PLAY LATER. IT'S YOUR OWN FAULT FOR BEING A GODDAMN GENIUS. ASSIGNMENT EXTREMELY IMPORTANT. BUT YOU'LL LOVE IT, TRUST ME. YOU CAN SHOW OFF YOUR NEW TOY.

YOU SAID THE MAGIC WORD, BOSS. I'LL BRING THE BOX AND CATCH THE NEXT FLIGHT OUT. WHO ELSE IS IN ON THIS?

YOU'LL FIND OUT WHEN YOU GET HERE. ALL TOP PEOPLE. SIGNING OFF NOW. SEE YOU TUESDAY.

Sumi came up out of the depths of his concentration, once more centering himself in the physical world around him. Must be something really big, he mused, if Great White Father himself is summoning the tribe.

Sumi's swarthy brow wrinkled in concentration for a moment. His dark eyes narrowed, almost seemed to glow briefly, and a crumpled pack of cigarettes on a nearby table rose up and slowly floated through the air and into his outstretched hand. His psychokinetic ability only worked with small, light objects so far, but constant exercising of this amazing psychic talent was steadily increasing its power. Sumi's researches had convinced him that PK and other psychic abilities were analogous in many ways to the muscles in the body; the more you used them, the stronger they became.

Finding one slightly bent cigarette left, Sumi lit it and inhaled a deep draught of smoke. He wondered whether Eris Campbell was going to be in on this assignment. He certainly hoped so. He had worked with her once before, and he didn't mind admitting, she knocked him out! What a woman! Of course, Chris Troy was out of his gourd over her, and Chris was a nice guy, but as Sumi remembered it, she apparently hadn't returned his ardor in kind. In fact, although a naturally warm, friendly woman, she had put the skids on any hint of a sexual overture from anyone. Rubbing his shaggy black beard, he smiled. Well, you never know, old son, maybe things have changed. Maybe we'll just take it slow and easy and find out....

Next the President turned his telepathic attention to Agent 5, Raymond Gaunt, sunning himself like a lizard in the peaceful winter warmth of the tiny Spanish island of Ibiza. A small, quick man, usually extremely active mentally and physically, Gaunt was enjoying one of his rare moments of quiet and relaxation. It wasn't often that his ferret-quick mind would stop running and churning long enough to allow him to rest, but through systematic application of his training in the esoteric art of alchemy, Gaunt had managed to strengthen his will enormously, transmuting the raw Mars-energy of his active nature into something more harmonious and controllable, as the ancient alchemists transmuted lead into gold. He knew he needed to stop and relax now and then; so he made himself do it. It was as simple as that. (Although actually it never lasted very long, because something more interesting always seemed to appear.)

Like the big brunette in the black string bikini who had just stretched herself out on the sand about three yards away. With one bird-like brown eye, Gaunt was admiring the incomparable engineering that had gone into the construction of that large honey-dark body. Christ, she must be six feet tall, he thought, beginning to steam inside like a pressure cooker heating up. I wonder if she's hung up about being seen with guys shorter than her?

As he lay there, listening to the harsh creaking of circling seagulls and the soft murmur of the Mediterranean surf and watching the girl begin to rub her arms and shoulders with suntan lotion, Gaunt decided that he was either going to have to make his move or vacate the area. The human endocrine system could stand only so much stress. His, anyway. Well, why not hit on her? he asked himself. Lots of women seemed to like him, attracted to his energetic brashness, and Lord knew he liked them! He'd only been on the island a few days and already he was getting restless. So far, nothing really interesting had attracted his attention, but this...*this* was something interesting! Maybe she was bored too.

He was on the verge of making his move, when he felt his Mentacom Medallion grow warm against his sun-warmed chest. Oh, no, he thought, not now!

But unlike the telephone, the MM couldn't be ignored—it was always something important. Closing his eyes reluctantly and concentrating, he heard the President's silent summons in his mind.

PSINET 21 CALLING 5. WAKE UP, 5, SIESTA'S OVER. TIME TO GO TO WORK. URGENT ASSIGNMENT.

PSINET 5 HERE, 21. BOY, YOU SURE CALLED AT THE WRONG TIME. YOU SHOULD SEE THE LOVELY THING HERE NEXT TO ME OILING UP HER MACHINERY.

Tom grinned.

JUST AS WELL I CAN'T. DON'T NEED THE EXTRA STRESS.

Gaunt chuckled, swiping at a bothersome sand fly that seemed determined to use his stomach as a landing strip.

WHAT'S UP?

FILL YOU IN WHEN YOU GET HERE. TAKE THE NEXT PLANE OUT TO D.C. EXPECT YOU ON TUESDAY.

SHALL I BRING MY ALEMBICS AND CRUCIBLES?

NO ALCHEMY THIS TIME, SORRY. BUT BRING MARIELLE. WE'LL NEED HER. CONTACT ROW AS SOON AS YOU ARRIVE. HAVE FUN, BUT WATCH THE CLOCK. 'BYE.

OKAY, CHIEF. TO TELL THE TRUTH, UNTIL NOW I WAS GETTING BORED HERE ANYWAY. MARIELLE TOO. SEE YOU TUESDAY.

Raymond Gaunt sighed, scratched his mustache and rolled over on his stomach. Well, hell, he thought, at least this'll be something new and exciting. Glancing over at the shining brunette who was now doing her thighs, he again calculated his chances of jumping those big beautiful bones. It would have to be a quickie, he told himself, if I've gotta be back in the States tomorrow. Well, why not? Let's give it a try.

Picking up his towel, Gaunt walked casually over to the girl and stood next to her. "Ah, excuse me, miss...but if you'd like someone to do your back...."

* * * * * * *

Next, President Warren contacted Gabrielle Bane (6) and André Renard (8), on assignment together in Louisiana. They reported briefly on their success in locating fresh water on a small island off Grand Isle, utilizing Gaby's X-ray dowsing powers and André's gift of clairvoyance. The President was pleased and told them to come to Washington immediately.

Finally, he contacted Eris and Chris in Cairo, and received a brief report on what was happening there.

HOW SOON CAN YOU AND 17 GET HERE IN THE *DAWN WING*?

the President asked. Eris knew she could push the plane to Mach 4—over 3,000 miles per hour—if she had to. The landing gear and nose wheel, which had been slightly damaged in their narrow escape earlier, had been fully repaired and the little craft was ready to go at a moment's notice. They could probably make the 5,822-mile trip in under two hours.

WE CAN LEAVE TOMORROW MORNING AND BE THERE BEFORE WE LEFT.

she replied mentally.

COUPLE OF HOURS, I'D SAY.

GOOD. WE'LL MEET WEDNESDAY MORNING.

And the President's strong mental presence faded away.

"I wonder what *this* is all this about? asked Eris. "If it involves the quake, wouldn't he want us to stay here and try to find out more about it?"

Chris shrugged. "Beats me. But I'm sure he has a very good reason—he usually does." Chris stood up, trying to stretch the fatigue out of his body and breathing deeply the dry cool air of Egyptian twilight. From the balcony of his hotel room, they could see Cairo spread out like a glowing jewelbox all around them. He smiled at Eris' worried face, wanting to erase the lines of concern there. He came over to her, laying his hand gently on her shoulder, feeling the tension coiled within her body like a spring trap. "Come on, pal, let's get an early night and then tomorrow morning we'll get up with the chickens and buzz out of here."

Eris smiled back at him, then moved into his arms for a hug. "Okay," she murmured against his shoulder, secretly loving the solid warmth of him. "We'll leave at 0800 in the morning. Will you call Colonel Zaid and tell him?"

"Sure. By this time tomorrow we'll be breathing that good old Washington winter air—cold and clear as crystal. And not a grain of sand for hundreds of miles !"

Eris closed her tired eyes and tried to imagine what Washington looked like now, under a mantle of soft white snow.

But all she could see was sand. And a great stone image, dark and brooding in the flames of the setting sun.

Yea, he did fly upon the wings of the wind...his pavilion round about him were dark waters and thick clouds of the skies.

—Psalms 19:10-11

CHAPTER EIGHT

DEATHFLIGHT

SOMEWHERE OVER THE NORTH ATLANTIC: 3 NOVEMBER 2020

The steadily retreating sun lanced argent fires from the silver needle that was the *Dawn Wing* as it hurtled across the deep bright sky. Forty thousand feet below, the shimmering blue-gray expanse of the North Atlantic was visible only intermittently, a secret jealously guarded by massive mounds and towers of brilliant whipped-cream clouds.

Inside the small pressurized cockpit, Eris was feeling better with every passing mile. At three and a half times the speed of sound, they seemed to be suspended silently in a vast azure bowl. There was no sound, no real feeling of movement, only the occasional hum and chitter of digital instruments and the almost inaudible hiss of oxygen being recycled in the cockpit.

Once more at the controls of the finest, most responsive airplane she had ever flown, with Chris by her side, smiling his enjoyment of her uplifted spirits as well as his own, Eris felt her mental and physical exhaustion drop away like discarded garments. As she threw the little craft across the great blue vault of sky, she felt refreshed, renewed...almost reborn. She loved Egypt deeply, its past and its people, but the terror and pain and death of the recent months, and especially the

84

last few days, had begun to weight her down like stone. She was happy to be heading home.

Home. The word sounded strange in her mind now. She felt as though she had been away and gone from her roots for centuries. But memories began to crowd into her mind now, memories of childhood....

As a little girl in Long Beach, California, she recalled entertaining herself for hours with picture books of airplanes and old comic books reprinting vintage strips such as *Smilin' Jack, Flyin' Jenny, Skyroads*, and *Tailspin Tommy*. Eris, an only child, vicariously soared high with her collection of model airplanes, remote controlled from the ground. Then, when she was twelve, she broke her leg in the first test flight of a homemade hang-glider from the top of her two-story house. The doctor told her parents she was lucky it hadn't been her neck.

Grounded but undaunted, she spent that summer in a cast reading about the insane gallantries of the fliers in World War I: the astonishing feats of the German aces—von Richtofen, the notorious "Red Baron," and his Flying Circus; Lt. Franz Max Immelmann, who shot himself down twice with his own machine guns before German engineers learned to synchronize the firing mechanism with the propellor's revolution; and others—particularly impressed her. She watched endless flights of aviation movies on DVD: *Hell's Angels, Wings, 12 O'Clock High, The Spirit of St. Louis*, and many others. She read about Billy Mitchell and Wiley Post and Wrong-Way Corrigan and Charles Lindbergh; she drank in the soaring poetry of Antoine de Saint-Exupéry and Richard Bach; she spent hours pondering the mysterious fate of Amelia Earhart, with whom she identified strongly; and when her favorite uncle brought her a stack of his crumbling old pulp magazines with titles like *War Birds, G-8 and His Battle Aces, The Lone Eagle*, and *Dusty Ayres and His Battle Birds*, she thought surely she would explode with joy and excitement.

A few years later came one of the high points of her young life: her first actual ride in an airplane—a cross-country trip to visit her grandparents in Missouri. From the moment she looked down upon the vast multicolored patchwork of land below as the great Boeing 787 climbed smoothly up into blue immensity, Eris Campbell knew she must be a pilot or die of longing for the sky.

All through high school she worked—baby-sitting, clerking, odd jobs, whatever she could scrape up—and hoarded her money like the miserly financier Hetty Green. Her mother practically had to take her by the hand and force her to go out and buy clothes for herself, a situation almost unheard of among teenaged females.

Although an excellent student, with a natural aptitude for math and science, Eris participated little in the social life of her school. Boys flocked around her, drawn to her ripening honey-golden beauty like bees to a flower, but, as politely as possible, she ignored them all. A soul that longed for the sky like a caged eagle could find little satisfaction in the mundane adolescent rituals of dates and dances and parties and hot fumblings in the back seats of cars.

When she turned 18, she was able to take the first real step toward her dream: flying lessons. Her family, frankly disapproving of her infatuation with flight, had forbade it previously, but now she was eighteen, a woman and on her own, and soon she was soaring high above the world in a bright new Cessna trainer twice weekly.

She graduated from Long Beach State College with high marks in engineering and math and immediately went to work for the Cosmodyne Corporation as an aerospace engineer. On weekends, she flew. She flew high and alone, communing with the sky and the sun and the clouds, drinking in the indescribable exhiliration of flight. It was everything she had always imagined it to be, and more. It filled her soul and she was satisfied. She wanted, needed nothing else. Or so she thought.

Until that weekend at the International Air Show as she watched the stunt competition fliers loop and roll and streak through the air like mad birds, trailing long plumes of white smoke as they danced across the sky in an incredible aerial ballet. Her heart pounding in her throat, Eris watched the brightly colored bi-planes and single-wings, vintage aircraft carefully and lovingly restored, cartwheel through maneuvers she had often read about but had never observed. It

86

didn't seem possible that aircraft and pilots could take such punishment and survive, but they did. It looked like the most wonderful thing she could imagine. She had to get in on this! She had already been putting away part of her salary toward purchasing her own plane; now she began socking away even more.

Then, on a glorious September afternoon at an air show near Long Beach, the winner of the stunt competition waggled his wings, landed his red and white De Havilland Chipmunk and walked across the field straight toward Eris. When she realized he was approaching her, she suddenly dissolved into a heady swirl of amazement and confusion. He walked up to her, took off his helmet and said, "I've been watching you for months at these shows. You're the most beautiful woman I've ever seen. I'd like you to have dinner with me this evening."

Imagine Errol Flynn—a young Errol Flynn with hair like wheat in sunshine and a flash of white teeth in a smile that could melt an iceberg. Eyes like the sky itself. Asking you to dinner. She mumbled something stupid which must have been a yes, for that evening, Eris Campbell found herself dining in the most expensive restaurant she had ever seen with Jordan Wingate Austin III, winner of almost every aerial race and stunt-flying contest in the world.

That night, Eris lost two things, her heart and her virginity, in that order, but both were given gladly. Jordy Austin was well known as a spoiled, rebellious daredevil whose sole ambition in life was to win, to be number one, to excel at more and more difficult and dangerous aerobatics in the sky and to constantly add to his list of conquests in bed.

But Eris Campbell brought all that to a halt. She was that something different he had been looking for unknowingly all his life, a woman as beautiful and warm as a summer sunrise and as enchanted with the sky as he. "It was love at first flight," he often quipped to friends later, but the truth of it was raw, inescapable magic sparking like invisible arcs between them. Eris discovered with astonished joy that night that she had a vast unsuspected country, bright and hot, within her soul, an unspoiled landscape waiting to be discovered and claimed by the right explorer. This lush golden woman, naïve as a child about love and sex, suddenly experienced the molten core of herself and knew that she was changed forever. Henceforth, the two of them would no longer ride the skies alone, but together.

One week later, Jordy asked Eris to marry him and she accepted. Jordy's jet-set friends and former lovers—and especially his father, president of the powerful and prestigious Austin-Hammerfield Advertising Agency—were amazed at the change in him. This bright young Icarus who could charm the birds out of the trees had in turn been charmed by a beautiful bird with whom he could soar high and far. They hoped she would give him a reason to live, not a compulsion to die in foolish daredevil boasting.

For a while it worked. But gradually, as they flew together, stunted together, entered competitions together, dark clouds began to gather in Jordy's heart. Instead of being proud of his wife's natural prowess in the air, he began to resent her. She had asked him to teach her stunt flying, and she had turned out to be even better at it than he was. Innocently, not realizing what it was doing to him, Eris continued to win competitions, often just a few points ahead of Jordy in mixed singles, but those points began to stretch into a vast gulf between them.

Instead of confiding his feelings of resentment to Eris, he chose to keep them bottled up, and his immaturity and pride led him to hurt her in return by becoming cold and distant at home, by drinking and stretching himself further and further into the area of foolhardiness in the sky.

Eris tried to talk to him, reason with him, but she might as well have been talking to the wind. Finally, desperate, she forced him into discussing their deteriorating relationship, but the discussion soon disintegrated into a terrible screaming fight. He said things and she said things and he slapped her and left her stunned as he slammed out of their apartment and spent the night in a bar trying to drown his hurt and frustration in a cataract of alcohol.

The next morning, still drunk, he took his De Havilland up for a practice run. No one ever knew exactly what happened, but at the top of a steep climb, the plane stalled, nosed over, then dropped 500 feet like a stone. It slammed nose first into the fairground and burst into a huge ball of greasy orange flame. By the time the fire trucks arrived both the plane and the golden boy who had so often flung her through the skies in breath-taking exhibitions of daredevil wonder were charred and smoldering corpses.

Chris' hand on her shoulder blessedly snapped Eris back to the present, away from the scarlet agony of her memories.

"Eris, are you all right?" he asked, concern soft in his smoky eyes. "You're white as a ghost and you're gripping that stick like it was going to fall apart or something."

She closed eyes that had been staring into yesterday, eyes that had no more tears left in them and now felt raw and scratchy. "I-I'm okay, Chris. Just daydreaming again." Her eyes were bright and warm now as she smiled at him. "Not a very smart thing to do at close to Mach 4, is it?"

But they both knew that the part of her mind and reflexes, razor-honed to perfection, that actually flew the aircraft was on the job, not drifting with the painful tides of memory but separate, alert and keen as steel.

"I'm not worried about that...but I do worry about *you* sometimes, Eris. How long are you going to carry around this big black ache in your guts? I know there's something in your past that's eating at you and keeping you from leveling with me about how you feel. You can tell me...."

She shook her head, avoiding his eyes. "Chris, I'm...just not ready to talk about it yet. I'm sorry...I know it's causing you pain, but—"

"It's causing us *both* pain, Eris. We—" Chris broke off suddenly, a startled look on his face as he stared past Eris out into the sky. He had seen a bright glint of silver, something moving fast.... There it was again! "What the hell is that?"

Eris followed his gaze and saw a gleaming argent speck heading toward them from the east at incredible speed. Her smooth brow furrowed. "It's no plane, nothing I've ever seen before. There's no scheduled traffic up here either."

As it rapidly closed with them, they could see that it was a thin wedge of metal glittering like a blade in the retreating sunlight, hurtling toward them at a speed greater than their own.

"Eris, it's a spacecraft—a UFO! But I've never seen one shaped like that before, have you?"

"No," she replied, dark feelings of danger beginning to uncoil within her like ebony snakes. "The space visitors have all had ships that are roughly saucer-shaped, nothing like this."

They could see it more clearly now, looking more ominous each second. It was a few hundred feet beneath them, shaped like a crescent moon with a third point at the center of the trailing edge. With a start, Chris suddenly recalled exactly the image he had been searching his mind for: the damn thing looked just like the swinging blade in the Edgar Allan Poe story that had scared the pants off him as a kid, "The Pit and the Pendulum." Poe's vivid description of it jumped into his mind from that long-ago, child-scaring time:

> *...its nether extremity was formed of a crescent of glittering steel, about a foot in length from horn to horn, the horns upward, and the under edge evidently as keen as that of a razor. Like a razor also, it seemed massy and heavy, tapering from the edge into a solid and broad structure above. It was appended to a weighty rod of brass, and the whole* hissed *as it swung through the air.*

This memory did nothing to ease Chris' apprehension; as he watched the thing slash through the high thin air toward them, he could almost hear it hiss like that blade in his mind. "I don't like this, Eris...that thing's bad news...and I think it's after us."

"Maybe it's new space visitors...people who haven't been here before, just checking us out...?" Eris looked at Chris and they shook their heads in unison. "Uh, uh...neither of us is buying that one. I'm afraid you're right, Chris—my back is crawling. Every subliminal sense I've got says 'get away from it!'"

Now it was climbing toward them, fast as a thrown knife. Then suddenly, an emerald-green beam leaped from it, barely missing the nose of the *Dawn Wing*.

Eris clamped her teeth together, her eyes beryl ice. "*That* does it! Whoever they are, they're out to skrag us. Okay, let's see what they've got."

Chris felt the pressure of acceleration slam him back in his padded seat as Eris punched up the throttle buttons to max. "Oh, shit, here we go again," he muttered between clenched teeth.

The little ship leaped forward into emptiness like a gazelle running from a cheetah, the glowing green numerals of the airspeed indicator flicking toward Mach 5. And let's see what *we've* got while we're at it, Eris thought grimly. She knew the ship was not meant to go much beyond Mach 5, but no one had ever tested its real limits, had they? She had a feeling they were going to find them now.

Twisting her head slowly around to glance astern, Eris saw that their jump ahead had gained them only moments; they were flying balls to the wall, yet the crescent-shaped craft was right on their tail and again closing rapidly. As the *Dawn Wing* hit Mach 5, a warning light began to blink like a hot coal on the instrument panel. Above it, the ship's computer frantically flashed a readout on its display screen in glowing red letters: DANGER. DO NOT EXCEED MACH 5.0. The plane began to shudder slightly, then more violently, like a man naked in Arctic cold.

Eris throttled back down to 4.5 and the red light and display winked out. The shuddering stopped and the plane flew smoothly again.

"Well, we can't outrun them," she said. "That thing might be capable of near light speed, for all I know." She winced as another verdant bleam sliced close to the plane. "Damn! I sure wish I had some weapons on this crate! Then I'd give 'em a run for their money. Well, we can't sit here like a duck in shooting gallery! At least we don't have to make it easy for 'em...hang on to your teeth, babe, mama's gonna show those bastards some stuff they've never seen before!"

Chris groaned. "Why is it every time I fly with you I end up owing you new seat covers?"

Eris grinned in spite of the seriousness of their situation. She suddenly felt fine; fear fell away like dark sand; Chris' keen sense of humor warmed her as it always did, yanked her up out of the dark well of depression and despair always deep inside her, yawning to claim her spirit. She felt the old familiar thrill of adrenalin beginning to pump into her system as she yanked the stick back into her stomach and kicked down the flaps. The little plane leaped upward in a steep climb, then banked into a sharp left turn. The pursuing ship followed, mirroring her maneuver. After a few more moderate moves, Eris tried a few aerobatic tricks, loops and rolls, experimenting. She began to feel with dismay, as the crescent ship imitated her exactly, that it must have some kind of visually activated navigation computer locked on her, automatically duplicating any maneuver she made. She knew also that the spacecraft could handle with ease G-forces that would kill an aircraft pilot.

No matter what wild stunt she tried, she couldn't shake the ship; it clung to her tail like a lamprey on a shark. But at least she was keeping them too busy to fire at her—

A flash of brilliant green suddenly filled the cockpit and she was almost deafened by a sharp *crack*, followed by a howling shriek as air began to rush out of the cockpit at unimaginable speed. Shit! she thought, wrong again! She knew immediately what had happened: the green beam had narrowly missed her head and had punched through the thick plexiglass of the cockpit. She could see two perfectly round holes in the canopy, each about the size of a half dollar.

She glanced over at Chris to make certain he was okay; he managed a weak grin. She couldn't make herself heard over the horrid shrieking of the rapidly depressurizing cockpit, so she pointed to the oxygen masks which had automatically popped out of their compartments beneath the seats. He nodded, understanding: at 40,000 feet, they had less than a minute before the sacs in their lungs would rupture from their own internal pressures of water vapor and carbon dioxide, their blood streams would die from oxygen starvation and hypoxia would bring them unconciousness and death.

The fierce suction of escaping air tried to rip the masks from their hands as they hastily donned them. An Arctic chill filled the compartment: the heating system was out. Even with the masks on, they could die from hypothermia at this

92

altitude, dressed as they were only in light non-thermal G-suits.

Eris knew that she had to descend quickly to a warmer altitude. She couldn't outrun the ship, couldn't outfly it; maybe she could lose it down there in a cloud bank. But there were none on the horizon at this height. Where are the goddamn thunderstorms when you need them? she asked herself wryly.

She eased the stick forward and the plane nosed down in a steep dive, the thin air whistling through the holes in the plexiglass like a demented tea kettle. At 15,000 feet she leveled off and looked back. The blade-like ship was still on her tail, apparently unshakable. The air in the cockpit was still cold, but bearable.

Spotting a patch of puffy white altocumulus clouds to the north, Eris headed the plane directly into it, kicking up her speed as she did so. As the little craft shot ahead, Eris exulted once again in its smooth, instant response. She couldn't let anything happen to this plane! It was such a honey and the only one of its kind! And so was Chris, she thought immediately, glancing over at him. She couldn't bear the thought of losing someone else in a flaming crash. Oddly, her own death didn't seem to matter at this moment. Somehow, she had to save Chris and the plane—she had to figure a way out of this. But how? She felt like a target in an obscene video game in the sky with an unknown player looming gigantically somewhere in space, feeding in dollars....

Another emerald lance sizzled through the air, nearly taking a chunk out of the fuselage, as the *Dawn Wing* disappeared into the cloud bank. Eris was outraged to see a long, ugly black scar where the beam had kissed the nose of the plane. Inside, they seemed suspended in a gray, formless limbo. Eris' only hope was that if the navigational computer in the pursuing ship was locked onto her visually, this might break the link. If it was heat-locked, with sensors zeroed in on her exhaust, then this game of hide-and-seek in the clouds would be futile.

After a few minutes of level flight though the dull fog-like cloud, Eris abruptly threw the little plane up and out of the top, breaking though bright whipped-cream rolls into the clear blue sky. Her heart leapt with joy: she had shaken them! As she continued to climb, she saw them break out of the clouds beneath her. She could sense their rage. She threw back her head and permitted herself a brief laugh of triumph, although it sounded faint and strangled beneath the oxygen mask.

Chris shook clasped hands at her in a victory salute and she could sense him grinning beneath his mask; but she knew their edge was only temporary. Already the crescent ship was wheeling up toward them; in seconds it would lock on them visually once more and the deadly game of cat and mouse would begin again.

Then a wild, harebrained possibility occurred to her, if she could only pull it off. It seemed so farfetched that at first her rational mind rejected it. But what if—? She had no weapons on this aircraft—or did she? Perhaps there *was* one, if she could only get into position to use it....

Raising her voice, she yelled to Chris to brace himself, then horsed back on the stick, kicked the flaps down and the elevators up and shot up and over in a tight inside loop. Lt. Franz Max Immelmann, the World War I German ace who invented this stunt that bore his name, had intended it as a "chicken" maneuver: at the top of the loop, he did a slow half roll until upright again, then hightailed it for home base, leaving a perplexed Allied pilot behind who until then had had the advantage of the German, outflying him and on the verge of shooting him down from the rear.

But Eris knew she couldn't outmaneuver this strange ship; she had something else in mind. She wasn't doing a true Immelmann turn: instead of a rollover at the top of the loop, she continued down the other side, pulling up above and slightly behind the pursuing craft. She held her breath to see if it would duplicate the maneuver, but apparently she had acted before it could lock in again.

She was flying at exactly the same speed as the crescent ship now, directly above it. She was close enough to notice that there were no visible observation ports on the top. Hopefully, the effect to the ship's occupants was as if she had vanished into thin air!

Puzzled, the silver blade-ship wheeled in a shallow turn; Eris' hairtrigger reflexes banked her plane with it, precisely maintaining their respective positions. Two can play this game, she thought with grim glee. Gradually, she began to decrease the distance between them, maintaining the same speed exactly. Chris looked puzzled but said nothing; he knew she had something in mind and he was willing to bet it would be good.

The crescent ship arced up into a climb, the pilot probably thinking that more altitude might somehow reveal the whereabouts of his prey. Eris climbed with it; then, as it leveled out again, she continued to lower her craft slowly toward its broad, flat top.

Soon she was hovering only yards above the wide metallic surface, carefully pacing her speed to match the other's. She could see every detail of this strange ship now: the polished silver hull was smooth and seamless, with a light green iridescence like that on a butterfly's wing sheening it. Its only other feature was a hatch about four feet in diameter, located toward the center of the leading edge. It was decorated with an ominous symbol: a cobra's head reared above its flared hood, ready to strike.

Chris began to squirm despite himself. He felt icy sweat bead his forehead but said nothing, not wanting to distract Eris, fighting to trust her skill and judgment.

This was precision wingtip flying; Eris and Jordy had done it together many times, thrilling crowds at the International Air Shows. But she had never done it with an unknown spacecraft and an unknown pilot who was probably not even human! Now she was flying only a few feet above the crescent ship; she had to gamble that it would make no more sudden climbs, for she was too close now to get out of the way in time. At supersonic speed, even a momentary touching of the two craft would send them spinning out of control and destroy them both.

Thank God, they seemed to be holding steady, Eris breathed. Now for the really long-shot part of this crazy maneuver. This was her last trick; if this didn't work, they had bought the farm.

The *Dawn Wing* carried no armament, true, but it had one incredible weapon that she was now in position to use. The exhaust from the little plane's experimental plasma engine was unthinkably hot: six times the temperature of the center of the sun! The heat-resistant materials that shielded the engine had been provided to PIA scientists by friendly space people; she hoped fervently that this craft was not made of that same stuff!

Slowly, very, very slowly then, Eris eased back on the stick, carefully maintaining exactly the same speed as the ship beneath her. Slowly the *Dawn Wing*'s nose tilted upward. She knew she could maintain this position for only a few seconds before she would begin to climb, but a few seconds might be enough.

It was extremely ticklish, for if the tail nozzle bumped the top of the crescent ship....

And then the angle was correct: the full raging force of a jet blast of ionized matter hotter than a star billowed downward onto the surface of the alien ship.

The results were astonishing. The spacecraft was constructed of an alloy of metals far stronger than anything known on earth, designed to withstand velocities in excess of 20,000 miles an hour, yet where the pulsing blue-lavender beam touched, metal simply exploded into nonexistence! Molecules of titanium, iridium, silicon, and manganese screamed into instant white-hot annihilation. A huge contrail of vapor and metallic gases streamed out behind the alien ship into a miles-long tail. Around the center of the rapidly widening hole the surrounding metal glowed white, shading off into yellow and cherry red.

At the moment of contact, Eris eased forward slowly, flicking throttle buttons higher, moving across the top of the spacecraft as she slowly eased upward in a gentle climb, the nova-heat of her exhaust opening up the ship like a blowtorch through a stick of butter.

And then she was up and away, looking back to see the entire ship now glowing crimson. Black smoke billowed out of the gaping white-hot wound on its back. It suddenly split apart like a rotten apple, the two crescent horns of it whirling away into the air like spinning blades, and out of the center of it, two worms wriggling, humanoid figures flaming like torches, hurtling down through the clear cold air to finally sizzle out in tiny white plumes of spray as they hit the Atlantic almost three miles below.

A great cataract of relief swept over Eris; impossibly, she had done it! They were safe!

Heedless of the cold thin air, Chris ripped off his oxygen mask and gave a great warwhoop, then grabbed Eris, pulled off her mask and kissed her, full and warm, on the mouth. She was so surprised that she responded, waves of heat washing through her body like tides of sunlight. His mouth on hers felt so good and once again they had come so close to death....

Then she pulled away, remembering that she was still the pilot of a plane moving faster than sound, not willing to surrender to Chris' eager warmth just yet....

"Hey," she said with a mock frown to disguise her flaming cheeks, the triphammer pounding of her heart, "don't distract the pilot. It's against FAA regulations."

He just grinned like a fool, squeezing her strong brown hand, now steady as a rock on the stick. "Whatever you say, lady, whatever you say. I feel like we just shot down the Red Baron himself. If they ever give Nobel Prizes for flying, I'm gonna see that you get one."

She laughed, her eyes on the darkling skies ahead. And as she looked, she thought she saw a faint, ghostly outline forming: a phantom plane, perky in red and white, a familiar shape sweeping down the sky, the pilot laughing in the open cockpit, hair pennanting in the wind like wheat in summer. Eris forgot to breathe, then, as the apparition swooped near and the golden-haired pilot flashed her a thumbs-up signal. Eris thought: Jordy would be proud of me. And like an echo from a faraway place, came an answering thought: *Yes. He is.*

The phantom plane waggled its wings then, dissolving into blur and ripple as Eris' eyes overflowed. For a moment she allowed the tears to cascade down her cheeks, then bravely blinked them away. The ghostly ship was gone, only the open sky stretched before her. A trick of fatigue, an atmospheric illusion, a daydream....

She smiled at Chris, knowing he understood, needing no words between them in this fine moment. Then she turned back to the controls. She had a plane to fly.

Battered but proud, the victorious *Dawn Wing* hurled them home.

Being formed by the union of the first odd and even numbers, 5 was considered of peculiar value and used as an amulet or talisman powerful to preserve from evil and when inscribed on a portal, could keep out evil spirits; it is found almost everywhere in Greece and Egypt.
> —W. Wynn Wescott, NUMBERS: THEIR OCCULT
> POWER AND MYSTIC VIRTUES

CHAPTER NINE

PENTAD

WASHINGTON, D.C.: 4 NOVEMBER 2020

Dr. Gideon Stack, Director of the Psychic Intelligence Agency, was angry. He had been summoned to a ten o'clock meeting this morning in the President's office at which six of his best agents were going to be sent out on an assignment that would probably turn out to be no more than a wild goose chase at best and an embarrassing waste of money and manpower at worst.

When the agency had been created in 2010, with Dr. Stack as its director, it had been intended primarily as an intelligence-gathering organization, expanding the conventional spying capabilities of the CIA into dimensions beyond current espionage technology and providing competition to the Russian advances in psychic research, not as some half-ass psychic Peace Corps, with valuable Psi-Spies galavanting all over the world on missions of mercy and good will. These things could be done by other psychics who were not also highly trained secret agents!

Dr. Stack frowned, his high-domed forehead, surrounded by cottony wisps of white hair, gleaming dully in the soft lighting of his plush office. He was a small, rather bulbous man of sixty-two, with thick horn-rimmed glasses and a snowy goatee that made him look like a cross between a mad scientist and an irate gnome. But behind that forehead was an intelligence and a wit as keen and brilliant as a sword of light.

It was all the President's fault, Dr. Stack mused angrily. Ever since he had become convinced of the validity of psychic research, President Warren had bulled his way into the management of the agency and ripped the reins of control from Stack's hands. The President had insisted that the top Psi-Spies report only to him; although not psychic himself, he had demanded to be assigned an occult number and a Mentacom Medallion so that he could keep in telepathic contact with "his" agents at all times; and now, without so much as asking the director's opinion, he was sending them out all over the world on assignments that had nothing to do with espionage—the very thing they had been trained for!

Now this latest crackbrained idea—a five-man expedition to Egypt to look for a buried pyramid and an alien superweapon to ward off an invasion from space! It all sounded like the plot of a low-budget science-fiction movie. There wasn't an iota of hard evidence to support the necessity for such a costly mission. Yet, he mused, we now know extraterrestrials do exist, and there's no reason to suppose they're all friendly.... If there *is* something behind all this, and such a weapon as the Immobilizer does exist....

Dr. Stack knew that he would have to be very, very careful from now on. There was a chance—a slim but intriguing chance—that great power might be his if he played his hand in this game with extreme caution and finesse. Enough power to put the PIA back in his pocket, where it rightfully belonged....

Throwing some papers into his briefcase, Dr. Stack steamed silently to himself. Internationally recognized as a top authority in the field of psychic research, he was by far the best qualified man to head the PIA, but if he made too many waves about the President's taking over, he would be out on his can, regardless of his credentials. Dr. Stack was not one of your ivory-tower scientists. He knew all about

100

Washington politics and intrigues and he knew when to speak up and when to shut up. He liked his job; it was exciting and challenging, even if he was not really pulling the strings anymore. Besides, it provided him with a salary that would choke an alligator. His goal was to entrench himself in his position, make himself so valuable that the administration could not do without him, much as J. Edgar Hoover had done in his long reign as head of the FBI. Hoover had seen many Presidents come and go, and Stack would do the same. Perhaps the next President wouldn't be as involved in psychic affairs and the reins of power would return to the hands of the one truly qualified driver—himself.

Dr. Stack smiled tightly as he got up from behind his massive walnut desk and walked stiffly to the door of his sumptuous office. He was not without influence in Washington, he knew. President Warren had made plenty of mistakes and not a few enemies during his first term in office. There might be ways of working behind the scenes to ensure that this first term would be his last. Behind their coke-bottle lenses, his pale blue eyes glittered bright malice as Gideon Stack began to formulate his plan.

At precisely ten o'clock, the President sat down at his desk in the Oval Office, crossed his hands before him and looked intently at the men and women seated in the comfortable chairs before him. Initially, he liked what he saw. They were a strong, intelligent group, each with a special psychic talent that set him or her apart from ordinary people. Could they work smoothly together? He would soon find out.

Eris' aqua eyes were alight with barely restrained eagerness to hear what the President had to say to them. She glanced over at Chris, who sat next to her. He seemed relaxed enough, but she could tell he was as alert as she: almost imperceptibly, a jaw muscle twitched his curiosity.

Avram Sumi was quiet and reserved, his keen dark eyes taking in every detail of this bright seat of power and the people assembled here.

Next to him sat Raymond Gaunt, smiling and bristling with barely repressed energy. He almost seemed to hum and crackle as he crossed first one leg then the other, fingers

101

dancing on the arm of his chair as though he were absently playing some invisible musical instrument.

Seated side by side, Gabrielle Bane and André Renard made a striking couple, her shoulder-length chestnut curls and large expressive eyes the color of a summer sky a vivid contrast to his wheat-blond hair and warm brown eyes. Their obvious love for each other seemed to flow between them like an invisible current, but now, like the others, their attention was not on each other but on the President.

Behind the six agents, like a distant thundercloud threatening a clear day, sat Dr. Stack. He had been the last to arrive and had been greeted cordially by the President, who had hoped to enlist his approval and cooperation by inviting him to this meeting. Dr. Stack had responded in kind, with only a hint of a cool wind blowing around the edges of his smile. Now he too awaited what the President had to tell them, but his mood was tense and dark.

"I'm glad you were all able to come," the President began. "The mission I'm about to entrust to you will be the most important you have ever undertaken.

"I'd rather exaggerate than downplay this situation in any regard. I feel that this assignment is going to require the utmost from each of you—mentally, physically, and spiritually. It concerns the gravest challenge this planet has ever had to face."

He paused to survey the faces before him, now sober and galvanized with eagerness to hear more.

"As you may have guessed, it has to do with the earthquake in Cairo last week. That quake was not an act of God...nor was it caused by human means."

"*Mon Dieu!*" André Renard exclaimed. "What does that leave, Mr. President?"

"It leaves a nonhuman entity from another star system, André...an alien agent who is here on earth masquerading as a woman. A very powerful woman, protected by a carefully organized empire of vast wealth and power."

"Jesus Christ," Raymond Gaunt said impulsively, eyes snapping with excitement. "Are you *sure*, sir? I-I mean—"

President Warren smiled, amused by Gaunt's reaction. "I know this sounds like a scenario from the funny farm,

102

Ray, but so did UFOs and our friendly space people...until they happened. After all, now that we know there's intelligent life and advanced technologies out there, is it so hard to accept the idea that maybe not all of it is friendly? It's a damned unpleasant and disappointing thought, but we have to face it. Apparently, we've just been lucky so far that our space visitors have been humanoid-type nice guys. Believe me, I wouldn't be wasting my time or yours if I weren't convinced that this is true. I believe our planet to be in deadly peril—*right now!* We have to act immediately before it's too late."

"Who is this woman, sir?" Eris asked, leaning forward in eagerness to learn more. A phrase from the Sphinx's message to her began to echo ominously in her mind, a distant cry across centuries, slowly glaciering down her spine: *Beware the Daughter of Set, She-Who-Is-To-Be-Feared; beware the Shaker of Worlds....*

"We don't know yet, Eris, but we're working on it. We hope to find out for certain at a reading with Jaca I've scheduled this morning at 11:30."

Eris nodded, but her mind was buzzing off elsewhere. Set...Set...something about that name was beginning to connect with something else....

"Keep this strictly top secret, all of you," the President said."If the Press should get wind of what's going on.... "

He left the sentence unfinished, but Dr. Stack could have finished it for him. It was tempting. Rancor gleamed darkly in the director's eyes as he envisioned the lurid headlines: ALIEN INVADERS AMONG US, SAYS PRESIDENT. PRESIDENT IN EARTHQUAKE COVERUP. But no...Stack might be dragged down with the rest of the administration if Congress investigated. And if Warren ever found out where the lead came from, it would be Stack's ass. Besides, if the public bought the story, they'd have a panic on their hands that would make Orson Welles' 1938 Martian invasion look like a tea party. No, he decided, it wasn't worth the risk. There were other ways....

"For now, our cover story is that the earthquake was a natural one," the President continued, "and the QEWPIE

System malfunctioned and failed to pick up the pre-tremors in time to warn us."

"But what happens when the technicians check out the system and find it's okay?" asked Avram Sumi. "Won't they proudly announce that to the Press and blow your cover?"

"They have orders to keep quiet about it. We'll square it with them later. I'm stalling President Fahey too—I told him as little as possible. He wasn't happy, but he said he'd go along with me for now."

"Mr. President," Chris asked, his tanned face solemn, "getting back to this alien woman. Do you know which planet she's from—which star system?"

"Yes, we were able to learn that much. She's from a world in the system of Algol."

Eris suddenly sat bolt upright. "Algol! That's incredible, sir!"

The President looked at her quizzically. "Why, Eris?"

"Well...I wanted to keep this until later, when we briefed you on what happened to us in Cairo, but at the risk of interrupting your train of thought, sir, I think this is the time to bring up something I experienced the day before the earthquake."

"By all means, Eris," said the President, smiling at her earnestness. "Go ahead and derail the damn thing if you have anything that'll help us."

Eris then told them of the warning dream about the plea for help from the Sphinx that had preceded the cataclysm; the battle with the Arab thugs and the bizarre destruction of their bodies by apparent spontaneous combustion; and the strange psychic message of warning she had received from the Sphinx itself: *Beware the star that blinks*, it had said. The star that blinks! "That's Algol, isn't it?"

André, whose hobby was astronomy, leaned forward, his eyes sparking excitement. "That's right, Eris. Algol is an eclipsing binary star—the most famous one, in fact. It has a larger darker companion star which revolves around it, periodically cutting off its light from our view, making it seem to 'blink.' The early Arabs felt that this was an ominous sight in the heavens and named the star Algol—the demon."

104

"Yes," Gaunt agreed. "And even today, astrologers consider Algol to be a malefic influence."

"Apparently they're right," Warren said grimly. He noticed that Dr. Stack's remote, disdainful demeanor had momentarily vanished and that he was listening intently to what Eris had to say. Stack knew her psychic talent to be impressive; if she had corroborative evidence to offer, it was not to be dismissed without consideration, even if it had come to her from a very strange source.

The President took a sip of cooling coffee, wishing he could lace it with a drop of the good Irish he kept handy for less public occasions. "Good, Eris. This is the first confirmation we've had from another source that Jaca's reading was correct. Go on—what else did the Sphinx tell you?"

Eris smiled, feeling a little foolish. "You...don't think I'm going off the deep end with all this, do you, sir?"

"Hell, no, Eris," the President replied reassuringly. "You're a highly trained psychic—one of our best agents. If you can bring in this kind of information from a supernormal source, nobody's laughing. Believe it. Now, was there anything else it warned you about?"

"Yes...it also told me to beware of someone called 'the Daughter of Set, She-Who-Is-To-Be-Feared.' It added, 'Beware the Shaker of Worlds,' then just faded away and I couldn't pick up anything else. God, it was frustrating!"

The President drew in a deep breath between clenched teeth. "Never mind, Eris...in light of what's happened I think it told us plenty."

"But there's something else, sir," Eris said, "something that's been batting around in my head trying to make a connection. Set...Chris, wasn't Set the Egyptian god of evil or something?"

"Yes, Eris," replied Chris, "According to ancient Egyptian mythology, Set was the equivalent of our Satan. He killed his brother Osiris and drove Isis and her infant son Horus into exile. When Horus grew to manhood, he returned and battled Set, defeating him and avenging his father's murder."

Eris put her hand on Chris' arm excitedly, squeezing it. "Wait a minute! Wasn't there something about one of the forms of Set being a giant snake?"

"Yes, and he's come to be associated with snake worship...."

"That's it!" Eris yelped. Then she related the story of their perilous flight from Egypt in the *Dawn Wing* and how they were almost shot down by a strange-looking spacecraft with *the symbol of a snake on top!*

"Well, this 'Daughter of Set,' whoever she is, seems to be well named," said Warren. "Apparently she's here to prepare the way for an invasion force from Algol. The Algolians have provided her with an ultra-sophisticated weather machine: she can create earthquakes and other climatic disasters with the flick of a switch, anywhere in the world. Now according to the reading we had, there's only one thing that can stop her—some kind of machine called the Immobilizer, left here by an advanced race of aliens centuries ago. Your job is to get this machine before Lady Set does."

"Where is this Immobilizer supposed to be located, Mr. President?" Raymond asked.

"In a pyramid buried somewhere under the Giza Plateau," the President replied.

"The Hall of Records!" exclaimed Eris, her beryl eyes shining with excitement. "'Between the Sphinx and the river....' Just like Edgar Cayce said, years ago. The hidden pyramid we've always dreamed was down there with all the records of man's true history—*it really is there!* And we're to be the ones to find it? My God, how exciting! I can't believe it!"

"Apparently so, Eris," said the President, enjoying her excitement. "You five will report directly to me via the medallions, as usual. You'll be taking some special equipment along and you're scheduled for a crash refresher course in physical and psychic training, plus some special preparation, at PSI-QUARK during the next two weeks. André, I want you to document every step of the mission with photographs. Ray, Marielle will record everything for us on tape. Is she ready to go?"

"Yes, sir," replied Raymond, beaming happily.

"Mr. President..." said Gabrielle, a troubled look on her face.

"Yes, Gaby."

"You've been talking about five of us agents—a Pentad—going on this mission. But there are six of us here today."

"That's right, Gaby. I was going to explain that to you. You will have another assignment, the exact nature of which is not yet clear, but it will be no less important to the mission."

Gabrielle and André traded looks of shock and disappointment. "You mean Gaby won't be going with us to Egypt?" André asked.

"That's right. I'm sorry, but that's the way it has to be, I'm afraid."

Gabrielle nodded, fighting hard against tears that suddenly threatened to inundate her big blue eyes. She won, but the sunlight that had come into the Oval Office with her was gone now.

André put his hand on her arm to comfort her. But who would comfort him? he wondered.

"The first thing I've set up for you is that reading with Jaca this morning," the President said. "Hopefully she'll be able to give you further information and details concerning your mission, including your part in all this, Gaby.

"Now before we adjourn, does anybody have any questions or anything further to contribute? How about you, Gideon?"

Dr. Stack had been holding himself back throughout the meeting, but he decided that now was the time to speak up. He was preparing a plan which would require a convincing cover and he recognized this as the perfect opportunity to establish it.

"Yes, Mr. President, I would like to say something," he exclaimed, scorn dripping like acid from each word. "Since you've asked for my input—which in itself surprises me—I feel that this entire enterprise is extremely premature. All I've heard this morning are unrelated incidents, suppositions, and expositions of myths and legends which seem conveniently to tie in, no matter how remotely, to this far-fetched theory you all seem so anxious to embrace, despite the lack of any hard evidence whatsoever.

"As far as I can gather, Mr. President, you are ready and willing to assign six of our top psychic agents, at a cost of thousands of dollars of our already inadequate and overtaxed budget, to a wild goose chase in the Egyptian desert without one single shred of evidence that there indeed is a menace to the safety of the world from another planet. The only evidence we have of this wild supposition and its supposed link with the earthquake in Cairo comes from Jaca Ciencé's crystal ball!"

Seeing the President's face darken at the mention of Jaca's name, Dr. Stack moderated his tirade a bit. He didn't want to overdo it, after all. "Now I mean to cast no aspersions on Ms. Ciencé or her gifts of crystallomancy, but psychic information of this nature should not, in my opinion, be used as the sole basis for making costly and possibly politically embarrassing decisions of this magnitude."

Seeing Dr. Stack pause for a breath, Warren said evenly, "You're correct, Gideon, when you say we don't have any hard evidence on this thing. However, the circumstantial and psychic evidence we do have is so compelling, and its source, in my view, so impeccable, that frankly I don't think we can afford to take the chance of not acting immediately. I'd rather gamble an expedition and a few bucks than take that chance. If we do nothing, we have an awful lot to lose."

"Well, can't you at least send one agent to check out the situation first, instead of commiting five at once? Six, if you include Gabrielle's assignment, which seems to be totally unknown."

"Gideon, we're receiving very specific guidance on this situation from the inner plane teachers. They want us to send five agents on the expedition because they feel that five is a powerful protective force against evil. And apparently Gaby has an important role to play in all this too."

Dr. Stack feigned further indignation. "Then I take it, Mr. President, that your mind is made up on the subject?"

"I'm afraid so, Gideon."

"Then I have nothing further to say. If you will excuse me, I have things to attend to."

Without any further words to anyone, the Director of the Psychic Intelligence Agency marched stiffly across the bright room and was gone. Tension seemed to lift like fog with his departure.

The President glanced at his ringwatch. "This has taken longer than I intended. It's almost eleven—I don't want you to be late for your reading with Jaca."

He stood up and the six agents got to their feet also. After hasty handshakes and farewells, they were ushered into a presidential limousine and whisked away through the leaden afternoon to Ciencé Park.

Back in his office, Dr. Stack made a phone call without activating the video unit. After a few seconds, a thin, faraway-sounding voice answered.

"Yes?"

"Sender?"

"Affirmative."

"This is Jerubaal. Meet me at the usual place at two o'clock this afternoon. The time has come for you to pay your bill."

There was a hollow silence, then the reedy voice replied, "I'll be there."

Dr. Stack smiled his cold smile. "Good."

He was well pleased with his performance this morning. He was certain the President had bought it. He had wanted to appear a disbelieving skeptic, someone who would have no further interest in what those five agents would be looking for in Egypt.

But he *was* interested...very interested.

As he began to sort through the paperwork on his desk, Dr. Gideon Stack hummed tunelessly to himself.

What is evil lives forever.
    —Spanish Proverb

CHAPTER TEN

FURCA THE FOOL

WOLFE ISLAND: 4 NOVEMBER 2020

Warmly clad in a white mink-lined jacket, white slacks and black mink-lined leather boots and gloves, Nicasia Bane crunched rapidly through the two-foot-deep snowdrifts that covered Wolfe Island this chill gray morning, heading for the stables. There she told the stableboy to harness one of her horses to an old-fashioned sleigh.

"Which one, m'lady?" the groom asked.

Nicasia scanned the animals cooly. "That one," she said, pointing to a large gray.

As she and the stableboy approached him, the big horse rolled his eyes and snorted white plumes of fear. When the boy opened the stable gate, the animal bolted out of his stall, then stopped, rearing and whinnying his terror.

"Look out, m'lady!" yelled the stableboy as the horse reared again, striking out at Nicasia's head with an iron-shod hoof.

But Nicasia's reflexes were cat-quick; she ducked, throwing up an arm to protect her head, and the horse's hoof struck her forearm a glancing blow.

She stepped back out of reach, holding her bruised arm. She knew it was not broken, but it hurt like hell. Her eyes blazed molten gold as she glared at the trembling, snorting animal.

"I don't know what's wrong with him," cried the terrified stableboy. "He never...."

He trailed off as Nicasia walked slowly and deliberately up to the horse, rubbing her arm, tiger eyes boring into the animal's. He pawed the ground and whinnied, but did not rear again.

"What's his name?" she asked the groom without taking her eyes off the horse.

"Ah...Galahad, m'lady."

"Okay, Galahad," she told the horse in a low soft voice like velvet over barbed wire, "pay attention. You settle down *right now* or you end up inside my twenty-two-foot snake before the day's out. He would consider horsemeat a real delicacy. Understand?"

The horse did understand, for Nicasia accompanied each word with a strong mental image which she projected forcefully into his mind. Galahad stopped his snorting and pawing immediately, although his eyes still rolled in fear.

Still shaken, the groom harnessed the animal to the sleigh, and a few minutes later Nicasia hissed away through the snow in a merry jingling of sleigh bells.

As she rode briskly through the icy morning, past dark skeletons of trees clawing at gray sky, Nicasia began to enjoy the bite of the wind on her face and the smoky clouds of her breath. Her anger began to subside and her arm pained her less. She looked forward to her meeting with the black magician who awaited her in his laboratory.

This strange and sinister dwarf was something of a mystery to her. He had never revealed anything about his background or nationality, claiming to be "a citizen of hell" and the incarnation of the infamous fifteenth-century Marshal of France. Gilles de Rais. "I had only begun my magical experiments in that life," he had told her. "In this incarnation, I have learned how to make the demons dance for me, my lady, and I will make them dance for you as well."

She had first met him at a Black Mass in London five years ago and learned that he was an adept in the black arts. He called himself merely Furca, after the mysterious figure in the Major Arcana of the Tarot deck. Furca the Fool, the Juggler, the card with the numerical value of zero, symbolic of man's lower consciousness, separate and dreaming, poised on the edge of a precipice with his head ever in the clouds. Furca loved the irony of it, yes, and the appropriateness of it also, for, like the Fool, he juggled frightful spells and incantations for his own dark purposes, ever mindful that the slightest mistake could be his last, could hurl him over that yawning precipice into everlasting night. But also mindful that the other half of this powerful symbol from the time of earth's beginnings was the Magician, the first of the Major Arcana, the occultist, the superman, the master of all magics, black and white, with the four magic symbols before him on the garlanded altar and Eternity itself above his head. For a small man, Furca dreamed great dreams of power and carefully, thoughtfully, bided his time....

Despite his grotesque appearance and uncouth personal habits, Nicasia knew that he would prove a valuable ally in melding the dark principles of sorcery on this planet with the advanced science of her home world. A mind as carefully conditioned as Furca's could open dimensional gates and provide a direct pipeline to the inexhaustable power source of Darkness itself.

So Nicasia had taken Furca into her organization and given him free reign with his magical experiments, an isolated laboratory in which to conduct them and all the young subjects he needed as sacrifices to his insatiable thirst for occult power and his perverted lusts, apparently a holdover from his previous existence. Several miles out in the forest, no one could hear the screams.

She had never seen his face uncovered; he always wore a ski-mask or other covering, except when alone. Some speculated that he had been horribly burned; he had told Nicasia once that his ruined face was the result of his first experiment in calling up a demon. He had not been as careful as he should with the pentagram and had come close to losing more than his face. One of his eyes was a mechanical-optical device; the other one burned darkly with a lust for obscenity and pain.

This morning, Furca was disposing of the remains of last night's excesses in the small nuclear furnace that served as crematorium and power source and provided ample heat for

112

his dwelling, when his keen ears picked up the faint jingle of sleigh bells approaching. He waddled hurriedly into his bedroom, located a pair of dirty wool trousers and a baggy, moth-eaten black wool sweater and pulled them on. Then, shoving his feet into a worn pair of boots, he reached for a red woolen ski-mask and carefully adjusted it over the horror of his face.

Moments later, the insistent knocking came and Furca admitted Nicasia into his cluttered domain with a mocking bow. "Welcome, mistress. To what do I owe the honor of this visit?"

Nicasia looked around at the filth and disarray amid which this strange creature chose to live, her nose wrinkling in disapproval. "Don't you ever clean up this pigsty, Furca?"

The dwarf grinned behind the mouth-hole of his mask. "You gave me no warning of your visit, my lady, or you would have found the place spotless."

Nicasia smiled at his small insolence, carefully calculated to amuse rather than enrage. "You're such a liar, you little freak. I suppose you would have conjured a genie to clean it all up in ten seconds?"

"*Two* seconds, my lady. I am not without experience in Arabian magic. The jinn are fast workers but hard to control. Far simpler would be merely to alter your perception of reality here—like this."

He made a few quick passes in the air with both hands, muttered something in a tongue never meant to be spoken by human lips, and suddenly Nicasia saw the room around her *blink* like an eye, darken for a fraction of a second, then reappear spotless, everything in its place, floors clean and swept, piles of old books back on shelves, windows sparkling like crystal. Her eyes widened in amazement; before she could say anything, Furca snapped his fingers and the room blinked back to normal, chaotic and familiar.

Nicasia shook her head, rubbed her eyes. "Shit, Furca! Don't do that again!"

"Disorienting, is it not, mistress? But it does make you begin to ponder the true nature of reality—"

"Never mind the philosophy, wizard," she cut in, irritated by the thought of such power over her perception. "I

113

don't have time to ponder this morning. I need you and your magic to provide some information."

"Ah. Past or future?"

"Both."

"Then perhaps the Tarot—"

"Too vague. I want hard facts. Grab your bag of potions and paraphenalia and let's go to the crypt. You know what to do. We've done it before."

An evil grin writhed beneath the mask. "At once, my lady," he said, bowing mockingly.

Minutes later, Nicasia and her small companion set off through the snow toward a small cemetery about a half-mile away. Surrounded by a rusting iron fence, it was traditional and sad, a few small tombstones, now mostly obscured by snow, scattered here and there. In the center rose the imposing mass of a large mausoleum constructed entirely of imported Italian marble. A few naked trees stretched bony branches on either side of the forbidding structure.

Nicasia brought the sleigh to a halt in front of the large iron gate, unlocked it, and the two walked directly into the crypt, Furca's small legs lagging behind the purposeful strides of his mistress. Behind him he dragged a large canvas bag which left a deep round impression in the snow.

They entered the mausoleum, grateful to be out of the icy winds that still gusted the morning, rattling the bare branches of the agonized guardian trees. Two small high windows admitted a sickly gray light into the chamber. Their breaths steamed in the meat-locker cold and gloom as Nicasia moved slowly over to the single marble sarcophagus in the center of the large bare room. Almost tenderly she moved a gloved hand over the smooth cold top, pausing to read the words chiseled there with the precision of a master stonecutter: "Here lies Sir Harcourt Bane, beloved husband of Nicasia and father of Gabrielle. Born February 11, 1947; died April 30, 2012. *Requiescat in pace*." Her lips curled in an ironic smile at the traditional Latin phrase. "Not yet, my dear departed husband...not quite yet...."

She nodded, and with surprising strength for one so small, Furca wrenched the heavy stone cover off the tomb and set it down carefully to one side. Then he reached into his bulky canvas bag and withdrew two iron braziers which he set upon tripods at the head and foot of the coffin.

As Furca prepared for the ritual to come, Nicasia gazed thoughtfully at the remains of her multimillionaire husband. Had any of his other relatives been there at this moment, they would have been profoundly shocked by three things: first, that the body was perfectly preserved; although it had lain here for eight years, it showed not the slightest sign of decomposition. Nicasia had seen to that: among his other talents, Furca was well versed in the ancient Egyptian arts of the preservation of the dead; indeed, had improved upon them immeasurably, so that the skin of the corpse had not become shrunken and leathery like that of Egyptian mummies, but looked as though Lord Bane had died only this morning.

Second, the mourners would have been appalled to see that the corpse was naked: instead of the customary funereal attire befitting a man of his position, the body was wound about by garlands of dried green and purple-blotched leaves, from which a faint disquieting smell still arose.

Finally, and most ominous of all, was a large black iron cross which the corpse's hands clutched to its chest in the inverted position.

Now the dwarf was constructing a magic circle next to the coffin, drawing with colored chalk on the dusty stone floor. He divided the inner circle into four quarters, carefully chalking in strange names and sigils: around the perimeter of the outer circle he inscribed the names *Raphael, Rael, Miraton, Tarmiel, Rex*. Then, bowing low, he said, "If my lady will step inside the protective circle, we may begin."

Furca's dark eyes, both real and false, glittered with anticipation as he looked up at Nicasia stepping into the center of the circle to stand next to him. Drawing himself up to his full height of four feet, he warned her, "On no account move outside the circle during the operation, my lady. Although it is a relatively simple conjuration, there is still danger—"

"I know, I know," she replied impatiently. "Get on with it, will you?"

He bowed, and reaching into the bag once more, brought out a glass jar containing an ugly greenish powder. He threw

115

a handful on each of the braziers, which he had previously filled with smoldering charcoal. A flash of green flame and an evil stench arose in clouds of gray-green smoke. Next he lit four large black candles which he had placed at the four corners of the sarcophagus, muttering incantations as each one sputtered into life.

"Now we may begin," the wizard said in a low voice. "This should properly be done at midnight, but we can...compensate." Removing a large thin knife of dark metal from his bag, Furca began to inscribe invisible signs in the air with it, closing his eyes and muttering strange, guttural words and phrases in a monotonous tone. After a few minutes of this, he intoned in a louder voice, "*Exurgent mortui et ad me veniunt.* Rise, ye dead, and come unto me. Infernal powers, those who bringeth disturbance into the universe, quit thy somber habitation and render up him whom we do summon in the name of the Dark Father, of Ashmedai the Destroyer, of Abaddon the Waster, of Astaroth the Searcher of Souls, of Ophis the Serpent of Hell, and all other infernal and subterraneal intelligences and spirits who may hear our call. If thou dost hold in thy power him whom I call, I conjure thee, in the name of the Master of Shadows, to release his spirit for a time into our care."

Furca then withdrew a handful of earth from his bag and carefully scattered it over the corpse. "May he who is dust awake from his sleep. May his spirit once more enter the dust and answer all demands we may make in the name of the Father of Ultimate Night."

A slight tremor shook the ground, accompanied by a distant rumble that might have been thunder but was not. The greenish fires that had been smoldering suddenly turned a vivid scarlet, painting the cold stone of the tomb a murky crimson. There was the smell of an abbatoir in the air.

Furca turned to Nicasia, a bit uncertain for the first time. "Blood, mistress! They demand blood. This is the token—the compensation they insist upon for this daylight summoning."

Nicasia regarded the little man coldly. "What kind of blood? Animal or human?"

"Either will do. Perhaps the horse—but we cannot leave the circle in safety—"

"Never mind. How much?"

"Only a few drops, but—"

"Give me your knife."

Furca hesitated, disturbed by the cold yellow fires that glared down at him. Reluctantly, he handed over the black blade.

Nicasia grinned, the ruddy light crimsoning her teeth as though she had been drinking from a jugular. For a moment she held the knife, feeling its weight and balance, her glance hypnotic as she contemplated the misshapen figure, watching fear begin to dance in his one good eye.

"M-my lady, the operator must not—"

"Don't worry, wizard," she purred. "I wouldn't take your blood for this. You don't have enough to spare." Still smiling, she stripped off her left glove and quickly drew the dark blade across her wrist, just deep enough to break the skin. A scarlet line of blood welled up, and holding her hand over the corpse, she let several drops fall upon its upturned face. Then, still smiling, she handed the bloody knife back to a visibly relieved Furca.

The guttering flames changed color once again, returning to their original murky green, and as she wrapped a silk handkerchief around her wrist and drew on her glove, Nicasia could feel a slight lessening of the tensions that had built up in the chamber.

As Furca began muttering again in a vile, discordant language that bore little resemblance to a human tongue, the air in the tomb seemed to thicken; the wan light coming in from outside seemed to dim away almost to darkness; the already frigid temperature seemed to drop suddenly to new depths. Nicasia looked up to see hoar frost beginning to form on the ceiling and walls of the vault. The flames of the four black candles turned blue and began to diminish, dancing in some sudden silent wind that affected only them.

"The spirit comes!" exclaimed Furca, excited now. "Behold, mistress!"

Nicasia's attention was drawn to the space directly above the tomb; in the darkening gloom she could see a hazy

117

blue cloud begin to form, whirling within itself like a miniature cyclone. As it gradually became larger and clearer, she could make out what looked like the features of a face—darker holes for the eyes and mouth—the face of her late husband.

Furca cried out in a loud rasping voice, "We summon thee, Harcourt Bane; return for a while to thy earthly prison, tell us what we wish to know. We command thee, we hold thy chains, ye must obey!"

A great, shuddering sigh seemed to fill the chamber then, as the whirling smoky cloud spiraled down and into the forehead of the corpse. Immediately the body began to twitch and jerk, as though electric current were flowing through it; the eyelids and mouth writhed in tic and rictus and hideous low groans began to issue from deep within the spasming corpse. The dried herbs wrapped around it jerked and rustled like snake rattles.

Gradually the horrid dance subsided and the corpse's eyelids flicked open to reveal dead eyes staring far into other realities.

Nicasia's own eyes gleamed in feral anticipation now as she bent over the corpse. "Harcourt...can you hear me? Answer me!"

From far away beyond imagining, a low, moaning voice, sepulchral, slurred with pain, replied in halting words:

"Nicasia...why have you...called me...again?...Release me...please...release me...I loved you...I want to go on...out of the darkness...toward the light...please...."

"When my plan is complete, then I will let you rest. The chains that bind you are your own, you know. Not even I could hold you now if you had not forged them yourself during your lifetime. There were things done in your youth, Harcourt, people ruined, careers destroyed, even a few lives lost here and there, I believe.... No, my dear departed husband, it's not I who keep you in the darkness. I merely make use of your own sins for my purposes. Now tell me what I want to know."

Another great sigh heaved up out of the Stygian depths of the tortured spirit's despair. "What...do you...wish...to know?"

118

Nicasia succinctly described the situation with the lost cobracraft, sent out to intercept and destroy the American agents' unarmed plane over the Atlantic. "Show me what happened there, Harcourt."

The corpse shuddered and twitched, rustling the poisonous-looking wreaths around it, and the pale eyelids snapped shut. A few moments later, an eerie blue glow began to form on the far wall, rapidly spreading to encompass almost the entire area. Gradually, the image of a vast body of blue water became visible below a blue sky; a silver dart appeared, rapidly became a sleek plane being pursued by an ominous blade-shaped craft spitting lethal green beams at it. Nicasia's eyes became saffron slits riveted on the aerial scene being recreated for her. She watched in fascination as the small plane tried and failed to shake the cobracraft, finally bolted into a cloud bank to re-emerge temporarily free of the adversary ship. Nicasia gritted perfect teeth. "Those stupid horn-heads," she hissed. Then she watched in amazement grudgingly mixed with admiration as she saw the little plane loop over and pull out above the cobracraft, gradually lower itself, then tilt and sear the top of the blade-ship with its exhaust until that ship turned cherry-red and exploded into flaming wreckage, hurling its hapless occupants out and down to a fiery death.

"Well, I'll be God damned...." Nicasia breathed incredulously. "I don't believe what I just saw. An unarmed plane outwitted and blew away a fully armed Algolian cobracraft, one of the most vicious fighting machines in the entire galaxy!" Before the pale image could fade, Nicasia demanded, "Harcourt—I want a close look at that pilot! I wish he were working for me, instead of those idiot goats!"

As if a zoom lens had been shooting a scene in a movie, the image of the victorious little plane rapidly enlarged until a clear view of the occupants could be seen. Nicasia gasped. "A woman!"

Furca replied with excitement. "Those are the two that fought us at the Sphinx!"

Feeling a bit threatened and annoyed by the sight of Eris' pure honey-gold beauty, Nicasia asked in a harsh voice,

"Who is that pilot, Harcourt? And the man with her—I want both their names and who they work for."

The image on the murky wall grew hazy and faded away as the corpse's bloodless lips twitched once more in reply:

"The woman...is...Eris Campbell...a test pilot...the man is...Christopher Troy...Egyptologist...both work for...PIA...."

"The PIA! I might have known! That's the outfit Gaby's in. They're Warren's people. He's recalling them home to reassign them, I'll bet. What does he know about me? Does he know who I am yet?"

"No...but he knows...someone from Algol...caused...earthquake .... He is...preparing...to send...a team of agents...to Egypt...."

Suddenly the corpse moaned and twitched. The gnarled hands jerked, unclasped, and the heavy iron cross slipped to the side of the body with a thump.

Furca, who had been observing the unearthly dialogue in silence, now grew rigid with alarm. "Mistress! The cross— he released it! It must be replaced or we may lose him!"

Seeing that it was impossible for Furca's stumpy arms to reach the cross, Nicasia carefully retrieved it and placed it back in the hands of her late husband, head down. His skin was cold and dry to the touch, like a serpent's, she noted with amusement.

She stroked her perfect chin, peering into distance, her mind churning with plans. So, President Warren was already acting...well, that was to be expected. She would be able to deal with his people when she arrived at Zeinhom. But that woman, that pilot, disturbed her.

"I want this Eris Campbell, Furca. I want her. She's cost me four Arabs, two goat-men and a cobracraft. She owes me for that...and she's going to pay."

Furca grinned evilly and said nothing.

"Okay...I've heard enough," Nicasia said. "Send him back to his keepers and let's get out of here."

The small magician bowed, then began the arcane ritual that would allow the spirit of Harcourt Bane to return once more to the dark limbo of its own captivity.

I am thy father's spirit...
The serpent that did sting thy father's life
Now wears his crown.
　　　　—William Shakespeare, HAMLET,
　　　　　ACT I, SCENE 5

CHAPTER ELEVEN

GABRIELLE'S MISSION

WASHINGTON, D.C.: 4 NOVEMBER 2020

Jaca Ciencé, radiant in a long aquamarine gown that bared the snowy beauty of her arms, shoulders and back, welcomed the six Psi-Spies in her spacious foyer. Her emerald eyes were deep with feeling as she embraced each of them.

The visitors removed their snowy boots and shoes and put on soft white slippers, then followed Jaca down the long hallway, admiring the paintings and other art objects as they went.

Soon they were in the beautiful tower room, seated cross-legged in a semicircle facing Jaca across the jeweled mandala. She closed her eyes in concentration and in a few moments the great crystal globe began to descend in its glittering golden net. They had all had readings from Jaca before, but they never ceased to marvel at this beautiful sphere of frozen light and the visions it offered to her special talents.

Jaca was in a light trance now, eyes closed, and the beams of color began to rise and stream gold, rose, azure, violet and emerald into the faintly perfumed air. The agents

121

felt a tingling warmth bathe their bodies, relaxing yet energizing them at the same time.

"He is with us," Jaca said in a soft, low voice, opening her eyes to the images and symbols beginning to swim within the crystal. Her voice deepened then, became more formal, vibrant with high power perfectly controlled, as a presence from the inner planes began to speak through her.

"I bring you all greetings from the Light," it said, radiating a peace and warmth that seemed to fill the room like incense. "I am called Klorian and I come to give you further information concerning the great mission you are about to undertake.

"Christopher Troy, your main role in the upcoming drama will be to guard Eris Campbell with your life and if she falters, aid her. At some point her energy may be drained from her selfless efforts as leader of your group."

"Leader?" asked Eris incredulously. "Me?"

"Yes. You have been chosen."

She bowed her head in silent humility and gratitude for the great trust placed in her. As rainbow light caressed her face and golden hair, Chris glanced over at her. She looked at that moment almost like a creature of light, ethereal and impossibly beautiful.

"The rest of you also have important roles to play," continued the spiritual teacher. "Each of you was chosen for your specific psychic abilities and spiritual qualities. How you choose to utilize them on this mission will determine its success or failure, so each of you must strive to reach your highest potential.

"All of you must keep your energies as high as possible in order to pass through the psychic barriers erected millennia ago by a great Atlantean magician named Hept Supht. He erected special energy fields around the buried pyramid and in the passages leading to it, so that no one except those who walk in the Light might enter them. Now the time has come for the ancient secrets to be revealed to mankind, lest it be cast again into countless centuries of darkness. The lifting of the time-lock which has guarded the subterranean vaults has been accomplished and the entrances are once more perceptible to human senses. But they are guarded by vibrational

122

codes; there are no physical keys, only spiritual ones. Your vibrations alone, if they are correctly attuned, will permit entry into the secret places."

"You mean the Algolians can't enter the passages?" asked Raymond Gaunt.

"That is correct," replied the teacher. "Their energy patterns are filled with hate and lust and the glorification of the ego, so they cannot penetrate the vibrational barriers. However, they are cunning and resourceful and may find ways to circumvent this obstacle, so haste is essential. You must locate the ancient device called the Immobilizer and take it safely to Washington before they can reach it. That is your primary goal. When you reach Ka-Ren, the Ruby Pyramid, far under the sands of Egypt, you will meet those who will provide you with further assistance and information."

Eris' eyes widened in excitement. "A ruby pyramid? Wow! How beautiful! And who are these people who'll help us?"

"This information will be revealed when you reach your destination," the voice replied gently. Then a more somber note colored its words. "Now before I leave you, I have a painful piece of information to impart. We have finally been able to penetrate the psychic barriers guarding the identity of the woman who is the head of the Algolian force on this planet."

The six agents sat bolt upright at this, alert and eager to learn the identity of their adversary at last.

"Who is she, Klorian?" asked Eris.

There was silence for a moment, then the spiritual teacher replied, "She is Nicasia Bane, Gabrielle's stepmother."

Gabrielle sat rigid, her eyes widening in horror at the awful revelation. She looked as though someone had slapped her. For a moment she tried unsuccessfully to speak, then, "I—I don't believe it! It can't be! Not Nicasia! I mean, she's a cold woman, even cruel at times, and we don't always get along, but she's been the only mother I've known since my real mother...."

She trailed away; then, after a shuddering breath, anger began to shrill in her voice. "No! It's not possible! My father loved her! He would never have married such an evil woman! It can't be true!"

André put his arm around her, trying unsuccessfully to calm her.

Klorian's gentle voice cut in: "I am deeply sorry, but it is true. Your stepmother has been using your father's vast financial empire to further her ends. She is your enemy. However, she does not know that you are aware of her true identity, so this is why your mission must be different from that of the others."

Hysteria began to filter into Gaby's voice. She jumped to her feet, eyes blazing. "No! I won't believe this! I want to go to Egypt with André and Eris and everybody! I don't want a different mission!"

Then, a strange and ominous thing occurred. The air in the room began to grow cold; a feeling of uneasiness and despair began to creep over the little group, already shocked by the dreadful information they had just received.

"Wait," Klorian said in a warning voice. "Something— or someone—is approaching.... It wishes to communicate.... I must leave you temporarily, to give it a channel. I will return afterward...."

Then, abruptly as thought, the powerful presence was gone, its warmth replaced by an impression of gloom and sadness that chilled the assembly like Arctic air.

All eyes were on Jaca, then, as she suddenly stiffened, clenching her fists. An agonized shriek ripped from her lips, shattering the silence like a strike of lightning. She gripped her forehead with both hands, rocking back and forth in apparent agony. *"My God, my God, the pain, the pain—"*

Chris was instantly on his feet, darting around the rainbow mandala to her side. "Jaca! What is it? What's hurting you?" The others had half-risen also, alarm flickering like wildfire across their faces.

"No, she groaned, eyes squeezed shut, "not me...someone else...*his* pain ...terrible psychic agony.... I see black chains...he wants to come through...."

Then her face relaxed, and her hands fell limply to her sides. Her eyes opened and it was like looking into the murky depths of the Styx itself. A masculine voice, dark with pain and despair, spoke through her scarlet lips.

"Gabrielle...."

It seemed to well up from unimaginable depths.

Gaby's flushed face turned white, her eyes great circles of blue flame. She stood rigid as stone at the sound of her name.

The eerie call came again.

"Gabrielle...." Her reply was only a whisper, yet every-one in the room heard it perfectly. "Daddy...?"

"Jesus," gritted Chris between clenched teeth, but he moved back away from Jaca, knowing not to touch her when she was in a mediumistic trance.

"This...is...your father, Gaby...," said the hollow voice. I...must warn you...."

"Daddy!" Gaby fought to keep from screaming it. "Is it really you? Oh, my God...."

"Listen to me, Gaby...I have very little time...you must listen to what Klorian tells you...it is true.... Nicasia is evil, a monster from another world.... She murdered me...and now holds me...in her power...I cannot go on to the Light.... She will do the same...to you.... Stay away from her...."

The voice grew weak, dropped to a whisper, and was gone. Jaca's eyes closed and she slumped to the floor, her spun-gold hair flowing out around her head like a tide of sunlight. Still Chris did not touch her; after a few moments she got up, shaking her head, her eyes clear emeralds again. "Good Lord," she murmured shakily. "That was awful...that poor spirit...I've never felt such psychic agony before...."

"Are you all right?" asked Chris gently, now touching her shoulder to reassure her.

Jaca smiled assurance that she was, then she saw Gabri-elle, still white and stricken, bent over as though her stomach pained her, her eyes still wide with shock. "Gaby...what's the matter? Who was that?"

"My father," replied Gaby in a small voice, tight with agony. She sat down shakily, her knees suddenly turned to mush, and great hot tears overflowed and coursed in torrents down her pale cheeks.

André held her in his arms, rocking her back and forth gently and murmuring to her in French until the tears were done and she looked up at the group again. As she wiped the wetness from her face, she said, "I-I'm sorry, I'm acting like a baby.... Yes, that was my father, Harcourt Bane.... He came to warn me...I don't know how, but.... It must be true, then...oh, Jaca, my stepmother murdered him and now she won't let him rest! She still controls his spirit somehow! That's horrible! How can she do that?"

"She must be an adept at black magic," Jaca replied gently. "She has acquired the power to keep his spirit from moving on to its proper spiritual plane in the next life. She probably makes use of him for necromantic divination."

"What's that?" asked Gaby.

"She can compel him to come at her call and reveal things about the past and future. No wonder she doesn't want to let him go! It's the equivalent for her of the information and guidance the teachers give us through my crystal."

"Can't we release him somehow?"

"Yes—there is a kind of exorcism that could free him from her bondage, but it would be very dangerous to attempt it. You'd have to go to Wolfe Island, to the place where he's buried, and—"

I'll do it!" Gaby cried. "I'll do it! Oh, Jaca, tell me how!"

André started to protest, but she gently shushed him. "I'm not afraid of her! He's my Daddy...oh, God, how I loved him...." She could feel the hot pressure of tears welling up again.

"And that love will enable you to free him, Gabrielle," came a familiar voice then, strong and warm and full of peace. Klorian had returned, and Gaby suddenly felt as though wrapped in a warm blanket of security and comfort. "This is why your mission must be different from that of your five friends. They will form a Pentad, a team strong and potent against evil. You must go home to Wolfe Island to observe your stepmother's movements and keep the President informed. Only you can do this, Gabrielle, because of your unique relationship with Nicasia Bane. Your mission is as important as the other. You will be in great peril, but she

126

does not suspect you, and if you are careful, you can allay her suspicions for some time."

"I'm not afraid. I see why I must go...."

"Jaca will tell you what you must do. Remember that the Light is always with you, my child, no matter what bitter valleys you must walk through in the days to come. Call upon the Light when you are in need and you will be answered. Never despair. May the Light be with all of you on your journey."

And then the powerful presence was gone.

The little group looked at Gabrielle with admiration and love as she rose, smiling now, determination and courage bright in her eyes. She was no longer afraid. She would do what was necessary, even though it meant separation from her beloved André and the others and deliberately walking into danger.

"All right, Jaca," she said, tilting her chin bravely. "Tell me what I have to do...."

For dogs have compassed me:
the assembly of the wicked have enclosed me....
                                    —Psalms 22:16

CHAPTER TWELVE

THE ASSEMBLY OF THE WICKED

WOLFE ISLAND: 6 NOVEMBER 2020

Luxuriating in the steamy flower-scented fragrance of her own bathtub once again, it almost seemed to Gabrielle as if she had never been away; the old familiarities of Wolfe Island, the mansion, her room still exactly as she had left it, all had clicked back into place with startling clarity the moment she had stepped off the plane at Kingston Airport. All the fascinating, exciting events of the past three years— joining the PIA; the rigorous training of her mental, physical and spiritual abilities; meeting and working with the other Psi-Spies; even meeting André and their passionate romance—seemed to be blurring, fading away in her memory like some fragile dreamstuff dissolving.... But no! not André! His handsome laughing face was still bright and vivid in her mind, and she missed him, missed him terribly, already.

Smiling, her eyes closed, she recalled the sweet, fierce pleasure of their last night together in Washington. The urgency and pain of his need for her had been matched by her own for him and she had surprised herself with the complete abandon and uninhibited fire of her response. She could still see with heartwrenching clarity the curve of his cheek in the firelight, the dreamy, shadowed depths of his eyes inches from hers, cloudy with love, could still feel the hot sliding of their bodies, slick with their own perspiration.... God, how

128

she loved him! It was a long time before she had fallen asleep with her chestnut curls billowing across André's warm chest, listening to the soothing thumping of his good Gallic heart.

Enough of *that*, girl! she told herself firmly, feeling the warm tingling in her loins. I don't want to have to take a cold shower after this nice hot bath. She wished she could stay here forever, floating in this fragrant womb far removed from the cold realities that awaited her this evening. Nicasia had insisted on some kind of a silly "welcome home" party tonight, just another excuse for one of those boring and ruthless business bashes she loved to throw at the drop of a skirt.

But after the party, Gaby had something else to do, something that had to be done in utmost secrecy, the most important task she had ever undertaken. The bathwater seemed to turn to ice as she thought of her poor father, murdered and still bound even in death.

The thought of her father brought with it a new flood of memories, no less bittersweet than the others. Harcourt Bane might have been one of the richest and most influential men on earth when he died, but to Gaby he was always her kind, tall Daddy, smelling of pipe tobacco and cologne, always patient and loving with her, calling her his "little princess" and making her feel as though she were his real treasure, not all the money and investments he had scattered throughout the world.

Often, on cold winter nights, she would curl up beside the great roaring fireplace in her father's library and there would be hot mulled cider for her and coffee and brandy for him, and he would tell her tales of his days in the Royal Military College nearby and of his boyhood in his beloved Scotland. "Someday I'll take you back there with me," he had promised her. "Someday when I have time to do it right. You won't believe the beauty...."

Gaby and her father had shared a warm secret world that no one else could enter, and he had often provided a kind of bulwark for her against the unpleasant incursions of his wife, whom Gaby had never liked or felt easy with. Oh, they got along well enough most of the time, but it was at best an uneasy truce. Gaby had usually given in to Nicasia's wishes,

129

not so much for herself as to avoid causing her father any trouble. Her real mother had disappeared under mysterious circumstances when Gaby was four years old and was presumed dead. It was officially assumed that she had been kidnapped, but no ransom demand was ever delivered.

As England's Ambassador to Canada and later, as Ambassador-at-large for the Crown, Lord Bane had taken Gaby and Nicasia with him on trips throughout the world. He had proved to be an astute businessman and, with Nicasia's help, had amassed a staggering fortune in oil and land without ever incurring a hint of scandal or conflict-of-interest accusation.

But then, time ran out forever for Harcourt Bane. Gabrielle could feel the heat of tears building up behind her closed lids as she recalled how his sudden and unexpected death had brought her world crashing down around her ears like an avalanche. It was as if all the light had been taken away and she had been left in a dark closet. Great gulfs of depression and grief alternated with feelings of rage against her father for deserting her and leaving her to the chill ministrations of her stepmother.

The fact that Harcourt Bane had left an estate valued in excess of fifty billion dollars, $800 million in cash and the rest in U.S. petroleum shares, Arabian oil and real estate in Egypt, Canada, England and America, had meant nothing to Gaby, sunk deep in the morass of her pain and grief. The bulk of this enormous inheritance had gone to Nicasia, but $100 million dollars and the Wolfe Island estate had been left to his daughter, placed in trust in Switzerland until her twenty-first birthday.

Only the fact that this money meant freedom to live an independent life for herself, free from the influence of her stepmother, kept Gaby from cracking up completely. Her naturally ebullient temperament won out at last over her anguish and resentment, and on her eighteenth birthday she decided to go to Washington and make a career for herself in some type of foreign service so that she could travel extensively.

At this time, the top secret Psychic Intelligence Agency was being organized, and when Gaby heard about it through

130

the Washington grapevine, she knew this was what she wanted. She lost no time in securing an interview, and after a demonstration of the remarkable dowsing powers she had often used in her father's behalf and a security clearance, Gabrielle Bane had been trained and graduated as a Psi-Spy. She had been personally welcomed by President Warren, whom she had liked immediately and with whom she had felt a warm and genuine rapport.

The President had been delighted with her immediate success in locating several deep water wells in drought-stricken areas of the U.S. and abroad.

She loved the excitement and intrigue of her job, and the fact that she was able to put her ESP talent to use helping others made it absolutely perfect.

Her thoughts were suddenly interrupted by a shock of cool air against her face. She opened her eyes to see a tall, thin blonde slouched against the door, staring at her with cold, deep-set eyes.

Damn! thought Gaby, I should have locked the door. Aloud she said, "What do you want, Kathy?"

Slowly shutting the bathroom door behind her, the woman sauntered insolently over to the tub and stood looking down at Gaby, a smile like a wound on her face. She had the high cheekbones of a model and would have been pretty except for the hard, predatory look that tightened her mouth and eyes.

"Still the haughty little princess, eh? Didn't you learn any manners out in the big wide world, Gaby dear?"

Gaby slipped down into the water as far as she could, hoping there were enough suds left to cover her. Angrily she replied, "I hardly think breaking in on somebody's bath qualifies as good manners, 'sister' dear. I learned plenty out in the big wide world, including not to take any shit from the likes of you. Now get out of here and let me finish my bath!"

Kathy's brown eyes began to glow with dark fires. She sat down on the edge of the ornate Victorian tub and stroked Gaby's slippery shoulder with a thin crimson-nailed hand. "Now, now, little sister, that's no way to say hello after three years away from home. I'm just playing with you. I missed you. Now that you're back, I don't see why we can't be friends...."

Gaby's azure eyes were dark with anger. She shrugged her shoulder, trying to dislodge the repugnant caress. "Beat it, Kathy, and keep your claws to yourself. We never were friends before."

The clinging hand remained despite Gaby's twisting and shrugging; she couldn't move very far without revealing herself.

"You should put aside your old resentments, darling," said Kathy, undaunted. "I'm willing to, and the others, too. You're much too beautiful to be so cold and mean. Oh, I'll admit I was jealous of you before, but now that you've come home again, I'm really happy to see you."

Kathy brought her sardonic face so close to Gaby's that she thought the woman might try to kiss her. If she does, Gaby decided, I'll throw up all over her. Oops! Now that wandering hand was reaching under the water, stroking her breast....

Gaby grabbed the hand firmly with her wet one and flung it away. Something about the hunger in Kathy's dark eyes frightened her. It wasn't merely a hunger for her body.... "Cut it out!" she warned. "I don't appreciate you pawing me now any more than I did the first time you tried it. Women don't turn me on. Now *get out!*"

Undeterred, Kathy licked her thin scarlet lips sensuously and rubbed the wet spot on her wrist, caressing herself languidly. "How do you know women don't turn you on?" she purred. "Have you ever tried one? I'll bet I know a few things you didn't learn out there—"

Gaby had had enough. Abruptly, she stood up in the tub, spraying her surprised visitor with soapy water. Her lush young body glistening with rivulets of cascading water and snowy patches of soapsuds, she looked like Venus rising out of the sea. "Okay, Kathy, is this what you came in here to see?"

A look of raw lust flamed across Kathy's thin face like a brush fire.

Gaby scooped up a double handful of water and dumped it over her stepsister's head, turning her long straight blond

132

hair into a tangled mat of weeds. Kathy screeched like a cat on fire and jumped up, shaking herself frantically. "You little cunt!" she screamed, hurling herself at Gabrielle, scarlet claws outstretched to rip. Bracing her feet against the sides of the tub, Gaby blocked the assault with her forearms and delivered a hard wet slap to Kathy's face that sent her reeling back against the commode. Unfortunately for Kathy, both the lid and the rim were up, and she plopped right into the bowl with a loud splash and stayed there, stuck tight as a beetle in a thimble, her long legs waving and howls of rage and horror issuing from her throat like steam from a ruptured calliope.

Gaby tried not to laugh, failed miserably, then stepped out of the tub and leisurely wrapped a big fluffy towel around herself.

"Get me out of here!" screamed Kathy, looking like a scarecrow after a rainstorm.

Grabbing her stepsister's frantically waving hand, Gaby yanked her up and out of the commode's sodden embrace. "That ought to cool off your hot pants," Gaby said, planting a wet foot on Kathy's soaked rear and propelling her out into the hall. "Next time go hit on your sisters and leave me alone. This is as close as you're ever gonna get to this body."

Instead of the screamed obscenities she expected in reply, what Gaby heard as she shut and locked the bathroom door chilled her. In a low, acid voice like bone breaking, Kathy grated, "Don't be too sure of that, you little bitch.... When the time comes, I'll have your precious lily-white ass on a silver platter, and when I'm finished, there won't be *anything* left. Gabrielle, you're going to wish to God you'd never come back here...."

Amen to that, Gaby thought as she inspected herself in the large bathroom mirror. I already do. The flush of anger was receding from her cheeks and she felt cold and a little weak, wobbly in the knees.

She drained the tub, then took a quick hot shower to revive herself. As she toweled her auburn curls dry, she began to feel much better. She had come off pretty well in her first confrontation, she decided. André would have been proud of her. She smiled as she thought of relating the ludicrous episode to him and hearing his full, hearty laugh. She laughed aloud herself, remembering how ridiculous Kathy looked with her ass stuck in the john.

Cautiously she unlocked the bathroom door and checked to make sure no one was lurking in the hall. If she knew Kathy, it wouldn't take long for her to tell the other "stepsisters" of Gaby's "attack" and plan some kind of group reprisal. Well, I'll deal with that when it happens, Gaby decided, padding damply into her room, a little haven of familiar security with all her dolls and teddy bears neatly lined up on her bed just as she'd left them.

As she searched her closets for something to wear to the party, there was a light tap on her door. At least this one knocks, she thought. "Come in."

Nicasia swept into the room, looking radiant as a dream in a full-length rose-red gown with a neckline that took a stunning plunge all the way to her navel. A silver tiara glittering with diamonds and rubies adorned her midnight hair.

"Nicasia, you look absolutely gorgeous!" Gaby gushed, knowing what her stepmother wanted to hear. "That gown is unbelievable! Where did you get it?"

Nicasia smiled grandly. "Thank you, darling. I'm glad you like it. I had it flown in from Paris last week especially for your party. Etienne Saint-Moreau, you know; he's all the rage this season. And look—" Devilish gleams danced in her tiger eyes as she swept open the front of her gown, which parted up to the crotch in a hidden separation. "A little surprise for the crowd when I start dancing."

Gaby caught a stunning glimpse of long, white legs, then saw that Nicasia was not wearing underwear. "Mother!" she gasped as the dress floated back together like a theater curtain closing.

Nicasia laughed heartily. "You always were a little on the prudish side, Gaby. After all, this *is* 2020, you know— not 1990. I like to give my guests a little something scandalous to talk about for the next week or two." She turned a critical eye on Gaby's pale rainbow-colored gown of spun chiffon which, by contrast, looked quite demure. "That's very pretty in a girlish way, dear, but it hardly does you justice. That neckline is pathetic. It should show at least a little

134

cleavage. I want everyone to see that my daughter's become a beautiful woman, Gaby, not make them think you're trying out for a remake of *The Wizard of Oz!*"

Oboy, thought Gaby. She's really into the "friendly mom" bit, isn't she? "Oh, mother, do you really think it's too tame? I mean, this *is* a party and not an orgy we're having tonight, isn't it?" She twirled before the full-length mirror, surveying herself thoughtfully. "Hmmmm...maybe you're right, though. After all, I'm not exactly Rebecca of Sunny-brook Farm any more, am I?"

"Not if what I hear about you and that Frenchman is true."

"How do you know about him?"

"I have my ways of keeping an eye on things—and people, my love. Especially in Washington. As it so happens, I approve.... You needed to find out what life is all about. What's his name—André something?"

Gaby smiled in a foolishly love-smitten manner. "André Renard...he's a freelance photographer, does marvelous work. Maybe you've seen some of it—he's in all the magazines."

"Well, you must tell me all about him later, when we have time. Right now we've got to find you something more suitable to wear." Nicasia burrowed into Gaby's closet, re-emerging in a few minutes with a slinky gown of emerald satinex. "Ah! This ought to do the job." Holding it up to Gaby she added, "Yes, this will go nicely with your hair, darling, and show you off properly. And go a little heavier on the makeup than you usually do, will you?" She handed the dress to Gaby, patting her gently on the cheek. "I'll be back in a little while to inspect. I'm *so* glad you've come home, Gaby. I've really missed you, you know. I'm afraid we weren't very close while your father was alive, but we'll have time to really get to know each other now, won't we? I'm sure we'll become great friends."

Gaby felt that hot yellow gaze on her, intense and probing. "Yes, mother...I'd like that," she lied masterfully.

Then Nicasia was gone in a rose-colored rustle, and Gaby breathed a sigh of relief. She walked slowly over and looked down at her faithful old black cat, Damon Runtyon,

ESQ, who was having a nap on one of his favorite places in all the world—his mistress' bed. He was ecstatic that she had returned at last; he'd never doubted that she would. She reached down to pet the head of the only friend she had on all of Wolfe Island. "Somehow, I don't think we're in Kansas any more, Q," she told him wistfully.

"Q" opened one eye and was rewarded with a view of the most angelic of all human faces in his world smiling down upon him. He cranked up his rusty old motor and began to purr.

By 10 P.M. the Bane mansion was filled with several hundred international guests: U.S. senators, high-ranking members of the Canadian parliament, top officials of banks and utilities, Arabian oil sheiks and Texas oilbarons, jet-set beauties with their year-round tans and perfect teeth, a few famous high-fashion models, all glitter and cheekbones, and a smattering of video and film stars to add a little spice to the assembly. Gaby recognized the famous 3D pornovision star, Yoni Cassolette, undulating through the crowd, surrounded by a clutch of slavering male admirers.

Colored spotlights lanced rainbow fire off the huge glittering crystal chandeliers and great wall mirrors that lined the immense ballroom like the Palace of Versailles. The heady mix of expensive French perfumes blended and softened the harsher smells of tobacco, coke and alcohol, and a live Slimerock band pumped out bizarre black songs of death and degradation.

Gaby recognized them as the Cisterns, one of the top recording groups, grateful to have her thoughts distracted for a moment. She felt rather embarrassed in the super-sexy green gown Nicasia had chosen for her (when had she bought *that* dress? Nicasia must have picked it up for her on one of her shopping trips to Europe), which enticingly revealed the supple contours of her back—all the way down to her buttocks! Between her bare back and the lack of material covering her chest, Gaby was glad of the almost tropic warmth of the great ballroom.

A cold, dry hand, soft as petals, touched Gaby's bare shoulder. She jumped, startled, and turned to see a pair of

136

ink-dark eyes staring intensely into hers. "Oh, hello, Tina," Gaby said, attempting to keep the revulsion out of her voice.

Another of her "stepsisters," Tina, like Kathy, also just missed being pretty, with her long, dark hair and light coffee skin. But she always wore too much makeup and her fingernails were ridiculously long. They looked like meathooks covered with dried blood.

"I hear you dunked Kathy in the commode this afternoon, little sister," Tina said without a hint of humor on her unsmiling face.

Gaby nodded, saying nothing, not wanting to encourage a conversation with this one.

"Well, she probably deserved it," Tina said. "She's always too pushy. She's tried to make it with all of us at one time or another. But I'd be careful if I were you. Watch your step. Kathy was really pissed. She's not the kind to forgive and forget, you know."

Gaby felt a strange weakness beginning to suck at her brain, the same kind of feeling she had noticed during her confrontation with Kathy this afternoon. Tina's low, flat voice and huge black eyes were hypnotic.....

Gaby shook her head to break the spell. "Uh, thanks, Tina, I appreciate the warning...I really do." She flashed Tina her best fake smile. "Look, I...uh, have to go find Senator Wilson now. Nicasia says he's looking for me. I'll talk to you later."

Gaby wrenched herself away from the black vacuum of Tina's gaze, somehow feeling that she had to escape or be pulled inside out. As she whirled away through the crowd, only the slightest discernable reaction could be seen on Tina's wooden face: a faint upward twist of one corner of her mouth. Then she began to survey the eddying throng, her hungry eyes sweeping like spotlights, searching for her next encounter....

As Gaby passed near the sumptuous buffet tables, laden with a feast fit for Louis XIV, she saw Kathy devouring a large sandwich stuffed with bleeding roast beef. As if sensing Gaby's presence, Kathy turned as she passed by and gave her a look that could melt metal. Gaby ignored it, but felt a chill ladder down her exposed backbone.

Hooking a glass of wine from a passing waiter, Gaby made her way to an unpopu!ated niche near one of the entrances leading into a broad hallway. The dark liquid burned slightly going down, but Gaby was grateful for the feeling of warmth it provided. She heard a slight ringing in her ears when she finished the wine; her cheeks felt hot.

She spotted another of her "stepsisters"—Lola, the prettiest one, and the friendliest to Gaby—in a bizarre zebra-striped outfit that showed off her long bronzed legs to striking effect. She was dancing with a balding, heavily bearded man wearing sunglasses, clinging to him like ivy and smiling up at him like an ad for some new toothpaste guaranteed to get your teeth as white as a film star's $10,000 cap job.

Time crawled. Gaby tried to look as though she were having fun, always wary of her stepsisters' eyes on her. She danced with a few of the less blatantly lecherous men who asked her, but dismissed them politely but firmly afterwards.

Finally, her moment seemed to come. Gaby carefully surveyed the room. For an instant she seemed to be in the clear. Two of the girls were dancing with their prey for the evening; Kathy had returned to stuff her face again at the buffet table. She couldn't see Nicasia—no, there she was, deep in conversation with an Arabian sheik in Western dress. Beautiful! This was her chance.

Gaby quickly ducked around a large couch, made her way to a nearby exit and hurried down a long hallway. She felt a little unsteady from the wine she had drunk and gulped in huge breaths of fresh, cool air whenever she passed an open window. Her heart was pounding like a jungle drum, but she felt good.

Carefully avoiding anyone wandering through the mansion and particularly watching for servants who might be instructed to report on her movements, Gaby made her way upstairs to her room. There she quickly dug out the flight bag she had brought with her. Apparently it hadn't been tampered with. Good. She grabbed a heavy coat and put on the warm boots next to her nightstand.

Glancing at her Piaget voxwatch, Gaby asked it the time and the little electronic voice replied: "11:45 p.m.." According to Jaca's instructions, the ritual she was going to perform

138

had to take place exactly at midnight. She'd better get moving! Quietly she hurried downstairs and out the back entrance into the cold black night.

The chill hit her like a fist after the superheated atmosphere of the ballroom, but it cleared the last cobwebs from her head. She breathed deeply of the icy air, savoring it like sparkling wine. She looked up and gasped at the wonder of the stars flung in crystal splendor across the dark, then hurried toward the east garage, where she knew the electric hovercars were kept. She had considered using her old favorite riding horse, Sinbad, to take her out to the cemetery, but she didn't want to take the time to saddle and bridle him. No, let him sleep in his warm stable—no need both of them freezing their buns. A hovercar would get her there faster and quieter anyway. She hoped they had been properly maintained and charged during her absence; the small vehicles were used mostly by the caretakers to reach all parts of the eighteen-mile-long island, as they could navigate as easily over water as land.

As Gaby reached the garage, her breath pluming into steam, she saw that the door had a large padlock on it. Oboy, she thought. Now what?

A distant owl hooted mournfully, like a boat lost in fog. Then Gaby remembered the small laserpen André had given her. After a quick scrabble through the bag's arcane contents, she located it, a slim silver tube no larger than a penlight. She switched it on, and a thin scarlet beam hissed out, quickly searing through the heavy lock like wax.

She quietly lifted the heavy metal door, eased it shut and switched on the fluorescents. No one from the house would be likely to notice a small rim of light around the doorframe, she hoped.

There were six of the small, two-seater hovercars lined up, gleaming like multicolored beetles. She flicked on the ammeter of the car nearest to her: half-charge. Too risky; she couldn't take a chance on the car dying on her halfway to the cemetery. The next car, a blue one, showed a full charge. She got in and switched on the electric motor. A welcome whining hum reached her ears and the smell of ozone briefly touched the chilly air and was gone. She hopped out of the car, turned off the lights and carefully raised the garage door; then she jumped back into the car and, holding her breath, engaged the powerful ventral fans that lifted the vehicle and held it a constant twelve inches in the air. The rushing hum of the fans sounded like the loudest sound in the world, but she revved up the engine, swiveled the propulsion fans to the rear and shot out of the garage into the starbright night.

She did not switch on the headlights; the brilliant starlight provided a cold bluish glow adequate to drive by. As the little car hummed down the snowy road, sending up white plumes behind it like the wake of a ship, Gaby checked the time: 11:49. Close, but she would just make it.

Her watch murmured "11:53 p.m." as she pulled up in front of the cemetery and killed the engine. The hovercar gently settled to the ground, crunching into the icy snow. As she stepped out of the car and grabbed her bag, she thought that the mausoleum, standing pale and stark in the wan starlight, surrounded by the gaunt ghosts of trees, resembled nothing real, seemed as eerie and insubstantial as a dream.

A quick burst from the laserpen took care of the gate's rusting old padlock, and a few moments later, panting white steam into the still and frigid air of the crypt, Gaby stood trembling like a bird beside the marble sarcophagus of her father.

I'm here, Daddy, I'm here.

A faint grayish illumination from the small high windows gave barely enough light to see by, but it was enough. Summoning all her strength, Gaby eased the heavy marble lid off the coffin until it fell to the stone floor with an ear-splitting crash. Rummaging around in her bag, she brought out two large white tapers made from pure beeswax and personally blessed by the Archbishop of Washington. She placed them at the head and foot of the coffin and lit them; a soothing golden glow seemed to spread out like summer sunlight, sending huge dancing shadows to play on the veined stone walls and ceiling.

Now she looked at the figure resting on the plush satin cushions for the first time and a knifeblade of agony turned in her guts. Harcourt Bane looked the same as when she had last seen him on the day of his funeral! She had expected to

140

find only a bleak skeleton, but seeing him untouched by decay, seeming merely asleep, unnerved her. Also, the fact that his body was naked and wound about by garlands of poisonous-looking dried herbs shocked her; but she quickly mastered her feelings and began to proceed as Jaca had instructed her.

She ripped off the hideous wreaths and tossed them aside. Then she pried loose the grim iron cross from his rigid fingers and turned it upright, replacing it in this position in his gnarled hands.

Quickly she constructed a protective circle beside the coffin from a diagram Jaca had drawn for her, after carefully erasing the remains of one drawn previously, no doubt by Nicasia, she surmised. Standing in the center, she closed her eyes and imagined herself enclosed in a capsule of brilliant white light as a further protection against evil influences.

After a few seconds of this visualization, Gaby opened her eyes and removed a small ceramic jar from the flight bag, handling it gingerly. Opening it, she carefully poured the contents, a thick, aromatic oil, over the body, drenching it thoroughly. A pungent odor hung in the air like a presence, reminding Gaby of the incense she used to smell long ago at Mass in Kingston, mixed with various exotic spices old when Egypt was young.

Next, Gaby extracted the crumpled piece of paper Jaca had given her, smoothed it carefully, and began to read in a loud, strong voice the ancient ritual of releasing. She stumbled several times over the unfamiliar words, most in Latin, some in a language she did not know. She repeated the indicated sections three times loudly, concentrating all the force of her will on seeing in her mind the black astral chains dropping away from her father's spirit:

> *"O angeli! Supradicti estote adjutores mihi petitioni et in adjutorum mihi, in meis rebus et petitionibus. Anoor, Amacor, Amides, Theodonias, Anitor, Salam, Amabael, Cetarari, Samax Rex, Carmax, Ismoli, Paffran, o vos omnes, adjutore atque contestor per sedem Adonai, per Hagios,*

141

*Theos, Ischyros, Athanatos, Paracletos, Alpha
et Omega....*"

As Gaby continued the incantation, she began to feel
tingling waves of power surging through the chamber; once
or twice she thought she heard the distant beating of mighty
wings. She felt flushed and warm, bathed in the aureate glow
of the consecrated candles; a tension, a straining of the very
air began to make itself felt, as though a battle were being
waged on some astral battlefield unimaginably far away, yet
all around her. Jaca had warned her not to be distracted by
anything she might see or feel during the ritual, so she continued on to the end of the arcane invocation, then stopped,
silence rushing in upon her like a great dark wave.

She bowed solemnly, once to each cardinal point of the
compass, then carefully lifted the candle from the head of the
coffin and held it up over the reeking corpse, now saturated
with the holy oil poured over it.

> "In the name of the Father and of the Son and
> of the Holy Spirit, I release thee from the
> bondage of the dust!"

It was done. Now all she had to do was release the candle
and let it—

Like a steel vise, a huge dark hand suddenly closed
around her wrist, and a voice like ice splitting down into the
Arctic sea rumbled, "What the hell you think you're doin',
girl?"

Gaby's heart froze in her chest. She screamed in fear
and surprise, the shrill cry richocheting off the smooth stone
walls in a deafening bullet of sound. She whirled to see a
terrifying black shape with eyes like emerald furnaces towering over her. O dear God! Had she somehow called up a demon?

No, as the dark figure moved into the amber glow, she
could see that it was human—a huge man whose eyes re-
flected the candlelight in eerie pools of phosphorescence,
like a cat's.

142

"Answer me, girl," the man demanded harshly. "What you doin' out here in the middle of the night?"

Gaby tried to free her trapped wrist in vain, spattering white droplets of molten wax on the man's black sweater. She gritted her teeth in pain; it felt as if the bones of her arm were grinding together. "Let me go! I'm Gabrielle Bane, Nicasia's daughter!"

A humorless chuckle rumbled up like a bubble of tar. "I know who you are...I wanna know what you're *doin'* out here with all this crap."

Gaby decided to try to bluff it out. "I'm visiting my father's grave. This is a little religious service for him. Nicasia said it was okay. Now let me go! You're hurting me! Who are you, anyway?"

"My name is...Reaper." He kept his hand locked tightly around Gaby's throbbing wrist. "Not bad, little lady. I could almost believe you, except that you look like you fixin' to torch your old man's body. Now what kind of religious service is that?"

It wasn't working. He wasn't buying it. Anger swept Gaby like a hot wind. Damn this man! Had she come this far only to be stopped at the last inute by one of Nicasia's goons?

Reaching suddenly with her left arm, Gaby grabbed the second candle from the foot of the coffin and swung it at Reaper's head, spattering hot wax across his face.

He roared thunderously in surprise and pain as the molten wax seared his skin, momentarily blinding him. Then she jammed the sputtering flame into his imprisoning hand, forcing him to let ho with a curse as he tried to wipe the wax out of his eyes with the other hand. The stench of burnt hair was sharp in the air.

Split-second decision: Gaby could duck around Reaper and run for it...or she could stay and finish what she had begun before he could recover. No choice. "Daddy, you're free!" she screamed as she plunged both candles into the coffin.

Instantly the corpse erupted with a *whoosh!* into intense, bluish-green flames, almost exploding with the heat of the inferno, sending thick, choking clouds of greasy black smoke

143

into the air. Gaby's lungs seemed suddenly filled with ice and fire; the smell of myrrh and natron and ancient spices was strong in her nostrils. She felt deliriously happy, despite her aching arm and the hot pain in her chest. She'd done it! Now she had to get out of here before—

She never even saw the great dark fist that whipped out of the roiling billows of smoke and exploded against her right temple like a sledge hammer. A pinwheel of brilliant sparks erupted behind her eyes and she felt herself falling into a bottomless well of night; or was she falling up into the stars? As unconsciousness closed in on her like a Stygian tide, she felt a warmth suddenly envelop her and a distant voice, no longer sad, seemed to whisper, *Thank you...oh, thank you, my little princess....*

Then cold and dark swept over her and she knew nothing.

*He made the treasurer of the East Pyramid
an idoll of black Agate, his eyes open, and shining,
sitting upon a throne with a lance; when any look
upon him, he heard of one side of him a voice,
which took away his sense, so that he fell prostrate
upon his face, and ceased not till he died.*
        —*John Greaves,* PYRAMIDIOGRAPHIA, *1646*

Walking on water wasn't built in a day.
        —*Jack Kerouac*

CHAPTER THIRTEEN

PSI-QUARK

WASHINGTON, D.C.: 6 NOVEMBER 2020

The white crane, graceful as a willow sapling, lifted her head, sensing her surroundings, keen eyes focused on the danger slowly approaching her. She was not afraid, merely alert, every nerve in her body tingling with readiness to defend herself against attack.

Before her, the snake slithered forward in a slow reptilian glide, weaving his body hypnotically. The crane ached to strike, her sharp dagger-like bill extended; but she must wait, pick the exact moment of moments....

The moment arrived! The crane felt it in the deepest wellspring of her being, and in a blurring movement almost too fast to see, struck, bill plunging toward the heart of the snake. But the snake was fast, agile, strong; he parried the movement and twisting aside, launched a blinding strike at the bird's unprotected side. The crane was not caught unprepared: she blocked the blow and before the snake could

145

strike again, focused all her consciousness into and beyond the point of her bill, centering herself in the tides of universal energy that swept through her, and struck a blow that traveled no more than six inches. Yet her opponent hurtled back several feet and was down.

But only for a moment. Master Sho Shin leaped agilely to his feet, smiling. He bowed to his opponent. "Excellent, Eris. You have truly mastered the way of the white crane. You have learned the lessons of grace and self-control it teaches. You were too anxious when you began your kung fu training, as I recall. Now you allow patience and stillness of mind to lead you into the flow of your *chi*, the universal life force that makes you forever one with all creation."

Eris bowed, flushing slightly at the praise from her *sifu*, or master. "Thank you, Master. You taught us this in our aikido lessons and it seems to work in any style of martial arts we use."

"Indeed it does, Eris. Think of the martial arts as a strong oak tree with many branches; each branch is in some ways different, yet all are branches of the one tree; and the *chi* is the sap, or life force, that nourishes them all. Now let us see if you are as proficient in the other systems."

As she had not merely assumed the posture of a crane, but temporarily in her mind *become* the crane, Eris now became the sinister praying mantis, squatting back on her left leg, right arm extended high above her head, an antenna intercepting all stray motion, analyzing, waiting....

"The way of the mantis is the most perfect system of all," Sho Shin had told her. "It requires extreme alertness, as it intercepts everything. It is a soft system, embodying the essence of pure defense. Yet the mantis strikes quickly when the prey comes within reach."

Now as the Chinese instructor circled warily near her, Eris whipped down a Knife Slash Blow in a blur of motion, a mantis striking at a careless insect. But this insect was not careless; the shoulder for which the blow was intended was gone. The Master danced aside in a quick graceful motion, almost seeming to float upon the air, and launched a Lightning Kick at the mantis.

146

Not quite quick enough, Eris whirled to parry the kick with the Whipping Branch. She caught most of the force of the blow on her shoulder, tried to recover her balance, but failed and toppled to the mat, gracefully blocking her fall with her arms.

She sat there, panting and laughing, as Master Sho Shin again bowed to her and smiled. "It seems the mantis is not quite as alert as the crane today. Remember that you are not merely the mantis and I the prey; you and I are one, we coexist, locked in a time that is not time. When I decide to strike, you must feel it as I do and be ready to turn my force—which is your force—aside. But you are progressing well. It will not be long before your brown belt will darken into black. Rest now."

Again he bowed, black eyes twinkling. Then he turned to the others, who were sitting cross-legged at the edge of the canvas mat. "Now let us see what the rest of you have retained from our last session. Christopher, show me what you know of the way of the tiger."

Eris scrambled to her feet and walked over to sit with Avram, André and Raymond and watch Chris work with Sho Shin. She smiled at Chris' seriousness as he assumed the hunch of a stalking tiger, his fingers curling into lethal cat claws, his body advancing and retreating with feline grace. The mimicry was perfect: as Eris had become the crane and the mantis, Chris was now a great jungle cat circling around the Chinese teacher in the most aggressive of the systems, one to be used only in response to extreme provocation. Eris could almost see the tip of a long striped tail flicking among moist jungle leaves, almost hear a thunderous feline snarl rumble through the gym.... Then the Tiger Claw leaped out to rake his opponent, but the Master was not there; he was suddenly out of reach and in almost the same motion seemed to lift off the mat like a ballet dancer and hurtle toward the tiger with a Dragon Stamp Kick that, had it landed full force instead of stopping just short of it, masterfully controlled, could have torn Chris' head from his shoulders. The tiger shifted sideways, his right knee grazing the mat, as he deflected the blow upward with his left forearm in a Leaping Deer Block. But even so, the force of it broke this concentra-

147

tion for a moment, long enough for a Side Hammer Blow to make his head ring as Sho Shin hurtled past him.

Shaking his head like a great cat, Chris recovered and circled to face his agile opponent once more. The training continued....

After a session of Hatha Yoga and *siddhi* meditation, the five agents had a light breakfast of dried seeds, nuts and fresh fruit. Then they went to a small classroom, furnished with only a large Indian rug on the floor. They seated themselves side by side, crosslegged, and waited for their instructor to appear.

A few moments later, a small, aged, brown-skinned man with a bright cherubic smile entered and bowed to the group. "*Namasté*," he said, greeting them in the traditional way of the yogi. He was filled with ageless energy and peace, which immediately communicated to the five. Bald and beardless, Yamaharindra wore the saffron cotton loincloth of a Hindu monk with the end draped over one thin brown arm, on which a gold digital wristwatch dangled incongrously, like an ill-fitting formica top on an antique coffee table.

Seating himself in full lotus position at the opposite end of the rug, he said, "My friends, it is good to see you all again. I am sorry that we seem to meet only in times of crisis, but such is the way of things here. As before, I will be instructing you in mental concentration and control.

"But before we begin our lessons, I have been asked to communicate to you some more details of your mission to Egypt."

Yamaharindra raised his right hand, palm toward them, then rotated it ninety degrees. Immediately the blank wall behind him glowed into life, revealing a realistic three-dimensional color image of the Giza Plateau, the Pyramids and Sphinx prominent.

Without looking at the picture, Yamaharindra continued in his dry, heavily accented voice. "Chris and Eris, you are the most familiar with this location, having just come from the Giza Plateau. This is the area within which your quest lies. Nicasia Bane is attempting to purchase this territory in order to keep you or anyone from gaining access to the secret passageways beneath the monuments which lead to Ka-Ren, the Ruby Pyramid. So far she has not been successful in her negotiations; the President of Egypt is still doing everything in his power to prevent the sale. We do not know how much longer he can hold her at bay; that is why your training must be completed in as short a time as possible and why you must get to this place as soon as you can."

The little guru raised his hand again and the picture dissolved to a close shot of the Great Pyramid alone, its immense bulk of jumbled stone towering into the bright blue sky of Egypt.

"This is *Ta Khut*—'the Glorious Light'—known to the world as the Great Pyramid and erroneously attributed to the IVth Dynasty pharaoh Khufu, or Cheops. It is actually far older than most archeologists believe. It is within this ancient temple that your mission begins."

The wall picture changed to a cutaway diagram of the interior of the Great Pyramid. The old yogi rose to his feet and walked over to the screen, pointing to the largest room, near the center of the structure. "You will spend the night in the King's Chamber, here. Then in the morning you will remove a certain three-ton stone block from the wall, revealing the entrance to a secret passageway. This passageway will eventually lead into the tunnels constructed ages ago, which wind steadily downward until you reach your destination—the buried city of Amentet-Nefert. In the center of this city you will find Ka-Ren."

"Apparently legends of this lost city became the basis for some of the beliefs about the Egyptian underworld," said Eris. "But Guruji, I'm confused about something."

"What is it, my child?"

"I always thought the entrance to the underground city was through the paw of the Sphinx. Wasn't that what Edgar Cayce said in his readings?"

"You are correct, Eris," replied Yamaharindra. "The original entrance is indeed located in the right paw of the Sphinx. Edgar Cayce said that the Hall of Records, which is inside the Ruby Pyramid, lies 'as the sun rises from the waters—as the line of the shadow (or light) falls between the paws of the Sphinx; that was later set as the sentinel or

149

guard, and which may not be entered from the connecting chambers from the Sphinx's right paw until the time has been fulfilled when the changes must be active in this sphere of man's experience. Between, then, the Sphinx and the river.'

"However, those who constructed the tunnels did not foresee the technological achievements that later generations of Egyptians would become capable of. The ancients built the passages to withstand catastrophes of nature such as floods, earthquakes and sandstorms; but they could not anticipate the slow, insidious damage from below which would occur as a result of water diverted by the Aswan High Dam constructed many years ago."

"You mean the steadily rising ground-water level has now flooded the tunnels?" asked Raymond.

"That is it. All the pyramids in the Nile Valley, as well as the Sphinx, are slowly sinking and being eaten away from below by the ground water accumulation. As many have long conjectured, there is a system of subterranean tunnels and temples connecting the Sphinx to the Great Pyramid, but these are also inaccessible now because of flooding. Only a single passageway remains: the one leading from the King's Chamber. Apparently it was constructed with greater care than the others; our clairvoyant viewings show that it is still clear. This is the one you will use."

"But, Guruji," asked Eris, "if this passageway runs through the Pyramid, how come it's never been discovered before?"

"It is guarded from discovery by a psychic field which warps all energy particles around it; thus, it remains invisible to any X-ray or cosmic-ray probes, just as does the legendary secret chamber inside the Pyramid which has yet to be revealed."

"Guruji," Chris asked, "you say that we'll have to move a three-ton stone block in the King's Chamber to reveal the passageway. How are we supposed to do this?"

"That's my department," answered Avram, who had been silent until now. "I've been working on a psychokinesis augmentation device which will enable us to levitate the block out of its resting place. So far I've only been able to

150

lift a thousand pounds with it, but with practice I think we can goose it up to three tons. But it'll require all of us feeding psychic energy into it at the same time. We'll practice with it every day, until we're able to lift the required tonnage. My own PK input will naturally be considerably stronger than yours, since I've been working on it for years, but I'll need all your help to pull this off."

"You can do it," said the ancient instructor. "One of the reasons for this class is to teach you how to accomplish that task. I will show you how to focus your concentration and visualization to a fine point; Avram's machine will amplify and focus your psychokinetic powers toward the stone in order to lift it."

A closeup view of the interior of the King's Chamber now filled the wall screen. "There is another reason for you to use the passageway in the Pyramid," said Yamaharindra. "Although it is no longer used for this purpose, perhaps you recall the real functions of the King's Chamber in past ages?"

"Well, it certainly wasn't a tomb, as people have been saying for years," replied Chris. "Cheops' body was never found; the stone sarcophagus in there is plain and unadorned. It's only symbolic."

"Yes...the 'Glorious Light' was built as a temple of initiation to the Ancient Mysteries, as well as a symbolic representation in stone of All That Is. The King's Chamber was known as the 'Holy of Holies.' On the day of initiation, the candidate had to enter the sarcophagus and spend three days there alone. The pyramidal energies that penetrated his body represented the energizing ray of the universe impregnating the fecund womb of Nature. Emerging from the tomb on the third morning, the neophyte personified the resurrection of the spirit after death.

"The postulant also represented the solar god—the all-vivifying orb that 'resurrects' itself each morning to impart life to the earth. The sarcophagus itself was symbolic of the feminine principle in Nature."

"Then it was actually a vessel, a symbolic female-shaped container holding the germs of life?" asked Eris.

151

"Yes. Our golden sun makes the earth potent and the silver moon makes it fertile. In fact, the whole Nile Delta, which resembles a lotus, beautifully symbolizes this relationship. The triangle-shaped Delta represents the *yoni*, or female genital, and the Nile entering it is the *lingam*, or male organ of generation."

The old yogi walked slowly back to his end of the rug and reseated himself in the lotus position. Behind him, the wall screen faded out. "We feel that by your spending the night in the King's Chamber, you will be subjected to the radiations which are focused within that room; in the positive and disciplined frame of mind you will possess when you enter the chamber, the pyramidal energies should prove highly beneficial, strengthening you both mentally and physically, as they did the ancient neophytes long ago."

"Not to mention sharpening enough razor blades for the entire trip," quipped Raymond.

The old man chuckled like a stream bubbling over rocks. But then his face turned serious.

"Now, my children, there is one thing further which I must impart to you at this time. I must warn you of the *Aner-sa*."

Chris' eyebrows shot up. "The what?"

"The *Aner-sa*—the Stone Sentinel—that was placed in the passageway as a guardian against the intrusion of anyone who might somehow circumvent the psychic barriers at the entrances. We have been able to learn very little of the possible perils and obstacles that may await you along the way, but we do have sketchy information from Coptic writings as to the existence of a great stone statue which supposedly guards the tunnel. It is made of black agate and sits on a marble throne with a lance in its hand. This image is reputed to have the power to produce a 'whispering sound' which causes an intruder to lose consciousness and die. You must be wary of this guardian statue and approach it with extreme caution—if indeed it does exist."

"You mean we can't assume it'll know we're the good guys?" asked Raymond.

"That is correct. It has undoubtedly been programmed to resist any intruder."

152

"Apparently this little expedition into the interior isn't going to be all fun and games," said Raymond, nervously smoothing his mustache.

Yamaharindra smiled. "Indeed. You may encounter dangers during your journey for which we cannot prepare you, situations beyond our conjecture. That is why you must all be functioning at your peak levels, physically, mentally and spiritually. Now I will dismiss you, for others are waiting to have their ways with you. Are there any further questions? If not, then I bid you good day and will expect you at the same time tomorrow, when we will begin our mental exercises in earnest."

That evening, after lights out at 2200 hours, Eris stretched out naked on her bunk, her body still tingling with the excitement and exhiliration of this incredible day. My God, she thought, and this is only the *first day!* Gonna be one tough two weeks! There would be meditation, running, Tai-Chi, kung fu, biomanipulation exercises, flotation chamber trips into the past, PK drill, biofeedback, and tests, tests, tests: Ganzfeld, Zener Cards, RNGs, PK video games, and on and on and on. Enough to wear you out just thinking about it. In fact, she should be exhausted now, after all she'd been through since 0500 hours this morning.

But she wasn't. The energizing effects of meditation and breathing exercises were still with her. She felt as if she'd been popping uppers; maybe she'd have to hypnopsych herself to sleep tonight.

Raising her arms above her head, she stretched luxuriously in the darkness, like a great sleek cat. No, she wasn't tired at all; she was amped, wired, bursting with energy and ...something else.

Something she'd been trying to put out of her mind all day: the image of Chris' strong, agile body stalking and whirling in lightning mock combat this morning, half man, half tiger. It was indelibly burned into her brain. She couldn't dislodge it, no matter how hard she tried.

Come on, she chided herself, let's admit it—I know why I'm so hyper tonight. I'm horny as hell and I *want* that guy! I love him and I want him! Now why can't I face that?

153

This had been coming on for a long time. She'd known her feelings for Chris were intense and true ever since that moonlit night at the Sphinx when she'd almost lost him to that Arab thug; and again, after the narrow escapes from the falling radar tower and the pursuing spaceship, she'd shuddered at the thought of losing him as she'd lost Jordy....

But now she felt that her late husband's ghost was exorcised from her heart at last. She was ready to commit herself again...wasn't she? It was time to grow up and stop hiding in the past behind a black curtain of resentment and guilt.

Eris sat up, her eyes searching the darkness and seeing only Chris' face, his laughing smoky eyes, dark hair touseled by dry desert winds .... *Life* was what she wanted now...life and love, without which life was only a kind of death. As quickly as a key turning in a lock, then, Eris made her decision. She couldn't stand the thought of another cold shower, another empty session of stroking herself to release, only to have the burning sweep back over her like a brushfire once again. It wasn't just fucking she wanted, it was a closeness, a sharing; she wanted to be held in strong arms and told she was beautiful and loved.

And she could have it. Now, tonight. Chris' room was only two doors away down the hall. No one else would know.

She was as familiar with her little cubicle in the dark as a person blind from birth. She made her way over to the small closet and wrapped a white terrycloth robe around herself. Then she found her bag, took out a candle and a book of matches and let herself quietly out into the hall.

A dim night light at the end of the corridor provided sufficient illumination for Eris to locate Chris' door. She knocked, softly.

"Come in," was the immediate response.

Eris struck a match and lit the candle, then slipped inside the room and quietly shut the door. The warm glow from the little flame revealed Chris lying on his bunk, naked except for boxer shorts and with a look of surprise on his face.

"Eris!" he exclaimed softly. "What—"

"I couldn't sleep," she said, feeling her pulse hammering.

"Neither could I." Chris patted the bed beside him. "Well, don't just stand there looking like Lady Macbeth—come sit."

She walked slowly over to the bed, placed the candle on the nightstand and sat down next to him. He looked at her steadily, not saying anything. In the golden light he looked to her like an Attic god cast in bronze, and she suddenly felt herself trembling. Shrieking silent control commands to herself, she said to him, very seriously,"Chris, I want to tell you a story. A long story. And when it's over, maybe you'll understand why I—"

Smiling that wonderful smile that made her heart do backflips, he interrupted her, gently laying a finger against her trembling red lips. "No, lovely lady...not now. Talk to me like this now, my love...."

He reached out strong brown arms to her and before she knew what had happened she had thrown herself into them, exulting in the feel of their warmth and strength as they pulled her close to his hard bare chest. This was it!

All recriminations fled away into the darkness and suddenly there was nothing else but the heat of the two of them together, golden in the night, 200 feet below the frigid Washington soil in a tiny room that was suddenly as big as the universe itself.

She had time for only a tiny moan before the bonfire that was his mouth crushed hers. His tongue probed hers like a hot animal with a life of its own, teasing, dancing; his teeth nipped her playfully, gently, maddeningly. She had never dreamed that there could be so many variations, so many nuances to kissing. She squirmed, she smoldered, she flamed in his arms, wanting to pull away and kiss his body yet not able to detach herself from the searing magnet of his mouth on hers.

At last, with a supreme effort of will, she ripped her mouth away, breathless and panting, trembling with want. "My God, Chris...I never dreamed...why did I wait so long...?" she whispered as he gently eased the robe from her shoulders and dropped it soundlessly to the floor. The magnetism between them fairly crackled as he held her at arm's length for a moment and looked at her. In the aureate glory of her nakedness she was the most beautiful thing he had ever seen or imagined. He could hardly believe she was here now in his arms after so long....

She sank into his arms again, pressing her breasts hard against his chest, loving the feel of the curly hairs there teasing her nipples, now rigid as bullets. His hands began to stroke the long smooth curve of her back, cupping her buttocks, as their mouths locked again in a frenzy of wet heat.

She couldn't stop trembling all over, as if a mild epileptic seizure had taken her; she felt the heat in her loins raging like a furnace.

But Chris was in no hurry. He wanted to savor this female feast as long as possible. He's going to drive me right out of my mind! she screamed silently, loving it, as he bent his head to her nipples, licking and sucking the throbbing rosy points, biting gently, flicking his tongue over them, driving her crazy, crazy, *crazy!*

Then the incandescent mouth was gone, leaving her heaving breasts to tingle and cool in the air; then back again, blazing a trail of liquid fire down the lush contours of her body. She squirmed and moaned, almost weeping with passion. His tongue circled around and dipped into the shallow cup of her navel, then began tracing hot circles on the incredibly sensitive surfaces of her inner thighs. She gripped his dark hair with both hands, knowing where he was heading, wanting and not wanting him to—

Then he was at the fiery core of her, probing, flicking, nibbling, licking gently, inhaling her sweet musky perfume, and she exploded in a violent climax that shook her as a lion shakes its prey.

Moaning and crying, she felt sweat begin to dampen her writhing body as she reached down and gently pulled his shining face up to hers. Somehow she found the strength to whisper, "Put it in me, Chris, oh, God, I want you so...."

And then he was pressing the hot length of his body to hers and she reached down to touch him, to feel him enter. He paused at the steaming portal of her center and she opened to him like a wet flower. As he slid into her she had

156

another orgasm, a smaller one. She felt filled and complete at last; he was like a red-hot poker inside her as he began to move, slowly at first, gently, then gradually building, his superbly trained athlete's body pacing the rhythms, his hands busy as butterflies, stroking every part of her he could reach, her long golden legs gripping his hips tightly.

Then his burning mouth found her breasts again, the hollow of her neck, behind and below her ears, her armpit; he seemed to know every secret sensitive place on her body as if it were his own.

Now he was thrusting so deep into her she thought surely she could feel him in her throat. Her legs and arms flung wide now, she felt herself begin to whirlpool toward another climax, saw his face, too, contorted now in sweet wild agony. Then he groaned, and she felt him throb and burst within her, triggering her own release, a shattering, wrenching orgasm that almost swept her consciousness away with it. She screamed, biting into his shoulder to muffle the sound, and he pressed his mouth into the side of her neck, panting like a runner.

As they relaxed in each other's arms, sharing the sweat that drenched them both, she could feel her heart pounding like some insane drum, so hard it almost hurt. She had a sudden wild desire to talk, to babble, to tell Chris how much she loved him, but instead she kept her silence, eyes closed, reveling in the weight of his body pressing on hers, not wanting to move ever, feeling the two of them cooling down like two engines switched off and come to rest....

Later, the candle flame guttered low, sending flickering shadows to play like dark children among the hollows and curves and strong lengths of their cast-bronze bodies as they slept deeply and happily.

But just before dawn, Eris' rosy dreams began to fade and darken and a familiar lion-bodied figure bulked against a lowering Egyptian sky. A huge storm was brewing: clouds like dirty water eddied and roiled overhead; a seething spear of violet lightning smashed into the earth near the Sphinx, fusing the sand into glass. A cold wind began to blow out of the north, whipping up blinding billows of sand. Thunder boomed and muttered in the distance; more lightning crack-

157

led through the rapidly darkening sky like brilliant lances of shattered neon. Eris began to run, the sand scouring her face like tiny razors, great gusts of icy wind battering her. She ran toward the haven of the Sphinx's great stone paws, the only shelter she could see. A large entrance seemed to yawn open in its breast as she ran between the paws; inside she could see only blackness. Then, as she was about to plunge inside, a great ebon figure with blazing eyes reared above her, stepping out of the darkness and raising a lance that pulsed and blazed with white fire. The flaming spear hurtled toward her breast and she awoke with a strangled gasp into the familiar darkness of Chris' room, remembering instantly where she was, feeling his sleeping body strong and secure next to her.

She let out a shuddering breath, careful not to wake him, and lay there, her heart pounding. Was this nightmare another prophetic dream like the one about the Sphinx? And if so, what did it mean?

She lay awake for a long time in the darkness, listening to the steady breathing of her lover and feeling his warmth pressed against her. But she was neither comforted nor warmed now.

Toward morning she slipped at last into a deep and thankfully dreamless sleep.

PART TWO

THE MISSION

A workman walks by carrying a pink torso.
The storerooms are full of hearts.
This is the city of spare parts.
　　　　—Sylvia Plath, "THE STONES"

CHAPTER FOURTEEN

THE CITY OF SPARE PARTS

WOLFE ISLAND: 7 NOVEMBER 2020

Gabrielle slowly fought her way toward a glimmering of light, a swimmer painfully clawing up out of dark depths to the surface of consciousness. For a moment, she didn't know where she was, nothing looked right, then recognition returned and she realized that she was back in her room, lying in her bed. ESQ was gone, with only a few black hairs on the bedspread to mark his presence.

She tried to sit up, groaning at the throbbing pain in her right temple. Gingerly she touched the area, discovered a large painful bump there. The images of last night's events rushed back over her then, pain and triumph intermingling in a jumble of eerie blue-green flames, thick, choking clouds of smoke, the huge menacing man with the green cat's eyes....

He must have hit me when I wasn't looking, she thought, but no matter. I did what I came to do.

Gaby suddenly noticed that she was naked under the bedclothes. She wondered who had undressed her last night, hoping it wasn't that man.

The door opened and Nicasia entered the room, her face stern and cold. Behind her loomed the dark figure of the man who had attacked Gaby last night. What had he said his name was? Reaper? It fits, thought Gaby.

161

"I see you're back among the living again," said Nicasia without humor. "How do you feel, Gabrielle?"

Finding the effort of sitting up too much for her at the moment, Gaby fell back on the pillow, pulling the covers up to her neck. "Like a truck ran over my head."

"Sorry Reaper had to rough you up, but he says you put up quite a fight. That wasn't wise, Gaby. But then neither was what you did out there last night. In fact, it was very, very stupid. What did you think you were accomplishing by burning your father's body? Giving him a Viking funeral?"

Gaby decided to play it straight. "*You* know what I was doing, mother! You're a witch and you were forcing my father's spirit to serve you in some horrible way! I had to free him! And I'm not sorry I did it!"

Nicasia glided forward and sat on the foot of Gaby's bed, her face thoughtful. Reaper remained standing, massive arms crossed, glaring at Gabrielle as though she were a bug he was waiting to step on.

"This is nonsense, Gaby," said Nicasia. "Who filled your head with such crap? Who gave you that mumbo-jumbo spell and all that silly junk in your bag?"

"It's *not* nonsense!" Gaby cried, anger beginning to well up inside her. "My father came to me in a...a séance, and he spoke to me! He told me you had trapped his soul and warned me not to come home. But I *had* to come, don't you see? I couldn't let you keep tormenting him like that!"

"I'm surprised at you, Gaby," Nicasia said cooly, her eyes shards of yellow glass. "I always thought you were a rational, level-headed girl. Now, in just a few short years away from my care, I find you messing around with spiritualism and magic, accusing me of being a witch and desecrating your poor father's body. These are not the acts of a sane person, Gaby."

"Oh, yeah? Then answer me this, Nicasia: Why wasn't my father's body decayed? It was perfectly preserved! And who wound those dried leaves around him—and why? And what about the remains of a magic circle I saw on the floor of the mausoleum? Who drew that? Mice?"

Nicasia's mouth twitched ominously. "I'm sure I don't know what you're talking about. You must have been hallu-

162

cinating. Were you snorting coke at the party last night? I haven't seen your father's body since he was buried.... I don't know anything about any leaves or magic circles...except the one you drew. Your poor father's body is just ashes now, Gaby. What a terrible, sacreligious thing to do!"

Gaby hung her head, trying to look contrite. "Well...maybe...maybe you're right, mother. It does all seem kind of foolish, I guess, now that I see it from your point of view...."

Nicasia smiled, but there was no warmth in it. "That's better. You've had your brains scrambled down there in Washington by all this spiritualism nonsense. I'll admit, some of those people can be very convincing, telling you just what you want to hear. But they're all fakes, Gaby. Stay away from them in the future. Now I think you need some more rest until that bump on your head goes down." She stood up, looking down at Gaby intently, as if trying to tell whether the girl was sincere. "Oh, by the way...one other thing." Nicasia reached into her skirt pocket and took out Gaby's laserpen. "Where did you get this?"

Again, Gaby decided to tough it out. "Oh, that's a gadget they gave me as part of my training in the PIA. Standard issue. I figured it'd come in handy if the cemetery was locked."

"I see," said Nicasia, frowning slightly and fondling the slim silver tube absently. "Well, I'll just keep it for now, until you're better. Now we'll give you something to make you sleep and help heal that bump. Reaper."

Gaby's eyes grew wide with alarm as the big man drew an ominous little compressed-air hypogun from this pocket. From another pocket he took a small vial of a colorless liquid which he inserted into the bottom of the instrument like a clip of bullets.

"Hey!" she cried, attempting to scramble out from under the bedclothes, heedless of her nakedness. "What's that? I don't need any sedation! I'm okay! I'm not crazy!"

Disregarding her cries, Reaper stepped forward, grabbed her bare arm roughly and quickly pressed the barrel of the gun to it. There was a sharp hiss and Gaby felt a stinging pain in her arm. Almost immediately she felt the strength begin to ebb out of her. Her vision began to blur and the room began a slow whirling motion.

Nicasia leaned down, bringing her face close to Gaby's, tiger eyes coldly aflame. "Did President Warren send you here to spy on me, Gaby? Is that why you suddenly decided to come home?"

Gaby shook her head feebly. "No...I quit...PIA...because they wanted me to...didn't believe what they said about you...."

"What did they say about me, Gaby?"

"Said you were...from 'nother world...crazy stuff...didn't believe...."

Feeling a swirling vortex of darkness rising about her, Gaby tried valiantly to maintain her cover story even as she slipped into unconsciousness. If only she could convince them that she was just a silly, superstitious girl, she might still have a chance....

The last thing Gaby saw before night swept over her was those two tawny flames probing deep into her soul....

Nicasia stood up, regarding the sprawled nakedness of her stepdaughter thoughtfully. She pulled the covers up to Gaby's chin, then turned to Reaper, who had obviously enjoyed what he had seen. "Don't get any bright ideas, Reaper. She's not for you. I have a far better use for her."

Reaper shrugged, removing the empty vial and replacing the hypogun in his pocket. "You think she's on the level?"

"You mean do I think the only reason she came home was to free Harcourt's spirit? Frankly, no. I think Warren put her up to this. She'd be the perfect spy, wouldn't she? Well, no matter. We'll see that she doesn't communicate with him or anyone. That drug will keep her on ice until I'm ready for her. When she wakes up, we'll all be in Egypt."

Reaper's thick eyebrow lifted. "Oh? We pullin' outa here?"

"Immediately. I'm moving our base of operations to Zeinhom. I want us there when Warren's agents arrive, so we can...welcome them properly."

Reaper barked a short, ugly laugh, then he and Nicasia left Gaby's room, locking the door behind them.

CAIRO: 25 NOVEMBER 2020

Eighteen days later, Eris and her four companions found themselves in the midst of the incredible assault on the senses that is the heart and soul of downtown Cairo. An overall aroma of lamb, mixed with the odor of coconut oil, seemed to predominate, permeating the city like an invisible fog. As the driver of the government Mercedes sent by Colonel Zaid inched his way cautiously through the chaotic swarm of traffic, the five agents also experienced a dizzying jumble of secondary odors, wafting in and out of the open car windows. The rich, heady aroma of fresh-brewed Arabic coffee mixed with the delicious pungency of exotic herbs and spices would make them gasp in delight, only to be replaced by the sickly smell of overripe mangoes in a passing fruit stall or the odor of fresh donkey dung in the street. Ears were bombarded by the constant hoot and clamor of traffic. The discordant wail of Arab music from numberless portable radios formed a plaintive background for the rumble of ancient wooden cart wheels on granite cobblestones and the hiss and roar of the ever-present red-and-white buses, battered and overflowing with sweltering passengers.

Eyes were overwhelmed by the eddying riot of shape and color that was the people of Cairo. They were everywhere: thronging the pavements, pouring out of offices and shops, milling unconcernedly in the paths of careening, blaring automobiles and trucks, herding slow-moving flocks of sheep and camels down the center of the streets. Dark-eyed peasant girls in print dresses and colorful scarves; ebony Nubians with powerful torsos naked to the waist or wearing turbans and snow-white *galabias*; women in black shawls, like shadows; fierce bedouins, burnt almost black by the sun in their voluminous striped robes; gaunt-faced civil servants in Western dress; groups of laughing schoolchildren; all merged into a fascinating kaleidoscope of humanity through which the snailing government car cautiously inched its way.

And over all, eternally, the dust: thick, acrid, mixed with sand blown in from the desert, forming a constant pall over the city, together with the raw stench of petrol fumes and the

165

greasy smoke of mutton kebabs being cooked at curbside stalls.

All this was old and familiar to Eris and Chris, who loved the city as one loves a disfigured and cranky old friend, overlooking obvious faults and turning irritating idiosyncrasies into charming eccentricities. But to Avram, André, and Raymond, their first taste of Cairo was bewildering and almost overpowering.

As they drove, Eris spotted some evidence of earthquake damage which had not been repaired, a few cracks here and there in buildings, occasional piles of rubble extending into the streets, but overall, the damage to the center of Cairo had been slight.

She spotted a white van spraying the air with a disinfectant that billowed out behind it like a grayish fog, reminding her of a still further horror hovering over the stricken city like a curse from some vengeful pharaoh's desecrated tomb. Cholera—always a menace in Cairo—was once again on the march, sweeping through the city from the shattered western districts in a ghastly tide.

Eris felt anger begin to burn inside her as she thought of all the terrible, needless suffering, destruction and death deliberately and cruelly wrought by that demonic alien woman, merely as a demonstration of her power. But as quickly as she felt it, Eris dismissed the anger as negative and nonproductive. Instead she closed her eyes and visualized a huge shield of white light covering the entire city, healing its populace and protecting it from further devastation.

A great sad sigh that penetrated even the constant cacophony of the Cairo streets brought Eris suddenly out of her reverie. She recognized it instantly; she had heard it often during the past two weeks. She turned to André, who was sitting next to her, staring out the window but seeing nothing of the passing spectacle. He was terribly worried at having heard nothing from Gaby since she left for Wolfe Island. She had promised to call him on her Mentacom Medallion in a few days, but no call had come. President Warren had received nothing either and he too was worried. When they had attempted to reach Gaby mentally, there was no response. It was as though she had ceased to exist. The President had

166

then ordered one of the orbiting U.S. surveillance satellites to home in on Wolfe Island, but the resulting tapes had revealed no trace of Gabrielle on the grounds.

Then, about a week ago, the spysat had revealed that the entire contingent of the island seemed to be making preparations to leave. During this operation, clear images had been obtained of servants loading Nicasia's private jets with cartons and luggage. She herself could be glimpsed frequently, directing the activity, but there was never a trace of Gaby. Finally the party had vacated the island, their destination a place called Zeinhom Gardens in Cairo, which Nicasia had bought from the Egyptian government several years ago and converted into another walled citadel.

Eris squeezed André's hand, causing him to turn and give her a bitter smile. "I know, I know, goddammit! But Eris, I can't help worrying about her. I mean, I can understand her not being able to communicate by phone—Bane probably has them all bugged—but not to hear from her on the MM...*that* I can't understand. What could have happened to her? Surely Nicasia wouldn't murder her own stepdaughter...?"

"I don't think so, André. If for no other reason, Gaby's dowsing ability is too important to waste, even if Nicasia found out she's really a spy. Maybe Gaby discovered that they have some kind of psychic bug as well and is afraid they could monitor even her mental communications if she tried to contact you." Eris' aqua eyes were deep and warm with concern as she tried to lift André's spirits. "Although she may be a prisoner, there's every reason to believe she's still all right, André. Don't automatically assume the worst."

André tried to smile again and made a mess of it. "It's my gloomy French nature. And on top of that, I have this...feeling that she's in real trouble, and I feel so damned helpless!"

"We know how you feel, pal," said Chris from the other side of Eris. "It's awful not knowing what's going on. We never figured on Gaby's MM being cut off. But I think she's okay, too. She's too valuable to Nicasia for her to kill the golden goose. As a matter of fact, Gaby's probably here in Cairo right now."

167

André brightened for the first time. "Christ—do you really think so? Then let's get Colonel Zaid to order a raid on that place!"

Avram leaned back over the front seat, his dark face grim. "On what grounds? We'd have to get a court order first, and that would take weeks over here. And then even if we got in and searched the place, I'm sure they'd hide her where we'd never find her. No, André, I'm afraid you're just going to have to bite the bullet with the rest of us and wait it out. Don't forget, we've got a mission to perform, all five of us, and we can't let anything delay us."

André nodded gloomily. "I hear what you're saying, Avram, and I know you're right. But it's so damned hard...."

André's dark mood was contagious, spreading throughout the car like a cold mist, and there was no more conversation until the driver finally pulled up in front of the venerable old Continental Savoy Hotel at 10 Opera Square, in the heart of Cairo.

Eris had decided to book them at the hotel where she and Chris had stayed before for several reasons: she was familiar with it and liked the old-fashioned, spacious rooms with their high ceilings, even if they were often a little shabby. The general consensus was that Nicasia probably knew who they were and why they were here, so an elaborate cover was unnecessary; still, officially they were merely a party of scientists and Egyptologists in Cairo to do some research inside the Great Pyramid. Chris' professional reputation was well known in Egypt, and Sumi's bearded face was familiar to many since his Nobel Prize award and subsequent appearances on talk shows and the cover of *Time*. Raymond was another scientist, working with Sumi; André was there to photo-document the proceedings, and Eris was their pilot. Together, they made a believable team for the Egyptian officials and news media.

As the five agents entered the lobby, cluttered with colorful guests and ornate furniture, none of them noticed the tall, gaunt, fair-haired man sitting in a chair not far from the registration desk. But he noticed them. He began to stare at them intently, peering over the top of the magazine he had been pretending to read. His pale, almost colorless eyes

168

seemed to glow like clear sapphires as he gazed at the little group, now at the main desk awaiting their turn to register. The man seemed utterly absorbed in them. His face grew even paler than it was normally, he began to tremble slightly. Small beads of perspiration, almost invisible against his high forehead, appeared. His heartbeat increased until it seemed like a drum pounding in his ears.

The man kept his eyes locked on the agents with this same eerie intensity until they had completed registration and had entered the elevator for their rooms. Only when the elevator doors closed behind them did he relax. He sat, pale eyes closed, trembling like a man with fever. He breathed deeply, feeling his heartbeat slowing. A brief smile flicked across his lips and was gone. Then he got up and headed for the bar and a well-deserved drink.

Washington, D.C.: 25 November 2020

Almost six thousand miles away, another man sat in a room to which only he had access and stared intently at the glowing blank screen of a video monitor. His gaze was almost as intent as that of the man in the hotel as he waited impatiently, occasionally glancing at his ringwatch.

Suddenly a ripple of movement appeared within the dancing electronic static on the monitor. An image began to form, spread out, take on color and dimension. The man watching moved closer to the screen, eager to catch every detail of the scene unfolding there.

What he saw was a perfect three-dimensional image of Eris, Chris, Avram, Raymond and André in the lobby of the Continental Savoy in Cairo as they walked up to the registration desk. The scene continued until the doors of the elevator in the lobby hid them from sight. Then, it faded away like a mist and the screen was blank and glowing blue once again.

The man watching nodded and smiled to himself. As he reached out and switched off the monitor, he began to hum softly, off key. He looked again at his ringwatch. In exactly thirty minutes he would place a scrambled call to a certain hotel room in Cairo. He smiled again.

Dr. Gideon Stack was well pleased.

CAIRO: 25 NOVEMBER 2020

After unpacking, the five agents rendezvoused at the hotel's charming outdoor cafeteria for lunch, enjoying the sight of Cairo's gray-and-white vastness spread out before them, modern steel and glass office buildings and high-rise apartments mingling with ancient mosques and minarets and shabby tenement areas.

As they relaxed from the ordeal of the noisy and interminable ride from the airport over cups of hot, thick *ahwa turki mazboota* (Turkish coffee, moderately sweet, but still enough to make your head ring), they planned the rest of their day. After lunch they would meet with Colonel Zaid and brief him on their plans. He would greet them officially, give them President Fahey's blessing, and promise them any assistance they might need. It would be arranged that all tourist traffic (what there was left of it) would be forbidden entrance to the Pyramid until they re-emerged and twenty-four-hour guards would be placed in front of the entrance to assure their privacy. To the outside world, they would be camping in the King's Chamber, conducting important experiments for an unspecified length of time.

After meeting with Zaid, providing they could dodge the press, the rest of the afternoon and evening and the following day would be theirs to sightsee or do whatever they wished. Then, tomorrow evening at sunset, they would go out to the Pyramid, enter it and prepare to spend the night in the King's Chamber before entering the secret tunnel at dawn of the following morning.

A few hours later, Eris was heading down the Sharia Talaat Harb toward the deluxe Nile Hilton on the Corniche el Nil, overlooking the gray-green expanse of the great river. Colonel Zaid had told her that the Hilton management had volunteered the only slightly damaged hotel as an emergency hospital, since most of the other hospitals and hotels in the area had been completely devastated. Eris had wanted to spend a few hours there with the injured, using her psychic healing powers to help however she could. She felt a tre-

170

mendous bond of empathy with these ravaged people; after all, she too had been Egyptian in countless lives....

Chris had offered to go with her, but she had graciously declined; he would be too much of a distraction for her. Instead, she suggested that he show André, Ray and Avram the sights of Cairo; she would meet them back at the hotel for dinner.

Eris closed her eyes and settled back in the worn upholstery of the old Mercedes limousine she had rented from Limousine Misr. It was a little more expensive than a regular car rental agency such as BITA or Avis, but the drivers were more experienced and the cars more comfortable. As experienced as she was in the ways of the city, she didn't feel up to driving herself through the insanity of afternoon traffic.

She smiled as she pictured again in her mind the wild sweet passion of her night with Chris. From there, her thoughts flew backwards like bright birds to the day they had first met. It was in a crowded bazaar near the Mouski in Cairo. He had saved her from making an expensive purchase of an extremely clever copy of a scarab fraudulently extolled by the merchant as being over six thousand years old. Impressed and grateful, Eris accepted his offer of dinner that evening, and as they sat in an open-air restaurant on the east bank of the Nile, relaxing over cinnamon tea and watching the sun fall slowly down the western sky in a welter of rose and crimson and gentle lavender, Eris gazed at the ageless, grainy hulks of the Pyramids, awe-inspiring in their dark geometries even from this distance, and thought that perhaps she had found the real reason for her journey to this land.

Ostensibly she had come to Egypt as a means of putting her tragic past behind her; after Jordy's estate was settled, she found herself a wealthy woman, but this meant little to her. She used the money as a way to throw herself into forgetting, first as a flying instructor, then, when that palled, she applied and qualified for a job as a test pilot, soon earning a reputation as one of the most daring and skilled in the business.

But even this was not enough to purge the bitter memories from her heart; the thrills and danger of her job only served to intensify the dark feelings. So she decided to leave the country and travel, see other lands, hoping that an infusion of new and different scenes and people might bring her some measure of peace. She had always been fascinated with Egypt; many of the retrocognitive experiences she had had, ever since her teenage years, had concerned former lives in this ancient land.

So she left the sky and came to Cairo, where apparently destiny had arranged a meeting with a man who might—eventually—help her out of her abyss of sorrow and self-recrimination. She had liked this Dr. Troy immediately; something about his open, smiling face and strong athletic body sparked the same kind of electricities that her husband had, it seemed so long ago. And she could see his admiration for her glowing in his warm gray eyes like embers in ash. She felt relaxed, content in his presence; with a shock she realized that she had not felt this way since long before Jordy died. And as she turned to watch the last sullen gleamings of sunset, she realized also that for the first time she was not seeing the colors of blood and fire and death.

So she encouraged his friendship but kept him at a distance, not wanting to reveal the torment of her past, hoping that their closeness could somehow grow without sex, hoping that he would be man enough, human enough, to understand. And because he knew almost instantly that he loved her, that she was precisely what he had been searching for in ancient, dusty tombs and temples all his life without knowing it, Christopher Troy did understand and decided that he was willing to wait until she could come to him freely.

When she told him of her retrocognitive experiences, Chris was amazed. He too began to see more than coincidence in their meeting. He told her that he also had a psychic gift—clairaudience—and suggested that she return with him to Washington, where he wanted her to meet some very important and very special people.

Those people were, of course, Dr. Gideon Stack and the President himself. After an intensive course of testing and training, Eris Campbell became Psi-Spy #12. She realized then that this was what she was supposed to do with her life. And she loved it.

Eris suddenly realized that her car had stopped and the driver was speaking to her, a worried and apologetic look on his face.

"It is not the petrol, Miss Campbell, I personally checked the tank before we left."

Eris leaned forward, scanned the dashboard. She could see nothing wrong, the car was not overheated. "Then what is it, do you know?"

The driver shook his head forlornly, turned back and tried the ignition. Nothing, not even the grinding of a weak battery. "A moment ago it was running smoothly, then suddenly it sputtered and stopped. And now it won't start again."

Eris shrugged, "*Maareish*," she said with a grin. Not to worry. These things happened all the time in Cairo, where automobiles were patched together and run long past their prime. She could always walk the rest of the way to the Nile Hilton; they weren't far away now. It was a pleasantly mild day and she could (God help her!) take a taxi back to the Continental Savoy later.

The driver was all smiles now and continued to apologize profusely, charmed by Eris' use of the Arabic word and her reasonable attitude, not often encountered in visiting Americans. He hopped out of the stalled car, heedless of the screaming horns and Arabic curses which lacerated the air. He opened the door for Eris, and as she stepped out and pressed a generous tip into his hand, she noticed that theirs was not the only vehicle stopped in traffic. Dozens of cars, trucks, buses, and even a motorcycle, within a radius of about sixty feet were stalled dead in the street. Just ahead of them, the driver of a battered Toyota pickup full of spare automobile parts had raised his hood and was gazing perplexedly at a motor that had simply stopped functioning.

Eris looked around, a tingling sensation beginning to make the back of her neck crawl as though ants had invaded it. She felt uneasy as she watched the angry and bewildered drivers cursing and shouting at one another and their recalcitrant vehicles.

Then she heard the shouting turn to screams of alarm and astonishment; people began to look up and point into the sky.

What in God's name is going on? wondered Eris as she glanced skyward, following the pointing fingers. Directly over her stalled limousine, about thirty feet in the air, hovered a bright green circle of light! It seemed to be about six to eight feet in diameter and Eris could see a kind of hazy shimmer surrounding it, like heat waves in summer, making the tall buildings in the distance dance and waver slightly.

For a moment she thought she was hallucinating. But she could hear cries of "*jinn!*" and "UFO!" around her in Arabic and English, so she knew others were seeing it also. The driver was standing next to her, his eyes bugging out like ping-pong balls as he watched the incredible phenomenon in the sky.

Suddenly the green circle was flushed with yellow and a chartreuse beam hurtled down out of it, encircling Eris and the driver in a tight cone of light. Eris felt every muscle in her body grow instantly rigid; she felt as if she were being submerged in champagne—an effervescent tingling sensation swept through her. She tried to speak but could not, nor could she move a muscle. Next to her, she could see out of the corner of her eye that the driver was experiencing the same thing.

She felt giddy and weightless as the beam began to draw them slowly up toward the pulsing circle of light. She could dimly hear people screaming in the street.

Within seconds, Eris and the driver were levitated up to the circle and swallowed by it as though they had never been. Then the green light winked out of existence and the sky over Cairo was clear once more.

Seconds later, dazed and frightened drivers were discovering that their vehicles would now start, and soon traffic on the Sharia Talaat Harb was back to its normal chaotic condition.

174

On evil days though fall'n, and evil tongues.
In darkness, and with dangers compass'd round,
And solitude; yet not alone...
　　　　—John Milton, PARADISE LOST

CHAPTER FIFTEEN

WHERE EVIL DWELLS

CAIRO: 25-26 NOVEMBER 2020

Nicasia Bane surveyed herself in the mirrored wall of her master bedroom. The long black hooded silk robe she wore was embroidered with strange characters and sigils in gold and silver, some totally unrecognizable, even to magical adepts on earth; some were so alien as to almost hurt the eye that looked directly at them. She was barefoot, toenails and fingernails painted a glossy black, and she was naked beneath the robe. The caress of the silk on her body as she moved stimulated her; tonight would be an important and fulfilling night. The thought of the forthcoming conjuration filled her with excitement and even an icy ripple of fear, for she and Furca would be dealing with powers so great as to defy comprehension by those unversed in the black arts. The slightest slip could mean disaster and consequences so unthinkable that death would be infinitely preferable.

Nicasia twirled before the mirror, the two sides of her unfastened robe billowing out to provide a brief glimpse of the white flame of her body before settling back into place like clouds covering the moon. She smiled without humor, then glanced at her bedside clock. 11:30. Almost time. The conjuration had to be performed precisely at the stroke of midnight or they would have to wait another thirty days. She was impatient to proceed: tonight that treacherous little bitch of a stepdaughter would be initiated into the service of the Dark Father, and from then on, she would be under Nicasia's complete and total control.

As she applied a coat of dead-black lipstick to her lips and then to each of her nipples, she became a bizarre monochromatic vision, beautiful and terrible as Death, stark as a woodcut, her only color the burning amber of her eyes. At last she was ready.

"Tina," she called softly, and an instant later the dark girl appeared, garbed in a robe identical in design to Nicasia's, except that it was a flaming scarlet and lacked the embroidered characters.

"Is it time?" Tina asked eagerly.

"Yes. Go and wake Gabrielle and prepare her for the ceremony. Make sure she's completely under control, understand? We don't want any slip-ups tonight."

The girl nodded and was gone.

Once again the black mists of drugged sleep parted and Gaby awoke to find Tina's midnight eyes boring into her own, only inches away.

"Tina...? Whuzzit? Where...?" She felt groggy and weak, sunk deep in a lethargic twilight in which every movement was a supreme effort of will. There was a metallic taste in her mouth and her lips were dry and cracked.

Tina thrust a bowl of hot soup into her hands as she struggled to sit up. "Here, Gaby, eat this. It's good for you."

Gaby accepted the soup gratefully. It tasted kind of funny—bitter—but it was warm and satisfying. As she ate, she looked around the room, found it unfamiliar. She could dimly recall waking several times before, being fed and led to the bathroom, but it all seemed like a hazy, amorphous dream. What had become of her own room in the house on Wolfe Island, her own bed? Where was she?

"Tina...what is this place? Why do I feel so weak? What's wrong with me?"

"We're at Zeinhom—mother's house in Cairo. You've been in and out of a coma for two weeks now, ever since that blow on the head. We've all been so worried about you. Lola and Kathy and Bianca and I've been...taking care of you."

176

Gaby vaguely remembered the party, the mausoleum where she had burned her father's body, Reaper hitting her.... Then something Tina had just said struck a sudden chord of hope in her heart: Cairo? They were in Cairo? Wasn't that where André and Eris and the others were going? Was she in the same city as André? She tried to push these joyful feelings into the back of her mind as she ate the soup. Tina was watching her like a hawk. And what was that silly-looking robe she was wearing?

Tina appeared nervous now. "Hurry and finish that, Gaby. We mustn't be late."

"Late for what? We having a costume party or something? I don't feel like going to any—"

"It's a special ceremony—in your honor. Don't worry, you'll be fine. That soup will fix you up. Here's a robe for you." Tina held up a robe similar to her own, except that it had no hood and was pure white.

Gaby looked at Tina in surprise. She realized that she was still naked beneath the bedclothes. "You're kidding! You expect me to wear *that?* With nothing on under it? What is this—one of Nicasia's orgies?"

Tina's dark face turned mean, her sable eyes narrowing slightly. "You're asking too many questions, Gaby. Get up and put on this robe."

To Gaby's horror, she found her body obeying Tina's command like an automaton, while some distant lost portion of her mind screamed contradictory orders to it silently and uselessly. She struggled groggily out of bed and put on the white robe, wrapping it around herself as closely as possible. As she did so, she caught a glimpse of herself in a full-length mirror and was startled to see how thin she looked. She could see her ribs standing out in gaunt relief beneath her breasts. She shivered as Tina grabbed her arm and shoved her out of the room.

They padded down a dark corridor and down a long flight of stairs, then through several large rooms, through a heavy wooden door and down another flight of stairs. It seemed to Gaby as if they were descending into the very bowels of the earth.

Finally they arrived at a heavy iron door in the shape of a Gothic arch, with bizarre and obscene figures in bas-relief covering its surface. Tina knocked three times using a heavy brass knocker in the shape of a phallus; it sounded like someone pounding on a metal coffin....

The door was opened by a girl in a red robe identical to Tina's. As they entered, Gaby saw it was Lola, another of her "stepsisters."

Gaby's eyes grew wide in horror and disbelief as she gazed around her. She was in an immense subterranean chamber carved out of solid rock, the high arched roof lost in darkness and supported by huge black stone columns upon which grotesque and monstrous bas-reliefs seemed to writhe and twist as if alive in the dancing scarlet light from two large flaming braziers. At one end of the room sable draperies fell from the ceiling like theater curtains, framing a large flat altar of dead-black volcanic stone. An inverted pentagram in vivid crimson was painted on the front of the altar, and on either side of it a striking and bestial figure was embroidered on the draperies in stunning detail. To the left was Baphomet, the infamous Goat of Mendes, God of the Witches, with a woman's nude torso, head and horns of a goat and great feathered wings. On the right was the Scarlet Woman of Revelation, clothed in a robe of purple and red which left most of her body naked and lasciviously posed, draped with precious stones, pearls and golden ornaments, and holding high a golden chalice over whose rim a filthy black ichor dripped. She was seated on the back of a hideous scarlet monster with seven heads and ten black horns. Gaby gasped in revulsion: the face of the woman was that of Nicasia Bane!

Directly above the altar was the blasphemous centerpiece: an enormous brass crucifix suspended upside down by a long black chain. Where the traditional figure of Christ should have been, the withered, mummified carcass of a huge vampire bat was fastened to the cross with scarlet nails.

Slightly in front and to either side of the altar was a large iron candelabra, each holding seven black candles that burned with a horrid green flame.

178

A heavy, musky incense that smelled like semen and seaweed burned Gaby's nostrils, and a thin, monotonous wailing from some unseen flute-like instrument filled the cavernous air. She wanted to throw up, but nothing would come.

"Welcome, Gabrielle Bane, to the Cathedral of Darkness," intoned the chillingly familiar voice of Nicasia Bane from across the vast chamber. Gaby seemed to notice for the first time that others were here also, dressed in robes which hid their faces from a distance. She sensed that they had been waiting for her entrance with intense expectation, a fact which did nothing to ease her steadily mounting anxiety. Nicasia, in a black robe, was standing next to a squat, grotesque little man who could only be Furca, also robed in black. Before him was a small lectern, on which an ancient leather-bound book lay open. They were standing in the center of a large magic circle drawn with colored chalks, the outer edge of which was composed of a mixture of salt and crushed garlic, adding its heady reek to the already noxious air.

Next to this circle was a larger one, identical in design, within which stood a group of about a dozen people, all garbed in red like Tina, who was still standing next to Gaby, holding her arm. She thought she recognized three of the figures in front as Kathy, Bianca, and Lola.

"Tonight you are to be consecrated to the service of Our Father of Darkness, Lord of the Lower Depths, Master of Shadows, Emperor of the Eclipse and Glorious Exalter of the Ego," continued Nicasia's stentorian litany, rolling away into the gloom like muted thunder. "You are to be honored as few are honored by the Dark Powers: tonight you shall receive the favors of none other than Lord Ashmedai of the First Hierarchy, King of Seventy-Two Legions, Prince of Wantons, Conqueror of Solomon, Serpent of Ryanneh, Chief of the Power of Amaymon, Dark Angel of Chance, Despoiler of Virgins. He shall ascend at our invitation from the black flames of despair to initiate you with the cold seed of damnation.

"Sister Hel and Sister Lamia, escort the neophyte to her bridal couch." The unthinkable horror of what her stepmother intended broke through the drug-clouded murk of

Gaby's mind then. They were going to summon a demon up from Hell itself and watch while it...it.... She couldn't make herself accept the hideous reality of it. She tried to scream "No! No!" but nothing escaped her parched lips except a strangled squeak. She tried to wrench her arm from Tina's grasp and run, but her feet seemed nailed to the floor.

Then Tina and another red-robed woman—Bianca—were leading her across the cold black stone floor toward the altar. There, they quickly threw her down supine on the grainy surface and shackled her arms and legs in a spread-eagled position with iron manacles she hadn't noticed before. Bianca flipped open Gaby's white robe, so that she lay naked and obscenely spread before the robed congregation, ready for...what?

The girls left her and went back to their circle, carefully stepping over its salted outer rim. Spreading her arms, Nicasia cried out, "The Bride of Darkness awaits her lover! Let the conjuration begin!"

Gaby couldn't believe this was happening to her. It all seemed like some horrid fever dream. But no—despite her lethargy and inability to focus her mind, she knew it was real: the horrible smells, the wailing of that damnable music, the monstrous flickering shadows and the ruddy glow of the braziers on her exposed white body, the feel of the cold gritty sone against her arms and legs. All too terribly real.

She watched Furca waddle up to the lectern and raise a slim hazel wand engraved with arcane signs and names. In a loud voice and as low a tone as he could manage he warned the congregation: "From this moment on, no matter what any of you may see or hear, do not, under any circumstances, leave the circle, or you will die!"

Reaching into a small storage space at the base of the lectern, Furca brought forth a cloth garment that resembled a priest's alb and held it above his head as he recited the opening invocation:

> "ANTON, AMATOR, EMITES, THEO-
> DONIEL, PONCOR, PAGOR, ANITOR, by
> the virtue of these most holy angelic names
> do I clothe myself, O Lord of Lords, in my

vestments of power, that so I may fulfill, even
unto their term, all things whatsoever I desire
to effect through Thee, IDEODANIACH,
PAMOR, PLAIOR, Lord of Lords, Whose
kingdom and rule endureth forever and ever.
Amen."

At the amen, Furca let the garment fall about him. Then
he brought out a small iron crucible, which he set in front of
the lectern, facing the altar. Small blue flames began to
flicker in the bowl, and the little magician cast a handful of
incense into it, saying as he did, "Holocaust. Holocaust.
Holocaust."

The flames in the crucible rose higher and a new smell,
sickly sweet yet harsh, rose into the already malodorous air.
Furca pointed his wand at the altar, which was surrounded
by a large green triangle painted on the stone floor. The apex
of this triangle extended several yards to the right (north) of
the altar; within its boundaries were drawn a series of strange
characters, also in green, the demonic symbols of Ashmedai,
or Asmodeus, as he is better known.

The dwarf continued his bizarre invocation, speaking in
loud, firm tones:

"BERALANENSIS, BALDACHIENSIS,
PAUMACHIA, by the most mighty kings and
powers, and the most powerful princes, genii,
Liachidae, ministers of the Tartarean seat, I
adjure thee, I invoke thee, I conjure thee, I
strongly command thee by the power of the
ineffable Names ADONAI, ELOHIM, JEHO-
VAH, TETRAGRAMMATON, AMIORAM,
ZEBAOTH, AGLA, SADAI to appear before
me at this hour, O great ASHMEDAI, agent
of our Father of Darkness and of his beloved
son, LUCIFUGE ROFOCALE, Inciter of
Lust, Prince of Flesh, Destroyer of Innocence!
Come and appear before me, I command,
mighty ASHMEDAI, by the power of the pact
I have with thee, and by the power of the

hierarchy of superior intelligences and spirits who shall constrain thee against thy will to do no harm, *venite, venite, venite, submiritillor,* ASHMEDAI!"

For a moment there was silence in the great chamber as the last of Furca's invocation rumbled away into the gloom. On the altar, Gaby forgot to breathe. Her exposed body shone with sweat in the flickering light.

Then, green smoke began to issue from Furca's crucible, smelling like burning hair and fish entrails. A hot wind began to blow in the sealed hall, making the candle flames and flaming braziers dance madly. At the apex of the green triangle appeared a whirling cloud of yellow fumes, gradually enlarging into a sulfurous funnel about the height of a man. A new stench, of burning metal and brimstone, made Gaby choke and gag. She noticed that several of the spectators were coughing as well.

The yellow fumes ceased their spiraling and began to dissipate toward the ceiling, revealing the totally naked figure of a large man with bright red skin standing in the apex of the triangle. His head and body were completely devoid of hair, and as he stood there, hands on hips, looking out at the hushed assembly in the shadowy hall, Gaby's mind leaped with a sudden wild hope. Whatever she had thought might appear, it was not this! Perhaps the whole thing was just an elaborate charade for her benefit! Just stage effects. Just a naked man with red body paint playing the part of a demon. She felt her cheeks blaze as her eyes were drawn to the huge scarlet phallus, already half erect, that jutted out before him. Well, if she had to be raped, at least a man was better than a—

But then all hope fled screaming as she heard the scarlet man speak:

"I AM HERE. WHAT WOULDST THOU HAVE OF ME? WHY DISTURBEST THOU MY DUTIES IN MY FATHER'S NAME?"

This was no human voice. It roared out into the dark chamber like molten rocks tumbling down a volcano's side, burning with hatred and evil. Gaby could also see with horror that the creature's mouth was filled with yellow flames which flickered and danced like sulfuric tongues as he spoke.

"Welcome, O most noble prince," cried Furca, bowing grotesquely. "We have summoned thy presence among us, thy worshipers, for a duty that thou wilt surely find pleasing. We call thee not to constrain thee or demand favors of thee, but to offer unto thee the fair one thou seest on the altar, that thou mayest make of her in thy father's name a Bride of Darkness."

The demon turned and surveyed the terror-stricken girl.

"I AM PLEASED THAT THOU WASTEST NOT MY TIME WITH FRIVOLITY. I SHALL DO AS THOU WISHEST. I FIND THE MAIDEN PLEASING."

He began to stroke his organ obscenely, making it swell to an impossible size. The demon's skin seemed to shimmer with heat, as though he were made of metal and heated from within by a roaring furnace. Even his eyes now seemed blank bright pools of yellow fire; sparks sizzled out of his mouth. Then, chuckling lewdly, he began to walk slowly toward the altar.

Gaby's horror increased as she felt a wave of heat and lust pulsing out from the demon as he approached her. She saw that his naked feet left smoking molten footprints on the black stone floor.

Sweat was pouring off her in streams now. She closed her eyes and tried to pray, but somehow she couldn't seem to remember the words coherently. Her mind was too fuzzy, too disjointed. *Our Father Who art in...hollow be Thy Kingdom...our daily bread...*It was no use...the words wouldn't come.... Frantically then, she hurled a wordless prayer out into the universe, forgetting the structured rituals and litanies of her Catholic childhood, a silent plea from her heart. *Dear God, save me please save me....*

Her mind seemed to clear a little and she could remember the words Klorian had spoken to her at Jaca's that terrible afternoon:

> *Remember that the Light is always with you, my child, no matter what bitter valleys you must walk through in the days to come. Call upon the Light when you are in need and you will be answered. Never despair....*

The Light! The Light! She visualized strong, pulsing waves of pure white light surrounding her, as Jaca had taught her. She imaged André's handsome face, aglow with love for her; she called up the faces of her closest friends: President Warren, Jaca, Eris, and her beloved father, who seemed to whisper to her, "Don't be afraid, little princess, you cannot lose your soul to Evil unless you choose it...."

Then her concentration was shattered by a terrible grinding laugh and a wash of blistering heat over her naked body. She opened her eyes to see the scarlet figure of the demon looming over her, smoking with lust, yellow fires blooming in his mouth and eyes, black-clawed hands poised to rake her helpless form in a hideous parody of a caress. Steam seemed to curl up from the gigantic crimson organ which the demon was preparing to ram between her open thighs.

She closed her eyes again, unable to look, feeling as if she were being fed into a fiery furnace. *The Light! Don't despair! Believe in the Light! Save me please please don't let this happenGodJesusMaryOurFatherWhoartinHeaven—*

There was a blinding flash then, light so bright that it burned through her eyelids like an arc, a crackling sizzle like a high-voltage wire, and a horrendous scream of hate and fury that sounded like all the wails of the damned belching forth at once out of the deepest pit of Hell.

Gaby opened her eyes to see an amazing sight: the demon had grown to enormous height, at least fifteen feet tall, and was raging with incoherent fury, clawed hands futilely trying to clutch her trembling body. Each time he reached for her, brilliant white sparks spat into the air, repelling his grasp painfully. It was as if she were enclosed by an invisible electric fence!

The baffled demon continued to roar and scream the foulest curses in an appalling tantrum of fury that seemed to blister the very air. Hot winds swirled shrieking through the hall, and the floor rumbled and shifted, as if the earth beneath it had moved. Then, as the thing screamed and gibbered in insane wrath, it suddenly split the red shell of its body down the center like a butterfly's cocoon; what emerged was so monstrous that even Furca felt his knees quaking. He knew well the incredible power of an enraged demon and could only hope that the triangle would contain it and the circles protect him and the others from its wrath.

Ashmedai now appeared in one of his true forms, a three-headed abomination seated upon a squamous black toad belching fire; one head resembled that of a black bull with blazing red eyes, the second that of a ram, and the third was human, a fat, loathsomely debauched face covered with horrid fleshy growths and suppurating sores and wearing a crown. All three heads also breathed fire. The monster had webbed feet and hands and a serpent's tail that lashed back and forth like a whip.

"SHE IS PROTECTED! HOW DARE THOU OFFEREST ME A PROTECTED ONE! SUCH AN INSULT MAY NOT GO UN- PUNISHED!"

the demon roared through his human head.

Furca tried to apologize. "A thousand pardons, great prince, we did not know. There was no way we could tell—"

The demon wavered, flickered, grew taller and changed his shape once again. Now he towered up into the gloom a full twenty feet high, roughly man-like in shape but covered with iridescent greenish-black scales like a peacock's tail. His hands and feet were clawed and webbed, and his fearsome face had a fish-like appearance, with great glowing saucer eyes and a yawning bellowing mouth full of dagger-like teeth. He resembled a nightmare hybrid of shark and man, and an overpowering effluvium of rotten seaweed and dead fish issued from him.

Gaby once again ached to throw up, but she was still so weak that nothing would come. She kept trying with all her might to maintain the mental white light barrier around herself, but she was terrified of this roaring, raging monster so close to her. How long could she maintain her defense?

This latest transformation was too much for Serabi Khadiz, the Egyptian Finance Minister, who had been one of Nicasia's invited guests at this ceremony. He had insisted on a position near the edge of the magic circle where he could see everything, but now he wished fervently that he had never come. As he jabbered near hysterical prayers to Allah and Mohammed to save him from this abomination, his body betrayed him. He never even felt it when his bladder let go, sending a warm stream of urine down his bare inner thigh and onto the stone floor. As the puddle grew in volume, an unevenness of the floor caused it to flow toward the edge of the magic circle, where it rapidly dissolved a two-inch portion of the salt and garlic mixture which formed the outer perimeter. All eyes were on the roaring creature near the altar, so no one noticed the break in the circle.

But some Thing did.

Quick as a cat pouncing on a mouse, the huge demon whipped an enormous scaly arm across the intervening space and plucked the terrified minister up like a toy figure. The monster held the screaming, squirming man high in the air, then threw back his monstrous head and laughed horribly. It sounded like a volcano belching flame and lava deep beneath the sea.

> "THY FEAR HATH CONDEMNED THEE, THOU PITIFUL SCRAP OF OFFAL! IF I MAY NOT SLAKE MY LUST ON YONDER MAID, I SHALL SLAKE ANOTHER APPETITE ERE I DEPART."

Before anyone could fully comprehend what was happening, the demon brought the struggling Egyptian to his fanged and yawning mouth and quickly bit off his head, like a child biting off the end of a candy bar. Blood fountained out of the ragged neck as if from a fire hose, some of it spattering Gaby's body. It pattered on the black stone floor like red rain. Then the demon turned and spat out the head like a watermelon seed. With unerring aim the head hurtled across the chamber like a cannonball, pinwheeling a red spray through the air, and struck Furca in the chest, bowling him over like a tenpin. The robed spectators screamed and Nicasia nimbly dodged as Furca tumbled toward the edge of the protective circle and the awful head went bouncing away into the darkness. Fortunately for him, the little magus was able to stop himself before reaching the circle's edge, but he saw with dismay that the lectern had been knocked over and the book of incantations and the hazel wand had fallen outside the circle.

Tina had had the presence of mind to quickly stoop and repair the break in the other circle, so they were all safe again—for the present. But without the book and the wand Furca could not banish the demon back to where he came from. They were trapped in a ghastly stalemate: the creature would simply wait them out until some other mistake was made or someone panicked and bolted in fear.

The demon was still laughing thunderously, his scaly jaws and chest streaked with great gouts of the blood that was still spouting from Serabi Khadiz's headless corpse. He calmly proceeded to dismember the body, pulling off legs and arms and popping them into his cavernous maw like a man eating a baked chicken. The sound of crunching bones was like splintering wood.

"STRINGY AND TOUGH. A POOR OFFERING TO COMPENSATE FOR SUCH A DISAPPOINTMENT. WHO SHALL BE NEXT?"

He pointed a great clawed finger at Furca, his black robe sodden with blood, who was just struggling to his feet, trying to recover from the shock of being bowled over by a flying human head.

"AND THOU, O MIGHTY MASTER OF MAGICS," the demon sneered, "THOU TINY DAB OF DONKEY DUNG WHO WOULDST PRESUME TO COMMAND A PRINCE OF THE PIT, WHERE ART THOU NOW WITHOUT THY BOOK AND THY ROD? THOU CANST NOT BID ME DEPART, CANST THOU? I SHALL STAY AND WAIT FOR THEE, FOR TO ME, TIME IS NOT. EVENTUALLY THOU WILT ATTEMPT TO LEAVE THE CIRCLE, AS WILL ALL OF YE HERE ASSEMBLED. THEN SHALL I FEAST!"

"Isn't there anything you can do to control him, you fool?" Nicasia hissed, but Furca merely shook his head in despair. "N-not without my b-book and wand," he stammered, still thoroughly shaken by his near brush with death.

Nicasia dropped to her knees, as near the edge of the circle as she dared, and reached out for the book, which seemed to lie almost within her grasp.

With a reptilian bellow of laughter, the monster bent forward from the waist and a black, slime-coated tongue yards long shot out, adroitly snapping up the book from the floor and reeling it back into his gory mouth. It all happened in the flick of a second, exactly like a frog's tongue shooting out to snare a fly.

Nicasia drew back her arm in alarm and fury. *Damn that girl!* she fumed. The whole thing was Gaby's fault. Nicasia had assumed that she would be too fuddled and weak to protect herself spiritually from the demon's ravages. Someone must have taught her how to guard herself temporarily—

Temporarily. That was the important word. In her weakened state, Gaby couldn't possibly maintain such concentration indefinitely. Soon she would falter, and the demon would be on her like a shot. Hopefully, he wouldn't kill her, but in his present state of murderous fury, he might just decide to pop her down his gullet like a gumdrop....

Similar thoughts were pounding through Gaby's horror-blasted mind at the same time. She felt herself slipping, losing her grip on consciousness; the tiny part of her mind that could still reason had been stressed to its utmost limits; it had to retreat into oblivion now or risk insanity. The fragile psychic barrier that was protecting her from the blasphemous horror towering above her was crumbling. All she could hope for now was that maybe the demon would be furious enough to kill her quickly, as he had Khadiz....

As if reading her thoughts, the creature suddenly turned toward Gaby and bending down, grasped not her, but the altar stone, and with one mighty heave, ripped it up from the floor. Holding it high above his hideous head, the creature thundered,

"HER PROTECTION FALTERS. I MAY YET HAVE THIS TENDER MORSEL THOU HAST PROMISED ME. PRAY TO MY FATHER THAT THIS BE SO, LEST I FEAST ON THY FILTHY MORTAL CARCASSES ERE I DEPART THIS PLANE."

Gaby's eyes were tightly shut now; she dared not look down at the demon's ravening maw and the stone floor twenty-five feet below. She tried valiantly to maintain the white light around herself, but she could feel her powers of concentration leaking away like water down a drain....

And then, born of ultimate desperation, a prayer suddenly blossomed in her mind, whole and complete, like some bright star, the prayer to the great archangel Michael she had loved as a child. A sudden calm descended over her mind like twilight. She began to recite the prayer:

(*St. Michael the Archangel, defend us in battle.*)

as the demon brought the altar slowly down
(*Be our protection against the malice and snares of the Devil.*)

to the level of his gigantic lidless amphibian eyes,
(*We humbly beseech God to command him and do thou,*)

189

cold and merciless as the deeps of Arctic seas.
(*O Prince of the Heavenly Host, by the divine power,*)

Ashmedai looked closely at his young victim
(*thrust into Hell Satan and the other evil spirits*)

and wondered why she was not screaming in terror.
(*who roam through the world*)

In fact, she looked strangely
(*seeking the ruin of souls.*)

at peace.
(*Amen.*)

Was she dead? the demon wondered. He thrust a cautious claw at her, found only weak resistance, and touched her breast. It was warm. Her protection was gone. Ashmedai howled in triumph. He would have his bride at last. He would—

A curious sound reached the monster's ears then; it was like a wind soughing through trees and it came from the mortals assembled out there in the hall.

It took the demon a second to realize what it was: a great gasp of horror and fear, taken in unison. It was rapidly followed by cries and screams of terror. The fools were pointing at something behind him. Ashmedai the Destroyer, Prince of Wantons, King of Seventy-Two Legions, turned ponderously.

And trembled.

For high above, yet rapidly descending toward him, was a brilliant cross of white light, brighter than the sun itself, yet strangely, it did not illuminate the gloom of the chamber. The light seemed somehow selective; it seared into the demon's eyes like shards of shining glass. Furca, Nicasia, and the spectators were almost blinded also as they tried to shield their eyes from this incredible apparition.

Gaby, still held aloft by the demon, opened her eyes and smiled. O *thank God thank God*, she breathed. She could see

190

through the shining glory of the light what it really was. The glow, though brilliant, did not hurt her eyes; she could discern features of a sort near the top of the cross, vaguely human yet as far beyond human as man is beyond the microbe. She could see now that it was not really a cross at all: the outstretched arms were actually radiant wings of glimmering light.

Then a voice like great golden bells ringing filled the chamber:

> "CREATURE OF EVIL, THOU HAST NO POWER OVER THIS SOUL. RELEASE HER AND DEPART, LEST I SMITE THEE WITH THE SWORD OF POWER THAT SMOTE THY INFERNAL MASTER ERE TIME CAME TO BE!"

With a titanic howl of rage and frustration that shook the very foundations of the chamber, the demon vanished instantly in a great burst of crimson flame and foul-smelling black smoke. Gaby's support vanished at the same time, but as she slipped away at last into merciful unconsciousness, she saw a great hand of pure light reach out and catch the altar, depositing it on the floor as gently as a falling feather. A wonderful feeling of great peace and joy swept over her; the last thing she remembered as darkness claimed her was the bursting open of the manacles that bound her to the altar stone, and the *cracking* of that stone in half beneath her body.

The angelic brilliance seemed to expand then, to engulf the entire hall, illuminating the very souls of the evil assembly now writhing in terror on the floor.

As the light blasted through her tightly closed eyelids, Nicasia threw up an arm to protect herself from blindness and saw the bones standing out vividly, as in an X-ray.

Then the light winked out and was gone.

There's only one way to hurt a man who's lost everything.
Give him back something broken.
        —*Stephen R. Donaldson:* WHITE GOLD WIELDER

CHAPTER SIXTEEN

PAINSONG

CAIRO: 25 NOVEMBER 2020

Eris felt like a fly trapped in amber; she hung suspended in the greenish-yellow beam of light that had lifted her and her driver up and into...what? She couldn't move, she couldn't speak; she could only see what was directly in front of her, part of a large circular room with metallic walls and floor. Banks of computer-like machines with blinking colored lights were arranged around the curving walls. She could see no windows.

Then she got her first look at her captors. A large goat-headed humanoid clumped into view and stood looking up at her as she hung helpless several feet off the floor. As the creature glared at her with baleful yellow slit-pupiled eyes, Eris could see that its face and head were covered with silky, grayish-white hair. It had a tufted beard, two straight six-inch horns on its head, and was dressed in a tight-fitting metallic garment with black-and-silver gloves and large black boots. Its body was heavy and powerful and slightly taller than a man's.

Suddenly her attention was drawn to a mark on the goat-man's left breast: a cobra head facing forward, with flared hood, ready to strike! She had seen it before! The memory hit her like a blow: those two tiny silver specks falling to a fiery death from the spacecraft she had destroyed! This was

192

one of those same creatures! She was probably inside another of those ships now, one that must have been hovering invisibly over the city, tracking her, waiting for a chance to kidnap her. Were these Nicasia's creatures? If so, she must have sent them to get her. But what were they going to do with her? Ransom her?

She had a sinking feeling she was going to find out—soon.

As if in agreement, the goat-man suddenly turned and lumbered over to a bank of controls nearby. He pushed a button and the yellow-green cone of light winked out. Eris and the limousine driver fell to the metallic floor heavily, still unable to move. Eris felt nothing when she hit the floor; her whole body was anesthetized.

The goat-man clumped back over to her and picked her up as effortlesssly as if she had been a pillow. Ignoring the driver, whose eyes were bulging with terror, the creature carried Eris over to a wall screen and activated it with the touch of a finger to a translucent panel beneath it. The panel glowed green and in a moment, a swirl of colors on the screen resolved into the face of one of the most beautiful women Eris had ever seen. But it was the cold, relentless beauty of evil, and the two yellow eyes that blazed out of that perfect face were pools of hellfire. The crimson mouth was tight with anger. "What is it, Caprix?" she rasped impatiently.

"Pardon, Queen, but we have captured the woman pilot as you commanded," the goat-man bleated in barbarously accented English.

The face softened into a pleased expression. "Ah! Good. Let me see her." The creature held Eris up.

The face on the screen Smiled coldly. "Yes! She's the one—I marked her face carefully in my mind. Well, my dear," she continued, speaking directly to Eris, "I'm sure you know who I am. I'm Nicasia Bane, and I know who you are. You're Eris Campbell, the pilot who's caused me a lot of trouble and who is responsible for the deaths of several of my servants. That annoys me greatly."

Eris felt her blood turn to ice water as she listened to the honeyed poison of her adversary's words. So this was Nicasia Bane! Eris wished she could talk back, scream her anger and outrage at this gloating monster, as beautiful and terrible as Hel, Goddess of Death.

"Shall we kill her, Majesty?" asked the goat-man.

Nicasia's smile was like a fresh wound. "No...not quite. Give her to Kathy, Caprix. Tell her to use the Agony Machine."

Eris felt her heart pounding wildly. She began to tremble, the first movement she had been able to make since the beam hit her.

"We have one other earthling, Majesty, an Egyptian driver who was accidentally drawn up with the woman. What shall we do with him?"

Nicasia waved a hand in dismissal. "He's of no use to us, but we don't want a witness. Kill him."

The goat-man bowed stiffly, still holding Eris like a sack of potatoes. "It shall be done."

Nicasia's blazing eyes bored into Eris'. "Goodbye, my dear. You're very lovely...now. But if we should ever meet again, I doubt very seriously whether I'll be able to recognize you."

And with a ringing, glacial laugh, the image faded.

The goat-man carried Eris across the room and dumped her on a metal platform that resembled a doctor's operating table. At its foot was a console of buttons and instruments that resembled the keyboard of some curious musical instrument. Above that were two video monitors, and before it all was a padded seat on a pedestal that rose out of the floor.

Eris was using every ounce of self-control to hold back the black wave of panic that threatened to engulf her at any moment. She was beginning to feel a pins-and-needles tingling throughout her body now; this meant that sensation was returning. If only she could regain even partial use of her limbs before—

Her eyes widened in apprehension as she watched the goat-man walk casually over to the cringing driver, who had apparently regained some motion already. His arms and legs were twitching like a wounded beetle. As the creature approached him, he tried to hunch himself backwards frantic-

194

ally. He had heard what Nicasia told the goat-man. His efforts to escape were pitiful and grotesque. And useless.

Eris tried to scream at the alien, but her vocal cords were still paralyzed. Nothing emerged but a feeble squeak of breath. Hating her helplessness, she saw the goat-man reach down with one gloved hand and hoist the driver off the deck in one quick motion, holding him by the throat. Then, as unemotionally as a farmer's wife wringing a chicken's neck, the goat-man began to squeeze.

The hapless man struggled and squirmed as his breath was cut off, but to no avail. The creature held him at arm's length as easily as if he had been a doll. He began to turn a brilliant scarlet, and his eyes looked as if they would pop from their sockets at any second. A purple tongue protruded, thrashing about like a fat snake looking around for a way of escape.

Eris wished desperately that she could close her eyes and shut out the sight of the man's agony. Her eyelids fluttered; there! Just as he began to turn a deep magenta, she managed to shut her eyes. Silently she prayed to Allah for the man's soul. It was all she could do.

The driver turned slate-blue then, and it was all over. The goat-man dropped the body contemptuously to the deck, then turned and lumbered out of the room.

Alone now, Eris concentrated all her energy on moving her limbs, visualizing the blood circulating through her body, restoring feeling and motion. After a few moments, she found that she could move her arms and legs slightly. She began to squirm toward one edge of the table....

The rapid clack of a woman's high heels approaching made her stop. Damn! she thought. Just a few more minutes and I'd be able to—

A tall, cold-looking blond woman appeared, dressed in the same tight silver suit the goat-man wore, with spike-heel black boots and black gloves. Over the woman's left breast Eris noticed the cobra-head insignia.

"Well, well," said the woman, coming closer in a sinister gliding motion that gave Eris the creeps. "So you're Eris Campbell, the hot-shot pilot who's been giving my mother such a hard time."

She moved closer, her vacuum eyes boring into Eris's as she caressed Eris' cheek softly with a thin gloved hand. "It's a real pity to have to...alter...such beauty. Under other circumstances, I'm sure that you and I could have become real...friends."

Eris tried to move her face away, but her neck muscles wouldn't obey yet. Then the woman leaned down and kissed her, full and sensuously, on the mouth!

A surge of weakness and revulsion swept over her.

The blonde stood up, laughing nastily and licking her thin red lips. "Now let's see what the rest of you looks like." She bent over again and began to remove Eris' clothes. "Oh, by the way, Eris," she added, "my name is Kathy Bane."

At first Eris tried to squirm, but seeing that this didn't hamper Kathy's efforts at all, she relaxed and lay there limply as her garments were stripped from her.

When she was naked on the cold table (sensation continued to return, yet she still could make no broad movements), Eris felt as embarrassed at Kathy's smoldering appraisal of her body as if she had been a man.

Kathy walked around to the foot of the table and sat down in the pedestal chair before the keyboard. Eris heard a switch click, then a soft hum of machinery beneath her, and the table top began to glow with a cold blue light. Desperately, she poured all her will into moving her right arm, and did move it several inches, but it was too late. Like the lid of a coffin, a black metal carapace rose up from beneath the table and fitted itself snugly over her body, leaving only her head free. Before it settled around her, she caught a glimpse of the underside of the thing: it was crowded with myriads of complex instruments and long wires. Some looked like electrodes, others bore a horrifying resemblance to dental tools and surgical instruments.

Next, a helmet-like device settled down over the top of her head. It felt cold and hard. Her vision and breathing were not obstructed, but she could not move her head.

"What the hell is this thing supposed to do?" Eris suddenly found herself croaking, her voice finally returned.

Kathy's smile was cold as sleet. "Ah, you've got your voice back! Good.

196

"I was waiting for that. For that is your essential contribution to my...composition. Now this next proceedure will be a little unnerving and slightly painful, but it's necessary." She sounded like a doctor trying to prepare a patient for some complex medical test.

Then, horror. Eris began to feel things—cold metal wires and probes—crawling and writhing over her naked skin like metallic worms. Prodding, insinuating their ways into her flesh with tiny invading pricks and thrustings; she felt them burrowing deep into her, tracing veins and arteries, searching for sensitive nerve ganglia, carefully, blindly seeking out all the most sensitive areas of her body. She bit down on her lip when she felt something cold enter her vagina, her urethra, even her anus. Another invaded her navel, two others attached themselves gently to each of her nipples. She began to sweat. *I'm not going to be able to stand this*, she screamed silently to herself.

From out of the helmet, more of the nasty little probes invaded her ears, her nostrils, and one snaked into her mouth, fastening itself to her teeth. She tried to bite it off, but it was too hard. Her mouth tasted of metal. Something with a cold blunt nose was nudging itself into her armpit; something else came to rest against the soles of both feet. She fought back a tremendous urge to cry from the fear, the revulsion, the awful feeling of violation she was experiencing.

Finally, everything was in place and the invasion ceased.

At the keyboard, Kathy nodded in satisfaction. She flicked two more switches. "Good. Now. These two monitors give me a view of your entire body inside the cocoon, Eris, so that I can see what's going on in there, plus a computer simulation of what's happening with your nervous system, internal organs and circulatory system. I think you should know that I had two years of pre-med, so I know quite a bit about the human body and what it can sustain without dying. I probably won't kill you, except by accident. You'll beg me to, of course, but I won't.

"So instead of becoming a doctor, I've become a composer of sorts. And what do I compose on this fascinating example of alien technology? I call them *Schmerzenlieder*...Painsongs. As I play this keyboard—and I've become very proficient at it, I might add—*things* will happen to and in your body. Unpleasant things. They will cause you pain—of various kinds and in varying degrees. They will cause you to make sounds: whimpers, moans, shrieks, gasps, cries, screams—sounds I'm sure you never dreamed the human voice was capable of. You will sing for me, Eris, *a capella*; you will sing like a bird, like an opera star, like a city burning. And I will record your songs, Eris, mix them, edit them, augment them electronically, until I have a new masterpiece of agony for those who listen with delight to my compositions: the High Court of Caput Algol, my adopted mother's home planet."

Eris tried to think of something to say, but her mind and throat were choked with horror and fear. Somehow, nothing brave or defiant presented itself. The thing in her mouth tasted like cold electricity. She thought of Chris, then, his brave, gentle face tortured with worry for her, and hot tears squeezed themselves out of her eyes at last. She felt sorrier for him at this moment than for herself. Even if she survived this ordeal, she would probably be scarred and maimed hideously. She thought of the others: jaunty Ray, serious Avram, gallant André; Gaby, her sweet adopted little sister, also imprisoned somewhere by this insane alien woman; she saw President Warren's grave, handsome face, etched with the burdens of his office, and Jaca's lovely green-eyed beauty, calm and powerful. If only she were here now.

Kathy's broken-glass voice cut through: "Any questions about what we're going to do?" She slowly removed her black gloves and flexed her fingers, like a piano virtuoso preparing to play for a concert audience.

Eris opened her eyes and looked at the gaunt face of her tormentor, blurry through a cascade of tears. "Just one," she said weakly.

"What's that, darling?"

"How can you, a human being with a soul, willingly do the bidding of a...an alien *thing* like Nicasia Bane? She's opposed to everything human, *everything*, Kathy! She's vowed not to rest until the entire world—every man, woman and child—is ground to dust under her heel. She not only wants our resources and our bodies—she wants our very *souls!* Don't you know that? Do you think she'll spare you or any other human? She'll take your soul like all the others and hurl it down into the Pit to feed the filthy, obscene Darkness she worships!"

Kathy smiled sardonically, almost pityingly, her eyes as empty as the spaces between the stars. "I'm afraid not, my dear...you see, I don't even have a soul anymore...."

Then she rested her scarlet-clawed hands on the keyboard and began to play.

"Jesus Christ, where the hell *is* she?" Chris' voice was ragged with worry as he paced his hotel room like a caged tiger. It was seven-thirty, a full hour and a half after Eris had promised to meet them back at the hotel for dinner. Twilight was sifting down over Cairo like soot and galaxies of lights were twinkling on across the broad expanse of the darkening city. "I mean, she's a responsible woman—she'd have phoned us if she got held up for some reason, wouldn't she?"

Avram, slouched in a comfortable but somewhat motheaten armchair with a cup of hot mint tea, sighed. "You'd think so. Maybe she just got caught up in helping the casualties and lost track of time. Or maybe she stopped to do some shopping."

Chris stopped pacing, turned to face his friend. "But you don't really believe that, do you?"

Avram looked at the floor. "No, I don't really believe that. I wish I did."

"But his first suggestion is possible, Chris," said Raymond, as cheerily as he could manage. "That scene at the hospital must be pretty traumatic, right? She could just be completely wrapped up in it. Look—why don't you call over to the hospital and see if she's still there?"

Chris took a deep breath, inhaling the cool, dry night air. "Okay, maybe I'd better. I've been thinking about doing that, but I guess I just haven't wanted to know..." He glanced at the doorway, thinking, Dammit, she's going to walk in that door any minute now, looking tired but gorgeous....

Slowly, like a man going to his own funeral, Chris walked over to the phone and asked the hotel operator to connect him with Dr. Abu Moustafa, who was in charge of the temporary hospital operations set up in the Nile Hilton. After a wait of several minutes, the doctor came on and said that no, Miss Campbell had not been there this afternoon, but he would be delighted to see her any time.

Chris hung up, his face ashen. "She hasn't been there."

André turned from the window, where he had been absorbed in his own gloomy thoughts of Gabrielle. "*Merde!* That *is* bad, Chris. Perhaps a traffic accident...?"

Avram shook his head, his dark eyes somber with concern. "I don't think so. We'd have heard something by now. She'd have called us...or somebody would...."

The phone rang, the loudest sound in the world. Four men froze. Their eyes locked. *Was this it?*

Chris approached the clamoring instrument as if it were a snake. Gingerly he picked it up. "Yes?"

It was the desk clerk downstairs. "Dr. Troy? I have a special delivery for you in the lobby. It is quite large—a crate. If you would be so kind as to come down—"

Chris' breath went out of him in a rush of annoyance. "A crate? I'm not expecting any deliveries. What the hell can it be? Christ, not now...." He put his hand over the mouthpiece and turned to his hovering friends. "There's a crate for me downstairs. Shit, talk about rotten timing...."

He turned back to the phone. "Listen, I'm just on my way out. I'm not expecting anything, so it must be either a gag or a mistake. Can you hold it for me until I get back?"

The desk clerk was distinctly upset. "A thousand pardons, Dr. Troy, but it is really quite large. It is in the lobby. It looks very peculiar there, sir. I'm afraid we really have no place to put it. If you could only spare a few moments to open it. The manager—"

"Okay, okay, I understand. The manager's on your ass to get the thing out of the lobby so the guests won't be inconvenienced, right? I'll come down in a minute."

Chris hung up. "Come on, guys, let's go see what the hell this is all about...."

200

Downstairs they encountered the distraught desk clerk fluttering like a wounded bird around a large wooden packing crate.

"*Wen-Nabi*, by the Prophet," he dithered apologetically, "I am dreadfully sorry to inconvenience you gentlemen at this time of night, but this is most irregular—"

Chris waved him silent, looking at the thing curiously. It was just a plain wooden crate with no marking on it, except for his name and the name and address of the hotel stencilled on one side. It measured approximately six feet high by five feet wide and five feet deep. "Who delivered this?" he asked the clerk. "Did you see them?"

"Oh yes, sir," the man replied, his head bobbing like a yo-yo. "They were a most peculiar pair: a large Nubian and a dwarf with a mask over his face."

A dark, dark bell rang somewhere deep in Chris' memory. His hackles lifted. "Did you say a large black man...?"

"Yes, sir. He said you were expecting it."

"Get me some tools to open this with!" Chris snapped. "A crowbar, if you have one! *Move!*"

"Of course, sir, right away, sir!" The little man scurried away and in a few interminable minutes, returned with a rusty iron bar.

Like a man possessed, Chris hurled himself at the crate, ripping out the nails and tossing the boards aside carelessly. A curious German tourist who was standing nearby almost got a board in his chest, but Raymond intercepted it just in time. The man stepped well back, away from this American maniac with the crowbar.

As the desk clerk scurried around trying to pick up the discarded nails, boards and slivers of wood that were piling up on the Continental Savoy's somewhat worn lobby rug, Chris wrenched the last board loose and hurriedly pulled out large wads of packing material.

At last the crate's contents stood revealed: a traditional carved sarcophagus of larch wood, painted and gessoed in bright colors with a carved human head and breast supposedly representing the occupant within. Chris' blood flash froze as he saw that the face had been viciously slashed and mutilated, so that the features were unrecognizable. An in-

201

scribed band down the center of the case which had been a prayer in hieroglyphics was also mutilated, and Chris noticed that a separate wooden cartouche had been glued over the center of this band. On it was a painted hieroglyph of a seated being with a long curved nose and long ears, holding a scepter. With an added chill, Chris recognized it as the character determinative of Set.

"What in God's name...?" breathed Raymond.

"A mummy?" André said. "Who would send you a mummy?"

"Come on, you guys!" yelled Chris, lifting the heavy case out of the remains of its crate and lowering it to the floor. "Help me get this thing open!"

The outer lid came off easily, revealing a smaller, more elaborately decorated inner coffin made of cartonnage, a material consisting of successive layers of linen and papyrus soaked in plaster and moulded to fit the body while soft. The entire case was highly varnished and beautifully painted with texts from *The Book of the Dead*. Like the outer case, the face on the inner one had also been mutilated.

Working feverishly, the men quickly stripped the linen backing off the inner case and unfastened the lacings that held its contents inside.

The moment they lifted out what was inside, they knew it was not a mummy. Although swathed from head to foot in linen wrappings, it was limp and still faintly warm. The bandages were mostly soaked through with encrustations of dried blood and some that were still a vivid scarlet. A terrible smell arose from the thing.

Fighting back the vomit that threatened to spew forth at any moment, Chris knelt down and unwrapped the head of the "mummy," silently screaming a garbled prayer: *Please, please, don't let this be—*

Then he saw the first lock of golden hair. His stomach heaved and tossed like a boat in a typhoon, but grimly, he made himself continue unwrapping the head he held in his lap.

When the last blood-soaked strip had been unwound, Chris stared in cold black horror at a face that was almost unrecognizable as human. Virtually every inch of it was

202

slashed, bruised, lacerated, punctured, and burned. The lips were cracked and bloated like obscene sausages, oozing pus. Only the terribly familiar cascade of honey-golden hair served as identification.

Then, slowly, a mangled eyelid raised itself, revealing a beautiful aqua-blue eye that rolled up and looked at Chris. The mutilated lips parted and a voice as weak as a baby bird whispered: "You'll be...proud...of me...darling...I didn't...sing...worth a damn!"

The eye closed and the terrible wrapped body was silent.

A great wracking sob heaved itself up out of Chris' gut like a huge fish surfacing, along with the remains of his poorly digested lunch. The desk clerk's eyes bulged in horror as he saw his rug forever desecrated by this mad American's awful indiscretion.

André was on Chris like a flash, holding him, whipping out a pocket handkerchief to wipe his mouth. Avram was pale and shaken with horror. It was Raymond, also stricken to his very soul, who noticed the piece of paper pinned to the front of the pathetic bandaged figure. Like a man in a dream, he slowly unpinned it and looked at it. For a moment the words on it wouldn't focus, but finally he could read it through hot tears. It said:

> *We thought you might like*
> *this mummy returned to you,*
> *although it's not in very good*
> *condition any more. Hardly a*
> *museum piece.*
> *Who wants to be next?*

At the bottom was a hooded cobra's head, hand-drawn in fresh human blood.

There is only one thing
pain is good for
It teaches you to love
God bless pain.
        —Joey Goldfarb, "AVATAR"

CHAPTER SEVENTEEN

THE HEALING

CAIRO: 26 NOVEMBER 2020

Southwest of the Old City of Cairo, in the crumbling elegance of the seedy southern district called El Saiyida Zeinab, lay Zeinhom Gardens, for years a large, irregularly shaped public park rarely visited by tourists. To the west of Zeinhom were the state-controlled slaughterhouses and tanneries, to which were regularly driven herds of sheep, camels, goats and other animals, creating a constant snarl of traffic in the area, and from which rose daily a charnel stench foul enough to deter even the hardiest explorer of the byways of Cairo. Also to the west were the Christian cemeteries, and to the southeast the vast Mohammedan cemeteries, the sprawling City of the Dead, occupying almost two square miles and containing the tombs of the Mamelukes and the Khalifs. The southernmost corner of the Gardens nestled up to the ruined Roman aqueducts which surrounded it on two sides.

Nicasia Bane had found Zeinhom, surrounded by death and antiquity, the ideal location for her Egyptian base of operations and had induced Harcourt to purchase it from the Egyptian government two years before his death. As they had done with Wolfe Island previously, the Banes immedi-
204

ately closed the park to all visitors. They erected a high stone wall around its perimeter and constructed a European-style, three-story, thirty-room mansion on the grounds, which were re-landscaped to suit Nicasia's rather bizarre taste. A pool and a landing pad for helicopters and hovercraft were added behind the house, as well as several outbuildings for storage.

Now, as the sun set in a fiery welter of bruised violet and crimson beyond the stark black points of the Pyramids, Nicasia gazed from her third-story balcony across the gleaming copper ribbon of the Nile toward the Giza Plateau, whose hidden secrets and treasures she knew would soon be hers. At her feet, coiled into squamous knots of darkness, the great serpent Typhon slumbered languidly, his blood cooled by the evening chill.

As the last embers of sunset were painting Nicasia's perfect face the color of old blood, Tina came out onto the balcony, silent as a shadow in the deep turquoise of twilight.

"Excuse me, Mother, but it's my turn to watch Gaby. Just thought I'd let you know."

Nicasia turned slowly, her dark hair rippling in the dry breeze like clouds of ink. "Thank you, Tina. How is she doing? You girls are getting your fill for once, aren't you?"

Tina smiled, which she did rarely. "Her energy level's way down, mother. She still has no idea what's happening to her. The drugs keep her mind totally smacked, so she can't focus her will. And we're constantly visiting her...."

Nicasia smiled a dark smile of approval. "Good. Just be careful not to drain her too much. I don't know what happened at the ceremony, how she managed to protect herself. Whoever gave her that ritual of releasing must have taught her more than I thought...." She broke off, shuddering as she recalled the terrible singing fire of the angelic presence that had come and driven the demon back into Hell and looked deep into her soul....

"Well, whatever, Mother, it doesn't protect her from us, does it? Gotta run now...it's my turn...and I'm hungry." Her sable eyes glowing with anticipation, Tina slipped away into the dark house.

Alone again, Nicasia gazed into the night and thought about her "stepdaughters." It had been a masterstroke to gather about her these young girls, carefully selected from hundreds of young women Nicasia had encountered during her international business trips with Harcourt.

They were all in their early twenties, from different backgrounds and social positions, but they all shared one trait in common: they were psychic vampires. Without being consciously aware of why, they found themselves feeling always listless and empty when alone, lacking energy and tormented by a vague hunger that was not of the body. They never came truly alive except in the presence of others; the closer proximity the better. They made it a point to attend as many parties and group functions as possible; they glowed and shone in crowds, sucking the vital electrical and psychic energy from one person after another, leaving each one exhausted, dull and listless and forever unable to determine why.

Sex was the ideal way of acquiring this necessary energy on a one-to-one basis, so all the girls competed to be as stylish and seductive as possible, taking lovers, using them up and discarding the husks like empty potato-chip bags, all under Nicasia's expert guidance.

Most humans who were in this lamentable condition of psychic vampirism (and there were many, Nicasia knew) had no idea they were what they were; had no conscious knowledge that somewhere along the great road of lifetimes they walked, they had used their free will to make the deliberate soul-choice to turn away from the Light forever, to abandon their karmic debts and default on salvation, their soul-essence stripped of its awareness for all eternity and returned in oblivion to the Source of All That Is.

Thus, these creatures were no longer truly human, although the majority of men and women they encountered could never tell the difference. They were bodies occupied solely by ravenous egos, without any spiritual guidance to control them. They were human sharks: to them, other people were merely prey. Nicasia's contribution, with Furca's sorcerous help, had been to make these girls aware for the first time exactly what they were and how to make the most advantageous use of it. She had shown them how to augment and increase their powers of vampirizing others until they

206

had become virtually irresistable. Of course, their appetites for human vital energy had increased also, Nicasia knew, but there was always plenty of unsuspecting human sustenance around.

Currently, that sustenance was Gabrielle. Soon the girl would be weak and malleable enough to serve the purpose for which Nicasia had intended her all along. So what if her soul was protected from the Dark Powers? Nicasia would control her mind and her body. That would be enough.

Yes, thought Nicasia, things were proceeding well. Without their leader, Eris, Warren's agents would be stripped of the power of five, and their pain and sorrow at her mutilation and Gaby's disappearance would hamper them in their efforts. But they would soon enter the Pyramid and begin the search anyway, and undoubtedly eventually locate the Immobilizer. Then, she would strike, quick and deadly as the cobra that served as her symbol, using the one instrument none of them would ever suspect.

Pleased with her prospects of success, Nicasia smiled again into the cool Egyptian night.

As Tina reached Gaby's room, she was surprised to see Kathy there. Lola was just prancing off down the shadowed hall, full of stolen vigor and energy. "Hey," said Tina angrily, "what are *you* doing here? It's my turn."

Kathy turned slowly, fixing Tina with the glacial glare that was her specialty. "Oh, really? It's so hard to remember who's supposed to go in when. I just happened to be nearby and Lola was ready to leave, so...."

"Dammit, Kathy, that's not fair! We agreed on a certain schedule, and it's my turn now!"

Kathy's hand shot out like the lash of a whip, grasping Tina's wrist in a strong grip. She twisted the wrist cruelly, making the dark girl gasp in pain.

"We're switching schedules, honey," Kathy said coldly. "Got it? I'm going in there now...alone. You can find something to do for an hour, can't you? *Can't you?*" She emphasized the last two words with another twist of Tina's wrist, and the girl sank to her knees, hissing in pain.

Kathy released her and Tina got slowly to her feet, rubbing her sore wrist, her eyes sullen inky pools of hate. Abruptly she turned on her heel and stalked off down the corridor, cursing under her breath.

"Don't worry, darling," Kathy called mockingly after her, "there'll be plenty left for you. Her battery's not quite dead yet." She smiled thinly as she unlocked Gaby's door.

Kathy entered the dimly lit bedroom, quietly closing and locking the door behind her. Gabrielle sprawled naked on the sweat-soaked bed, the sheet twisted around her waist. She slept fitfully, tormented by dark dreams. Kathy noted with satisfaction that Gaby's once lush body was now gaunt and wasted, her hair a stringy tangle.

Kathy licked her thin red lips and began to remove her clothes. When she was naked, she moved to the side of the bed and called softly,

"Gabrielle...."

Slowly, Gaby fought her way up through drug-saturated layers of sleep to groggy consciousness. She opened sticky, burning eyes to see Kathy towering over her, blurry and wavering, as though seen through tears.

Then, as her vision cleared, she noticed that Kathy was naked. "Where...where's y'r clothes, Kathy?" she mumbled.

Kathy reached over and took Gaby's thin face between her two scarlet-clawed hands, thumbnails alarmingly close to Gaby's eyes. Her own eyes, bright with lust, bored steadily into Gaby's, seeming to reach down inside her and suck out her very soul.

Softly, Kathy said, "You can't make love properly with your clothes on, little sister...."

Alarm, recollection, revulsion, panic all blossomed in rapid succession in Gaby's fuddled mind like the poisonous flowers in her stepmother's garden outside. "No!" she cried. "Let me go! Get away!"

Kathy removed her hands from Gaby's face, which was now twisting from side to side. Kathy drew back her right hand and slapped the girl across the face, hard. Gaby's eyes grew wide with pain and shock as a crimson handprint bloomed on her white cheek.

"Now, you can make this easy for yourself, Gaby, or you can make it hard. Either way's all right with me. I've waited a long time for this and I've taken a lot of shit from you. Now I'm through waiting. I'm going to take what I want now, while there's still enough of you left to make it interesting. Understand? Easy or hard. It's your choice, darling...."

Gabrielle felt something inside her whimper and die at that moment. She shut her eyes, blotting out the sight of that terrible black-hole gaze fixed on her face, that dread emptiness demanding to be filled. If only I could think clearly...fight back...do something.... The Light...even the Light couldn't save her this time from such a totally physical assault. She just couldn't summon up the energy to fight back....

Then, as she felt Kathy's cool, dry hands begin to rove over her body, she also felt something else begin to coalesce inside her mind, a kind of formless energy gradually shaping itself into...a face? Yes: warmth and peace and love radiated from this mental apparition, soothing Gaby's tormented mind.

Now she could see two great pools of aqua blue, shining like the sea...was it, could it be...*Eris?*

Gaby had to bite her lip to keep from screaming the name out loud. It *was* Eris! How could she be here? Oh, God, was Eris dead? Wait...she was saying something.... Gaby could see her friend's beautiful face clearly in her mind now...she was trying to speak to her. The tortured girl tried desperately to still her mind, to ignore the violation of her body, to listen....

> *Gaby...Gaby...this is Eris, love, can you hear me?*
>
> *Yes! Yes! Oh, Eris, thank God! How—*
>
> *Hush, baby. Just listen now and do as I say. I'm visiting you astrally, Gaby. I'm out of my body now. My physical body is very sick, it may die, but before that happens I wanted to come and find you. Now listen to me carefully, Gaby: You are not a body! Your real, true self is*

not physical! What you really are is mind and spirit. Your physical body is only a vehicle for living in this earth dimension. You can leave that body, just like I'm doing. Will yourself out, Gaby, feel yourself leaving your body just like walking out of a room, see yourself rising up out of your body, free. Come on, baby, you can do it! Try!

Gaby had heard about astral travel; she wanted desperately to be able to do it now, to be with her beloved friend, to leave behind the nauseating things that were happening to her...no, not her...only to her body....

Summoning the feeble remnants of will left to her, Gaby tried to relax her body, to reject its clinging heaviness and the dense physical environment around her; she could feel strength and power pouring into her now from Eris. She began to lose contact with her physical self; now she could no longer feel Kathy's repugnant caresses. She held Eris' image strongly in her mind, desiring, willing with all her heart to leave her body and join her friend....

And suddenly she was free, floating near the ceiling of her bedroom! She opened her eyes, and for a second a feeling of disorientation and giddiness swept over her, but she soon steadied herself. She looked down and what she saw made her look away quickly. She felt a strong, warm hand clasp hers then, and she turned to see Eris, radiantly beautiful, hovering in the air beside her. Her welcoming smile warmed Gaby like the first sweet rays of dawn. Joyfully, she willed herself into Eris' arms and was instantly there without consciously moving. Her friend felt warm and solid to her.

"Oh, Eris, Eris, it's so good to see you," Gaby moaned, sobbing, astral tears sparkling like diamonds in the dim light.

After a long moment, Eris led Gaby up and out of the horrors and lusts of Zeinhom Mansion, out into the clear, clean Egyptian night.

"Where are we going?" Gaby asked excitedly as she and Eris hovered high above the twinkling lights of Cairo.

"Anywhere you like," replied Eris with a smile. "In our astral bodies, we can go anywhere in an instant, just by willing it."

"It's wonderful!" Gaby cried in sheer delight. "Oh, I'm so glad to escape from that prison down there.... I don't even know how long I've been in Cairo...all I've seen is the inside of a bedroom. They're keeping me drugged, Eris, I don't know what for."

"I'm sure Nicasia has some kind of plan in mind for you, Gaby, or else you'd be dead by now. Listen, let's go visit a friend of mine and we can bring each other up to date on everything."

Eris told Gaby to focus her attention on the Great Sphinx, a dark hulk in the moonless night, and they were there instantly, sitting on its huge right paw, looking up into the colossal stone face, battered by time and weather and man's folly, gazing inscrutably into eternity.

Gaby related all that had happened to her since she arrived at Wolfe Island, and Eris listened intently, appalled by the terrible dangers Gaby had been subjected to and filled with admiration for her friend's courage. Then she gave Gaby a brief account of her two-week training course with the other Psi-Spies and told the story of her bizarre abduction and torture by Kathy Bane. Gaby hugged Eris close, tears of pity and rage and terror flowing in shining rivulets down her astral cheeks.

"Kathy's a monster—she's as bad as Nicasia," Gaby sobbed. "Oh God, Eris, how could she do that to you...."

"Hush, baby, it's all right. I'm...I mean, my body's in the hospital right now in intensive care. I'm not dead yet, and they're doing everything they can for me. Chris and all the others are right there with me, pouring all the healing energy they can summon into me—and with their hopped-up psi powers, believe me, that's a lot. Besides that, they've contacted the President and he's alerted the entire Psi-Spy network to focus their light on me. And we're also getting help from Jaca and Klorian and our teachers on the inner planes as well. You watch—we're gonna show those doctors something that'll make 'em wet their pants!"

211

Gaby laughed despite her pain. She looked up at her friend's face, radiant with a shimmering glow in the darkness, and suddenly she felt better. She knew Eris would survive. With all this help—she just *had* to!

Suddenly a wonderful thought sprang into her mind: "Eris! What about André? Is he at the hospital too?"

"Of course he is, baby. You want to go visit him?"

Gaby leapt into the air, executing a graceful aerial pirouette, her eyes large and shining with hope. "Oh, Eris, could we? Can we go see him now?"

"Of course we can. Just close your eyes and imagine an intensive care ward with me in the middle of a group of doctors and our guys and all kinds of medical gadgets."

Gaby nodded, closing her eyes.

"Now will yourself to be there, Gaby. Desire—just wanting to be there—isn't enough. *Will* yourself there and—"

Gaby vanished in an instant.

"—there you'll be." Eris smiled up at the Sphinx. "That's my girl. Learns quick, doesn't she?" Then a sad, gray look touched her face. "Boy, I hate to go back there.... I hate to look at what that creature did to my body...but I know I have to, to help them help me. They can't heal me if I'm out playing hooky somewhere."

Eris sighed into the desert darkness and was gone.

She reappeared just outside and above the hospital, wanting to see once again the glorious sight she had witnessed with her astral vision as she left the hospital on her quest to find Gaby. Although invisible to physical sight, a shimmering, coruscating corona of white light played over and around the Dar el Shifa Hospital like an aurora, a dazzling scintillation of psychic and spiritual power lancing in from many sympathetic minds and spirits throughout the world, concentrated on this one location, this one tortured body. Healing energy. White Light, pouring in from the inner plane teachers, from radiant devas, Ascended Masters, from great high beings, themselves composed of pure light. An incredible vortex of canescent power focused on the physical body and aura of the woman who now watched its gleaming force in awe and wonder.

212

Breathing a silent prayer of thanks to all who were helping her, Eris willed her astral self into the intensive care
room, where she found Gaby anxiously awaiting her. Gaby
was standing next to André who, along with Chris and Raymond, was seated in the lotus position before a complex
computerized medical console. Their heads were bowed,
eyes closed, as they concentrated on sending healing energy
to the pathetic form that lay suspended in a cylindrical glass
chamber, gently cushioned on a constantly circulating, fil-
tered layer of compressed air. Eris' entire outer body was
covered with a thin layer of synthetic skin that locked in vital
body fluids and plasma while soaking up the debris and liquid wastes from the many burns and cuts. The body was kept
pain-free by electroanesthesia instead of by massive doses of
dangerously addictive drugs such as morphine. Eris could
watch all her vital signs being carefully monitored on beep-
ing oscilloscopes, could hear her own slow (but steady)
heartbeat thudding in the silent soundproofed room. On the
various monitor screens were computer-enhanced ultrasound
and NMR displays of her interior organs, circulatory system,
bone structure and nervous system. Other monitors displayed
color video images of the exterior of her body that could
zoom in to microdimensions when needed; a larger screen
displayed a beautiful rainbow-patched infrared silhouette of
her entire body, showing temperature variations throughout
it as the inner wall of the cylindrical chamber slowly rotated
the cameras and recording instruments to produce a 360-
degree picture.

Two doctors and a technician were in attendance, murmuring softly to themselves and occasionally making notes
on various charts. Machinery hummed and clicked sooth-
ingly, medicines and nourishment automatically dripped into
Eris' veins as preprogrammed by the diagnostic computer.

With her astral vision Eris could see laser-like streams
of white light pouring from the foreheads of Chris, André
and Raymond into the chamber, joining with the shimmering
nimbus of powerful healing energy bathing her body from
sources thousands of miles and even dimensions distant.

Then she noticed that Avram Sumi was not with the
other three men. He was working quietly in another part of

213

the room in his own unique fashion. In deep alpha concentration, he was using one of the microwave monitors to do what no doctor could do with even the finest scalpels or laser probes: utilizing his precisely honed powers of psychokinesis, he was slowly, carefully mending broken bones and damaged nerve tissue, making minute connections, welding and shaping molecules of bone and tendon, sealing and reattaching ruptured capillaries and veins, strengthening weakened tissues throughout the body. The finest doctors in Egypt and Israel had been called in and they were dumbfounded at what this dark, intense man with the glittering gaze was accomplishing with infinite patience before their very eyes.

A tear sparkled briefly in the corner of one luminous eye as Eris felt the strength and power of the love and devotion these men had for her, especially Chris. It beat against her in great warm waves of emotion, discernible in a way that would not be possible when she had returned to her body, she knew. They were true friends in the deepest, highest sense, five kindred beings soul-forged into one superb five-aspected instrument of light.

"Eris!" Gaby cried, sensing Eris' presence in the room and turning to greet her. "Where were you? God, this is fascinating! What a terrific way to travel! I love it! On, I don't *ever* want to go back to my body...."

Eris was beside her now, her arm warmly around Gaby's shoulders. "I know, sweetheart, but you have to...soon. And so do I. You shouldn't stay out too long, especially the first time. After all, you don't know what those creeps might be doing back at Zeinhom. If they think you're in a coma or even dead, they might write you off and feed your pretty little bod to the crocodiles."

Gaby's eyes grew very large. "Oh my God, would they really...?"

Eris laughed merrily. "I wouldn't put anything past that lovely bunch, kid. It is tempting to want to stay out longer, but I think we'd both better return now. You know how to do it?"

Gaby nodded solemnly. "Yeah...just visualize Zeinhom and will myself back inside and in my body again. Oh, Eris,

214

do I really have to go back now? I think I'd almost rather be dead than—"

Eris put her arms around the girl, feeling her sadness and fear spill out like dirty water swirling. "No, baby, don't give up now. We've both got tough times ahead of us, but we can't duck out. Too much depends on us. A whole world, maybe...."

Warmed and comforted by Eris' love, Gaby pulled herself together bravely, preparing to face whatever she had to face. "You're right, Eris. I'll hang in." She hugged the older woman tightly, then closed her eyes. "Goodbye, Eris.... God bless...."

And she winked out of the room like a light turned off. Eris' face was sober and drawn. "God bless, baby," she murmured, pleased that she had been able to lift Gaby's spirits a little. But who would lift hers? She glided over to where Chris' seated figure was projecting white light into the chamber. For a moment she moved to sit within him, intermingling her astral atoms and molecules with his physical ones, experiencing a feeling of oneness no physical union could ever provide, her astral heart pumping waves of rose-red love into his, her astral blood flowing through his veins, sharing spaces like two rivers coursing through one channel.

She could feel on one level that he was aware of her, but she did not want to disturb his concentration. Heartened, feeling well loved and protected, Eris moved inside the chamber and carefully, gently reintegrated her astral body with her physical one.

There was no pain. She was instantly deeply asleep from the sedation being fed into her system by the computer.

Meanwhile, Gaby had paused above the grim walls of Zeinhom Manor. Horror and loathing gripped her as she saw that the entire house was surrounded by a thick black fog, a shroud of psychic pollution formed by the negativity and evil thoughts given off by those inside. It was like those awful brown blankets of smog that covered Los Angeles and other cities so much of the time: but this was far worse—it was psychic smog. She shuddered as she saw that the thin glistening silver cord connecting her to her physical body disappeared into that murky mass.

Suddenly something horrible with flapping bat wings detached itself from the darkness and came shrieking and gibbering up toward her. It was not a bat, she could see: it looked more like a jet-black hog with fiery crimson eyes and fangs that glowed dully in the faint starlight. Gaby drew back instinctively, revolted and terrified. The thing made a pass near her, gabbling an obscene laugh. It seemed to grow bigger as she watched it circle around for another lunge at her. She could smell its psychic stench hanging on the air.

Suddenly Gaby knew what it was: Eris had instructed her briefly about the astral plane when they had talked earlier at the Sphinx. She had warned Gaby that she might run into some of the more unpleasant denizens of the astral world, elementals she had called them, negative thought-forms created by the force of dark minds. "They feed on fear and negative emotions," Eris had warned her. "If you're not afraid of them, they can't hurt you."

Defiance replaced the fear in Gaby's mind. "Scram, you flying fart, before I make batburger out of you!" She visualized a screen of white light around herself and laughed as the thing suddenly stopped its swooping flight, hovering uncertainly a few yards away. Shielding its burning rodent-like eyes with one scrawny black arm, it began to flap toward her again, hissing and babbling obscenely. But there was a feeling of caution in its approach now. It found itself suddenly bereft of nourishment and this was unsettling to it.

"Okay, toilet-breath, you asked for it!" Gaby visualized a laser-like lance of pure white light projecting outward from the spot between and just above her eyes, as she had seen André and the others do in the hospital. Instantly the thought became astral reality and the shining white beam struck the surprised elemental directly in the face, blowing it to dark shreds that quickly dispersed and vanished like wisps of smoke.

Gaby whooped in triumph. "Hooray! Watch out, you flying cesspools, here comes Gaby the Kid, fastest light in the West...or is it the East?" She remained on guard for a few minutes, watching the black cloud for any further elementals, but none appeared. Then, taking one last look at the jewel-like glitter of nighttime Cairo and breathing a silent farewell to the dark and distant lion-bodied guardian crouching on the eternal sands, Gaby sent her astral body hurtling down toward the dread mansion below.

Willing herself into the bedroom, she saw that her body was alone, still in a naked sprawl on top of the bedclothes. She breathed a sigh of relief, then slowly, gently settled her astral vehicle back into her body as Eris had instructed her, carefully reintegrating it with her physical self.

Gaby felt that too-familiar feeling of fuzziness and weakness sweep over her as soon as she re-entered her drained, drugged body. It was almost intolerable after the crystal clarity her senses had enjoyed outside; she felt terribly heavy and dense, as though she were made of lead and had gained 200 pounds.

Along with these unpleasant sensations, a sharp stinging pain bit deep into her torso, just under the left breast. She looked down and saw with alarm a round, raw wound, about the size of quarter, where her Mentacom Medallion had been! They had taken it! Nothing but a special solvent could remove the medallion from the skin, so good old Kathy had just taken the skin with it! Maybe Kathy had thought she was dead, although she knew that Kathy would have ripped it off while she was conscious if she had wanted to. Probably would have preferred it.

Well, they won't be able to use it, Gaby decided. They don't know the occult code number it responds to. Maybe they wouldn't be able to figure out what it was and would return it to her, she hoped, although she hadn't been able to use it either, in her weakened mental condition.

In the meantime, the wound left by its removal hurt like hell. She saw that blood had soaked the bedclothes under her left side; it was already beginning to dry and turn brownish-red. The wound itself was still oozing blood, so Gaby staggered out of bed and stumbled into the bathroom, hoping to find a bandaid or something to put on it. The pain had sharpened her senses somewhat, clearing her mind of the drugged fog, for which she was grateful. There was nothing in the medicine chest, so after washing the wound, she settled for a clean washcloth which she held pressed under her breast.

As she returned to her rumpled, bloody bed, she wished fervently for a change of linen and something to eat. Again, she experienced a flicker of fear that Kathy and the others might think she had died and would just leave her in here to rot....

Just then a key turned in the lock and Nicasia entered, a worried look on her face. She brightened when she saw Gaby awake and sitting up in bed.

"Oh, you're back with us again, are you? Kathy told me you'd passed out while she was examining you and she couldn't wake you up."

"Examining," Gaby thought with some amusement. Is that what she called it?

"Are you all right now?" Nicasia asked anxiously.

Gaby pretended to be as fuddled as usual. "Sure...m'hungry...want s'm food...hurts...." Gaby removed the bloody washcloth from her wound.

"I'll have the girls bring you some soup...and something to put on that." Nicasia's face grew hard. She held up the medallion, gingerly touching only the edges, as though not wanting to soil her hands with Gaby's blood. Gaby could see the round, gory piece of her skin still stuck to the back of it. "What is this thing, Gaby?"

Gaby hesitated, then mumbled, "Good-luck charm...."

"Bullshit! Nobody wears a good-luck charm soldered to their skin! It's some gadget the PIA fitted you up with, isn't it? What does it do?"

"Dunno...didn't tell me."

Nacasia shook her head impatiently. "Try again, Gaby, I'm not buying. I'm sure you know exactly what it is and what it does. If you want any food, you'd better tell me—now!"

Just then Kathy entered the room behind Nicasia.

"Oh, I'm so relieved, Gaby! You really had me worried there when you passed out. I thought you were in a coma or something."

Yeah, I'll bet you're relieved, thought Gaby. You're off the hook with Moms for damaging the goods.

218

"I was just asking her about this thing you rather drastically removed from her body, Kathy," said Nicasia with a frown. "She doesn't seem to want to tell us about it."

Kathy looked at the gleaming golden disc thoughtfully. "You know, Mother, I seem to recall seeing one of these things on Eris' body too. I didn't bother with it because she was already in the machine when I noticed it, but it was in the same spot—beneath her left breast."

"Oh, really?" said Nicasia. "Fascinating." She seemed to lose interest then. "Well, I'll send it up to Kalon 22 next trip. Maybe some of our scientists can figure out what it does. I doubt that it's anything important—it's not a bug, anyway."

Abruptly, Nicasia turned on her heel. "Bring her some nice hot soup, Kathy, and a bandage for that wound. Then leave her alone for awhile...I think she'll be all right now."

Gaby shuddered as the door closed behind them. She was grateful to be alone at last. Her side throbbed dreadfully. She knew that as soon as she ate the food they were bringing her, the mind-killing drugs in it would drag her back down into that terrible, fuzzy pit of helplessness. Once again, she would have to do anything they told her to. But she had to eat—or die.

"God help me," she whimpered, pulling the blood-stained sheets up over her emaciated body. She wanted to go out astrally travelling again, to escape the pain and the anguish and that awful feeling of hopelessness that kept trying to grab her in its mouth like a circling shark and drag her down and down.... But she knew she had to stay here now and face whatever Nicasia had in store for her.

However, if she could have seen what two of Nicasia's goat-men were offloading this very moment from a cobracraft just arrived from Kalon 22, if she could have known what it was designed to do, Gaby would gladly and unhesitatingly have chosen to die.

My cat a tuning fork?—
amplifier?—telegraph?—
doing secret signal work?

His eyes elliptic tubes:
there's a message in his stare.
I stroke him
but cannot find the dial.
            —May Swenson, "HIS SECRET"

CHAPTER EIGHTEEN

MARIELLE

CAIRO: 7 DECEMBER 2020

Monday, December 7, dawned crisp and clear; by 0900 hours, Eris had been discharged from Dar el Shifa Hospital into the joyful custody of her four companions. There were smiles and hugs and kisses all around and tears and laughter sparkling like fountains in the sunlight. A short and thankfully not too grueling taxi ride to the hotel later, Eris was enjoying her first non-hospital meal in almost two weeks.

Miraculously, she was whole again; there were now no scabs, no scars, no lingering internal pains or twinges. She laughed gleefully as she remembered the amazed and perplexed expressions on the faces of Dr. Bayoumi and the other physicians who had been called in to attend her. Only one doctor, an Israeli neurosurgeon, had fully understood what had happened there. Dr. Benjamin Eliezer, also a student of the Kabbalah, had watched with comprehending fascination the wonders that left his colleagues doubting not only their years of medical experience but their very sanity.

220

Eris' release had the four men in high spirits, especially Chris, who could hardly keep from constantly touching and hugging her, as if to convince himself that she was really here at last, sitting beside him in all her radiant, youthful beauty.

That afternoon, the agents gathered in Avram's hotel room, which had become a sort of unofficial headquarters for the mission. Sumi was making some last-minute adjustments on his "black box," the psychotronic device with which they hoped to move the great stone block inside the Pyramid. André was checking out the supplies and equipment in each of the agent's backpacks, which they would carry with them during the long underground journey. But it was on Raymond Gaunt that the focus of attention fell, for he had brought out the long-anticipated carrying case that contained his ultimate creation and major contribution toward the mission.

André was the only member of the group who had never met the occupant of the case, although he had heard the others mention her. He stopped his checking and came over to watch, joining Chris and Eris on a large worn couch.

Savoring his moment in the limelight, Raymond's eyes sparkled as he reached into the case (which had no air holes, André noted) and lifted out...a big, beautiful golden-furred cat!

"Marielle!" squealed Eris in delight, for this unusual creature was one of her very favorite "animals" in all the world. The cat appeared to be stiff and dead, a wondrous achievement by a master taxidermist, as Raymond set her down gingerly on the floor in front of them. As large as a small dog, she seemed a mixture of Persian, with a long, luxurious coat, and the Mau, or Egyptian cat, with a long, regal nose, large eyes and a faint scarab marking on her forehead between large, sensitive ears.

"*Marielle est une chatte?*" André asked in a puzzled tone. "A stuffed cat?"

Raymond grinned impishly. "'You might say that. But what she's stuffed with is two million dollars worth of the most sophisticated electronic microcircuitry in the world today, pal. Plus other surprises. Let's show 'em, old girl."

Reaching under her heavily furred stomach, Raymond pressed a switch and immediately the cat was no longer an inert work of art. It became a living animal.

Light sprang into the glowing emerald lenses that were her eyes, eyes that functioned as three-dimensional color video cameras, recording everything she saw onto a digital hard drive, for playback on any available computer or TV monitor. Her ears twitched into sudden life, capturing the sounds all about her with the super-sensitive omnidirectional stereo microphones deep inside them, sounds synchronized with the images on disk.

To the delight of her audience, Marielle casually looked at each of them in turn, then yawned a wide pink yawn and began to wash her gorgeous golden fur. A loud contented purr buzzed through the room.

"*Sacré nom*," breathed André in astonishment. "It's a robot cat!"

"Not just a robot, André," said Raymond, scratching his creation behind her ears. Her reaction was so lifelike, so typically feline, that all doubt as to her reality seemed to vanish in the minds of those watching her. She stopped washing and thrust her golden head against Raymond's hand, her eyes closed in ecstasy. Her purring intensified. "Marielle is a sophisticated audiovisual recording device that can go where no camera or cameraman can; her eyes are equipped with infrared lenses to see and record in total darkness; her nuclear-battery-powered brain is an iridium-sponge computer that responds to voice command and can store up to one trillion bits of information, including the contents of her disk, on artificial protein molecules. With her titanium-steel claws and endoskeleton, she can climb up surfaces no real cat can. She's virtually indestructible. Show 'em your stuff, kitty," he whispered into one furry ear. "Up and over."

Eris and Chris grinned in delight. They had seen this trick before, but it always enraptured them. Even Avram stopped to watch as Marielle casually ambled over to the nearest wall, stretched up to her full height as though preparing to sharpen her claws on the florid wallpaper, then sunk glittering steel needles into the plaster and calmly proceeded to walk straight up the wall!

André laughed aloud. "I see it...but I don't believe it," he said.

"Wait," admonished Raymond proudly. "As they say, you ain't seen nothin' yet."

Indeed. For when Marielle reached the ceiling, she paused only briefly, then with none of the trepidation of a real feline, continued her walk across the ceiling and down the opposite wall! When she reached the floor, she immediately resumed her interrupted bath, obviously feeling she had done enough showing off for one afternoon.

Eris laughed and clapped. "Oh, Ray, she's so wonderful! I just love her! I can't believe her either...but she *makes* you believe her!"

André shook his head, clapping Raymond on the back. "Truly a magnificent achievement, *mon ami!* Here I was thinking that Avram was the only genius in this group. Now I see we have two!"

Avram, who had gone back to his own, less dramatic, invention, pretended not to hear that last comment.

"There's only one problem, Ray," said Chris, looking at the feline robot (could you call her a febot? he wondered) thoughtfully. "Remember how last mission that German Shepherd almost chewed her up? Sure, she drove him off with those steel pig-stickers of hers, but all that equipment and documentation is too valuable to take a chance on losing—especially this time. What if she came up against a pack of dogs, or something even tougher? Could she defend herself adequately?"

Gaunt nodded. "Glad you brought that up, Chris. I thought of that too. Something new's been added since you last saw her.

"Marielle," he said, "show the folks your new defense system. Let's pretend that vase is a Doberman and he wants you for breakfast. What would you do?"

Chris marveled at the subtlety of Marielle's programming; she could respond not only to a direct command, but even to a suggestion. Raymond pointed out a large ugly vase sitting on a table across the room. Aureate fur arched on the feline's back as she faced the "enemy" rigidly. Her ears flattened on her head, while her tail began to twitch ominously.

223

Silent relays in her head racked over another kind of lens into her multipurpose eye sockets and suddenly her eyes glowed fiery red, like cauldrons from hell. A zinging hiss stung the waiting air as twin lances of crimson light speared out and blasted the hapless vase into ceramic dust.

"Hey!" yelped Avram. "They'll charge me for that!"

The others laughed, congratulating Ray again on this newest addition to Marielle's arsenal of wonders. Her foe vanquished, the cat's eyes lost their ruddy glow and returned to their normal emerald color. The much-interrupted bath continued.

"Lasers!" Chris exclaimed, impressed. "Perfect, Ray!" I pity anything—animal or human—that tries to mess with this kitty."

"Show André the playback, Ray," said Avram dryly from his corner.

Raymond hesitated for a moment, then said, "Wheel that TV set over here, will you, Chris?"

Chris, who was nearest the set, did so, while trying to hide a big grin. Eris joined him in poorly concealed merriment. They had seen this before. Gaunt called Marielle over, saying, "Okay, beautiful, we're going to show the nice people your playback system. I know it's an indignity, but...."

The wondrous robot feline stretched, yawned, then trotted over to her creator. She turned around and presented her rear to him, raising her fluffy plume of a tail high in the air. Looking somewhat sheepish, Raymond brought out a patch cord, plugged one end of it into the back of the TV set; then he inserted the jack on the other end into the proffered orifice, used for distinctly other purposes on a real cat.

André howled with laughter. "Of course," he managed between convulsions of mirth, "I should have known. You're much too good an engineer to waste a natural output channel!"

Raymond nodded as the others joined in the merriment. "Playback," he told the patient cat, who was attempting to assume an air of nonchalance about the whole procedure. In a few moments, the darkened TV screen lit up with a full-color sound replay of all that had occurred since Marielle had been turned on, including a dizzying feline's-eye-view of the ascent up the wall and across the ceiling.

André shook his head, still grinning. "What can I say? She's terrific!"

"I've always thought that's where most TV programming comes from, anyway," chuckled Avram sardonically.

"Yeah, Ray," put in Chris, "you oughta get this system patented for commercial use. You could call it 'RearVision.'"

"All right, you guys," said Gaunt in mock disgust as he unplugged Marielle from the set. "Can't you see she feels humiliated enough without all the wisecracks?"

Again laughter rippled throughout the room, high spirits providing a much-needed therapy for them all. It had been a long time since they had had anything to laugh about. And they all knew it might be a long time again before humor would touch their lives so freely and openly.

In that day shall there be an altar to the Lord in the midst of the land of Egypt, and a pillar at the border thereof to the Lord.

And it shall be for a sign and for a witness unto the Lord of Hosts in the land of Egypt.

—Isaiah 19:19-20

CHAPTER NINETEEN

KING'S CHAMBER

CAIRO/GIZA PLATEAU: 7-8 DECEMBER 2020

Toward evening, after supplies and equipment had been checked and rechecked, the Pentad had enjoyed one last meal at the Pharonic-Motif Restaurant in the Continental Savoy. By 1830 hours, they were on their way to Giza, heading south on the Corniche el Nil in a rented Volkswagen bus that had seen better days but had the virtue of being both inconspicuous and spacious.

By now, several of the bridges crossing the Nile had been repaired, and fortunately, the Giza Bridge was one of them. They passed over it without mishap, although traffic was heavy and they were forced to wait several times while herds of camels and sheep clogged the way.

Then they were on Ahram Road, which leads directly to the Pyramids. On both sides, vendors were selling sweet corn, watermelons and *qulla*, unglazed earthenware urns used to cool drinking water. The modern buildings gave way rapidly to a more rural community, blighted by a multitude of small shabby nightclubs, dark and deserted because of the diminished tourist trade. The cool benison of evening could not disguise the sad and desolate appearance of the area.

And then the massive geometries of the three Pyramids rose up before them, stark and imposing against the darkening sky, their immense shadows banishing the light from the great areas around them and dyeing those expanses a dense, almost preternatural black. Chris, who was driving, experienced the strange sensation that the Pyramids were somehow receding into the distance as the van approached them, that it would take forever to reach them.

But Eris found her heart quickening, as it always did at the sight of these ancient stone marvels. Behind them, the sun was an amaranthine ball of dying flame rapidly settling beyond the vast wastes of the Libyan Desert, coloring the monuments with a subtle wash of varied hues. As they pulled up at the foot of the Giza Plateau, Eris thought that the great forms looked eerily translucent in the dust and dimming sunlight, almost ghostly, as if they might flicker and disappear into another dimension at any moment.

Chris identified the company to the guards that Colonel Zaid had posted around the area ever since the abortive attempt to destroy the Sphinx; they were expecting them. What few tourists had been here earlier were gone now, and the parking lot was empty; even the ubiquitous camel drivers with their recalcitrant beasts were not in evidence.

A chill desert wind whipped Eris' hair into fulvous froth as she inhaled deeply of the dry evening air. This would be the last fresh air any of them would breathe for who knew how long, she thought. Silently, the five shouldered their backpacks, zipped up their jackets and began the short walk to the base of the Great Pyramid.

Marielle, her fur a golden flame in the evening light, trotted closely at Raymond's heels, tail held high like a proud oriflamme for the group, her supersensitive electronic eyes and ears recording everything.

At the base of the Pyramid, the sheer immensity, the feelings of power and permanence conveyed by the colossal jumble of stones as tall as a forty-story building were almost overwhelming to the little group. Chris and Eris silently shared dark memories of the last time they had stood here, on that moonbright night two months ago, when Death had sent a man mysteriously engulfed in cobalt flames hurtling down these massive stone courses and had made a pass at them as well.

They ascended the rocky north face in silence, heading for the cave-like forced entrance excavated by Caliph Al Mamoun in 820 A.D., after his failure to discover the original entrance, about fifty-five feet up, just a short distance above the forced one. Standing beside the cavernous entrance was an ancient Arab in a dark *galabia* and black skullcap, almost blending into the deep shadows there. He greeted them courteously with the traditional *"Salaam aleikum,"* bowing low and identifying himself as Abdul Afafa, the Keeper of the Pyramid.

"Wi'aleikum is-salaam," replied Chris, then introduced the party as American scientists with official governmental permission to conduct detailed experiments in the interior of the Pyramid. Afafa listened politely, obviously impressed, his hawk-nosed prune of a face bobbing like a fisherman's float on the Nile.

"Ah, yes," the old man replied in Arabic, "I have read of your coming in *El Ahram*. I would be most honored to act as your guide within the Pyramid. I can point out its many wonders to you and—"

As gently as possible, Chris explained that they did not require a guide, but would need him to unlock the gate and turn on the lights for them. Then, after half an hour, he could turn the lights off, lock up and forget about them, as they would be staying inside for quite a long time, several weeks at least. Chris also told the Keeper that no tourists would be allowed inside by the guards until the group had finished their experiments. In order to make up for the loss of revenue the old man would unfortunately experience, Chris presented him with a generous sum in American dollars. The Keeper bobbed and grinned in gap-toothed pleasure as he unlocked the heavy iron gate, switched on the lights and ushered the party into the Pyramid. He chuckled drily when he saw Marielle follow them inside, calling after them, "Did you think to be troubled by rats inside? You will find nothing living, my friends. Only death and silence and the weight of centuries awaits you...."

Eris shivered in the dim rough-hewn passageway. The old man's words disturbed her, but she shrugged them off. She had been inside the Great Pyramid once before with Chris, soon after they had met, but then it had been a light-hearted adventure as he had pointed out all the imposing architectural features of the chambers and passageways to her. Now, the dry cool air seemed oppressive and stagnant, and the ever-present aroma of lamb which permeated the tunnels from the thousands of visitors rubbing the remnants of their hand-eaten meals into the wooden handrails seemed cloying and unpleasant. As they proceeded further into the interior, she began to feel the sheer weight of tons of stone pressing down upon her, as if she were entering the gut of some great lithic beast, dormant for centuries, that might suddenly come to life and swallow her down as a whale swallows plankton in the sea.

Just ahead of her, Chris turned, sensing her discomfort. "You okay, honey?"

She nodded, forcing a smile.

About a hundred feet in, the Mamoun tunnel intersected the Descending Passage from the original secret entrance. At this point, a long, low, narrow corridor called the Ascending Passage angled upward at a steep gradient of slightly over 26 degrees just beyond the granite plugs which had sealed it millennia before and which were still in place.

"The people who built this thing must've been midgets," grumbled Avram as they trudged up the worn wooden slats that covered the slick granite floor. The passage was only 3'11" high and 3'5" wide, forcing them to bend awkwardly as they climbed. Although the corridor was well lit, Eris began to feel waves of acute claustrophobia surge through her.

She fought to restrain the black panic that nibbled at the edges of her mind; she was used to skies and open spaces, not this mole-like tunneling through stony entrails. She gripped the handrails until her knuckles whitened, grinding her teeth painfully into her lip to keep from shrieking aloud. Gamely, she forced herself forward with the others.

It was tough going for all but Marielie, but after what seemed to Eris like hours (really only minutes), they reached the north end of the 129-foot-long passage and entered the imposing Grand Gallery, 157 feet long and 6'9" wide, a continuation of the Ascending Passage at the same angle, but enlarged to a height of 28 feet.

As they stopped to catch their breaths, Chris pointed out a low horizontal passage directly in front of them that disappeared into darkness, leading to the Queen's Chamber. To their right was a black pit called the Well that wound down through the stone and bedrock for over 140 feet, through a cavity called the Grotto, finally intersecting the Descending Passage, which terminated in an unfinished subterranean chamber. In the floor of this chamber, Chris told them, was a deep shaft called the Bottomless Pit.

At the top of the Grand Gallery, they carefully surmounted a large block of stone three feet high, six feet wide, and eight feet thick called the Great Step and entered a cramped horizontal passageway leading to a small room called the Antechamber. The group looked around the twelve-foot-high room briefly, then entered another short, low passageway in the southern wall which led directly into a large room 34 feet long, 17 feet wide and 19 feet high, constructed of polished red granite blocks.

"Well, gang, this is it—the King's Chamber," said Chris, as they emerged into the room. Catching their breaths, the five looked around in awe at this great stone chamber which was their final destination, the heart of *Ta Khut*.

As she wiped dust and perspiration from her forehead, Eris was drawn to the lidless stone coffer at the western end of the chamber, carved out of one block of highly polished chocolate-colored red granite, one corner of which had been badly chipped away over the years by generations of souvenir seekers. Her boots echoed hollowly as she walked over and peered into its mysterious depths, an empty sarcophagus that had never held a pharaoh's body, nor was meant to.

As Eris walked back to rejoin the group, Chris was explaining some of the features of the chamber in hushed tones. Somehow being in this place gave one the same feeling as being in a church or library; loud voices seemed disturbing and undignified.

André felt his skin tingle as he looked around. "How is it we can breathe in here?" he asked Chris. "The air should be much more stale this far inside."

"The builders thought of that," replied Chris, pointing to two nine-inch-square openings in the north and south walls. "They installed a natural air-conditioning system: those holes are two air vents that run through 200 feet of rock, letting in air and keeping the temperature an even 68 degrees all year round."

Shaking his head in amazement, André dug out his camera and began shooting various angles of the chamber, electronic flash pulsing brilliantly like a small blue-white sun. Marielle explored the room in her thorough feline manner, sniffing and recording everything.

The others removed their backpacks and sat down against the cool stone walls, grateful for the chance to rest. As the perspiration cooled on her body, Eris began to feel much better. The constricting hand of claustrophobia that had gripped her before now lifted away and was gone. She felt safe and warm and protected here, as if the room welcomed her.

Then the lights went out, plunging them into a sudden silent darkness as profound as the void between the stars.

Eris laughed nervously, batting back a brief stab of panic that immediately left her for an even deeper sense of peace and security, as though the thick blackness were a blanket she could wrap around herself and hide in.

"Who forgot to pay the light bill?" quipped Raymond.

"That's just our friend the Keeper on the job," said Chris. "Don't anybody panic—I've got a battery-powered lantern in my pack somewhere."

"And I brought candles," added Eris. "Lots of candles...let's use them. It's a softer, mellower light."

Soon flowers of golden effulgence were blooming throughout the dark chamber, sweeping away great patches of blackness and sending shadows to dance in murky corners. Eris positioned four candles of white beeswax on the corners of the coffer and several more on the mysterious "altar stone" on the north wall. In the warm, mellow glow the group relaxed, drinking in the feelings of peace and contentment that pervaded the chamber.

After a while they meditated together, sitting in a five-pointed star before the sarcophagus, linking souls in reverent communion, a Pentad potent with the power of Light, asking for guidance and protection on their mission.

Afterward, they felt recharged, renewed by the powerful energies of the colossal psychic generator in whose heart they were gathered.

"Well, guys, it's 2200," said Eris, unsuccessfully attempting to stifle a yawn. "Our vibes should be high enough so that the Pyramid's rays will be beneficial to us. I can sure use a little extra charge after what I've been through, so I think I'll bunk in the sarcophagus tonight."

Avram nodded. "Good idea—that's the focal point of all the energy that's brought into the chamber."

The five unpacked their bedrolls and stretched out on the cold stone floor. Eris shooed an annoyed Marielle out of the coffer and climbed in.

Goodnights were exchanged and the candles extinguished. Each of the five wondered what tomorrow would bring, as darkness and silence settled down over them like a blind blessing, turning the great stone temple into a kind of isolation chamber, irradiating them with esoteric energies as old as time. Their anxieties and fatigues were swept away from them as they floated on a current of peace and harmony into sleep.

Just before Eris drifted into slumber, she thought she heard, very faintly, a sound like far winds blowing, winds that swirled and coalesced into a chant, a chorus singing, impossibly far away and impossibly sweet, like angel voices. She could not make out any words, but somehow the sounds seemed strangely familiar. She tried to concentrate, but darkness drowned her and she slept.

At 0500 hours, tiny electronic hums from their ring-watches woke the sleepers. Although it was still as dark inside the King's Chamber as it had been the night before, candles once more soon bathed the room in cheerful yellow

232

light. The group dug into their packs and took out the dehydrated rations and water pills that would be their only sustenance for the duration of the mission. These were highly nourishing concentrated foods loaded with vitamins and minerals, made from soy and seaweed extracts. There was also some fresh fruit, but this had to be eaten immediately. The secret of compressing molecules of water into a capsule had been contributed to the PIA by one of the friendly space visitors: when the covering of the capsule dissolved, the compressed molecules expanded instantly into a mouthful of purified water. It took about eight capsules to make a pint.

After breakfast, bodily functions were attended to using the ingenious devices called "baggie-potties" by Raymond, who had invented them. These were durable plastic bags, easily foldable, so that several months' supply took up little space. Attached to the mouth of each bag was a small delayed-action thermite bomb. After you finished, you pressed a button the the gadget, then stepped six feet or more away. After a ten-second delay, the incendiary device detonated, consuming the waste in an extremely hot flame for a few seconds, until nothing was left but ashes. Neat and efficient.

"Just make sure you don't accidentally press the button while you're still using it," warned Avram with a sinister grin.

Next, Avram removed the "black box" from his pack and set it up in front of the east wall of the chamber. It was about the size of a portable radio, with five wires leading from it, to the ends of which were attached copper electrodes. He switched it on and a soft humming filled the dry air.

Yamaharindra had told them that the stone they were to remove had been clairvoyantly seen as the central one, at floor level, so Avram instructed the Psi-Spies to sit in a semicircle behind the machine and focus their attention on that stone. He carefully attached the electrodes to the foreheads of each one; then, after adjusting the controls on the front of the box, sat down and attached the last electrode to his own forehead.

"Okay, people, now just relax," he instructed. "Take a few deep breaths, center yourselves and concentrate on the stone. Imagine it to be as light as a feather, as insubstantial as air. Use all your powers of visualization, just like we did back at PSI-QUARK...let yourselves *see* the stone vibrating itself loose from the ones next to it, see it slowly moving forward out of its place in the wall, *convince* yourselves this is happening. Believe it! Okay...here...we...go!"

Eyes closed, minds linked together and focused on one object—the stone—and one goal—its removal—the five poured the full power of their recently augmented psi talents into the machine, which began to hum at a higher pitch as it strained to translate will into action, amplifying their mental energies and transforming them into psychokinetic force.

For a few minutes, nothing happened. The agents kept their minds focused, pouring out energy, sweat now beading their foreheads.

Then, gradually, after what seemed like hours, a new sound became audible over the now shrill whining of the black box: a slow ponderous rumble, the sound of continents grinding against each other in the depths of midnight seas, a brutal, gritty sound, immensely *heavy*....

The whole chamber seemed to tremble; the five could feel the vibrations in their legs and buttocks. Excitement flared in their minds like incendiary torches, but they refused any distraction, kept the focus of their minds totally on the stone, mentally pulling, pulling, *willing* three tons of granite to move.

Avram opened one eye cautiously, still straining his own natural PK talent to its utmost capacity. He saw the great stone before them trembling, shuddering, spewing out chips of stone along its edges. Then, slowly...with agonizing slug- gishness, it began to move, to creep forward with a hollow grinding sound. Restraining his jubilation, Avram redoubled his efforts, could sense that the others were doing the same. The machine hummed frantically, like a bee gone mad; a sharp electric smell permeated the heavy air. Marielle sat some distance away, totally alert, recording everything, her emerald eyes brilliant in the gloom.

"Okay, group, let's rest now," said Avram hoarsely. Don't want to blow our fuses on this thing. We've got it loose and on its way."

234

Eris was drenched with sweat, her mind spinning from the intensity of her concentration. Grateful for the rest period, she popped a couple of water pills into her mouth, felt them explode into cool, wonderful moisture on her tongue. Stretching luxuriously, she understood for the first time why their training and discipline for this mission had been so strenuous.

Avram switched off the machine, then went over to examine the stone's progress. It had moved out from the wall about two inches.

A chorus of groans greeted his announcement, but their disappointment was tempered with the realization that *they were doing it!* The stone was moving, albeit with frustrating reluctance.

After resting for ten minutes, the Pentad again tackled the tremendous task, this time managing to pull the groaning, protesting granite block out a full foot.

It took them over two hours of alternately concentrating and resting before the massive stone was free of the niche in which it had rested for untold thousands of years. The final effort was to move it out far enough into the chamber to allow the group access to the tunnel behind it.

At last, the time arrived: panting and soaked with sweat, the agents crowded around the black hole that now gaped in the wall like a toothless maw. They were too tired to express their delight verbally; silently they peered into the darkness, trembling with anticipation. Marielle threaded her way sinuously through tree-like legs to the forefront, in order not to miss a single blink of action.

Eris picked up a candle and held it high. As she stooped to enter the cavity left by the stone, she hoped the entire tunnel wasn't going to be this low or they'd all be hunchbacks for the rest of their lives. The golden illumination flared against the stony walls on either side of her—the sides of the neighboring granite blocks—and she could see the deep horizontal scoring created by the slow, torturous emergence of the stone that once had rested where she now stood. She stepped further in, thrusting the candle ahead of her and feeling as Howard Carter must have felt, almost a hundred years ago, trembling on the verge of discovering the wonders of Tutankhamen's tomb....

The dancing radiance revealed—another stone wall! Eris' mouth fell open in dismay—there was no passage! Directly in front of her was only the blank mocking face of a limestone block almost exactly like the granite one they had just removed.

Prepare to go mad.
Prepare to break
split along cracks
inhabit the darks of your eyes
inhabit the whites.
        —*P. K. Page, "PREPARATION"*

CHAPTER TWENTY

GABRIELLE'S ORDEAL

CAIRO: 8-15 DECEMBER 2020

In a dim bedroom on the north side of Zeinhom Manor, Gabrielle lay in her stained and rumpled bed and stared at the ceiling. There was a long, thin crack across it that zigzagged from one side to the other, reminding her of a map of the Nile as it meandered down the length of Egypt. She imagined herself free of her prison and sailing down the sparkling blue waters of that great river in a *felucca*, just she and André alone under the clean, clear sky....

She smiled. She felt terribly weak, hardly able to move, but her mind was the clearest it had been in many days...weeks, perhaps. She had no idea how long she had been here. It seemed like forever. But ever since that wonderful night when Eris had come to her in astral form and taken her to the hospital to see André and the others, her spirits had soared. Since then, she had made a decision. Realizing that the food they brought her every day was drugged, Gaby had decided to fast for as long as she could, drinking only liquids—water and the occasional fruit juices she received. Experimentation had assured her that they didn't bother doping the liquids—only the solid food. So,

237

meal after meal, Gaby dumped the uneaten food down the toilet, and little by little, her head began to clear and her will began to return to her control.

Now, although she was so weak and thin she could barely make it to the bathroom, she had formulated a desperate plan. She prayed for the courage and strength to pull it off. Fearful that Gaby might kill herself, Nicasia had left her no razorblades or other sharp objects, but Gaby's mind was now working with a least some of its former agility: she had unscrewed the light bulb from one of the lamps in the bedroom and broken it in the sink. Then, saving one large shard of glass, she had ground up the others small enough to be washed down the drain. Next, after unplugging the lamp's power cord from the wall socket, she had managed to rip the cord loose from the base of the lamp, and by scraping the ends with the shard of glass from the light bulb, had exposed the bare copper wires for about two inches. Then, careful to keep the two exposed ends apart, she had plugged the other end of the cord back into the wall socket. Grasping it firmly around the still-insulated portion, Gaby had hidden the ends under the bedcovers.

Now all she had to do was wait.

As she waited, she drifted in and out of sleep, dozing fitfully, her exhausted body desperately attempting to replenish the energy being funneled away each day like water down a drain.

After several minutes—or was it hours?—her senses bolted to alertness as she heard the familiar metallic rattle of a key in the lock. Feigning sleep, she lay with her eyes closed, listening carefully to determine who was entering.

It was Tina. Gaby knew she would be bringing her food, food loaded with the mind-killing drug they all thought she was still ingesting.

"Gaby," Tina called softly, now standing by the side of the bed. Good, thought Gaby, her heart pounding hard, hold that pose. Summoning every ounce of courage and strength left in her wasted body, she swept back the covers and in the same movement rammed the two exposed ends of the live power cord against the metal bed tray Tina was carrying. There was a loud spitting pop and a flash of blue flame. Tina

238

shrieked and was hurled backward against the wall, the tray and several bowls of food crashing to the floor with a sound Gaby was sure could be heard in Alexandria.

She leaped out of bed and with her last remaining reserves of strength, grabbed the heavy metal tray and brought it down with all her might on Tina's head before the stunned girl could regain her senses. Tina slumped to the floor with a grunt and a sigh, a small rivulet of blood trickling down her dead-white forehead.

Gaby lay sprawled on the floor beside her, naked and sweating, panting like an emphysema victim, exhausted by this sudden explosion of activity. She couldn't believe her desperate ruse had worked. But what good would it do her if she couldn't get up now? Surely Tina wouldn't be unconscious very long. If she could only make it out of here before....

After a few minutes, Gaby painfully pulled herself to her feet, still breathing like a runner. The circular wound under her breast was stinging like fire from her exertions. Like a person moving under water, she slow-motioned Tina out of her sweater and skirt and put them on.

She peered out into the dim hallway; all clear. Her room was situated three doors from one end of the hall; she could see sunlight pouring in through a window there. She smiled to see it; the only window in her bedroom was barred and shuttered closed from the outside. She had not seen the sun in...how long?

After locking Tina in the bedroom, Gaby cautiously dragged herself over to the window and peered out. The sun felt warm and wonderful on her face. She noticed that this window was not barred, but she was on the third floor. No way of escape here. Behind her was a stairway, leading down into gloom. Could she handle it in her weakened state? She had to try. So far she had neither seen nor heard a trace of anyone else in this part of the house. Steeling her courage, she grasped the handrail and began to inch her way down the stairs.

She was almost to the bottom when the first convulsion hit her. As sudden as thought, a red-hot knife seemed to drive itself into her skull, directly between the eyes. An invisible steel vise suddenly clamped her temples, squeezing with unbearable pressure. Multicolored shards of light exploded behind her eyes like fireworks, and she heard a distant scream shatter the dim quiet of the house. She could not know it was her own. She tumbled down the few remaining steps heavily, arms and legs thrashing and trembling. At the bottom of the stairs she writhed like an epileptic for several minutes, heels drumming the floor, bloody froth bubbling at the corners of her mouth, back arched like a gymnast's. Finally she subsided with a deep groan into stillness. The trembling stopped and darkness swept down over her, bringing merciful oblivion.

In another room, a floor below, Nicasia flicked a switch on the console of a strange machine mounted on a pedestal and sat back, intently watching a small viewscreen built into it. The pathetic little figure of Gabrielle on the screen lay still, a crumpled rag doll at the foot of the stairway. Close about her inert form a pale luminescence flickered, a blue-gray radiance only dimly visible on the screen and totally invisible to the unaided human eye. Nicasia nodded thoughtfully, a half-smile dancing across her lips. Speaking to the two figures standing behind her, she said, "It works very well, doesn't it? And that was only the mildest dose...150 cps. It'll be interesting to see the results of say...twice that frequency."

The taller of the two goat-headed humanoids she had addressed replied in a bleating parody of human speech, "You must use care with the Aura Scrambler, O Queen of Darkness. The human aura is a delicate thing. Our experiments with kidnapped human subjects have shown that madness can quickly result from overexposure to the rays from this machine."

Nicasia swiveled in her chair to face him. "Yes, Caprix, you're right, I don't want to get carried away with my new toy here. I'll go slowly...I don't want to turn her into a raving lunatic. I have a much better use for her. I want just enough power to put her completely under my control once and for all and keep her there. My own private zombie."

Nicasia's face hardened as she turned back to the screen. "Those silly twits—my girls were supposed to be monitoring

240

Gaby's condition, draining off her energy and drugging her every day. Apparently, she figured out some way to beat the drug and outwit them; she's more resourceful than I've given her credit for. That's three times I've underestimated her. I won't do it again. Well, I won't have to depend on drugs now. You can tell the techno-priests that I am well pleased with this instrument."

The two goat-men bowed in unison, but Nicasia ignored them. She swiveled the machine on its pedestal, pointing it up and over toward Gaby's bedroom on the third floor. It resembled an obscene parody of a television camera, one that could see through solid wood and masonry into any room in the house, to target victims for the mind-destroying radiation it could beam into their brains with pinpoint accuracy.

The images on the monitor blurred as the instrument swish-panned over, then stopped, zooming in on the still figure of Tina, sprawled on the floor of Gaby's bedroom, surrounded by broken dishes and spilled food. A small puddle of blood had collected beneath her head and was soaking into the thick white rug.

"Stupid little bitch," snarled Nicasia. "How the hell could a drugged, weakened girl manage to knock her out, get out of a locked bedroom and halfway down the stairs?"

Swinging the machine back until Gaby was again centered in the monitor screen, Nicasia issued curt orders to the goat-men: "Caprix, go get Gaby and return her to her room. Let her sleep off this first treatment. I'll give her another dose before bedtime. Anthrix, you go with him—take Tina to the infirmary and have them take a look at her. Then bring her to me. I'll have a few things to say to *that* young lady!"

"Yes, O Queen," the aliens bleated in unison, backing out of her presence clumsily.

Nicasia watched the monitor until she saw the goat-man scoop Gaby's limp body up like a sack of dirty laundry and clump upstairs with her. Then she switched it off and leaned back in her chair, idly running her fingers over the cool metal surface of the frightful instrument.

The Aura Scrambler would prove to be much more efficient than drugs and work much faster, too. Time was an important factor now that the American agents had entered the

241

Pyramid. She had intended to start these treatments on Gaby sooner, but business matters in Canada had claimed her full attention for a few days. But now she could begin the task of harnessing her stepdaughter to her will, completely and irreversably, through the use of this marvelous machine of mental domination.

And during the nightmarish days and nights that followed, Gabrielle, her brief, bright hope of escape destroyed utterly, writhed and spasmed and screamed in agony as wave after wave of radiation was beamed at her in steadily increasing doses, bombarding her diminishing aura and inundating her tortured brain with invisible rays of mental disintegration and spiritual negation. In between these epileptic-like attacks, she floated in a near-comatose state of will-lessness, tormented by dreams of her father's fiery body trying to reach her, but always separated from her by a huge dark chasm, in which lurked some enormous and unspeakable *thing*, waiting to ensnare her like a spider waiting for prey.

She became too weak even to feed herself, so periodically they came and force-fed her, supplementing the now drug-free food with vitamin and mineral additives, as they did not want her to become so enervated as to be totally helpless. Day after day, Nicasia and her vampire daughters restored some measure of Gaby's physical strength as they sapped the last dregs of her mind and will.

She had no thoughts left that were her own; she had forgotten how to pray, or even whom to pray to. She was given simple but degrading tasks to perform as she regained some of her strength, things that she would never do of her own free will. Kathy and her sisters continued to visit her periodically, taking only carefully regulated amounts of energy now and subjecting her to cruel and obscene indignities to which she could no longer object.

Finally the day arrived when even the pale, thin, bluegray aura that had flickered wanly about Gaby was gone, distorted and refracted beyond even the supersensitive vision of the auric camera. The frequency indicator on the machine now displayed "1,000 cps." in cold electric numerals. Nicasia ordered Gaby washed and dressed and brought before her.

The thing that at last stood before her, the gaunt, pathetic shadow of what had once been a vibrant and beautiful young girl, almost shocked even Nicasia. But she was pleased by what she saw. Eyes that had once shone with the clear azure brillance of a summer morning were now glazed and unfocused, shards of pale blue glass sunk deeply into dark-ringed sockets. Her left eye and the corners of the thin colorless razor-slash of her mouth twitched almost constantly; from time to time, fits of uncontrollable shivering swept over her body as though she were standing naked in snow and ice. Her skin was sheet-pale and parchment-thin, stretched over cheekbones like knife blades. They had washed and cut her once luxuriant chestnut curls, but they now hung stringy and lifeless, and Nicasia noted with interest a two-inch streak of white that had appeared over her left temple. Her body was like that of a concentration-camp inmate; wraith-thin arms flopped like those of a marionette as she moved in a hesitant, slumping shuffle over to a chair next to Nicasia and sat down at her stepmother's command.

Nicasia smiled her most charming smile. "Do you know who you are?" she asked the girl gently.

"Yes...." came the hoarse, hesitant answer.

"What is your name, then?"

"Gabrielle...Bane." Nicasia could see her reaching, trying desperately to recall a name almost lost in the shambles of her mind.

"That's right, darling. Now, do you know who I am?"

"Yes."

"Who am I?"

"Nicasia...my...stepmother."

"That's right, and I've been taking care of you. You've been very, very sick for a long time. But now you're finally recovering. You must do everything I tell you if you want to get well and see your friends again. You know that, don't you?"

"Yes."

"And you'll do anything I ask you to do, won't you?"

"Yes."

243

"Good girl. Because if you do, I promise you won't have any more of those terrible headaches and convulsions you've been having. Do you understand?"

Gaby's pale face twitched, her skeletal hands clenched tightly, as she remembered the pain, the horror....

"Yes," she answered at last in a voice as weak as a dying man's.

"Fine. Now in a few days, when you're feeling a little stronger, I'm going to send you to where your friends are waiting for you. You'll like that, won't you?"

A tiny spark of something flashed in the lusterless eyes. An almost-smile flickered at the corners of Gaby's thin lips. "Oh, yes."

Nicasia leaned close to the girl, mesmerizing golden eyes boring into Gaby's skull like augers. "Good. Now listen carefully, Gaby. Here is what I want you to do..."

We do not know. But they know.
The stones know.
And they remember.
Airships were flying.
Came pouring a liquid fire.
Came flashing
The spark of life and death.
By the might of spirit
Stony masses ascended.
Scriptures guarded wise secrets.
And again all is revealed.
—Nicholas Roerich

CHAPTER TWENTY-ONE

BETWEEN THE SPHINX & THE RIVER

GIZA PLATEAU: 8 DECEMBER 2020

"No tunnel?" Avram's eyes were wide with shock and bafflement. "You're kidding!"

Eris shook her head. "Nothing but another block of stone, Av."

"You're *not* kidding," said Avram, looking like a man who's just been told his house has burned down.

"Honey, are you sure?" asked Chris, grabbing a candle and heading into the dark cavity. "Maybe there's a hidden lever or...or something."

"But we *know* there's a tunnel—several of us saw it clairvoyantly," said André in dismay. "I saw it myself. And the stone. It looked exactly like the one we moved."

"Yeah, but they all look pretty much the same," said Raymond. "Maybe it wasn't the floor-level stone, maybe the next one up—"

"*Non, non,* we all agreed: it was a center floor-level stone! And right behind it began a long, dark tunnel!"

"Then it *has* to be this one!" said Avram, rubbing his beard in agitation. "This is the east wall—the Nile's that way—and the quotation clearly states 'between the Sphinx and the river.' So the tunnel's got to be in this wall!"

Chris emerged from the hole, shaking his head. "I can't understand it. Nothing. Just another block of stone, like Eris said."

Eris put her hand on André's arm. "André...you say you saw the tunnel clairvoyantly before. Can you see it now? Try to image it for us again, okay?"

"Sure," he replied, sitting down in front of the wall and closing his eyes.

Eris motioned for the rest to be quiet as André tried to reach out with his psychic vision and "see" the tunnel that supposedly lay behind the ancient stone.

After a few long minutes, André shook his head in defeat, opened his eyes and got to his feet. "Nothing. I scanned the entire wall from side to side and top to bottom, all the way out into the sunshine. I could see nothing but limestone blocks."

Chris snorted in disgust. "Shit! I just can't believe that you and the others back at PSI-QUARK all saw something that wasn't there. And I also can't believe that Cayce's information was wrong."

Raymond scratched his moustache. "So where does that leave us?"

Suddenly a thought struck Eris like a slap. She began burrowing frantically through her backpack like a badger digging into a hillside. "Wait, you guys!" she exclaimed. "I've got an idea...." In a few moments she had what she was looking for: a wrinkled map of Egypt, which she carefully unfolded and spread out on the stone floor. "Look, fellas. Here's Giza, the Pyramid...and here's the Nile. Okay. We're assuming the tunnel leads from one toward the other, linking

246

up with the entrance in the Sphinx's paw on the way. And somewhere in the middle is Ka-Ren. Right?"

A chorus of solemn nods answered her.

"Well, what if Cayce wanted to be a little vague about his information, without actually lying?"

Avram looked puzzled. "What do you mean?"

"Look down here." Eris ran her finger down the blue ribbon on the map indicating the Nile's course to a region known as Faiyum, about sixty miles southwest of Giza. "This oasis, near Lake Qarun here, is one of the richest agricultural areas in Egypt. Why? Because it's irrigated by a man-made waterway called *Bahr Youssef,* Joseph's Canal, built during the Twelfth Dynasty, that forks off from a branch of the Nile." Her fingernail tapped a smaller blue line on the map.

"So?" urged Raymond.

"So...Edgar Cayce didn't say 'between the Sphinx and the *Nile*'...his exact words were, 'between the Sphinx and the river.' *But*...he didn't say for certain which river! Nor did he specify how far it was to that river!"

Chris' face brightened. "Then you think he meant this canal—an artificial river—instead of the Nile? God almighty, Eris, you might have something here!"

Avram's face was cloudy. "I don't know...a canal's not really a river. To me, the way he said 'the river' sounded like he definitely meant the Nile. Everyone knows the Nile's the only real river in Egypt."

"Well, he couldn't say 'canal,'" said Eris, "because then people would confuse it with the Suez Canal. Besides," she added, "we could both be right, Av. Look at this: If you draw a straight line from the right paw of the Sphinx to El Faiyum, you cross the canal, which after all, carries water in from the Nile, so in a sense could be considered part of the Nile. Then, if you extend the line farther, it eventually intersects the Nile itself as it curves to the west, down here. See? We always *assumed* that the shortest distance—straight east to the Nile from the front of the Sphinx—was what Cayce meant. But that was only our assumption! Ka-Ren could be buried anywhere along this line to the south and still be 'between the Sphinx and the river,' whether that river is the Nile or the canal. See?"

"Hmmm...I must admit you've got a point, Eris. Damn swift thinking." Avram scratched his beard thoughtfully. "And you feel that the tunnel from the Pyramid links up with the tunnel from the Sphinx, somewhere along the way?"

"Right. And theoretically, Ka-Ren could be located anywhere along that route, after that intersection."

"Ouch!" exclaimed Raymond in dismay. "That sure would put it a lot farther away then we bargained for. It's almost sixty miles to El Faiyum from here, and a lot farther on to the Nile. "We've been thinking in terms of something less than six miles. Well, I guess we've got enough rations to last us, if we don't pig out."

"Sure we do, Ray," Eris assured him. "Don't worry—nobody's going to pig out on the stuff we've got to eat." Then, turning her cheerful smile back to Avram, "What do you say, Av? My idea's worth a try, isn't it?"

"At this point, anything's worth a try. If your theory's correct, Eris, it'd mean the tunnel entrance is probably behind the south wall." Avram walked over to the wall and surveyed it, hands on hips. "Guess what, people—we've got to do it all over again!" He kicked the central granite block with his boot, an evil grin on his face. "This time we've got to pull out *this* baby!" It looked even larger and heavier than the previous stone.

"Before we do anything, though, let's be sure," said Eris. "André...try this wall. See if you can see anything behind it, will you?"

André nodded and seated himself in the lotus position before the south wall. He closed his eyes and once again brought his concentration to focus upon what lay behind the huge granite block. His far vision probed out, searching through solid stone, hunting for any kind of dark empty space, any opening....

Four people forgot to breathe as they watched their companion's face. Silence hung in the arid air like incense.

Then, a smile and a single soft word: "*Voilà!*" André opened his eyes and looked up at his anxious friends. "Yes. It is there. Behind the central stone."

248

Whoops of joy shattered the silence as André got to his feet. "You were right, *chérie*," he said to a delighted Eris. "It's a long, dark tunnel...the same one I saw before."

Chris crushed Eris to him in an ursine hug. "Sweetheart, you're a flaming genius! Boy, they sure knew what they were doing when the put you in charge of us bozos!"

Soon the five were again mind-linked with one another and the humming phychotronic generator. Once more they directed the full force of their powerful psi energies toward a huge block of red granite, clearly visualizing it as light, lighter, weightless, moving forward out of its ancient socket.

And, as before, slowly, grumbling and shuddering in gritty lithic protest, it came, inch by precious inch, foot by foot, until at last it rumbled free of the grip of its fellows, looking like a giant child's toy carelessly left in the middle of a playroom floor. Piles of rock dust and chips of stone littered the floorstones around it.

The five lay back, exhausted, their heads spinning from the tremendous mental effort, twice the amount they had thought would be necessary. For a few minutes, no one spoke. Finally, Raymond staggered to his feet, petting the purring robot feline who was rubbing against his legs, having again dutifully documented the entire operation. "All I can say is," he said with a weak grin, "that damn tunnel better be here this time, or cat and I are packing up and heading back to Ibiza. Man, I don't wanna have to do this again!"

The others slowly got to their feet and approached the yawning black cavity behind the great stone. This time Chris was the first to enter and inspect the space. His voice came back to them vibrant with triumph.

"You won't have to, Ray! Folks—we've got ourselves a tunnel!" Suddenly reinvigorated by the good news, they crowded around the dark opening, laughing and talking animatedly. The flickering candlelight penetrated only a short way into the blackness of the tunnel, revealing smoothly finished stone walls and ceiling and a steeply descending floor, more roughly hewn to afford adequate footing. The air was musty and stagnant, the smell of time itself suspended in stone for uncounted centuries. The passageway was disappointingly small: it was only about five feet high, slightly

249

higher than the Ascending Passage into the Pyramid, but low enough so that they would still have to stoop uncomfortably to negotiate it. In addition, the tunnel was only about three feet wide, so they would have to travel single file.

"Okay!" exclaimed Eris in delight. "Before we plunge into this lovely little hole in the wall, I'm going to contact the President and fill him in on the good news. While I'm doing that, why don't you guys break out the Headlights—we're going to need a lot more than candles down there!"

The four men began digging into their backpacks while Eris went over to the coffer, sat down on the rim, closed her eyes and concentrated on the small golden medallion beneath her left breast. As she felt it begin to grow warm, she mentally sent out a call, focusing on the occult code number that unlocked President Warren's mental frequency.

PSINET 12 CALLING 21. PSINET 12 CALLING 21.

Aware of the seven-hour time distance between Egypt and Washington, Eris knew it would be about 2030 hours there. She hoped she wouldn't catch the President in the middle of a big social function or a late dinner or—

The response came almost immediately, warm and cheerful.

PSINET 21 HERE. WONDERFUL TO HEAR FROM YOU, ER—12! The President chuckled mentally. OOPS! ALMOST FORGOT OUR "NO NAMES" RULE. HOW ARE YOU, 12?

TERRIFIC, FINALLY. BUT IT WAS HELL ON WHEELS THERE FOR A WHILE. THANKS FOR YOUR HELP...AND ALL THE OTHERS....

DON'T MENTION IT. WE NEVER DOUBTED YOU'D PULL THROUGH. WHERE ARE YOU NOW?

WE'RE IN THE KING'S CHAMBER. WE'VE MOVED THE STONE AND DISCOVERED THE TUNNEL ENTRANCE, ALTHOUGH WE HAD A FALSE START.

TELL YAMA IT'S LOCATED IN THE SOUTH WALL, NOT THE EAST. WE'LL BE ENTERING THE PASSAGEWAY IN JUST A FEW MINUTES. WISH US LUCK.

YOU KNOW IT—ALL THE LUCK IN THE WORLD! BY THE WAY, HAVE YOU HEARD ANYTHING FROM GABY?

Eris quickly recounted her astral visit with the girl, but sadly reported that she had heard nothing since. She could sense Warren's spirits take a nosedive at this information, but he tried to pull them back up immediately as Eris changed the subject.

LISTEN, THE OTHERS ARE ALL WIRED TO GO. THEY ALL SEND THEIR LOVE, ESPECIALLY MARIELLE. GIVE OURS TO EVERYBODY, WILL YOU?

SURE WILL. KEEP UP THE GOOD WORK—YOU'RE ALL DOING A TERRIFIC JOB. THE LID'S STILL ON BACK HERE. GOD GO WITH YOU.

As the President's strong mental presence faded from her mind, Eris thought, He's holding his end together—now it's up to us. She joined the others and related the gist of the conversation, watching with amusement as André and Marielle carefully documented the tunnel entrance with stills and video.

Soon they had all donned the leather-lined metal head-bands called "Headlights" that had been devised by the PIA scientists for their journey through dark underground passageways. On the right side of the band, connected to the right temple by a contact electrode, was a high-intensity quartz lamp, capable of brilliant illumination for a long distance ahead; on the left side, also connected by an electrode to the temple, was an extremely powerful high-energy laser which could be utilized either as a weapon or as a means of cutting through obstructions, including stone and metal.

251

Both devices were powered by tiny nuclear batteries like the ones inside Marielie, but their operation was a truly innovative triumph of paraphysics—a melding of mind and machine developed by Avram and several other scientists: both the light and the laser were controlled by thought alone. To turn on the lamp, the user had only to visualize the color white in his mind and mentally say the word "on." This silent command, conveyed from the brain through the electrode to the lamp's microcircuitry, activated the light, which would remain on until the operator visualized the white color again and thought the word "off." Similarly, the laser was operated by thinking of the color red and the command "on." The laser would continue to emit powerful pulses of coherent light until similarly commanded to cease.

Now they were ready at last. The dazzling blue-white illumination from the lamp sides of the Headlights bathed the King's Chamber in brilliant artificial daylight. Eris led the way into the steep, narrow passageway; Chris came next, followed by André and Avram. Ray and Marielle brought up the rear.

After about half an hour, they could feel the atmosphere growing damp and musty. Chris told them that they had passed through the body of the Pyramid and were now underground, where the rising water table was increasing the humidity. But they could see no traces of water in the tunnel; as the clairvoyants had predicted, this passage was still dry. It saddened Eris to think of all the other ancient subterranean passages, channels and temples linking the Pyramid with the Sphinx being flooded by the relentless incursion of underground water after so many centuries of remaining intact.

As the passageway grew damper, she could see large whitish patches of niter and encrustations of salt blanching the stone walls as though the tunnel itself were becoming blighted and leprous. The cold, heavy air now stank of mold.

There was little conversation among the five as they descended into the seemingly endless depths. They were forced to watch their footing carefully, for a misstep might send them all tumbling down into darkness.

Finally, Eris' light illuminated something. "Hey! I see a wall or a door ahead, fellas!" she cried, hurrying forward as fast as she could over the steep, stony floor. About twenty feet farther, the tunnel leveled out, much to the party's relief. At the same time, they noticed that the ceiling sloped sharply upward until they could stand erect with several feet to spare. As they rubbed cramped neck and back muscles gratefully, they examined the object ahead of them.

It appeared to be a door, constructed not of stone, but of metal, perhaps bronze. Its patina was dull, but it was not corroded or tarnished anywhere on its surface, which was decorated with hieroglyphics. Chris examined them closely without touching them. At length he ventured a translation to the anxious group:

"It seems to be similar to texts found in *The Book of the Dead*. It says, 'Homage to thee, O thou Lord of Brightness, Governor of the Temple of the Hidden Things, Prince of the light and of the thick darkness. I have come unto thee, bringing the bright flame of my heart as a gift for thee. I am shining, I am pure. All transgressions have been washed from me. Give unto me my mouth that I may speak the words of power unto thee, that thou shalt know me in my coming. I guide my heart at its season of flame and of night. Thou art the way and I would enter thy abode of life and be not repulsed.'"

"That's beautiful," said Eris, "like a prayer requesting entrance into the underworld. Do you see any way to open the door, Chris?"

Chris examined the door closely but could find nothing. The metal surface was smooth and unexpectedly warm to the touch. His fingers tingled slightly as though there were a minute electric current running through the metal.

"Time to use our heads," he said. "I've got a feeling this door is keyed to open only when someone who is as the prayer describes recites it. Some of these lines can be taken quite literally, I think: 'Give unto me my mouth that I may speak the words of power unto thee' may mean exactly that. If we assume our vibes are high enough to qualify us for entrance, then if we recite the prayer together, that may trigger some kind of sonic key which will open the door."

"Like the old 'Open, Sesame' bit in the Arabian Nights, eh?" said André, snapping several shots of the door. "Well, why not? Makes as much sense as anything else so far."

"Let's try it," agreed Eris excitedly.

Together they stilled their minds, concentrating on the sealed entrance before them, asking for guidance and grace, visualizing the door swinging open. Following Chris' lead, they recited the ancient prayer aloud in unison, then stood waiting silently.

Nothing happened.

"Hmm. Any suggestions?" asked Chris, disappointment thick in his voice.

"Maybe there are some unknown words of power we have to speak, as well," ventured Avram. "Or maybe we're not 'pure and shining' enough for the door."

"No, somehow I don't think it's that," said Eris thoughtfully. "I think our vibrations are okay. It's more like—"

Suddenly Chris slapped his hand violently against his forehead, as though he had been attached by a giant mosquito. "Dear God!" he yelped. "What an ass I've been!"

"Chris! What is it?" Eris was next to him in an instant, reaching for his arm. "You all right?"

He grinned at her like a demented Cheshire cat. "All right? Hell, no, sweetheart, I've been all wrong! I know why the door won't respond to our recitation! It can't understand us! *It doesn't know English!* How could it? This thing was programmed and inscribed by ancient Egyptians or Altanteans, thousands of years before anyone spoke a syllable of English, for God's sake!"

"Of course!" roared Avram excitedly. "You've got it, Chris! That has to be it!"

As the others scrambled to their feet, Raymond said, "Er...I hate to be a wet blanket, but...does anyone here speak hieroglyphic?"

Everyone looked at Chris, who replied, "I think I know enough to get through this inscription—it's pretty simple—although I'm much more used to translating hieroglyphics into English. And I can't be sure I'll be pronouncing the words the way they were actually pronounced, but it'll probably be close enough. Let me see now...."

The others maintained a taut silence as Chris began to recite the inscription in the sonorous, guttural tones of a language dead for thousands of years. It was an eerie experience, deep beneath the sands of the eternal desert, as if time itself had rolled back like a great wave, revealing the bare drowned bones of the distant past.

Chris finished the recitation and silence rushed in to surround them. Breathlessly, they waited for any sound, any movement. Then....

A low, grating sound began to emanate from the door, a hollow, gritty rumble that gradually got louder. Five people forgot to breathe. The massive door began to move, very slowly, rising upward into a stone socket above it. Its metal sides squealed in protest at being disturbed for the first time in over ten thousand years.

When the door was fully open, the rumbling stopped. Silence again settled upon the little group, but only for an instant. A chorus of ear-shattering cheers went up. They had passed their first real test.

Now they stared in fascination at what lay beyond the door. A large high chamber was revealed, about twenty feet wide, thirty feet long, and with an arched roof about twenty-five feet at its greatest height. It was empty, the smooth stone walls bare of any decoration. The only distinguishing feature was an odd round pit, about eight feet in diameter, in the center of the floor. Directly opposite them, in the facing wall, was another metal door identical to the one they had just opened, except that there were no hieroglyphics on its surface.

Before they could concern themselves with the problem of opening this new door, a hollow rumbling sound emanating from the pit stopped them cold. It seemed to increase in volume as they listened, as though something were rising up out of the black depths of that strange circular hole in the floor.

Eris started toward the pit, anxious to shine her lamp down into it, but something stopped her. She felt a chill begin to jitter deep in her bones.

They all felt that something critical was about to happen; André had his camera poised in readiness; Marielle's

255

eyes glowed like green furnaces as she crouched near Raymond's feet, her tail twitching nervously.

The moment they saw what rose up out of the pit, they knew exactly what it was.

"Oh, shit," said Chris in a low, tight voice."The stone Sentinel—the *Aner-sa* Yama warned us about. Watch yourselves, folks...."

A bulky statue about ten feet tall, made of gleaming black agate and seated on a marble throne, was thrust upward into the chamber atop a stone cylinder that fit flush inside the shaft of the pit. The cylinder stopped when it reached the level of the floor, and the rumbling of some distant mechanism far below died away.

The statue was awesome and ominous in the harsh light of their lamps; it wore the striped golden headdress of Egyptian royalty and a golden kilt about its loins, apparently garments of pure beaten gold. Its eyes were made of milky crystal and in its right hand was a long spear of some crystalline substance. Imbedded within the ebony stone of its body were waves, ripples, swirls of different hues, clouds, points of misty light glowing dimly. As the five gazed at this incredible dark colossus, they had the impression of staring into the deeps of space, of an infinite vista of stars, galaxies and nebulae frozen forever in a man-shaped void.

They watched it, rooted in place, nerves singing with tension and apprehension, waiting for it to move or threaten them in some way.

But nothing happened. Gradually they began to relax. André took several pictures of the statue, and Marielle prowled around its perimeter, recording a complete 360-degree view of it.

Eris realized that she was soaked with sweat. "It's the thing I saw in my dream," she whispered hoarsely to Chris. "The night we made love...I dreamt of this very statue, Chris. Only it was alive then, and it tried to kill me! Then I woke up."

"That was only a dream, honey," he whispered reassuringly to her. "This thing is made out of stone—it can't move." Then to the others he said, "The mechanism to raise this Sentinel into the chamber was undoubtedly triggered by

256

opening the door, but it looks like only a statue. Maybe it's become inactive after so long a time...or maybe the people who made it hoped its mere presence would frighten off anyone who saw it."

"I hope you're right," Raymond said. "As I recall, it's supposed to make a 'whispering sound' that causes unconsciousness and death. Anybody hear anything?"

"No," said Eris, unable to take her eyes from the sinister eidolon gazing at them with sightless crystal eyes. "Maybe it thinks we're okay since we managed to figure out how to open the door. Maybe it's only set to attack those with low or negative vibrations, if they should somehow manage to blow up the door or something and force their way in."

"Maybe," said Avram, rubbing his beard nervously, "but we can't assume that. It may be activated by proximity. I suggest we move cautiously around it, keeping as far away as possible, and head for that other door."

Eris nodded assent and the five agents began to move slowly around the midnight giant, keeping close to the right-hand wall. Gradually, Eris began to lose some of her apprehension. Evidently her dream had been only that, this time—a dream, not a prophetic warning. Just an overactive imagination, impressed by Yama's warning account of the *Aner-sa* and stimulated by the glorious night of lovemaking with Chris. She smiled secretly as she recalled the warmth and wonder of that night.

Then they were assembled before the exit door to the chamber. The stone image remained motionless, its great dark back turned indifferently toward them as if silently refusing to acknowledge their existence.

"Next problem, ladies and gentlemen," said Chris. "How do we open *this* door, which has no inscription? Any ideas?"

"Well," ventured Eris, "maybe if we just touch the door, the contact will—"

As she spoke, she touched the metal surface. The result was not what she expected. Although there was no visible reaction from the door, even before she could finish her sentence, a sudden low humming filled the chamber like a swarm of deadly bees. It seemed to stab deep within her brain like a million tiny needles. Then she heard another

257

sound, even more sinister than the terrible buzzing: a hollow grating rumble from behind them. Clutching their heads in agony, they turned to see the huge black statue swiveling on its pedestal to face them, no longer lifeless and distant. Now its crystal eyes were alight, incandescent with emerald flame, and the lance in its hand now pulsed and glowed ominously with a brilliant bluish-white radiance. The hazy clouds and points of colored light within the statue's agate body were now swirling and pulsing in a sluggish rhythm suggestive of some bizarre life process totally alien to humanity.

Eris felt terror clamber up her spine like a mad monkey; this was her nightmare coming true! The thing *was* alive after all! Contact with the door had triggered it, energized it into terrible and dangerous activity! The awful humming continued to emanate from the Sentinel, dropping down toward inaudibility as it increased in intensity. Eris felt as though her head were shaking itself apart; she had a vision of all their heads exploding like pumpkins blasted by a shotgun if this hellish vibration were not stopped.

Then, with a movement as unexpected as it was swift, the colossus lifted its lucent crystalline spear into the air and hurled it directly toward Eris' unprotected breast!

She had time for a flash of numbing horror as once again she recalled the awful dream in which the same dark figure had hurled its fiery lance at her.

But this was not a dream.

258

Hail to thee, King of the Gods, Atum Kheperi...making the names of the gods before mountains and desert, making the things under the earth...Thou didst make secret the Underworld.... Thou hast built a fortress of hidden name in the holy desert. Daily, forever, thou risest as morning before them.

—*Stela from the XXIInd Dynasty (945-730 B.C.)*

CHAPTER TWENTY-TWO

FAR BELOW

IN THE TUNNEL: 8-12 DECEMBER 2020

Time elongated and slowed in the next few moments. Eris was frozen in that time, unable to move, act, react, even scream, as immobile as she had been in the green stasis ray of the goat-men. All she could do was watch in mute terror as the fiery lance, glowing with unimaginable candescent power, seemed to float through the air toward her. Surely this was her last moment of life: she would be impaled, blasted, slain by the guardian of the secrets she had come to reveal....

But just inches short of her breast, the refulgent spear suddenly swerved in midair and hurtled up and over her head. It circled around and around near the ceiling of the chamber like a lightning bolt gone mad, sizzling ominously.

Astonished by her seemingly miraculous escape from certain death, Eris found that she could move now, but her eyes were locked on the glowing lance as it gyred insanely faster and faster in the heavy air, then suddenly dived like a hawk directly at the head of the implacable Stone Sentinel that had hurled it.

259

She heard Chris yell, "Watch your eyes!" and then the room exploded in a crackling, hissing thunderclap of white radiance brighter than the sun. Flaming chunks of red-hot stone and smoking gobbets of molten gold sprayed out into the chamber, miraculously missing all but one of the stunned agents, who had simultaneously hit the ground at Chris' warning, arms shielding their heads.

Eris looked up as she heard an indrawn gasp of pain from André and saw a nasty blackened gash in his left arm where a shard of hot rock had struck him.

As she got up from the stone floor and started over to André, she looked at the thing that now smoked and steamed in the center of the chamber. The huge dark Sentinel was now inert and headless, the black stump of its neck still bubbling with the reddish-yellow glow of molten stone rapidly cooling. The mysterious swirls and nebulous lights within its body were now still and lifeless. And the terrible sonic drone was silent at last.

Ears still ringing, Eris knelt beside André and attended to his wound with her emergency medpack, soothing on a layer of synthetic bioskin that would clean and close the wound without stitches and promote healing.

André grinned as she ministered to him. "Better my arm than my camera, anyway," he said lightly, and as soon as Eris had finished, he was on his feet, snapping pictures of the decapitated hunk of stone that only moments before had threatened to kill them all.

"Anyone else need medical attention?" Eris asked, looking around at her companions recovering from the shock of the blast. No one else was hurt, but they were still unable to make sense of the incredible events of the last few minutes.

"What the hell happened, anyway?" asked Raymond, checking Marielle carefully to make sure she was unhurt. "One second this animated coal bin is zapping us with some kind of killer buzz and tossing a light spear at Eris, and the next, its own weapon blows its head off! I don't get it!"

Then his eyes caught Avram's. A devilish grin had spread across the swarthy physicist's face. "Av—you sonovagun! You PKed the damn thing away from Eris and tossed it back at the Sentinel!"

260

Avram said nothing, merely continued to grin, but Eris, realizing the truth of Raymond's words, rushed over to Avram and gave him a big hug.

"You saved me, Av! That thing would have skewered me like a shishkebob if you hadn't deflected it. Hey, you're terrific, you know that?"

"If you got it—use it," Avram replied, keeping an arm around Eris' shoulders.

"Not to interrupt your well-earned thanks, Av," said Chris, a note of uncharacteristic curtness in his voice, "but has anyone noticed that the exit door is now open?"

They gathered around the portal to gaze into the tunnel beyond the chamber, now revealed by the opening of the second metal door, which had risen as a result of the destruction of the *Aner-sa*. The way was now clear for them to proceed into a passageway astonishingly different from the one they had just come through: it was much larger, about ten feet high and eight feet wide, spacious by comparison with the previous tunnel. It sloped downward also, but at a much gentler incline than the other. This passageway had also been hewn out of the rocky earth, but the walls were lined with long metallic panels, almost seamlessly joined and covered with colorful hieroglyphic writing and paintings depicting various scenes in the *Tuat*, the ancient Egyptian underworld, through which the souls of the dead journeyed.

But the most amazing aspect of this new tunnel was that it was illuminated by a soft, even light that seemed to come from the metal panels. Avram shook his head in wonder at the thought of an indirect light source of this intensity glowing steadily, far below the surface, for ten centuries.

With more than enough light to guide them, the agents mentally turned off their Headlights.

"Hey, Gaunt, tear yourself away from that corpse, will you?" Avram called. "I want your metallurgical opinion of these panels. You're gonna love this!"

"Huh? Oh, sure," Ray replied, reluctant to leave the still-cooling statue behind. "This thing's amazing, Av—I'd love to take it apart and see what made it move and glow inside like that. Can't even find a seam—"

261

"We don't have time to hang around and do a postmortem on it, Ray. We've got to keep pushing forward. We don't know how far we still have to go."

Ray nodded in agreement and joined Avram and the others in the mysteriously illuminated tunnel. As Avram had surmised, Ray was immediately absorbed by the glowing metal panels that lined the passageway. They were smooth and cool to the touch.

"Mmm," he muttered. "Looks like some kind of luminescent crystalline alloy...an actual fusion of metal and crystal somehow...beats anything I've ever heard of! I can't even identify this alloy! It's like it came from another planet or something."

Avram smiled, enjoying Ray's enthusiasm. "Maybe it did." He reached into his pack and brought out a pencil-sized Geiger counter with which he tested the panels. There were only a few random clicks, caused by the few cosmic rays that could penetrate this deeply beneath the earth.

He shook his head as he replaced the instrument. "Well, whatever makes it glow isn't radioactivity. I'm as amazed as you are, buddy. When you consider that this stuff has been shining steadily down here for longer than recorded history...what the hell kind of power source can it have?"

Eris had been sniffing the air in the passage for the last few moments. "Something else too, guys. Notice the air in here—cool and fresh as a spring garden. Not musty and stale like back there on the other side of the chamber."

"You're right," breathed Chris. "And the temperature's a nice comfortable 72 degrees. I'll be damned...Atlantean air conditioning!"

"With no ducts," said André between snaps of the panels. "How do you suppose the air is renewed and kept fresh like this? Does it filter through the stone in some kind of osmosis?"

Chris Shrugged. "It's all a mystery, André. I've got a feeling that our present level of technology—of which we're so godawful proud—is about to be reclassified somewhere between kindergarten and first grade, if what we've seen so far is any indication. And this is only the beginning!"

As they moved on deeper and deeper into the bowels of the Egyptian desert, the sameness of the softly illuminated tunnel turned time into timelessness; they lost all track of it, of the perception of days and nights, so far removed now from their reality. They ate when they were hungry, rested and slept when they were tired.

And kept on moving, down the ancient ever-descending passageway into the heart of the earth.

At length they came to another massive metal door like the one into the chamber of the *Aner-sa*. It too appeared to be made of something like bronze and was set into the left-hand wall of the tunnel. Chris supposed it to be the junction of the passageway from the Sphinx's right paw, and the others agreed. It looked undisturbed for centuries. It was a relief to know that at least no one had entered the tunnel this way before them.

Finally, after what could have been hours or days, they saw still another of the heavy metal doors blocking the way before them. As they approached it, they noticed that, unlike the first door, this one had no hieroglyphics embossed on it. It was smooth and featureless and gleamed softly in the lambent illumination.

As she walked forward, wondering how this door could be opened, Eris suddenly felt the floor beneath her boot give slightly. Instantly wary of a trap, she jerked her foot back and looked down to see a long narrow section of the polished stone floor slowly rising back up until it was once again level with the rest of the surface.

"What the hell is that?" asked Chris, right behind her. He knelt and ran his fingers over the place where the moving section had been. It was now invisible. He could not feel the slightest seam in the stone.

"Some kind of trap," he muttered, or...." Standing, he carefully placed his boot where Eris' had been.

"Be careful, Chris," Eris said.

He put his full weight on the spot, reflexes tensed to move at the slightest hint of danger. He felt the section of floor sink again, about a quarter of an inch. The silence in the tunnel was thick as fog as the five strained every sense, alert for anything.

263

Nothing happened.

Avram seemed disappointed. "Damn," he said with a dark grin, "I thought sure there'd be a falling two-ton rock or spears whizzing out of the walls."

"You saw too many movie serials when you were a kid, Av," Raymond said as they all crowded around the depressed section to examine it. It was approximately a foot wide and four feet long.

"Well, if it's not a trap, the other most likely thing is some kind of counterweight to open that door," said Chris, a puzzled look on her face. "The old Egyptians loved tricks like that. But this one isn't working."

"Wait a minute," said Eris as an idea suddenly hit her. "Maybe one of us isn't heavy enough alone. What if two of us step on it at once?"

Cautiously, she moved to stand beside Chris. The section sank a little farther...and this time a short, grinding rumble was heard, like a distant avalanche. Then, silence again.

Chris and Eris looked at each other, eyes bright. "Aha!" she exclaimed. "We got something—but still not enough. Come on, you guys, let's all pile on and see what happens!"

One by one, the others stepped beside Chris and Eris. At each new pressure, the stone sank a bit farther...and the brief rumbling sound was repeated, each time a little longer in duration. André, who had been taking pictures of the door and the depressed floor section, was the last to add his weight to the stone. The section sank a final distance, now about an inch and a half below the surface, and the muffled rumbling was repeated. But this time it didn't stop...it continued, getting louder and louder until it seemed to shake the very walls of the tunnel like an earthquake.

And the door began to rise, slowly, ponderously, grating against rock with a harsh metallic groan.

"That was it!" Eris yelped. "It needed all of us! See, there's just enough room for five people to stand side by side on the stone!"

Chris nodded excitedly. "Right—another reason for the Pentad. A party of fewer than five could never get past this point."

264

And then their feelings of triumph were hushed into awe by what they saw as the metal door inched slowly upward. At first, it was like looking into a blast furnace, but there was no heat, only light—pure white light, billowing out in fierce, writhing tongues of canescent power, silent as moonlight. It was an awful, eerie feeling to watch those ghostly flames twisting and dancing their uncanny soundless dance. There should be heat with such fury, and noise.

Then, as the door gradually disappeared into its niche in the tunnel ceiling, the flaring whiteness began to retreat and become less intense. The agents could now see into an enormous chamber beyond, about three times the size of the previous one. It was pyramidal in shape, smooth stone walls soaring up to an apex far above the billowing fountain of white light. Now they could see that the source of the light was a great gulf that bisected the floor of the chamber from wall to wall. There was no possible way to cross that gulf—except across a narrow stone bridge that spanned the abyss at its center. A path that led directly and deliberately through the heart of the raging white flame!

And the city was pure gold, like unto clear glass.
And the foundations of the wall of the city were garnished
with all manner of precious stones...
And the gates of it shall not be shut at all by day; for there
shall be no night there...
And there shall in no wise enter into it any thing that
defileth, neither whatsoever worketh abomination, or
maketh a lie.

—Revelation 21:18,19,25,27

CHAPTER TWENTY-THREE

AMENTET-NEFERT

GIZA PLATEAU/WASHINGTON, D.C.: 16 DECEMBER 2020

Corporal Mahmoud Bayoumi was uneasy. He did not like the desert at night, especially when there was no moon and it was as dark as the soul of Iblis. He regretted the loss of the nighttime *son et lumière* shows, the lack of tourists, the closing of the nearby nightclubs. With only one other guard for company, Mahmoud was bored and lonely, and the sharp desert wind cut icily through his thin khaki blouse.

He shifted the heavy automatic rifle he was carrying, grateful for its solidity in the eerie dark, and glanced uneasily for the hundredth time at the massive bulk of midnight stone that towered into the night beside him. He shivered, wishing he were home in his warm apartment with his beloved Sekina. She would soon make him forget the chill and this feeling of dread that seemed to wrap itself about him like mummy cloth.

Mahmoud was so lost in his thoughts that he did not notice the tall light-haired man until he was only a few yards

266

away. Sensing a presence, Mahmoud whirled, his weapon at port, prepared to challenge whoever might be out here at night where he had no business being. Seeing what looked to be just another American or British tourist out for a midnight stroll, Mahmoud relaxed. Probably wants to try climbing the Pyramid in the dark, he thought. Stupid tourists were always trying to find ways to kill themselves.

"Hello," he called out to the man in English. "You are lost perhaps?" The tall man came closer. Even in the dim gray starlight, Mahmoud could see that he had large, expressive—almost hypnotic—eyes. They seemed to bore right through him.

The man smiled. "Is this the Great Pyramid of Giza?" he asked in a voice as chilly as the wind.

"Of course," answered Mahmoud scornfully. This one was even dumber than most. Even the tourist children knew the Great Pyramid when they saw it. "Then I'm not lost," the man said. "But I'm afraid you are."

Mahmoud's mouth gaped in surprise as the blunt silenced muzzle of a large pistol suddenly appeared in the man's hand, like a coin in a conjurer's trick. Before Mahmoud could react, he heard the weapon cough thickly and simultaneously a red flower of pain exploded in his chest. He felt himself falling backward, but he never felt the impact with the sand. The dark night became much darker, darker than he had ever supposed night could be, as he died.

In a small secret office in Washington, Dr. Gideon Stack slammed his fist painfully against the desk top. "Damn!" he exclaimed as he watched the image on the video monitor in front of him, an image of cold-blooded murder occurring at this same instant almost 6,000 miles away. A murder seen through the eyes of the murderer.

Dr. Stack was angry and disturbed. He had told his agent to "use whatever means necessary" to accomplish his mission of grabbing the Immobilizer from the President's agents, but he hadn't intended murder to be one of the means. It was his own fault, he knew—he was fully acquainted with the man's criminal record before he began to work with him in secret, assigning him the descriptive code name "Sender"—but the man's incredible psychic power had made the risk seem worthwhile. Now he was beginning to wonder. He had watched, appalled and revolted, through Sender's eyes as Eris Campbell was unwrapped, more dead than alive, from a mummy case, and although he had subsequently seen her healed, it had shaken him badly. Obviously the enemy was more diabolical and devious than he had thought. That was not his responsibility, but this—this wanton killing of the guard....

His attention was drawn back to the monitor as he realized that Sender was now climbing up to the Pyramid's entrance, a gaping maw in stone black as the portal of Hell. A quick burst with a laserpen disposed of the rusty old padlock on the iron gate, and after stashing the body of the guard out of sight inside the entrance, the agent switched on a powerful electric torch and proceeded into the monument's interior.

Dr. Stack's eyes narrowed with interest as the rocky walls moved past Sender's field of vision. His resolution hardened. By God, he thought, he's doing it—he's in there and he's going to get that goddamn gadget for me. I can't let myself worry about a dead Egyptian soldier at this point. Even those Psi-Spies are expendable, if need be. I've got to have that Immobilizer—that's more important than a few lives. Much more important. He chuckled nastily, visualizing the President's face when his agents returned home empty-handed (if they returned at all) and he, Gideon Stack, had the only ace in the game....

CHAMBER OF THE FLAME/IN THE TUNNEL: 12-18 DECEMBER 2020

On the rim of the gulf across the center of the pyramidal chamber, the five agents stood and stared down into apparently bottomless depth, out of which the great pulsing fountain of white energy surged upward as if from the very heart of the world. Far below, they could see great crystals gleaming brilliantly, undoubtedly the generators of the flame.

"It's energy—raw energy," said Avram as he tested the phenomenon with his Geiger counter. "But a very special kind, unknown to modern science. No heat, no radioactivity...." He shook his head in amazement. Putting away the

268

instrument, he started across the bridge toward the shimmering curtain of light, now more concentrated around the center of the span. As they had entered, the flame had withdrawn, become less violent, seeming to invite them into the chamber almost as if sentient.

"Av!" cried Eris. "What're you doing? Be careful! We don't know what that stuff is—"

Avram grinned back at her. "Only one way to find out." He paused before the light, studying it, then cautiously extended a rod-like metal instrument from his pack into the silent snowstorm of energy burning in front of him.

Nothing happened. He withdrew his instrument. It was unharmed and cool. Nodding solemnly to himself, Avram next thrust his bare hand into the light, tensed to withdraw it at the slightest sensation of pain. He left it in for a few seconds, then withdrew it uninjured and raised it for the others to see.

"No reaction," he said. "Just a slight tingling sensation...and something else very weird...."

"What?" called Raymond, fascinated by Avram calmly using himself as a guinea pig.

"Resistance, like poking your hand through water."

"Maybe this big light show is just a bluff, then," Chris said. "Maybe it's just to scare us off—"

"No, I don't think so, Chris," said Eris thoughtfully. "That Sentinel was playing for keeps. I've got a feeling this is just as serious in its own way. Something else is involved here. Av—try to go through it and see what happens. But watch yourself!"

Avram nodded, shielded his eyes with his hand, and stepped into the cold inferno. Eris gasped as she saw his boots slip on the stone and he danced for a moment like a man on slick ice, half in and half out of the light. Then he regained his balance and was gone.

No one breathed. Endless seconds snailed past.

Then, "I'm through! It's safe, people!" Avram called from the other side, his voice echoing hollowly in the gigantic room.

"Okay," said Eris with great relief. "Here come the rest of us. Who wants to be next?"

269

"I'll go," said Chris, a note of annoyance in his voice. As he approached the energy barrier, Avram called out from the other side. "Be careful coming through, Chris—the stone just in front of and underneath the curtain is extremely slippery, like ice. Somehow the energy has canceled out friction in that area."

"Right," Chris replied stiffly. He looked back at Eris and smiled. She smiled encouragingly back. He felt a little silly, but he couldn't help but resent Avram being the first to cross the barrier. Probably did it to impress Eris, he thought; then, closing his eyes, stepped gingerly into the dancing blizzard of energy—and immediately felt the resistance Avram had mentioned. Simultaneously, he also felt a severe tingling sensation, like currents of low-voltage electricity pulsing through his body. There was a sizzling noise in his ears and he felt himself begin to grow warm. Alarmed, he tried to back out of the flame, but it was like moving through glue. His right foot slipped on the frictionless stone and he went down painfully on one knee.

"Chris! What's the matter?"

Hearing Avram's voice, Chris opened his eyes. At first the whiteness all around him blinded him, but then he could make out Avram's face, wavering and indistinct, calling out to him from the other side of the curtain. Conscious of his precarious footing on the narrow bridge, Chris carefully got to his feet. He felt like a fly trapped in soup, and noticed that all around him the white flames had turned slightly green where they touched his body, outlining him in a weird emerald nimbus.

"I'm stuck, Av!" he called to the physicist, who was now stretching out a hand to him from the other side of the barrier. It was getting hotter in there; Chris began to feel an itch of panic crawling deep inside as he realized he was trapped now. He could barely move at all.

Then Eris was running onto the bridge toward him. He could see her vaguely through the white curtain, like a shimmering wraith, as she called out to him, "Chris! Relax! I think I know what this thing is!"

One of Chris' hands was still outside the flames; Eris gripped it tightly as she talked to him rapidly and urgently.

270

"Listen, Chris, remember all that emphasis at PSI-QUARK about raising our vibrations? Spending the night in the King's Chamber to raise 'em further? Well, this is why—this energy responds only to people with high vibrations! Yours have dropped somehow. Why? What're you thinking? What's negative that could be holding you back?"

Instantly, he knew she was right. It was the only thing that made sense. And just as immediately, he knew what it was. But even in this uncomfortable predicament, he couldn't bring himself to admit it. He hedged. "Maybe it was our making love—"

"No way," Eris replied vehemently. "That was love, not lust. It's something else. Think, Chris, *think!*"

It was getting steadily hotter. Chris suddenly realized he was soaked with sweat. His knee ached. He turned slowly to see Avram's hand still stretched out to him, his distant flickering image taut with concern.

"Try to grab my hand, Chris," Avram yelled.

Chris felt a wash of shame surge through his body. It was jealousy of Avram that was lowering his vibrations, holding him back! The emerald halo dancing around him was that jealousy made visible by this incredible energy barrier that could be surmounted only by raising his spiritual vibratory level.

Eris seemed to read his mind. "It's Avram, isn't it, Chris? He likes me and you're jealous! Well, forget it—there's nothing between us but friendship. That's it. It's *you* I love, Chris!" she hissed into his ear ardently. "Kill that stupid green-eyed monster you created, sweetheart, before it kills *you!* Let it go!"

Chris closed his eyes, concentrated with all his mind-force. He saw Avram's dark anxious face, saw him as he really was, a good friend trying to help, visualized murky green webs of jealousy being washed away out of his heart by love's clear, cleansing waters....

And suddenly the verdant aura around him was gone, the gluey resistance vanished, and he could move, easily and freely, through the cool argent fires. He clasped Avram's warm, strong hand eagerly and gladly, and in another moment was standing on the other side of the light curtain.

271

"Thanks, pal," he said a bit sheepishly. Avram just smiled knowingly and nodded.

Breathing a sigh of relief at Chris' safe crossing, Eris stepped carefully onto the slippery section of the bridge and into the swirling snowfires. In moments she was through, effortlessly and safe.

Raymond came next, carrying Marielle in his arms. He experienced only minor resistance. Then it was André's turn. He had deliberately chosen to be last, so that he could snap pictures of the others going through, as well as of the energy fountain itself.

As he put one foot into the light, there was a strange hissing noise and a flare of blue-gray radiance danced around his boot. Puzzled and alarmed, he hastily withdrew his foot, which had become uncomfortably warm. He swore in French, then tried it again. The same thing happened.

"What's the matter, André?" called Chris from the other side of the flame. "Come on through—it's easy!"

"Not for me," the Frenchman yelled back. "Something's keeping me out.... I can't even get into the stuff!"

"What do you mean, something's keeping you out? It's your own consciousness, that's all.... Raise it, André, raise it. You'll make it, I did...we all did. Come on!"

"I tell you it's no use, my foot got stuck in something that felt like mud. I could hardly get it out. Did you hear that hissing sound?"

"Yeah, we heard it."

"That was my foot."

"Well, try again," called Eris. "We'll all concentrate with you, André.

You've got to make it through. This is the only way out of here."

"Okay," said André, worried but game, "here goes."

The group concentrated hard as André again put his left foot into the light, but he couldn't move it forward. He intensified his mental effort, trying to join with the others in raising his vibrations.

"It's no use, I'm stuck again. My foot feels like all the pins and needles in creation are sticking in it. And it's getting hot!"

From her vantage point on the other side of the chasm, Eris noticed the muddy blue light flaring around André's foot as he struggled to force himself into the resisting energies.

"André," she called, "I know what it is...it's Gaby! You're brooding and worrying about her! Drop it! You can't help her now! Don't let that hold you back! Release her for now!"

André shook his head, his forehead now beaded with sweat. "Yes, you're right...it must be that...but I can't help it! I can't get her out of my mind...I'm sorry."

Avram came over to Eris, stared gravely into her worried eyes. "Eris, we'll have to go on without him."

"We can't, Av...we can't leave him here. We need him!" Distraught, she called again to the Frenchman, who was now trying to extricate his foot from the light. His boot was beginning to smoke. "André! You've got to concentrate! You can do it! Think of your love for her! Imagine her safe and...."

But she trailed off, realizing it was no use. A deep, terrible silence filled the vast cavern for a moment, except for the sizzling of the angry flame around André's boot.

"Sorry, people," he called, "I can't make it. Help me get my foot out of this thing before it's barbecued!"

Chris, Eris, Raymond, and Avram joined hands and projected a powerful bolt of psychic energy through the dancing light to André. With a tremendous effort of will, he wrenched his smoking boot out of the flame and staggered back a few steps, losing his balance on the frictionless area. He stumbled dangerously near the edge of the narrow stone bridge, but managed to catch his balance in time to prevent himself from toppling into the bright abyss.

"André—are you all right?" asked Eris.

"Yes...I guess so," replied André, a disgusted note in his voice as he limped off the bridge and went over to one wall, where he sat down on the cool stone floor and removed his boot. The leather was almost too hot to touch. "Sorry to let you down, but that thing just gave me the great granddaddy of all hotfoots. You go on ahead. I'll sit here and meditate a while. I'm sure I'll be able to raise my vibes enough to make it through. I just have to concentrate on it. Don't worry about me—I'll be okay. I'll catch up to you later."

"I sure hope we don't run into any more gizmos that need five of us to work 'em," muttered Raymond despondently. The others echoed his wish silently, depressed by this unfortunate occurrence just when everything had been going so well. Reluctantly, they turned to go.

Ahead, they saw a small portal in the far wall of the pyramidal chamber. It led into a narrow unlighted tunnel, just large enough for them to walk erect, single file. The agents put on their Headlights again, and the powerful blue-white beams probed far ahead into the blackness as they made their way past smooth, unadorned stone walls.

Another timeless time passed. The four said little, each lost in his thoughts, now a little less certain about the outcome of this strange mission they had been sent on.

Then, suddenly, light: far away down the narrow black passage, a speck of cool, mellow light beckoned invitingly. As they approached it, they mentally switched off their Headlights, eager to see what would be revealed to them next.

Reaching the tunnel's exit, they stopped, catching their breaths in wonder and excitement at what lay before them. The passageway opened out into a gigantic cavern, ten square miles at least, carved out of the very bedrock of the planet, with a ceiling so high it was lost in the haze of soft golden illumination that bathed everything like muted sunlight. It seemed to come from everywhere and nowhere; it soothed and warmed the agents as if welcoming them home.

About a half-mile away, spread out across the cavern floor like a gigantic, glittering flower, was a city, beautiful beyond belief. A vast double circle of lush green gardens and sparkling fountains surrounded a twelve-pointed star of colored mosaic walkways, within which were delicate buildings and temples of alabaster and marble and crystalline substances of a thousand different colors. It looked like a dream city from the dawn of history, before Egypt was, deserted but somehow preserved for millennia in all its pristine beauty, waiting for its new inhabitants to arrive.

274

"Amentet-Nefert," breathed Chris in awe. "'The beautiful hidden place'...it really exists."

Then Eris shattered the spell with a delighted whoop. "There it is! Look, everybody! In the center of the city! Ka-Ren, the Ruby Pyramid! We made it, fellas, we made it!"

*He which built the Pyramid...because he saw in his sleep
that the whole earth was turned over...and the stars falling
down and striking one another...mountains closed upon
them, and the shining stars were made dark.... And there
remained a certain number of years to come, and he
commanded in the mean space to build the Pyramid. And he
built in the Pyramid thirty rooms, filled with stores of
riches....*
—*Ibn Abd Alhokim,* AKBAR EZZEMAN MANUSCRIPT

CHAPTER TWENTY-FOUR

KA-REN

GIZA PLATEAU: 16 DECEMBER 2020

Outside the immense black hulk of the Great Pyramid,
the chill desert wind whipped and tugged at a huge man-
shaped piece of the night that stood and glared with intense
cat-green eyes at the ageless monument.

Reaper Drum was puzzled. Behind him, an Egyptian
soldier lay sprawled, his life pumping like black syrup from
a slashed throat into the grayish sands. He had been an easy
mark for Reaper's silent approach and quick knife. No sweat·
But Nicasia had told him there would be *two* guards assigned
to the Pyramid. He had encountered only one, and a hasty
search around the structure had revealed no one else. Maybe
the other one went AWOL for awhile, Reaper thought. But
there were other strange and disturbing signs here....

Blood spots on the sand. And a trail as if something
heavy had been recently dragged across the sand toward—

The Pyramid. Reaper scowled, easing the heavy .357
Magnum from his shoulder holster. Every sense alert for
276

danger, he grabbed the thin arm of the wraith standing silently beside him and shoved her forward.

"We're going inside," he hissed into her ear. "Move it!"

Gabrielle was only dimly aware of the large man who
had brought her here. As he pushed her ahead, some automatic response not her own seemed to animate legs that were
somewhere far below, and feet like lead bricks shuffled over
the starlit sands toward the towering blackness that loomed
before her.

Together they climbed the crumbling stones toward the
entrance, silent as shadows. Reaper seemed to need no light
to guide him, as if his strange reflective eyes could see in
darkness like those of the animal they resembled. Whenever
Gaby lost her leaden footing among the stones, he would
yank her up roughly, like a puppet. But she was numb; the
brutal clutch of Reaper's fingers could not penetrate the De-
marol—like reality of her dream. She only knew that he was
taking her to a place where she would once again see her beloved André and her friends. Her stepmother had promised
her this. And in exchange, she was to do...something...for
her.... She couldn't remember what it was, but somehow she
knew that she would know when the time came....

Now they were at the iron gate guarding the Stygian entrance to the Pyramid. Reaper swore softly as he examined
the laser-fused padlock. Carefully, he eased open the gate. It
did not squeak.

As they started forward into the rocky passage, Reaper's
boot thudded into something soft. Instantly he knew he had
found the other guard.

He knelt, switching on a small wristlight to examine the
body. A neat bullethole over the heart told him what he had
already guessed. Somebody else was in here ahead of
him...somebody dangerous. But *who?* The American agents
wouldn't have done this. Who else was in on this game? Nicasia hadn't said anything about another faction being involved....

Grimly, he pushed forward into the rough-hewn passageway, dragging the unresisting girl with him. He sniffed
the dry, dusty air. Whoever was up ahead in the Pyramid was

a professional, and armed. Good—this little midnight delivery run might turn out to be fun after all.

Reaper grinned wolfishly and moved like an evil dream into the ancient darkness.

AMENTET-NEFERT: 18 DECEMBER 2020

The four of them stood there in the amber light, hypnotized like birds before the magnificent structure that dominated the central plaza of the ancient city. It gleamed in unearthly crimson splendor, a huge pyramid constructed of what looked like frozen laser light and topped with a glittering golden capstone of *orichalcum*.

This was Ka-Ren—the end of their quest. Inside this vermeil wonder was the thing they had come for—the weapon from the stars that could somehow turn back the dark hordes of Algol.

At last they started forward into the city, breathing a silent prayer of thanks to the Forces of Light that had brought them here safely. Feeling renewed energy and vigor pouring through their bodies in a tingling rush, the four agents hurried across the rocky cavern floor toward the entrance to Amentet-Nefert. A high wall of glittering amethyst stretched away around the perimeter of the city. In the center of this wall was a graceful arch of gold with a large *crux ansata* at its apex. As they neared the archway, they could see no sign of a gate—the city seemed open to them, to welcome their coming.

As they passed beneath the ancient sign of life into the city, each felt a brief mild shock, as though an electric current had coursed through their bodies momentarily. But they could see nothing.

"Another energy barrier," commented Avram with interest, "only this one's much more subtle and refined. The last test of the purity of our vibrations."

Eris' heart sang, her eyes riveted on the glowing ruby structure in the distance. The last psychic time-lock had been opened. They were the keys—and now all that had been hidden from mankind millennia ago would again be revealed.

278

Chris was totally fascinated by the architecture of this incredible city, with its glittering buildings of stone and crystal and self-cleaning fountains that sparkled like diamond flowers, just as they had for uncounted centuries. The style of the architecture was not Egyptian, he noted; it was far more sophisticated and delicate, yet here and there were hints of a kind of proto-Egyptian construction which would later be imitated and simplified, using the more prosaic building materials of limestone and granite available to the early Egyptians. The city was probably Atlantean, he decided, or perhaps even of extraterrestrial origin.

Soon they were on a broad avenue of rose tile that led straight toward the pyramid, through gardens green and fresh and thronged with exotic plants and brilliant blossoms of many hues. Most of the flora were unfamiliar; Eris marveled at how lushly they flourished without any apparent care. There were no weeds, no unwanted vegetation of any kind; everything grew as though a host of gardeners attended it each day. As they passed the gardens, delicious spicy fragrances teased their nostrils from the kaleidoscope of flowers all about them. None of them was recognizable.

Passing through a section of bright green shrubbery delicately shaped by some unknown artisan into topiary of strange animals and birds, the four found themselves at last at the base of Ka-Ren. The brilliant ruby structure was completely smooth and featureless on all sides, as they discovered by walking around it. It was about 250 feet high, a little more than half the height of the Great Pyramid far above, and constructed with the same angles and proportions. It looked as though it had been completed yesterday, showing no sign of age or wear, even though it had stood here in the center of the world for perhaps longer than recorded history. The gleaming golden capstone, itself a pyramid in miniature, glittered like a beacon high above them.

"God, it's gorgeous," breathed Eris, her golden hair and skin turned to rose by the pyramid's glow. "Is it really a ruby?"

Raymond stepped up to the glassy, slightly cool surface and examined it closely. "Well, gems are a little out of my line, folks, but this thing looks to be actually, literally, made out of pure, polished corundum—aluminum oxide. In other words, this sucker is the biggest damn ruby in the world!"

Avram nodded. "If this isn't synthetic ruby, it had to come from some other planet. You'd never find a pure stone this big on earth."

Chris too had been examining the pyramid's surface carefully. "It's beautiful, all right, but it looks like whoever built it forgot one thing—a door! How the hell are we supposed to get inside?"

"There must be a way," said Eris, but a close examination of all four sides revealed no sign of an entrance, not even a minute seam.

"Maybe we have to go in through the capstone," suggested Raymond.

"Terrific," said Chris. "Anybody here levitate? Or maybe there's a 250-foot ladder lying around some place."

Avram grinned. "Not likely. I can levitate other stuff, but not my—" He broke off in mid-sentence as an idea flashed into his brain. His grin broadened as he looked at his comrades. "Why not? 'Other stuff' includes you people, come to think of it. Who wants to go for a ride?"

"Don't look at me," said Raymond, backing away from Avram in mock alarm that wasn't entirely mock.

"Wait," said Chris, "Even if you could hoist one of us up there, Av, what could we do?" He paused, squinting up at the brilliant apex. "Say—what if we haul out your black box and all concentrate on lifting off that capstone! Think we could do it with only four of us?"

"Possibly," the physicist replied thoughtfully. "But somehow I can't believe the builders meant it to be this difficult. After all, we've passed all the barriers, run the gantlet, proved our worthiness to be here. You'd think they'd have the welcome mat out for us, wouldn't you?"

Eris' beryl eyes were bright with thought as she turned to face the silent scarlet stone. "Av, I think you've hit it. I'll bet it's not really difficult at all. Ka-Ren is offering us the last, greatest lesson we have to learn: If you want something, ask for it. All along, we've been depending on our own strength and ingenuity and wills to get us through. Now it's time to surrender ourselves to something higher."

She closed her eyes and Ka-Ren's splendor was there, burning crimson in her mind as if she were still looking at it. It seemed to be waiting for her to speak to it.

> *Ka-Ren*, she said silently, *we have come from a far place to find you, deep in the heart of the desert. We are the ones you have waited for since before history, the ones destined to unlock your secrets for a desperate world. We have passed the guardian and the fires; we have proven ourselves worthy. Now open to us, we beseech you. We surrender our wills to the Higher Will, to the judgment given you long ago by the mages who built you. We stand before you in harmony with the Light and ask that you now reveal to us your hidden heart, O Ka-Ren. Amen.*

For a moment she stood there, head bowed, eyes closed, concentrating intently on the incarnadine flame still blazing in her mind. The others, sensing she was offering them all to the pyramid's power, stood silently speaking their own supplications.

Then, gentle thunder: a huge voice boomed out of everywhere and nowhere into their shocked awareness. They seemed to hear it with their entire bodies, it sang through them like a great, kind wind, and it said:

"Congratulations, children of earth. You have passed the final test. We welcome you to Ka-Ren in the city of Amen-tet-Nefert."

The tension in Eris' muscles exploded then, and she jumped backward, coming down hard on Marielle's tail. A loud electronic screech ripped the air, startling the group further. Even in this joyous and sober moment, they had to chuckle when they realized what had happened. Raymond cradled the outraged cat in his arms, the abused tail switching angrily.

"She's not really hurt," Raymond explained at Eris' exclamations of contrition. "No pain receptors. Just a programmed response."

281

Eris stroked the golden-furred head, laughing. "You're *too* real, kitty. I'm sorry anyhow."

The great gentle voice spoke again. "Do not be alarmed, children. Nothing can harm you here. There are no further barriers before you. You may enter Ka-Ren."

Avram, his scalp prickling at the thought of being watched by invisible beings, asked, "Who are you...and *where* are you?"

The voice was bright with amusement as it answered, "You are among friends, Avram Sumi. We know you all. We have watched your progress with great interest and will answer all your questions in due time. Do not be shocked when we show ourselves to you, as the shortest of us is nine feet tall."

Eris forgot to breathe, excitement coiled in her chest like a tightly wound spring. "You're the ones Klorian told us about, aren't you?" she whispered. "The ones who'll help us?"

"Yes, Eris Campbell," came the response out of the golden light. "You may call us the Star Guardians."

Evil is indeed opposed to evil, but both to one good.
Good, however, is never opposed to good, but to two evils.
     —*Dion Fortune,* The Cosmic Doctrine

CHAPTER TWENTY-FIVE

BLOOD AND DARKNESS

Giza Plateau: 16 December 2020

Reaper Drum pushed cautiously into the midnight entrails of the Great Pyramid, straining every sense to catch the slightest clue to his adversary's location. His giant frame itched with danger; he knew the other was aware of his presence. Reaper had been inside the Great Pyramid before and had a rough idea of the interior layout of passages and chambers. As he inched his way along by feel alone, he knew he was about to enter the Grand Gallery, where he would be able to stand upright.

Silently breathing his relief, Reaper stepped into the great hall, feeling the cramped weight of stone lift away from him, sensing the free black space around him with his whole body. Bitterly he cursed the darkness; his peculiar eyes were of no use to him here, where there was not the tiniest speck of light to gather, and he dared not use even the small light on his wrist now. But at least he had the satisfaction of knowing that his opponent couldn't see either, plus the fact that Reaper had one tricky ace ready to be played if—

The darkness coughed. Stone screamed just above Reaper's head and granite splinters sprayed his face like ground glass. Cursing with pain and surprise, he hurled himself down onto the worn wooden slats that kept tourists from slipping on the stone floor. He tucked his large body tightly into the junction of the floor and the west ramp of the Gallery, his hands out before him pushing the .357 Magnum's long snout into the darkness.

Another cough, and another slug ricocheted off the ancient stone walls, inches above his head. Shit, Reaper thought, he's using a silencer—and he can see me! Must have an infra-red laser sight, too! Reaper had counted on being able to see his enemy's muzzle flash if they got into a firefight, but the silencer was preventing that too. With a nightsight, Reaper would soon be so much dead meat, unless—

He fired into the blackness, hoping the thunderous report would dazzle his opponent for a second. The sound crashed painfully into his ears in the confined space, echoed like doom down the inky passageway. But the man was a pro, and the huge muzzle flash of Reaper's pistol gave him an added advantage in aiming, which he was quick to use.

The next bullet slammed into Reaper's shoulder, sending a white sheet of agony through his arm. But he ground his teeth against the howling pain and blasted another round at his unseen opponent. Scrambling backwards awkwardly, he dropped behind the shelter of the beginning of the west ramp, where it had been broken off to reveal the Well Shaft years ago. This would give him some protection, but he had to be careful not to step into that yawning pit nearby.

This wasn't turning out at all like Reaper had planned. His enemy was too well equipped. But Reaper still had that ace, had anticipated he might need it if he got pinned down like this. He hadn't survived at his trade all these years without having a plan to cover his ass in a dangerous situation.

He cupped his hands around his mouth and roared down the Ascending Passage, "*Gaby! Now!*"

The shout barreled down the stone tunnel like a runaway truck. Reaper had left Gabrielle down at the entrance to the Pyramid, afraid she might make too much noise in her clumsy drugged state or get hit by a stray bullet. But he had also found a use for her, given her directions to be followed at his call, knowing that her robot-like mind would make her do whatever he told her.

284

She did. Bright white light suddenly flickered into being all along the Grand Gallery, starkly illuminating the tall straw-haired man atop the Great Step, pistol in hand. The unexpected light dazzled his sensitive retinas; he stood there for a moment like a bug in sunlight under an overturned rock.

"Good girl!" Reaper grinned ferally and threw down on the thin figure at the top of the Gallery, firing four times in rapid succession, ignoring the pain that gnawed his shoulder like a wild dog.

The figure disappeared; Reaper couldn't tell whether or not he had a hit, as his own eyes were dazzled after the long darkness.

Snapping the cylinder out, he reloaded quickly as he sprinted up the corridor, leaving a trail of bright scarlet drops behind him. At the top of the Grand Gallery, a sprinkle of someone else's blood on the stone floor told him he had a hit. Reaper grinned ferociously. Good. He didn't know how badly wounded the other man was, but he had only one way to go: into the King's Chamber. The crimson trail led through the Antechamber and beyond into the short low passageway before the King's Chamber.

As Reaper edged his way cautiously forward, he heard an unwelcome sound from the King's Chamber: the shattering of glass! Cursing, he began to run in a crouch. The bastard was still active, and shooting out the lights in there! Then with his infra-red nightsight, he would again have the advantage. Recklessly, Reaper hurled himself into the big room just as the last light died in a snowstorm of broken glass and arcing electricity. He had just enough time to see the blond man duck down behind the stone sarcophagus as he snapped off two thunderous shots. The heavy slugs spanged into the empty stone coffer, ringing it like a gong as darkness possessed the ancient room once more.

Reaper's shoulder and arm were becoming numb; he was losing a lot of blood. He slipped in his own gore scrambling back to the cover of the entrance into the chamber. He hoped like hell he wasn't going to pass out; then the other guy would have his ass for sure. But the stamina in his superbly trained body and the force of his hatred for this skinny yellow-haired tomb rat who dared challenge him kept him alert.

For a few loud minutes they exchanged gunfire, blasting away into the blackness, hot slugs gouging ugly scars in the time-worn stone, but neither scored. As Reaper reloaded again, a heavy silence settled over them like soot. The stench of cordite hung hot in the air, making it hard to breathe.

It looked like a stalemate. The only thing the blond man could hope for was to make a break for the entrance into the hidden tunnel opened by the Psi-Spies. But Reaper had spotted that entrance and knew where it was in the dark. He would probably hear the man's attempts to creep toward it and know where to aim. Stalemate.

Or...he could turn and leave, let the man go on into the tunnels, go back and get Gabrielle and let her follow him, as the original plan called for anyway. He hated to let the little shit go, but he was wasting time here like this. He couldn't see in the dark, and he was losing blood. Too much blood. The man could stay hidden behind the coffer for a long time. And he could see every move Reaper made.

Cursing silently and gritting his teeth against the pain every move now cost him, Reaper quietly retreated back down the low passageway, into the Antechamber, then cautiously down into the still lighted Grand Gallery.

By the time he reached the entrance to the Pyramid, his head was whirling and blackness was nibbling at the edges of his vision. Gabrielle was there waiting for him, patient as a pet dog, her hand still on the light switch he had told her to pull. Ignoring her, he stumbled to the entranceway and gulped in huge draughts of the cold night air. The chill freshness of the desert revived him, and after a few moments he turned to the blank-eyed girl.

"Thanks for your help, kid...as if you had a choice." He laughed nastily. "That little fucker in there almost took me out, you know. You'd've liked that, wouldn't you? Too bad. Well, time for you to go on with your assignment. You know what that is, don't you?"

Vaguely, she became aware that Reaper was speaking to her and that she had better listen. "Yes," she answered weakly.

286

"What is it?" he growled.

"Go...into tunnels...find friends...."

"Right. Find your friends and stay with them until they locate that weapon, the Immobilizer."

"'Mobilizer...."

"Yeah." He reached into his jacket pocket, brought out something small that gleamed metallicly in the wan starlight. He handed it to her, put it in her fist, closed her fingers around cold metal. "You know what this is?"

She looked at the ugly thing in her hand, trying to focus her attention on it. It felt like chilled lead. She nodded.

"It's an Ortiges 6.355 millimeter automatic pistol. Nice and light and easy to keep out of sight. You'll know when to use it. Now listen to me—" He grabbed her roughly, turned her to face his blazing emerald eyes. "Here's one more thing for you to remember. Somewhere up ahead in the tunnels you're going into is a man. He's tall and skinny, with light blond hair. He's dangerous. If you see him, kill him immediately, understand? He's a bad man—he wants to hurt your friends, so don't take chances. Kill him! Got that?"

Gabrielle nodded again.

"Good."

After making sure she understood all the instructions Nicasia had imprinted on her mind and checking the light pack of provisions strapped to her back, Reaper put the pistol in her jacket pocket and led her back up the passageway toward the King's Chamber.

Cautiously entering the chamber, Reaper sensed immediately that the other presence wasn't there. Predictably, he had made his break for the opening in the chamber wall. Reaper pulled a flashlight out of Gaby's pack, turned it on and put it into her hand. Traces of blood on the floor leading into the entrance confirmed his suspicions.

As Gaby disappeared into the dark tunnel, Reaper laughed at the thought of this frail, fuddled little bitch acting as his angel of vengeance.

He was still laughing as he turned and headed back out into the clear, cold night of the Giza Plateau, grateful to be done with this place of ageless shadows and silences.

O sages standing in God's holy fire
As in the gold mosaic of a wall,
Come from the holy fire, perne in a gyre,
And be the singing masters of my soul.
   —W. B. Yeats, "SAILING TO BYZANTIUM"

CHAPTER TWENTY-SIX

THE STAR GUARDIANS

AMENTET-NEFERT: 18 DECEMBER 2020

They stood there, at the base of the shimmering ruby heart that was Ka-Ren, momentarily stunned by the great voice that had just spoken to them out of empty space.

As someone in a dream, Eris walked up to the pyramid, expecting to see a door open automatically for them now that they had been accepted and welcomed by the Star Guardians.

But the polished wall remained unchanged. She reached out to touch it and the voice of the Star Guardian said, "We have told you there are no more barriers, save those you yourself create. Do not trust your physical perceptions in all things, my child. You may enter."

Eris closed her eyes, trusting in the benevolence of the great calm voice, realizing this was another test, and stepped forward. A part of her expected to bump into a solid wall of gleaming mineral and a part of her did not. A part of her believed.

There was a rush of coolness around her, as though she had stepped through a fine mist of spray—and she kept walking! A hard polished surface was now under her boots. Amazed and delighted, she opened her eyes.

288

She was inside! A triangular tunnel led away through the crimson gemstone, lit by a soft vermillion glow from the glassy walls, and vanished ahead of her to a point of rosy light. For a moment she stood bewildered by the perspective, since the tunnel seemed to recede into distances impossible inside a pyramid with a 400-foot base. Then she turned to confront the wall she had just come through, miraculously, as though the adamantine ruby had turned to vapor for her. She touched the wall; from this side it was again solid and impenetrable.

"Hey!" she called into the rosy dimness, "Thank you, Star Guardians...but what about my friends?"

As if in answer, Chris came striding through the wall like a ghost in a Hollywood movie.

"Chris!" she squealed. "Isn't this fabulous? They've got us walking through walls!"

Chris grinned, kissed her quickly in the red dusk and held her tightly for a brief stolen moment. Her lips were warm and hungry on his, and then they broke apart as Avram came through the crimson wall, grinning wickedly.

"Ah, ha! Turn my back for a minute...." He looked around, silently taking in the triangular passageway, the same trick of distance that had amazed Eris, and trying not to reveal his own amazement.

Then Raymond was through, holding Marielle in his arms while her glowing eyes recorded everything. "Hey! I thought I had to die to do this! What's next—walking on water?"

Chris laughed. "Why not? That's probably lesson five."

"Well, if there's any water down here, I'd rather bathe in it than walk on it," Eris said with a grin.

They waited for further instructions from the mysterious voice, but when none came they moved forward, down the long triangular tunnel, their boots squeaking on the highly polished floor.

The illusion of distance was no illusion: apparently the laws of time and space as they knew them were not fully operative here. They walked for hours, long enough to have traversed the interiors of dozen of pyramids Ka-Ren's size.

At length they rested, munched a few dried fruits and nuts and enjoyed the refreshing water pills. Moving ahead once more, they could now see that the triangular exit to the tunnel was coming nearer; a soft roseate glow penetrated inward from it, and they heard a faint sweet tinkling, like distant windchimes. It rode lightly on the dulcet air, a delicate, refreshing sound that made the four agents smile at one another.

At the tunnel's end, they found themselves in a vast, dome-shaped chamber hollowed out of the same red mineral, so huge it could not possibly be contained within a 250-foot-high pyramid, yet here it was! The mind-wrenching implications of this fact hardly had time to register before their attention was drawn to the floor of the chamber. There, a forest of complex, many-faceted crystals of a thousand different shapes, sizes and colors flourished in incredible profusion as far as the eye could see. They glowed and pulsed with interior lights of varying brilliance and duration: amethyst, indigo and amber, clear yellows and palest greens, delicate rose and deep bloody cinnabar. Eris saw a group the color of her eyes, the color of a deep tropical sea.

Rose-quartz seemed to predominate, coloring the air with its gentle light. Dazzled, the group descended a short flight of red stone steps into the crystal forest.

And the crystals—*sang*.

They burst into a fragile rippling sheen of sound like far waters tumbling over ice, a tinkling, lacy coruscation of harp-like arpeggios and glissandos, a shimmering paean of welcome that held the four friends stunned with its ethereal loveliness.

As the glittering crystals sang to them they walked, dazed with beauty, through the forest, guided by a series of winking white crystals that showed them the way like beacons.

At length they came to a clear space several hundred feet in diameter. Here, the crystals did not grow; instead, inset into the crimson floor was another wonder: a dome-shaped structure over 100 feet in diameter but of no great height, covered with a circular pattern of sparkling jewels in a red, blue and violet design of breathtaking beauty. Sap-

290

phires, rubies, opals, amethyst, a thousand varieties of precious and semi-precious gems formed a huge flower with myriad scarlet petals opening outward from a kaleidoscopic center of smaller blossoms and surrounded by a symmetrical crimson border of interlocking pyramidal crystals. Beyond this, another larger, darker red border flared out like dancing flames, gradually shading into streamers of royal blue, violet and deep indigo. It was a creation of staggering beauty, beyond price, a gigantic jeweled mandala in the center of the earth.

As she gazed in speechless awe at this glittering artifact, Eris was reminded of the smaller gem-flower mandala in Jaca's room, so far away and so long ago....

"You have now reached the end of your journey, friends." The huge gentle voice of the Star Guardian startled them. "Remain where you are for a moment, and all will be explained."

"Glad to hear the old boy's still keeping an eye—or whatever—on us," Chris ventured, "but where do we go from here?"

"Beats me," Raymond said. "That thing's mighty pretty, but it's not tall enough to—"

As if in answer to their questions, the great dome began to move slowly and silently upward atop a cylinder of dark blue-violet metal that gleamed dully in the crystalline light. In a few moments it reached its full height of about 150 feet and stopped.

Amazed, Chris shook his head and said nothing. The others too were silent as they waited for the next wonder to reveal itself. Behind them, the crystals blazed and hummed.

"Stand close together and remain perfectly still," instructed the Star Guardian's voice.

As they came together, Raymond whispered, "I wonder if we get to walk through another wall into that thing. These people sure don't believe in doors, do they?"

As if in answer to his query, a new note began to thrum through the crystal forest, much different from the ethereal music: a note of power.

"Look!" exclaimed Eris, who had turned to face the scintillating mass. The eyes of the others followed her point-

291

ing finger to see two large crystals *growing*, forcing their way up into tall spires higher than any of the others. Then, strangely, they stopped growing upward and a pointed, many-faceted extrusion began to grow outward from each tip, each shaping itself into a conical formation pointed directly at the agents. Abruptly the tall crystals were flushed with a brilliant violet light and the humming increased in volume. Eris noticed that the crystalline singing had stopped now.

"What in God's name?" began Chris, who was starting to feel uneasy, but he was cut short as a bright violet beam suddenly shot forth from each of the points on the crystal shafts. The two beams came together where the four stood rooted, bathing them in a sparkling lavender vortex that swirled around and through them, causing a faint tingling sensation. They felt warmer and *lighter*, as though they were losing weight, substance, as if gravity were somehow lessening where they stood.

Then sudden blackness slammed down like a trap as all consciousness left them.

If a feline robot could register astonishment, that was what made Marielle's emerald diode eyes widen and the synthetic fur bristle on her back, as she watched the bodies of her companions suddenly become enveloped in a bright violet beam of light, become translucent, then transparent, then disappear entirely. In a matter of seconds, where four humans had been standing, there was now only empty space.

Marielle shook her head, mewed plaintively, played back for herself the tape of what she had just recorded. Her replay showed the same thing happening again. No doubt about it—her people were gone, and it definitely did not compute!

Moments later, consciousness returned to the four agents; it had seemed like only a brief fainting spell, but now they were fully alert once more, feeling no ill effects.

Eris looked up—into the glorious red and blue and violet splendor of the great mandala dome, now high above them, forming a concave, cathedral-like skylight through which the roseate light poured like a benediction.

They were *inside* the huge metal cylinder!

292

"Good God," breathed Avram, his dark eyes quickly taking in their surroundings. "They teleported us in here? How the—"

"The crystals!" Eris said excitedly. "That's how! The Star Guardians use them as a power source, shaped by mental commands, probably for lots of different uses."

"Then the Star Guardians must be inside here somewhere," said Chris, looking around eagerly. But all he saw was the circular metallic wall that enclosed them. Around the wall, spaced at regular intervals, were seven large metal doors with strange hieroglyphics cut into their surfaces.

Examining the nearest one closely, Chris found the markings similar to Egyptian writing, yet oddly different, more sophisticated.

"Very interesting," he said. "This stuff could be Atlantean...it looks like the ancestor of Egyptian hieroglyphics."

"Sure," said Avram. "After all, this pyramid was supposedly put here by Atlanteans...and they had a technology based on crystalline power. But teleportation...?"

"Your conjectures are astute, friends," boomed the bodiless voice, louder in the confined space of the metal cylinder. "Now turn your attention to the center of this chamber."

As they did so, a shimmering began in the clear air, as though sudden heat waves danced there, then a slender silver ovoid began to appear out of nothing. Gradually it took on a metallic sheen and form, its outlines hardening into what was unmistakably—

"A spaceship," Eris whispered.

In seconds it was fully visible, a sleek silver saucercraft, its highly polished metal surface glowing with a soft violet aura. It hovered motionless about six feet off the floor, with no visible means of support.

"What a beauty," said Raymond. "Kitty, make sure you get a good shot of..." He trailed off, as he looked around for Marielle and suddenly realized she wasn't there! "Hey! Where's the fur?"

A brief search around the circular chamber revealed no trace of the robot cat.

"She must've been left outside," said Chris. "She didn't teleport!"

"Star Guardians, can you hear us?" Eris called out to the air. "Help! Our kitty, Marielle, is still outside the cylinder. Can you—?"

There was no vocal answer, but before Eris could finish her request, there was a light humming sound, and a spot of magenta light formed near the floor of the chamber. The golden-furred feline's body gradually began to materialize, tail switching with annoyance, looking very much like an irate inversion of Alice's Cheshire Cat.

When she was solid and the light had faded, Raymond scooped her up in his arms, comforting her.

The great voice boomed out, "We beg your pardon. We did not realize that the feline mechanism was one of your party. To our sensors it appeared as merely a small piece of electronic equipment." There was something that sounded like a chuckle, then: "The observation craft you see here has been waiting for many thousands of your years, and is your ultimate destination. Prepare to board."

Eris had seen no visible ports or hatches on the ship, but suddenly a triangular opening formed on the gleaming metallic surface, and brilliant white light spilled out into the soft rose-purple illumination of the chamber. Then a glowing ramp that seemed to be composed of the same snowy radiance extruded from the hatchway until it touched the dark crimson floor. Eris was the closest, so she set her boot on it and found it as solid as steel. Tingling with excitement and anticipation, she marched up the ramp, motioning her friends to follow her.

"Come on, you guys! This is one flight we don't wanta miss!"

They followed her up the ramp and into the bright interior of the ship, where they made their way through a short corridor with strange instruments and patterns of blinking colored lights on either side. Eris was secretly disappointed that the Star Guardians still had not appeared to greet them.

"I wonder how you get a window seat on this thing," muttered Raymond to Marielle, who was in good spirits once more and busy taking everything in.

The corridor led into what was obviously the main control room, a circular space about twenty feet in diameter with a domed ceiling about fifteen feet high. Running through the center of the room from floor to ceiling was a large column of semi-opaque glass. It was inactive and dark. Along the far curve of the wall was a control console which looked totally unfamiliar, even to Eris. She wanted to examine it more closely, but a line of green light suddenly formed beneath their feet on the metal floor, pointing them over to one of several closed doors leading off from the control room.

As they approached the door, it slid open silently and they entered a smaller hemispherical room with thick carpet on the floor and five comfortable-looking padded lounge chairs in the center. Soft, dim indirect lighting illuminated the blank, neutral-colored walls and domed ceiling.

"Oh, hey, does that look terrific!" Chris exclaimed, shrugging off his pack. "We haven't had anything soft to sit on for—how long have we been tramping around underground, anyway?"

Eris shook her head as she too dumped her pack onto the soft carpet. "Good question—I don't think any of us have been keeping track, have we?"

"Seems like months, but it's probably only days," said Avram, testing the resiliancy of one of the chairs.

The four made themselves comfortable in the lush chairs, which molded to their body contours without needing adjustment. A feeling of relaxation swept over them like a gentle breeze. Marielle curled up contentedly in Raymond's lap and began to purr.

Eris removed her boots with a sigh of ecstasy and settled back in her chair. Running her fingers through her tawny mane, she wondered when she'd combed it last. A shower and something real to eat would make this just about paradise, she thought.

The voice of the Star Guardian came through an unseen loudspeaker, intimate and well modulated now, instead of the stentorian tones heard earlier.

"Relax, friends. You have come far and must recharge your energies for what is to come. Refreshment will be served to you shortly. There are sanitary facilities through the blue door to your left, should you require them. Rest now...."

"Oh, Star Guardian...sir..." Eris said, "will we get to meet you soon?"

There was a tinge of amusement in the gentle voice. "I have a name, Eris. There is no need for formality here. As nearly as it transliterates into your tongue, it is Yod. The answer to your question is yes, you will see us very soon."

As the four lay back and closed their eyes, Eris found her heart still hammering with excitement. How are we supposed to relax? she asked herself. Here we are sitting inside a twelve-thousand-year-old UFO five miles under the earth, waiting to be interviewed by a bunch of E.T.s the size of statues, and we're supposed to relax? She grinned to herself, reached over to find Chris' hand next to hers and clasped it gratefully.

But her body was less impressed with all this than her mind, and it had every intention of taking full advantage of this welcome chance to rest. Her last conscious thought as she slipped away into darkness was how nice it would be to pee into something besides an exploding plastic bag....

Hours, or perhaps only minutes later, they awoke refreshed to the deliciously impossible fragrances of hot food and drink! Before each chair was a metal table with salads, vegetables steaming in butter, thick chunks of bread, soup...and mugs of a hot black liquid which could only be coffee!

Eris gave a cry of joy, instantly alert. "Hey! Real food! I'd almost forgotten what it looks like!"

Chris tasted the dark brew, pronounced it indeed coffee—and very good, too, with cinnamon in it—as the others began to put away the food like starving lumberjacks.

"I hope you find this food satisfactory," said the voice of Yod as they ate. "Evidently you do. It was synthesized from other elements of your world and contains no harmful chemicals. However, it does contain suitable nourishment."

"Thank you," said Eris through a mouthful of what tasted like tuna salad but wasn't. "We don't care what it was...whatever it is now is delicious!"

Raymond grinned. "We're better off not knowing. This pseudo-coffee is a real winner, though. If André was here, he'd have you try your hand at a bottle of Burgundy—"

Eris jumped as if she had been shot. "André! We forgot all about him! Has anybody tried to contact him?"

The others replied negatively, so Eris set down her sandwich and sat back to concentrate on her Mentacom Medallion, reaching out mentally for André, hoping that by now he had been able to raise his vibrations high enough to cross through the light curtain.

But her mind touched nothing. No answering response came to her mind-probe. She concentrated harder, filling her consciousness with his occult number, 8. Nothing.

She shook her head. "Can't raise him! I don't get anything at all—not even an awareness of his presence!"

"Let me try," suggested Chris. But he had no better luck than Eris. He tried again...and this time, something else happened. Chris began to *hear*. His particular psychic talent was clairaudience, and so far during the mission, he had had no chance to utilize it. But now...he heard a voice, harsh and evil. It was agitated, full of hate, and he could make out only a few words:

"*...kill you...frog bastard....*"

Jesus! What am I picking up? he wondered. He strained mentally, stretching his psi sense to hear more. That voice grated on his mind like a dental tool on a sore tooth, but he strained to hear it again.

This time he heard another voice, weak, desperate.

"Wait...help me up...can't get through...."

That was André's voice! And he's in deep trouble!

Snapping out of his semi-trance, Chris quickly told the others what he'd overheard. "We've gotta *do* something! André's in terrible danger! *Star Guardians!* Yod! Can you help us?"

"We can locate him with our sensors," came the response.

"Okay! Do it...please."

297

A spot of light glowed on the dome-shaped wall, then quickly widened into a large three-dimensional color image of the familiar cavern where they had left André. The angle was high; they could look down upon the silently roaring fountain of white light and see the narrow stone bridge through its center—

And then they saw him. He was dangling from that bridge by both hands, his body swaying high above the yawning abyss of alabaster brilliance below. And above him, a tall blond man with blood on his shirt and strange eyes bright with hate was slowly grinding his shoe into the tortured knuckles of André's right hand.

He saw; but blasted with excess of light,
Closed his eyes in endless night.
　　　　—Thomas Gray, THE PROGRESS OF POESY

CHAPTER TWENTY-SEVEN

BLOOD AND LIGHT

WASHINGTON, D.C.: 18 DECEMBER 2020

　　　Gideon Stack had become a video junkie. Since the entry of his agent into the Great Pyramid, and especially since the harrowing and totally unexpected firefight inside with the huge black man (one of Nicasia Bane's men?), Stack had been unable to tear himself away from the vivid drama unfolding on his monitor screen. He had set up a DVD recorder to capture the portions when his duties absolutely demanded he leave the small office where he had secreted himself, but he felt the need more and more to be there as it happened, to watch the action firsthand. He had become the ultimate couch potato, totally mesmerized by the real-time drama he himself had created.

　　　He had been having all his meals brought in now for days (or was it weeks?) and had lost all track of time. His secretary, totally unable to understand her boss' sudden erratic behavior, was quitting after fifteen years, but even this did not phase him. In fact, he was hardly aware of it—or of her. Even the President was beginning to wonder what was wrong with Stack, but he didn't trouble himself about it; he was glad to have him out of his hair for a while.

　　　So Gideon munched cold hamburgers, canceled all appointments, refused speaking engagements and fundraisers, even phone calls, and sat glued to his monitor, watching a bizarre and deadly series of events unfold through the eyes of another man, half a world away and miles beneath the earth.

CHAMBER OF THE FLAME: 18 DECEMBER 2020

André was deep into meditation when the boot caught him in the side and jerked him painfully back to reality. Reality was a tall blond-haired man with pale sinister eyes towering above him and pointing a very nasty-looking pistol at him.

André cursed vehemently in French, tensing to spring to his feet, but the look on the man's face stopped him.

"Hold it right there, Frenchy," he snarled. "No funny moves or you're dead meat."

André felt no fear, only anger and astonishment. Who could this joker be? he wondered. And how the hell could he get down here?

He didn't have time to speculate further. The man, obviously a pro, stepped back a few paces and motioned for André to get up.

"Who the hell are you?" André asked, fighting his anger and wincing at throbbing ribs as he carefully got to his feet.

"I'll ask the questions. Where are your buddies? How come you're here alone? Did they get swallowed up in that?" The man jerked his gun toward the towering white flames that burned in eerie silence in the abyss, then leveled it once again on André's heart.

"Those flames are a kind of psychic barrier," André replied. "The others were able to cross through them, but I wasn't."

"Oh?" The man raised a pale eyebrow. "Why not? What's your problem?"

"It's a long story, but basically you have to have a very high spiritual vibration to get through, and I was...worried about certain things and couldn't make it."

The man laughed, a nasty sound. "Well, now you got a few more things to worry about, Frenchy. Vibrations or no vibrations, I intend to make it through that bonfire, and you're gonna help me."

300

Now it was André's turn to laugh. "No way, pal. You're obviously somebody's rent-a-thug, and there's no possible way anybody with *your* vibes could get through."

An ugly light glimmered in the stranger's large, almost colorless eyes. "You got no idea who I am, Frenchy."

"You must be working for Nicasia Bane—who else?"

Sender shook his head. "I don't know who you're talking about. Just think of me as a government agent and let it go at that." He laughed again, amused by his own secretive humor.

André was puzzled now. "That doesn't make any sense at all! Is the CIA sending—"

"Fuck off, Frenchy. You talk too much. Come on, you and I are taking a little walk."

"A walk—where?" André asked, looking around the bare chamber.

"Out on that bridge," Sender replied, gesturing with his gun. "We're gonna take a close look at that fire—or whatever it is. And don't try to be a hero if you want to stay alive. Come on, *move it!*"

André shrugged and walked toward the stone bridge that arched out over the chasm, leading into the heart of the snowy flames. He saw for the first time that the man's shirt was soaked with blood on the right side. He'd obviously been wounded not long ago. But if he'd followed them into the Pyramid and down through the tunnel, who could he have been fighting with? Maybe one of the guards posted outside....

They went out onto the bridge, the blond man keeping a cautious space between them. When André had reached the white fires, Sender said, "All right, let's see what you did before."

André shrugged again and turned toward the flames. He had been meditating deeply for quite awhile before this ominous stranger had kicked him back to consciousness. He felt better about the things that had troubled him before, about Gaby, felt that he had mastered some of his negativity. Maybe he *could* make it through now! If so, he could leave this bozo stranded on the other side! Breathing a silent prayer, he steadied his nerves and stepped into the alabaster blaze.

For a moment he thought he was going to make it, but then, halfway in, he began to feel the familiar resistance, a sensation like pushing through thick mud. A dark blue aura sprang up around him and he could feel the flames heating up.

Damn! he thought. Still not enough. Disappointed and angry, he wrenched himself out of the clinging stuff. Glowering at the pale gunman, he said, "No use. You want to try?"

The man looked puzzled and uncertain for a moment. He swayed slightly, as though dizzy, then quickly recovered himself. His wound, thought André with a little surge of hope, it's giving him trouble. Maybe....

"Yeah," Sender said. "Maybe I will. At least it didn't fry you, so you may be leveling with me." His gun was rock steady now as he came toward André.

As he passed by the Frenchman on the narrow bridge, he suddenly struck out, slamming the gunbarrel against André's temple. André instinctively jerked his head to one side, but the blow still caught him heavily and a kaleidoscope of brightly colored lights exploded behind his eyes. His knees gave way and he dropped to all fours, fighting the ear-ringing pain that threatened to sweep him away into darkness. He felt warm blood sliding down his face.

Dimly, he heard the pale man's mocking words: "...don't need you. If you can't get through it, you're no use to me. So...."

André realized that this maniac was going to shoot him. Now. Forcing himself to ignore the pain and the encroaching blackness, he hurled himself at the man's legs.

As the Frenchman slammed into him, Sender fired, but the bullet whistled harmlessly over André's back, spanging off the stone behind him. His balance gone, the gunman fell backward, hitting the rocky surface of the bridge painfully. His breath went out of him in a grunt.

His head pounding and whirling madly, André gritted his teeth and clambered up Sender's body like a mad monkey, going for the gun. The blond man's face was distorted

302

with hatred as he struggled with André. He was stronger than he looked. He tried to bring his gun around, but the Frenchman put every ounce of strength into a hard chop to the gunman's wrist, smashing his gunhand into stone with paralyzing force. The pistol flew from his nerveless fingers, skittered across the bridge and plunged into the glowing abyss.

André grinned. Now they were even. Instead of continuing to grapple with Sender on the ground, André released him and jumped to his feet—or tried to. This was a mistake, for a wave of dizziness suddenly swept over him. He lost his balance and dropped to his knees.

In that moment of vertigo, Sender struck. A foot lashed out, catching André squarely in the chest and hurling him backward. The Frenchman's knees and legs scraped painfully on stone, then suddenly plunged into empty air! Frantically, he gripped the bridge's surface with his hands and arms to keep himself from hurtling into space, felt the skin on his hands rip as the weight of his lower body pulled him downward.

Then he was hanging from the bridge, swaying over brilliant emptiness, supported only by his hands! His head ached terribly as he fought to retain consciousness and find some way to pull himself back up onto the bridge.

And the blond killer was getting to his feet, grinning. Slowly he walked over to the edge and peered down at André's reddened face.

"Too bad, sucker, you were up against a pro. I hated to lose that gun, but I don't need a gun to finish you off now, do I?" His voice turned ugly. "I'm gonna kill you, you frog bastard."

Sender slowly raised one foot and pressed down against the whitened, straining fingers of André's left hand.

"Wait!" André ground out through his agony, seeking desperately for any possible delay. "Help me up! You can't get through without me!"

"Save your breath, Frenchy. You haven't got much left."

André watched the man's boot grind into his fingers, but oddly, he didn't feel anything now. It was as though he were watching somebody else's fingers being stepped on. In an almost detached manner, he saw the pale man smiling, savoring his sadistic game, saw him slowly press his boot down harder—

André saw his face suddenly jerk up in surprise and shock as a gunshot cracked through the bright air like a whip and a small, dark hole suddenly appeared near his throat. The hole bloomed a brilliant red flower as Sender reeled back. His mouth worked as though he wanted to speak, but nothing came out. Then he hit the outer edge of the flames. An ugly black nimbus, shot through with dark reds, grays and browns, flared out around him like a rotted cloak. Then the argent fire seemed to thrust him out of itself as though sentiently rejecting his psychic foulness. A scream ripped out of him then as, propelled by the impetus of the flames, he toppled off the other side of the bridge and hurtled headfirst into the chasm.

As if in a dream, André watched him fall for what seemed like hours. Then he instinctively closed his eyes and rammed his face into the shelter of one arm.

There was a faint shattering crash as of distant mirrors breaking and André felt a tingling rush of energy as the cavern filled with an immense flare of white light brighter than the sun. He could see the bones of his arms, the red veins in his eyelids, then darkness rushed into the cavern like a tidal wave. The fiery snowstorm was gone and he was hanging by his hands, suspended in ebony space.

After a long agonized moment, he saw a dim yellowish light bobbing toward him over the bridge. The light stopped and hit him in the eyes, making him squint. A soft, weak voice said, "André...?"

That voice galvanized him like high-voltage current. He almost lost his grip on the stone. "Gabrielle!" he croaked. "Is that you? Is it really you?"

The beam left his face and played over the face of the one who held the light, revealing a pale, wasted countenance, but one that unmistakably belonged to Gabrielle Bane.

André felt hot tears gush down his face thens but inside he was singing like a chorale. "Help me up, Gaby," he called out weakly.

Somehow (André was never able to recall later just how they managed it) the frail, gaunt scarecrow of a girl managed

304

to help the battered Frenchman haul himself up onto the bridge. They lay together there for a long time in the silent dark, trembling with joy and exhaustion in each other's arms, their only illumination the feeble firefly glow of Gaby's flashlight.

After awhile they got up and André limped stiffly down to where his pack lay near the entrance into the cavern. He put on his Headlight and the bright spear of blue-white light stabbed out into the darkness, lighting their way plainly. Then, arms wrapped tightly around each other's waists, they crossed over the stone arch together.

WASHINGTON, D.C.: 18 DECEMBER 2020

And in Washington, D.C., an old man with lank white hair whimpered and mumbled to himself as he stumbled into chairs and tables, searching for the light switch on the wall of his small office. He found it, fingers scrabbling against the wall like a pale spider trying to get back into its nest, but no light came on at the click. Nothing but thick, impenetrable darkness.

He had watched in horror the final moments of the fight on the bridge through his agent's eyes, had seen the chamber pinwheel around him as he pitched over and down toward an intolerable brilliance, a whiteness that had exploded into near nova intensity, transmitted psychically across thousands of miles into a small video monitor that couldn't possibly reproduce such brilliance, yet did, spearing a blast of light hundreds of times brighter than the heart of a star deep into his brain and searing his optic nerves into tiny twists of charcoal.

Now, as he fumbled for the doorknob in blackness, the truth rushed in on him as the light had and he realized that he was totally and irreversibly blind.

Alone in his terrible and personal dark, Dr. Gideon Stack began to scream.

And there appeared to me two men of very great height, such as I have never seen on Earth; and their faces shone like the sun, and their eyes were like burning lamps.... Their wings were brighter than gold, their hands whiter than snow. They called me by my name.
—THE BOOK OF THE SECRETS OF ENOCH

There were men from the sky in the earth in those days.
—HEBREW BOOK OF LIGHTS

CHAPTER TWENTY-EIGHT

MEN FROM THE SKY

AMENTET-NEFERT: 19 DECEMBER 2020

Naked, Gabrielle hung suspended like a pale wax mannequin inside an intricate mechanism of moving metal rods and crystals which hummed and glowed with multicolored light. Only Eris was in the room with her where she had been told by the Star Guardians to bring the ravaged girl. Here, they said, she would be healed of the terrible mental and physical wounds inflicted by Nicasia Bane during her captivity at Zeinhom.

There had been a joyous reunion when Gaby and André had arrived at the silver ship in the heart of Ka-Ren. In some eerie manner the Star Guardians had manipulated time as they had space inside the Ruby Pyramid so that André and Gaby had joined them only an hour after their ordeal in the chamber of the flame, instead of the extended length of time it had taken the rest of them (or seemed to) to reach Amentet-Nefert and finally the ship inside the cylinder.

306

Now, as moving rainbows of crystal light caressed Gaby's sleeping body and healing sonic vibrations pulsed and thrummed through the small room, Eris could almost see Gaby's wasted body filling out, her breathing now deep and normal. Her hair was beginning to regain its old luster, and the nasty circular wound under her breast, where Kathy Bane had cruelly ripped off her Mentacom Medallion, was almost healed.

But, Eris realized, they would have to wait awhile longer to see how Gaby responded to the most important part of the treatment: the healing of her mind. Could she be successfully deprogrammed from the terrible influences of Nicasia's alien drugs and machines? The Star Guardians had expressed optimism after a brief examination of her mind, but it was a guarded optimism. They would be able to restore her thinking processes, but there might still be hidden levels of hypnotic influence deep inside the brain that they could not reach. The others would have to keep a close watch on her, but Eris had confidence in the Star Guardians' ability to heal.

Eris' brow furrowed as she recalled how that confidence had been rudely shaken a few hours ago. Why wouldn't they help André when it looked like he was facing certain death? Was it because they could look ahead and see that Gaby would arrive in time to shoot the killer and save him? Or was it really as they had explained, that they were forbidden to intervene directly in the conflict between the people of this planet and Nicasia's dark forces? So what *was* "directly"? Eris wondered. Surely healing Gaby and removing her as a pawn in Nicasia's evil game was directly intervening...wasn't it? She shrugged. I guess they have their own rules about all this, she decided, grateful that they were at least helping the girl.

Eris looked at her ringwatch, saw that Gaby still had five minutes of treatment to go. Yod had warned her not to expose the girl to the power of the healing crystals for more than twenty minutes at a time. There were to be two more such treatments; then they would know whether she had responded to their effects as she should.

When Gaby's treatment was over, Eris helped her dress and they rejoined the group.

"It's all like some horrible dream," Gaby told them as she hungrily wolfed down her food. "I remember hazy images of my stepmother and Kathy and Reaper Drum and a long walk down a strange tunnel...and then finding André." She flashed him a dazzling smile.

André had had his wounds tended to and was feeling great. Smiling back, he wanted to ask Gaby whether she remembered shooting the killer, but decided not to. He started to say something about the small pistol still in her jacket pocket, but his thoughts were interrupted by the mellow voice of Star Guardian Yod.

"We are happy that you are all together again. Your separations have been painful...and there may be more such separations in the future. But for now, relax and let us introduce ourselves to you visually at last."

There was a rush of excitement as the light in the small room dimmed and suddenly the agents found themselves floating in the limitless dark of interstellar space, surrounded by millions of stars blazing like acetylene flowers. The holographic illusion was breathtakingly perfect as they seemed to hurdle through the void toward a central point of hazy blue-white that rapidly resolved itself into a spectacularly beautiful spherical galactic cluster. From the central core, high velocity explosions were shooting out enormous gouts of fiery material equal to the mass of thousands of suns.

"Several decades of your years ago," Yod told them, "a new galaxy was discovered by your astronomers and assigned the number M87. By your calculations, M87 is some thirty million light-years from earth and about one hundred times the diameter of your own galaxy. It is a great spherical island containing billions of stars, many of which harbor solar systems with habitable planets. At its center is an enormous white hole continuously ejecting into space plasma and gases which in time coalesce into new suns and planets."

As the unseen narrator paused, Avram asked, "A white hole? Then where is the ejected matter coming from? Another universe?"

"In a manner of speaking, yes. What you are seeing is material that is being absorbed and accelerated to near light speed by a black hole in another system of reality imperceptible to your observations. This island universe is symbolic of Creation itself, which is constant and ever-increasing by the will of the force we call the One and which you know as God.

"The term 'universe,' however, is a misleading one, as it implies a singleness. There are an infinite number of 'universes,' or alternate reality continua, separated from each other by vibratory differences and perceptual limitations. Perhaps the term 'multiverse' would serve you better. At any rate, you can perceive only one of these continua at a time at your stage of development. What your eyes see as you peer outward from your world into space, and the light and radio-wave emissions registered by your machines, do not actually exist in terms of concrete physical reality."

"Oh, wow!" exclaimed Ray, unable to keep silent any longer. "Getting in deep here, folks. You mean all...*this*...isn't real?"

"It is real to your perceptions, Raymond; you are perceiving your *conception* of what is, rather than what actually is. Your beliefs, together with those of all others sharing your plane of reality, form the reality itself."

"Hold it!" Chris said. "Are you saying that we—all of us on the physical plane—created all this? What about God?"

Yod chuckled. "The One, being spirit only, can create only spirit, my friend. It cannot be limited to spatial or temporal concepts. You are Its creation, to be sure, but only the immortal part of you. It created you to be co-creators with It, to explore the denser, lower areas of existence and experience, in order to extend Its own experience outward into infinity. To you, Its children, It gave the power to create an environment of your own design—an environment of physical 'reality'—knowing that eventually, when you tired of your toys and had learned all you wished to learn, you would return to It and enrich Its own experience with yours, ending your apparent separation from It."

They were silent in the silent deeps of space, then, deeply moved by the Star Guardian's words.

309

After a moment, Eris asked softly, "Then...what about you, Yod? Are you and your people...?"

"Part of creation, Eris? Of course...we too are children of the One, as are all the beings in all the myriad worlds and systems of reality. Creation is limitless and inconceivable in its richness and variety. You may think of us as your elder brothers, if you like."

Abruptly the group experienced the stunning illusion of hurtling forward toward the blazing heart of the galaxy, passengers in an invisible starship, until the burning mass separated into billions of individual multicolored suns whirling past them, finally slowing down to focus in on one single large white star toward the edge of the cluster with a family of twelve planets imperceptably wheeling around it like titanic clockworks.

"Our homeworld is the fourth planet outward, which we call Il. We are known as the Ilu to ourselves, but we have many names to many worlds."

They gasped in delight at the lovely blue and golden planet swimming in the dark, with its family of twelve tiny moons clustered around it like children.

"Ilu..." murmured Chris, "That's the ancient Akkadian word for 'deity,' isn't it? Literally, 'Lofty One,' the root of the Hebrew word El...."

"That meaning was assigned to it by some of the earliest peoples we visited on your planet, Chris. To them, we were gods—Elohim, in the Hebrew plural. Almost all your ancient languages stem from ours, as do long-standing customs, myths and legends of many earth cultures. But a number of your scientists and writers guessed this long ago, my friends. It is not new to you."

"Then the Bible is correct when it refers to 'gods' instead of 'God'?" asked Chris. "'In the beginning the *gods* created Heaven and Earth'...?"

"Those who wrote your book failed to make clear the distinction between created beings like ourselves who had a hand in preparing your planet for life and guiding it down the long path of evolution, and the actual creation by the One of the Earth Spirit which became physically manifest through Its children. We are undoubtedly the 'gods' men-

310

tioned in your book, but we did not create your world. We regret the centuries of confusion this misunderstanding has caused you."

"Why can't we see you?" Gaby asked in a hushed voice.

"Oh, but you can see us, Gabrielle," replied Yod, and instantly black space blinked into white dazzle and they were inside a vast soaring palace of alabaster and crystal and murmuring fountains and exotic greenery, and there, standing before them, dressed in long flowing robes the color of snow, were...the Star Guardians!

Three of them towered into the crystalline air like slender trees, twelve, fourteen feet high, with high-domed hairless heads and large, luminous, violet eyes. Their features were definitely humanoid, and their faces radiated an air of peace and wisdom and immense love. A slight violet cast suffused their golden skin, as though the blood coursing beneath were a royal purple instead of red. Their great height gave them an impression of dignity and agelessness and inexpressable power under absolute control, and standing there, welcoming smiles on their faces, they seemed as solid as the chairs holding the awed and delighted agents.

Forgetting herself and everything except the wonderful beings before her, Eris leaped up, dazedly walked forward and tried to grasp the slender, long-fingered hand stretched out to her, but her hand went through it like smoke.

"Oh..." she said, flustered, "you look so real...I...."

"We are indeed real," said the tallest of the group, smiling more broadly, "but not within your present time-space reference. We are communicating with you through an omnidimensional mental projection, what you would call a hologram. We are presently aboard our mothership, located about six thousand light-years from your solar system, approximately midway between the constellations Cygnus and Lyra. I am Yod, as you know from my voice, and these are my ka-brothers, Vau and Khu."

The other two beings bowed slightly.

Still feeling a little foolish, Eris sat down quietly, grateful for the absence of wisecracks.

"Excuse me," said Avram, a puzzled look on his face, "but if you're more than 1,800 parsecs away, how can you communicate sounds and images instantaneously? The speed of light—"

"We do not depend upon physical methods of communication, Avram," Yod replied, a touch of impatience in his voice for the first time. "Our communications can reach any part of any universe instantaneously, for they are entirely mental. The speed of thought is infinitely faster than the speed of light."

Avram nodded, obviously impressed but attempting to hide it.

"Now," Yod continued, "we will take you back in time thousands of years to show you our first contact with one of your earth civilizations. I think it will interest you."

A new hologram formed around them with stunning clarity. Sun-baked sand, hot blue sky. A group of dark-haired, brown-skinned people dressed in simple white garments were pointing upwards, hands shielding eyes from the relentless hammering heat of the sun. They babbled excitedly among themselves in an unrecognizable tongue as a huge silvery disc suddenly arced across the cobalt sky, rapidly becoming larger and larger.

Yod continued: "The people of ancient Khem—Egypt—had been told by their astrologer-priests that men from the sky would come to earth in this month, when Sirius, the Dog Star, was high in the heavens. Their prophecies had long foretold the coming of these beings, who would cross the seas of heaven in a great silver boat and teach them the secrets of the gods."

The huge saucership landed gently as goosedown on the desert sands a short distance away from the awestruck Egyptians. The illusion of being there was so real, Eris could almost feel the heat, the dry dusty air, the heart-stopping emotions of wonder and terror experienced by the brown people as they waited for the first sight of the gods from the sky.

Even though she knew what they looked like now, she could feel the base of her neck tingling as slowly, eerily, seven tall, willowy shadows began to form on the sand outside the ship. Gradually they took on color and substance, and in moments the Star Guardians stood revealed in the

312

harsh light of earth's sun—the three who had introduced themselves plus four others.

The Egyptians prostrated themselves in the hot sand, unwilling to look at the newcomers directly. Eris marveled that the thousands of years between the events they were witnessing seemed as nothing to the age of the Guardians: physically they looked the same, only now they wore tight-fitting suits of a silver metallic cloth that sparkled and glistened in the brilliant sunlight as though encrusted with diamond dust. Gloves and boots of a rich deep purple material resembling leather completed their attire.

The spacemen moved forward and gently lifted the people up, speaking to them in their own language, telling them not to be afraid, calming them, saying that they did not wish to be worshipped, that they came as friends to help and teach.

The hologram dissolved to an overview of a peaceful primitive agricultural village scattered around the Giza Plateau and along the banks of the Nile.

"Time passed, and the people of Khem came to accept us. We taught them methods of irrigation, crop rotation, planting and harvesting with the phases of the moon and planets. Finally, we instructed them in ways to utilize their mind power and conserve physical energy."

The agents now saw a small group of shaven-headed priests sitting crosslegged under a palm tree, receiving instruction from one of the spacemen. Looking closely, Eris was surprised to see that one of the priests was a woman. Her eyes were closed, a look of intense concentration on her face. Eris watched in delight as a large clay water jug in front of the woman wobbled, then slowly rose several feet into the air and floated there, shaking but not spilling any of its water.

"How 'bout that, Av?" Eris whispered, "Wouldn't the guys back at PSI-QUARK love to see this! She's almost in your league."

"Almost," said Avram, a little coolly.

Now the woman had safely lowered the vessel to the ground, still without spilling a drop. Eris clapped, even though she knew the woman couldn't hear her. "It's nice that you taught women as well as men, Yod. That period of history wasn't exactly famous for female equality."

"At this time, women were accepted into the priesthood of Khem as readily as men if they showed the same spiritual inclination and aptitude. In fact, in many cases, we found that women had a far greater aptitude for mental discipline than men. But the proper use of the mind was not easy for any of them to learn. We find that utilizing the natural polarity between the sexes greatly enhances the balance and harmony of feats of psychic power. On the three-dimensional physical plane, your instruments do not reveal any difference between the crystalline cell protoplasm in men and women. However, on a higher level of consciousness, there exists a molecular dissimilarity which, when linked together by mental energy contributed equally by a man and a woman, causes the completion of a psychoelectric circuit which makes possible feats of psychic power greater than can be achieved by either sex alone.

"We had taught the Atlanteans and the people of Mu before them, and civilizations on other worlds as well. The first step was to teach them how to cleanse their psyches of negative vibrations. This took several months of intensive preparation through systems of diet, concentration, meditation, and ritual. We could only work with those who had the highest spiritual energy.

"We taught them how to tap and utilize the spirit-force within, how to accumulate and 'store up' psychic energy in order to utilize it in manipulating matter. This is a very powerful force, as you have discovered in your own training, and must be handled with great discretion."

Again the hologram dissolved, this time to a scene of nine white-robed priests walking slowly down a desert road. Six feet over their heads floated an enormous block of cut granite weighing several tons, yet moving through the air as lightly as a helium-filled balloon.

Eris let out a squeal of surprise. "That's the scene I've seen in my past-life dreams! When I was in the hospital in Cairo I remembered being a little girl named Paoni in ancient Egypt watching people carrying stones over their heads just like that!"

314

"Yes, Eris," said Yod, "your particular psychic talent is the ability to mentally breach the barriers between different systems of reality and alternate probabilities to experience consciousness in other existences. Elsewhere and else*when*, you might say, part of your oversoul is also this little girl living her life in a time that seems to be far in your past, but is actually occurring *now* in simultaneous time."

"Whoa!" Eris exclaimed. "Are you saying that there's really no such thing as past lives or reincarnation?"

"Yes and no, Eris. You do indeed experience many different lifetimes, but it is only your three-dimensional frame of reference that sees them as 'past' or 'future' lives. Outside the physical plane of existence, time and space are meaningless concepts. All of creation takes place simultaneously in an eternal 'Now.' But you see this as the ring of reincarnation, the incurring and paying of karmic debts down through an apparently linear timeline, reinforced by your world's historic documentation. Through the use of this great illusion your soul can learn its lessons and eventually find its way 'back' to the One, Whom in reality it has never left."

Then, as the priests surmounted a high sandy hill, the huge block of stone still bobbing through the air above them, the agents could see, spread out on the vast plain beyond, a scene that set their pulses pounding with excitement and awe.

Almost as old as the framework of our continent, the earliest Egyptian civilization dates back to the ancient red race. The colossal Sphinx of Gizeh near the Great Pyramid is its handiwork. From the time when the Delta...did not yet exist, the huge symbolic animal lay upon its granite hill, before the chain of the Libyan Mountains, looking at the sea dashing against its feet where today the sands of the desert are spread.
—*Édouard Schuré,* THE GREAT INITIATES

CHAPTER TWENTY-NINE

PYRAMID AND SPHINX

AMENTET-NEFERT: 19 DECEMBER 2020

Locked in silence, the agents watched the awesome scene that was unfolding on the desert sands before them: thousands of brown workers were swarming like ants about a majestic and familiar structure in the process of construction. Everywhere groups of nine with huge blocks of stone hovering over their heads were being directed to various locations by overseers, while other, larger groups were raising gigantic blocks into place as easily as if they were made of feathers. Scattered in strategic places around the building site, the seven Star Guardians were keeping a violet eye on things.

"The Great Pyramid," Eris exclaimed at last. "That's what they're building, isn't it?"

"Not exactly, Eris," replied Yod. "This pyramid was the first ever built in Egypt...it is far older than the present structure you call *Ta Khut*. That pyramid was built upon the ruins of this one."

As the agents watched in fascination the spectacle of the huge pyramid taking shape, Chris noticed how different this scene was from that envisioned by most historians and archaeologists. There were no brutal overseers with whips, no masses of thousands of slaves groaning under the weight of huge blocks of stone pulled on wooden skids across impossible distances of desert, none of the complicated hoists or flotation mechanisms postulated by some scientists, no forced labor to build a pharaoh's tomb, just a few thousand people working willingly and with a great sense of spiritual achievement, using the power of their combined minds to construct a superb edifice of stone to the honor and glory of the Creator.

Chris recalled a passage in Book II of Herodotus's *History* in which the Greek historian had visited Thebes and been told that there was a tradition of priestly rulers there extending back 12,000 years! He was also told that the gods had come down from the skies and lived with the Egyptians for a generation, then returned to their heavenly home. But one question still intrigued Chris.

"Yod...we now know how the stone blocks were transported and assembled, but how were they quarried and dressed for use? They didn't have dynamite to blast the rock loose—did you give them lasers?"

"No...we wanted the entire project to be accomplished solely through the use of mental power, as a lesson to all mankind of the accomplishments possible through the constructive use of psychic energy. The granite was cut and polished using the full force of a tightly focused beam of psychic energy directed from the pineal gland, or 'third eye.'

"Another factor that helped us in our task was that some of the priests of Khem had been Atlanteans and already knew some of these techniques. They had built pyramids and other monuments this way in Atlantis and helped design and make the whole project less difficult by assisting their brothers and sisters to master these mental skills."

"It's obvious from what you've shown us that this all occurred a long, long time ago," said Avram, "much longer than historians believe. Most archaeologists think that any kind of civilization in Egypt doesn't extend much past 3,000

317

B.C., with primitive stone-age tribes as far back as 13,000 B.C."

Yod was amused. "As one of your great dramatists, Bernard Shaw, said in one of his plays, 'History will tell lies—as usual.' Of course, your scientists are not lying, but merely doing the best they can with the facts they have uncovered so far. They would be astounded to know that the events you are witnessing took place around 200,000 B.C., during the reign of King Hapi, long before the pharaohs. He was a highly advanced ruler, a priest, and eager to work with us to teach universal concepts and laws to his people. Together we put Egypt on the road to becoming one of the world's greatest civilizations. Unfortunately, as with Atlantis and Mu before her, she did not remain true to her spiritual heritage and eventually fell into a materialistic decline."

"Okay...that explains the Pyramid," said André, "but what about the Sphinx? Somehow the two always seem to go together."

"Indeed they do," replied the Star Guardian, and the hologram dissolved into an impressive view of a huge roughly rectangular bulk of pinkish-gray granite towering above the desert sands. Around it, dwarfed by its stark and rugged bulk, the seven Star Guardians stood in a half-circle. A closer view revealed their eyes closed and a look of intense concentration on their faces. In the golden morning light they resembled huge statues of precious metal, unmoving and eternal.

The agents were absolutely quiet now, hardly daring to breathe, sensing that the awesome mindpower of these space giants was being focused on some gigantic task before them, "revving up" to incredible intensity. Then, slowly at first but rapidly increasing, chips of stone began to spray out into the hot desert air; sections of the pink granite seemed to melt, flow and reshape themselves. As they watched in fascination and awe, the familiar figure of the Great Sphinx gradually took shape, emerging out of naked stone like some strange creature breaking out of a cocoon, tons of massive rock being molded like clay by the invisible mindforce of seven giant beings working as one.

318

Soon the incredible task was completed: where only minutes before had stood tons of naked rock, now a gigantic and beautiful figure crouched in awesome majesty on the desert sands, a figure to challenge and intrigue mankind down through the centuries as no other ever has. Polished and gleaming in its newness, the powerful lion's body with its huge outstretched front paws was topped by a handsome and serene human face in an Egyptian headdress, staring outward into infinity.

Slowly then, one by one the giants opened their eyes and walked forward to inspect their pristine creation.

Spontaneously, the agents broke into a round of applause which reverberated loudly in the small compartment in odd contrast to the apparent desert space around them.

"Bravo!" shouted André. "What a performance! Eat your heart out, Michelangelo!"

"That was wonderful, Yod!" exclaimed Eris. "How beautiful it is...was.... We've never been able to imagine what it looked like new, its face is so battered and mutilated now."

"Thank you. We wanted to create something for humanity that would symbolize man's purpose on earth. *Arq-ur*, the Sphinx, is humankind rising out of its animal consciousness; it is the Guardian of the Sacred Laws of the Multiverse and a symbol of our relationship to Eternity and to the One."

"But whose face is that on the Sphinx?" asked Eris. "It doesn't look at all like the face we see today."

"The Sphinx you see today was refurbished several times and given new faces over the centuries. It was first made in the likeness of Prince Coh, the deceased husband of Queen Moo of the prehistoric Mayans. She had come to Egypt, where she asked King Hapi to honor Coh, so they requested that his face be used for the monument. His countenance stood watch over the desert and the Nile for thousands of years, until the Sphinx was damaged and rebuilt with a new face."

"Yod, I have a question," said Avram, a troubled look on his face. "Several times now you've mentioned that these original monuments were damaged or destroyed and that the

319

ones we have today have been rebuilt. Can you elaborate on this? What destroyed them?"

"The Sphinx was not entirely destroyed, merely damaged a bit over the centuries. It alone withstood the furies that shook your planet, gigantic forces that collapsed even the most stable architectural design that exists—the pyramid."

The lifelike Sphinx, shimmering in the sunbaked sands, faded away into an emptiness of space with the bright points of millions of stars framing a large globe of the earth. It spun visibly on its axis for a few moments, the north and south poles indicated by small blinking lights. Then, suddenly, as if an unseen hand had twisted it, the globe tilted so that the north and south poles were now blinking at an angle of 45 degrees from the original axis. Eris caught her breath as the significance of what she was seeing hit her.

"This rather crude model will serve to show you what, in essence, has happened to your planet not one, but many times during past eons. Approximately every 12,000 years, the poles shift and change, usually rather suddenly, causing great storms, winds, tidal waves and gigantic earthquakes in some areas. Old land sinks, new continents arise. Areas that were buried under miles of ice become tropical, and steaming jungles find themselves almost instantly snowbound. This time, the pole shift caused a huge flood which wiped out the Giza Plateau, preceded by an enormous earthquake that changed the entire Mediterranean area. Our pyramid was destroyed almost completely, leaving only the Sphinx as a silent, eternal reminder of ancient days.

"Slowly the planet returned to normal, and during the thousands of years that followed, many different civilizations lived on and around the Plateau. The consciousness of humanity was raised once again to a high level and was flourishing, when in 9,000 B.C., the poles shifted slightly again, and Poseidia, the last remnant of the civilization called Atlantis, sank into the Atlantic Ocean.

"However, at least a thousand years before this event, many of the Atlantean initiates, priests, and artisans had resettled in Egypt, and using the techniques of meditation and mindpower we had taught their ancestors, rebuilt the old

320

pyramid, erecting the one you now know as *Ta Khut* on its foundations. The Sphinx was also refurbished at this time."

"So these periodic pole shifts have given rise to the legends of the Deluge which we find in the Bible and in the cultures of many peoples throughout the world?" Avram asked.

"That is correct," Yod replied.

"Did you come back to help the people rebuild the monuments?" asked Raymond.

"Yes, we did return for a short time to help restore the spiritual vibrations and supervise the reconstruction of the Great Pyramid and the Sphinx. Again, the powers of mind and spirit were used to quarry, dress, carry and fit the huge blocks of stone. The Pyramid was built in a much shorter time than your archaeologists believe and is far older than they think. The Pharaoh Cheops had nothing to do with *Ta Khut*, for it was never intended to be a tomb, but rather a temple of initiation for all who wished to inter their worldly natures and dedicate themselves to the Light."

"When was this?" asked Eris, curiosity burning like fire in her eyes. "Was this the period when you built Amentet-Nefert and Ka-Ren?"

"Approximately 10,000 B.C., many centuries after the time of King Hapi, we built the underground city as a duplicate of one constructed on the surface long before, during the first period, about 200,000 B.C. In the center of the city we built Ka-Ren, carved with our minds from a single ruby created from common sand."

"You mean you altered the sand atomically—transmuted it into ruby?" asked Raymond, fascinated by the alchemical inference.

"That is correct. Then we shaped it into a sealed chamber to conceal the spacecraft you are inside now, as well as other valuables we wished to preserve.

"Did the people of that time know about the city and Ka-Ren?" asked André.

"The leaders of the holy city of Aicerao, near what is now the Giza Plateau, knew about Ka-Ren and Amentet-Nefert. We revealed this information to them because our own teachers had instructed us to assist the leaders in preserving records of man's history, treasures and machines of various kinds, and certain other objects for posterity. So we did this, with the help of a specially chosen group of people who were sworn to secrecy. These people have reincarnated today...*and you are among them!*"

"Us?" exclaimed Eris. "You mean...we...we're the ones who...buried the records?"

"Yes, Eris," replied Yod gently, "each of you has a part in this great drama, the next act in the play you began 12,000 years ago. You were all alive during this part of Egypt's distant history."

"But who were we—where were we in all this?" asked Eris.

In answer, the present faded away once again into the distant past...a familiar glow of dark crimson surrounded them. They were dressed in robes of white linen, bordered with various colors. They were six, and behind them came others, softly chanting prayers and rituals of sealing and of protection. Ahead of them walked the tall, commanding figure of a man they knew to be Hept Supht, High Priest of Ra. Their minds were focused intently on long litters which floated before them, about four feet off the polished ruby floor, litters carrying myriads of different objects, levitated by their combined mental powers. Strange and intricate machines; papyrus and metal scrolls containing records of man's distant past; gold, jewels and artifacts of many cultures; musical instruments; art objects of incredible beauty; all these and much more were being transported deep under the earth to a place of storage, there to remain, carefully guarded by psychic barriers, until the time would come for them to be discovered by a far future generation.

"This was your promise," said Yod. "That having incarnated in this life to serve Ra...and to help bury these records and treasures for posterity, you would all reincarnate again and come together as a group in the distant future, when the time was appointed to unseal the vault and release the content of the Ruby Pyramid that you had buried so many millennia ago.

"Eris, you were a priestess named Net; André, a music teacher named Hes; Avram, you were an astrologer called Zant; Raymond, you were Tem, a healer and alchemist; and

Gabrielle, you were a man then, a priest of the Temple Beautiful named La-no.

"And so, my friends," concluded Yod as the scene faded and the dazed agents once again found themselves in their own bodies in the present, "you have fulfilled the promise you made together so long ago. You have returned once more to the Ruby Pyramid.

"But now we are finished with the past. We must turn our attention to the present. It is time for you to fulfill the more urgent purpose of your coming here—a purpose none of us could foresee thousands of years ago. The treasures and records you buried were not to be revealed until mankind was spiritually more advanced, but desperate necessity has changed that. Although we are reluctant to do so, we will now hand over into your keeping the device called...the Immobilizer."

PART THREE

THE WEAPON

I was struck dumb with amazement, and when Lord Carnarvon, unable to stand the suspense any longer, inquired anxiously, "Can you see anything?" it was all I could do to get out the words, "Yes, wonderful things."
—Howard Carter, THE TOMB OF TUTANKHAMEN

CHAPTER THIRTY

TREASURE AND TREACHERY

AMENTET-NEFERT/OVER EGYPT: 19 DECEMBER 2020

They stood again in the center of the huge cylindrical hall that housed the Guardian spaceship, regarding the seven bronze doors that ringed the chamber.

"Behind those doors you will find the records and artifacts you deemed worthy of preservation," Yod told them. "You may examine them briefly, but then you must leave this place. Outside, your enemy's plans come ever closer to fruition."

"I don't like the sound of that," Chris said to the others. "Yod's right—let's not forget what we came down here for in the first place."

"God only knows how long we've really been down here," André said, his arm tightly around Gaby, who smiled up at him.

"So how do we get into these rooms?" Raymond asked the air anxiously, hoping Yod was still "tuned in."

"There are seven doors," the Star Guardian replied. "There are six of you. Each of you must stand before one of the doors engraved with hieroglyphs."

Chris noticed that the seventh door was of a silvery metal, perfectly smooth and blank. A little chill tickled down his spine. Why was that door different...?

Yod continued: "Now each of you must concentrate intently on the writing on the door before you. Memorize it, visualize it in your mind as vividly as possible; imprint it on your brain."

After studying the markings closely, the six agents closed their eyes, visualizing the patterns in exact detail, holding the images brightly and clearly, as they had been taught to do at PSI-QUARK.

Then a strange thing happened: as they concentrated intently on their individual doors, their inner sight widened out much like a movie theater curtain pulling back to reveal a larger screen, and they suddenly saw all six doors at once! The realization came to them that the six patterns were linked, forming one single message written across six doors. And then—even stranger—they suddenly *knew* what the message was! Ancient memory came swirling back into consciousness across a bridge of centuries, and they recalled how they had stood here long ago with the high priest Hept Supht and carved this message for posterity into the metal doors *with their minds!* It read: "Herein do we, children of the Mother-Father God and citizens of Ararat, place all that we believe to be worthy of our world and our time, and times of old, when the Mother Empires ruled, and of times before that, unto the beginning of the world. Herein lie the records of man on earth and of the things which he hath done. Here may they lie protected from the knowledge of man and the ravages of nature, until the day appointed for their revelation is come. In the holy Name of Light, we seal these doors against all intrusion until that day shall dawn."

And as six minds reached back across the enormous gulf of time and reread what they had written so many lifetimes ago, they heard a hollow grinding noise, then a great serpent-hiss of air rushing into hermetically sealed spaces; then the grinding noise became louder, as if the world were shaking itself apart around them.

Opening their eyes, they saw the six doors slowly rumbling aside into stone sockets, revealing six large chambers filled with objects that seemed at once strange and familiar.

"The last of the seals have been broken," said Yod. "Enter and look upon your past."

The next few hours passed in a timeless blur of excitement and delight for the six companions as they wandered among a gleaming treasure trove of antiquity perfectly preserved in these six metal-lined chambers.

Here were artistic creations of incredible beauty and delicacy, crafted from gold, silver, ivory, ebony, alabaster and precious stones; jewelry, furnishings and utensils of all kinds; heaps of emeralds, diamonds, rubies, sapphires—many the size of a fist—glittering with rainbow fires in the same eternal illumination that had lighted the passageway from the Great Pyramid. They saw fantastic machines of metal and crystal, including electric generators and healing devices like the one on board the saucer; exquisite musical instruments: harps, lyres, flutes, sistrums, cymbals and other reed and stringed instruments; there were crystals that glowed with inner flame and sang when you touched them; coffers of seeds and grain, dried fruits and vegetables; vials and urns filled with delicious-smelling incenses, powders and perfumes that sent Gaby and Eris into ecstasies. There were several small, ornately decorated one- and two-seater ground vehicles designed to be powered by broadcast crystal energy; a fascinating array of medical and surgical implements was on display, including a curious electric scalpel; a number of metal chests contained clothing, garments of fine linen that looked as if they had been woven only hours ago. Raymond was particularly fascinated by several black marble coffers which contained ceramic urns and vessels filled with strange chemical compounds, potions, elixirs, unguents, attars, poisons, and other forbidding substances whose uses were set forth on rolls of papyrus laid in the chests with them. One of the objects that most interested Avram was a sheet of malleable glass that bent in any direction without breaking! And both he and Raymond pondered a long time over several large, sullenly glowing crystals they recognized as the legendary Firestones of Atlantis, capable of destructive energies surpassing even lasers or particle-beam weapons.

Two of the rooms were lined with thousands of scrolls of papyrus and paper-thin metal, stone tablets and small crystals that proved to be miniature audio-visual recordings. These were the actual Records themselves: written in a combination of Atlantean and Egyptian heiroglyphics, here was the entire history of Atlantis, and Lemuria before her, and of other civilizations only dimly dreamed of since the dawn of creation on this planet. Here, Chris found the culmination of all his life's work and study; this was indisputably the greatest archeological discovery in history. Knowledge of man's true past, hidden from him for millennia, could now be revealed, so that all the earth's people could at last realize their ancient roots, their proud intergalactic heritage, their kinship with all the peoples of the universe. Chris realized now that to reveal and interpret this knowledge for the world was really why he had been led to this place. He felt awe and gratitude at this wonderful privilege that had been given him. And everything was in a perfect stage of preservation! No crumbling papyri, no mummy-dust here!

A soft touch on his arm brought him plummeting down out of his archeological cloud-city to see, framed by a torrent of tawny-gold hair, a face more beautiful to him than all the secret treasures in all the treasure vaults of the world.

"Playtime's over," Eris said with a wistful smile that told him she knew exactly how he felt. "Yod says we've got to take the Immobilizer and leave." She nodded toward the mysterious seventh chamber.

His face was somber as he held her to him briefly, looking over her shoulder at that ominously blank silver door. He nodded in return, then they turned and went to join the others waiting for them in front of the door.

"This chamber you did not seal, my friends," said Yod. "We did...and we did not mean for it ever to be opened by humans. So we will open it...and we do so with great regret, for we had hoped that it would never again be necessary for this weapon to be used. Please stand well back."

By the seriousness of the Star Guardian's tone, the six friends knew they had better take him at his word, so they moved back several yards. Eris' mouth felt dust-dry and her heart was hammering in her chest like a mad drummer.

There was no sound in the cylindrical chamber, but the silver door began to glow with a brilliant white light; brighter and brighter it became, until the agents could no longer look at it, but like the flame in the chamber they had passed through, it emitted no heat. There was a steam-engine hiss of imploding air, such as they had heard in the other rooms, then the light faded, a small star brought to earth to die, and when they opened their eyes the door was simply gone, as though it had never existed.

Cautiously, the six entered the seventh chamber; the glowing metal walls cast pale shadowless light over their expectant faces. The room was identical to the other six, except that it was not packed with records and artifacts.

Quite the contrary: it appeared to be completely empty!

For a brief terrible moment Eris thought that Nicasia had stolen the Immobilizer, had somehow teleported it out of the room with one of her alien machines ....

Then Yod responded to their unspoken fears. "Do not worry...the machine is here, where it has remained undisturbed for centuries. But it is vibrating at a higher frequency than your human senses can perceive. Watch."

No one breathed as a shimmering circle materialized in the air before them, six feet above the floor. Quickly it took substance and became a flickering sphere of light about the size of a soccer ball. Then the coruscating lights dimmed and winked out, and floating in the air was a perfectly round metallic sphere, pale silver in color, with no exterior markings.

After a long silence, Raymond asked, "That's *it?* That's...the Immobilizer? The universe's most awesome weapon is an overgrown ball bearing?"

The others laughed, grateful for the shattered tension. Even Yod chuckled slightly as he replied, "Do not judge its power by its appearance, Raymond. It is compact, yes, but when activated it has an effective radius of one hundred miles."

Ray whistled softly. "Well, what does it do for a hundred miles? What does it immobilize? And how do we activate it?"

331

"You are naturally curious about this thing you have come so far to find, but we would rather not explain it at this time. There is still a chance that you may not be forced to use it...the mere threat of your possessing it may serve to restrain Algol."

Avram's scientific curiosity was seething inside him like a boiling cauldron and he was barely managing to keep the lid on. He stepped forward, reached out to touch the metal sphere, but found his hand stopped by an invisible barrier about a foot beyond the machine. The barrier seemed to extend all around the sphere, and as he put pressure against it, the sphere simply moved up and away from him until he stopped pushing.

"The Immobilizer is protected by a harmless but absolutely impenetrable force field," the Star Guardian explained. "Thus, once activated, the weapon cannot be harmed or turned off until its cycle of operation is complete."

Avram clenched his fist in anger. "So now we have the perfect weapon to use against Nicasia," he said, an edge in his voice, "but we don't know what it does or how to make it work. We can't even touch it! What the hell kind of deterrent is that? What if she calls our bluff?"

"If the time should come when you must use it, we will instruct you. We ask that you trust us in this matter." There was a note of sadness and perhaps even apprehension in the Star Guardian's voice that they had not heard before. It was as sobering as a shower of ice water.

"Okay," Eris said finally, as disappointed as the others. "We'll play it your way, Yod. We do trust you. You've helped us so far, and we're grateful." Then to the others, she said, "Come on, gang, let's take our doomsday beachball and go home."

As the others made preparations to leave Ka-Ren, Eris contacted the President on her Mentacom Medallion. He was delighted to hear from her: he'd been extremely anxious because of her long silence. After filling him in on everything they'd experienced, she told him the good/bad news about the Immobilizer.

The President's mind was still for a moment as he absorbed the mixed information. He decided not to get upset.

WELL...AT LEAST WE HAVE POSSESSION OF THE DAMNED THING. WE'LL JUST HAVE TO TRUST THE GUARDIANS TO COME THROUGH WITH THE INFORMATION IF IT'S NEEDED. PRAY GOD IT WON'T BE. BESIDES, WHAT CHOICE DO WE HAVE?

NONE, I GUESS, replied Eris. THE GUARDIANS ARE GIVING US THEIR SAUCER, TOO. IT'S INCREDIBLE! THEY'RE GOING TO TEACH ME TO PILOT IT.

GREAT! NOW LISTEN, 12—I WANT YOU AND 6 TO HIGHTAIL IT BACK HERE WITH THE IMMOBILIZER RIGHT AWAY. DON'T EVEN GO BACK TO YOUR HOTEL FOR A TOOTHBRUSH. I'M TAKING NO CHANCES ON EITHER YOU OR 6 OR THE MACHINE FALLING INTO NICASIA'S HANDS.

That makes sense, Eris thought (on another channel): Gaby has been through enough pure hell for one lifetime....

I WANT THE REST OF YOU TO STAY IN CAIRO FOR A FEW WEEKS TO KEEP AN EYE ON NICASIA, the President continued. *BUT BE CAREFUL!*

OKAY, CHIEF. NOW WHAT ABOUT THE RECORDS AND TREASURE HERE? DO YOU WANT US TO LOAD UP THE SAUCER AND BRING ALL THIS STUFF BACK WITH US?

GOD, NO...LEAVE IT. NO TIME FOR THAT. WHEN ALL THIS MADNESS IS OVER, YOU CAN ALL GO BACK AND CATALOGUE IT AND HAUL IT OUT THEN. WE HAVE A VISUAL RECORD FOR NOW, DON'T WE?

Eris smiled, remembering the delight André and Marielle had taken in carefully recording everything in the vaults.

WE SURE DO. BUT WHAT ABOUT THE EGYPTIAN GOVERNMENT? WON'T THEY OBJECT? AFTER ALL, THE STUFF REALLY BELONGS TO THEM.

NOT ANY MORE, IT DOESN'T. WHILE YOU GUYS WERE DOWN THE RABBIT HOLE, NICASIA FINALLY HAD HER WAY WITH THE EGYPTIAN PARLIAMENT. THE ENTIRE GIZA PLATEAU—EVERYTHING ON IT AND *UNDER* IT—NOW TECHNICALLY BELONGS TO HER.

OH, NO! INCLUDING THE IMMOBILIZER? BUT—The President grinned mentally. I SAID "TECHNICALLY"...AS ANY LAWYER OR FOOTBALL COACH WILL TELL YOU, POSSESSION IS NINE-TENTHS OF THE GAME. YOU JUST GET BACK HERE WITH THE BALL, AND WE'LL WORRY ABOUT LEGAL ENTANGLEMENTS LATER.

OKAY, 21, WE SHOULD BE BACK IN WASHINGTON BY TOMORROW.

With that, Eris signed off and relayed the President's instructions to the others. She felt a heavy sadness at the thought of being parted from Chris, and knew Gaby was feeling it too for André, but it was for the best...and besides, it would only be for a few weeks; then they would all rendezvous in Washington.

But now it was time to turn her full attention to the Star Guardian spaceship. A half-hour of instruction sufficed to thoroughly familiarize her with the alien controls. It was basically very simple—far simpler than any other craft she'd flown, including the *Dawn Wing*. Much of the operation was mental: for instance, she had only to visualize where she wanted to be and press a certain panel and the ship would instantly teleport itself to that location! Or she could fly it there by interacting manually with the colored lights and keys on the console. Gaby watched closely over her shoulder, fascinated.

"This baby's such a cinch to fly, I'll bet even you could do it, Gaby," Eris said, beaming with delight from the pilot's seat (somewhat oversized, she noted, for an alien rear much larger than hers—but very comfortable). Gaby shook her head. "No way, Eris. It's all yours."

Soon everyone was aboard and ready to go, the Immobilizer bobbing obediently behind them like the metallic beachball it resembled. Yod explained that it was now keyed to their auras and would follow any or all of them around like a pet until they agreed to release it into a sealed chamber similar to the one they had found it in.

Or until they had to use it.

Then it was time to bid farewell to the Star Guardians.

"May the One be with you and grant you victory in your struggle," said Yod. "If you should need us, think of us intently, visualize us in your minds, and we will contact you."

"Goodbye, Yod," Eris said for all of them, her voice choking in her throat. "And thanks for everything...We'll never forget you...."

When everyone was ready, Eris initiated the power sequence as she had been taught. For a moment nothing happened, but then a powerful humming began to throb through the craft. The glass cylinder in the center of the control room began to glow with rainbow light, and she could feel long-dormant electromagnetic energies building, building.

Eris grinned triumphantly at her companions, who returned her grin, then she pressed a green panel and a beam of violet light sprang up from the crystal lens and centered itself on her forehead, just above and between her eyes. She felt a slight tingling sensation for a second, then nothing.

She was now "connected" to the ship's teleportation drive. Closing her eyes, she visualized the surface of the Egyptian desert far above, and immediately a three-dimensional holographic representation spread out across the console before her. She layered details into the scene: imaging the sand's texture and color, silver-gray under the moonlight (instruments had told her it was night and a full

335

moon above), the ebon velvet of the sky, the Sphinx and Pyramids small stone ghosts in the distance.

Now the crystal column was glowing a rich blue-violet and full power thrummed through the ship. The six agents were rigid and tingling with anticipation: each of them knew there were miles of rock and sand between them and the surface, not to mention the enclosing metal chamber inside the Ruby Pyramid itself...but they trusted the Star Guardians and they trusted their pilot.

"Hang on!" Eris cried gleefully. "Going...*up!*"

She pressed the red panel beside the green one and concentrated on her destination...and nothing happened!

But something had. Although the occupants of the ship had felt nothing at all, the ship was now hovering 200 yards above the desert, a blue-green corona glowing brightly around its perimeter. Inside, Eris' destination-image faded, to be replaced by the real thing as the front section of the ship became transparent, revealing a magnificent panorama of the argent desert beneath them.

They were about forty miles south of the Giza Plateau. Eris switched the ship to manual and the violet beam winked out. The power cylinder glowed greenish-yellow as she sent the craft skimming over the silent sands toward the Plateau.

As they approached the Sphinx and the Pyramids, it became evident that Nicasia hadn't been wasting her time. Eris recalled with a shudder what Yod had told them: "*Your enemy's plans come ever closer to fruition....*" A twelve-foot chain-link fence topped with barbed-wire spirals had been erected around the entire Giza Plateau, and they could see clusters of temporary shelters and excavation equipment near the Sphinx. Eris breathed a silent prayer that the great stone sentinel was still intact...it looked undisturbed as she came closer.

Suddenly tiny sparks of light began to dance on the desert floor; Chris recognized them instantly as coming from automatic weapons.

"Watch it, honey! They're firing on us! The place is swarming with guards!"

336

"No sweat," Eris replied confidently. "They can't touch us in this baby, even with hand-held missiles. I just want to see what they're doing down th—"

A silver flash cut her words short; her smile died and she felt a hand of ice grip her spine. Something manta-like and very fast hurled itself up from the desert floor straight toward them, gleaming in the moonlight like an executioner's blade.

"Oh, shit," Chris muttered. "One of those cobra-ships, like the one we—" Eris knew her saucer had no weapons; she had only a split second before the goat-men would be within range and emerald death would spear out to cut them to slag. She slammed her hand down on the green panel, visualizing a distant deserted landing strip she remembered at Cairo International Airport. As a green beam lanced out from the oncoming cobracraft, she hit the red panel.

The goat-men bleated in astonishment as they watched their perfectly aimed ray slash through...nothing! Their quarry had simply winked out of existence before their eyes!

Hovering in the darkness over the airport, the agents said goodbye with lots of solid hugging and kissing all around. Then they split up: Eris lowered the craft to the ground and the four men and Marielle disembarked, melting away into the sheltering night.

Fighting back the potato in her throat, her lips still tingling from Chris' last kiss, Eris flicked the honey-gold hair out of her eyes and took the saucer up to 4,000 feet. Below, Cairo spread out like a glittering fling of jewels, reminding her of the fabulous trove of wealth they had left behind, far below.

"Well, kiddo, what'll it be?" Eris asked, turning to Gaby, whose eyes were glowing with excitement. "Shall I teleport us home, or shall we take the long way around?"

"Oh, let's go the long way," Gaby said. "This is so wonderful, Eris. Boy, will I be glad to see the last of Cairo!"

Eris laughed. "Well, we don't serve meals on board because the 'long way' won't take very long, but it should be a great flight."

337

As Eris turned back to the console, suddenly something happened in Gaby's brain. Something long buried, something ephemeral and very dark, uncoiled itself like a venomous snake and began to spread like inky fog through the girl's mind. Her eyes took on the glazed, haunted look they had had before. The posthypnotic command planted in Gaby's drug-sodden mind so deeply that even the Star Guardians' science could not root it out now blossomed like a poisonous plant. Part of her mind retained its sanity, knew with horror what was happening, but as the midnight tendrils spread, it knew also that she was powerless once more. It could only watch helplessly as her body jerked stiffly toward Eris, who was now preoccupied with the controls, as her hand reached inside her jacket and felt the cold metallic thing that was still there, as she brought out the pistol that had been given her long ago by Reaper Drum and which had saved her lover's life, shoved the barrel into Eris' mane of tawny hair...and pulled the trigger!

The report seemed as loud as doom inside the control room. Eris pitched forward without a cry, a bright spray of blood splattering the gleaming metal floor as her head struck it with the dull *thongk* of a melon dropped on steel.

Gaby gazed down at her friend's body as if looking at a bug she had just squashed, then seated herself in the control chair. But inwardly, part of her was screaming....

Then, the part that was no longer her own, remembering all that Eris had done, pressed the green panel on the console. The violet ray sprang up to link her to the teleportation drive, and she projected an image on the screen. Her destination.

The forbidding shape of Zeinhom Manor materialized, leprous under the moon's white kiss. Holding the sinister image in her mind, Gabrielle pressed the second panel, the one the color of spilled blood....

Why hast thou enticed thyself
Into the old serpent's paradise?
　　　—Friedrich Nietzsche

CHAPTER THIRTY-ONE

FOUR AGAINST ZEINHOM

CAIRO: 20 DECEMBER 2020

Consciousness trickled slowly back into the darkness of Eris' mind like water filling up an irrigation ditch. And with consciousness came pain: the back of her skull ached horribly; she could feel her hair matted and caked with dried blood.

Opening her eyes, she tried to sit up, but her vision blurred and the room wheeled around her like a carousel, so she lay back down, wincing at the contact of her head with even the soft goosedown pillow. Where in God's name was she? And how did she get here? Moments later her vision cleared enough to reveal a large well-furnished bedroom. She was lying on a comfortable queen-size bed; there was blood on the sheets.

She looked down at herself and was shocked to see that she was naked. She assumed that someone must have taken her clothes to prevent her from trying to escape. A quick self-examination revealed that she was otherwise unhurt.

Fighting back the pain in her head, Eris tried to reconstruct what had happened. The last thing she remembered was flying the spacecraft, preparing for the flight back to Washington D.C. She and Gaby were—

Gaby! Where was she? And then another thought hit her like a blow: Oh, my God—the Immobilizer! Where was it?

339

Eris recalled Gaby walking up behind her; she was about to say something to the girl when there had been a loud explosion, then blackness. Eris' mind writhed in horror, not wanting to accept what she now realized must have happened:

     somehow, Nicasia must have reasserted her control over Gaby and made her

Just then the bedroom door opened, and two people entered. One was a strikingly beautiful dark-haired woman with burning yellow eyes whom Eris recognized as Nicasia Bane herself; the other was a dwarf dressed in a black robe and a red ski-mask that covered his entire head. Eris grabbed the sheet to cover herself; she could feel the little man's lascivious eyes crawling over her like slugs on a plant.

"Well, Eris," said Nicasia, a sneer twisting her crimson lips, "I see from the look on your face that you remember me. This is my associate, Furca."

The dwarf made a mocking bow, but said nothing.

Nicasia continued: "I must say I'm amazed at the remarkable recovery you made after Kathy did her number on you, but you've only managed to prolong the inevitable for a little while. You may think you're lucky to be alive after my stepdaughter shot you, but I think you'll change your mind very soon. That would have been a nice, easy way to go.... By the way, either you have a very hard head or Gabrielle is the world's worst shot. Probably a bit of both, don't you think? The bullet seems to have only grazed your skull. In any event, before I leave you, I really must thank you and your friends for delivering my property to me. You've saved me a lot of inconvenience, you know."

"I presume you mean the Immobilizer," said Eris slowly. It hurt to talk.

"Of course...and that lovely ship parked outside. Far superior to our Algolian cobracraft. Our scientists will learn a lot from its design and construction."

"Where's the Immobilizer now?" asked Eris, as a quick glance around the room told her it wasn't with her.

"It's quite safe...with Gabrielle. It seems to like her...follows her around like a pet dog." Nicasia laughed icily. "After she tells me how to operate the thing, I'm going to have a *lot* of fun. And then I'm afraid her usefulness to me will be about over."

"She doesn't know how!" Eris blurted in alarm. "None of us does! The Star Guardians wouldn't tell us!"

Nicasia's face darkened. "So...I might have known *they* were involved in this.... Well, they can't help you now, my dear. And I don't believe you, of course—I'm sure they wouldn't hand over a weapon like that without explaining its operation. No...we'll get it out of Gaby...one way or another...."

Before Eris could protest further, Nicasia and Furca turned to leave. "Goodbye, my dear. We won't meet again, I'm afraid. But you won't be lonely long. A friend of ours will be coming to pay you a visit very soon...."

The dwarf cackled hideously, and they were gone, locking the door behind them.

Eris breathed a sigh of relief. She felt dizzy again, and sank back on the bed and closed her eyes. That last ominously enigmatic remark of Nicasia's bothered her, but she had other things to worry about immediately. With every bit of mindpower she could summon, she put out a mental call to Chris. Thank God they hadn't ripped off her Mentacom Medallion like they did Gaby's....

After a few anxious minutes, she succeeded in getting through to Chris, who was back at the hotel with the others.

ERIS! THANK GOD! he responded with intense relief. ARE YOU ALL RIGHT? WHERE ARE YOU? WHAT HAPPENED? THE PRESIDENT CALLED US TWO HOURS AGO WHEN YOU DIDN'T SHOW UP IN D.C. WE'VE BEEN GOING CRAZY—

WHOA, DARLING, SLOW DOWN...YES, I'M OKAY...I THINK. I GUESS I'VE BEEN OUT FOR SEVERAL HOURS. WHAT HAPPENED WAS THAT AS SOON AS GABY AND I WERE ALONE, SHE REVERTED BACK TO NICASIA'S CONTROL AND OBEYED A POST-HYPNOTIC COMMAND TO TAKE OVER THE SHIP AND BRING IT BACK TO ZEINHOM, WHICH MUST BE

WHERE I AM NOW. SHE TRIED TO SHOOT ME, BUT
THE BULLET JUST GRAZED ME....

GOOD GOD! DAMMIT, WE SHOULD'VE STAYED
WITH YOU! WE'VE UNDERESTIMATED THAT BITCH
NICASIA ONCE TOO OFTEN. WHERE'S GABY NOW?
IS SHE WITH YOU?

NO, SHE'S IN ANOTHER PART OF THE HOUSE WITH
THE IMMOBILIZER. CHRIS, YOU AND THE GUYS
HAVE GOT TO GET OVER HERE RIGHT AWAY AND
TRY TO BUST US OUT. NICASIA WON'T BELIEVE
THAT GABY DOESN'T KNOW HOW TO WORK THE
IMMOBILIZER AND I THINK SHE'S GOING TO TOR-
TURE HER TO FIND OUT. HURRY! CALL COL. ZAID
AND GET SOME MEN OVER HERE A.S.A.P.!

Suddenly a strange bumping, rustling noise intruded on
her mental conversation. It seemed to be coming from the
ceiling of the bedroom. Unable to maintain her concentration, she signed off weakly.

CHRIS...SOMETHING STRANGE...A NOISE...I CAN'T
TALK ANY MORE RIGHT NOW...I LOVE YOU....

Opening her eyes, she sat up on the bed, alarmed by the ominous sound. It was like a very heavy weight being dragged
overhead. She heard something scrape metal, and her eyes
went to the ceiling grating of the air-conditioning duct.
What the hell is that? she asked herself.
Her answer came almost immediately: the grating
popped out of the duct with a twanging sound and what
looked like a gigantic black firehose burst out of the opening
and cascaded to the floor like oil gushing from a pipe. Eris'
eyes widened in horror and she scrambled back against the
headboard. The thing seemed to take forever to pour its immense length out of the duct. Then out of the pile of massive
ebony coils, a huge head rose, swaying like a dancer, slitted
green eyes fixing hers with Arctic intensity, black forked
tongue flickering.

This must be the "friend" Nicasia had in mind, thought Eris, panic clawing at her spine like a cat. *That's the biggest goddamn python I ever saw...and it's up for a late supper— me! Now I know why they took my clothes—this thing doesn't like "dressing" on its salad!*

As the monster moved closer, Eris tried to recall everything she knew about pythons. It wasn't much. She did recall that they weren't poisonous, but were constrictors—they liked to crush their prey to death before they ate it, or at least squeeze it so tightly that it couldn't breathe and died of suffocation. Lovely! She tried to force herself to keep calm and beat back the waves of terror that threatened to inundate her reason at any moment. She was naked and unarmed...and the snake was beginning to move onto the bed. She looked around the room for anything she might use as a weapon. Suddenly her eye caught a heap of khaki thrown carelessly in one corner: her backpack! A flash of hope swept through her and she hurled herself off the bed and over to the pack in a blur of speed that surprised even her. The snake was in no hurry, confident of its prey. Its massive black head swiveled to follow her, began to move leisurely toward her. She scrabbled frantically through the pack, but her heart sank: they had been through it thoroughly and had taken anything that might have been used as a weapon, including her Headlight band.

Crouched in the corner, she looked up into the coldest eyes she had ever seen, hungrily riveted on hers. Then horror compounded itself a hundredfold: inside her mind, the snake *spoke* to her!

No usssse, it said, the syllables slithering through her brain like icy worms. *Misstresss ssaysss you're...mine!*

Relentless as time, the giant python heaved itself slowly forward.

They stood in front of the massive iron gate to Zeinhom Manor, four shadows drenched in shadow. Above them towered the forbidding twenty-foot-high stone walls that surrounded the estate.

The urgency in Eris' call had made Chris and the others unwilling to waste time trying to contact Colonel Zaid and mobilize a strike force against the manor, and the police would have required a long explanation, since officially the four men were only American scientists. And in any case, the damnably frustrating truth was that there was no evidence to point to Nicasia Bane's having kidnapped anyone. Not a scrap.

So they had come alone, dressed in dark clothes, faces hastily smudged, to face the old serpent in her lair. Avram cursed the "scientists" cover story that had made it impossible for them to bring any weapons into the country, but Chris reminded him that they did have weapons of a sort: the powerful lasers in their Headlights.

Now one of those beams (André's) blasted the gate's heavy lock to molten slag, and the four men cautiously entered the spacious grounds, Marielle following close behind, silent as a thought.

Chris breathed a prayer of thanks that the moon had set by now: The darkness provided the essential cover that could make the difference between success and failure. Nicasia had relandscaped the entire park area, planting thick groves of towering eucalyptus and date palms to keep out dust and sand and to provide a further screen for her activities. This would help them, too.

As they paused to size up their surroundings, they were engulfed by the deceptively peaceful ambience: only the rustle and hiss of leaves in the cool evening breeze and the distant susuration of city traffic reached their ears. The trees extended to within twenty yards of the house, which loomed ahead like some sinister medieval citadel. Lights blazed from several windows, seeming unusually bright against the enshrouding darkness.

André and Chris closed their eyes, sending their psychic senses out to probe for the girls' whereabouts in the house. Chris' clairaudience picked up a babble of sound, none of it meaningful, much of it in Arabic and a gruff alien tongue that he felt must be the goat-men's language. After a few futile minutes, Chris gave up in impatient disgust.

From the disappointed look on his face, André had apparently had no better luck with his psychic vision. He had searched through many of the thirty rooms—had even

344

glimpsed Nicasia once—but there was no sign of either Gaby or Eris anywhere.

"Several rooms seem to have psychic barriers around them," he said. "I couldn't see inside. Maybe the girls are in there." Chris nodded, his face grim and taut. "Okay, guys, let's go. And keep alert...be ready for anything...."

Silently, they moved forward through the trees, completely unaware of the video cameras that peered out through knotholes in the trunks of the shaggy eucalyptus, recording their every movement.

In another of the many bedrooms inside the manor, Gaby once again confronted her old nemesis, Kathy Bane. The tall blonde was dressed in the metallic jumpsuit she wore when on assignment with Nicasia's goat-men, an odd-looking Algolian beam weapon at her belt.

"Nice work, little sister," she sneered, hard eyes glinting like shards of broken bottles. "You came through like a champ for us, didn't you? Took out your pal Eris and delivered the machine, all according to plan."

Gaby's reddened eyes and tear-streaked cheeks betrayed the agonies she had been suffering ever since returning to Zeinhom. A few hours later, the dark command that had taken over her mind had released its hold and dispersed, its function accomplished. Gaby was in control of herself again, but was now tortured by horrible anguish at what she had done. They had told her that she had succeeded in her mission: killed her dearest friend (false) and delivered the Immobilizer into Nicasia's hands (true). This news had devastated her utterly, as it had been calculated to do. Although mercifully Gaby had no memory of what she had done, the fact that she was here with the machine floating innocuously beside her bed was proof enough for her that what they said was true. How could André ever come near her after this? How could she live with herself?

"Now, my bedraggled princess," Kathy said nastily, "you have one more task to perform. We need to know how to operate this gizmo here. Since you're the only one left, you're elected to play show and tell for us."

345

Gaby, wracked with the pain of guilt and loss, was almost completely numb. She sat up on the bed and tried to speak, but the words sounded weak and far away. "I...don't know how...to work it. They didn't tell us...."

Kathy's gloved hand whipped out like a crack of lightning, smashing Gaby across the mouth. "Bullshit! You know, all right. You *all* know—they wouldn't have given it to you without showing you how to use it! Doesn't make sense."

Abruptly her mood changed. Her thin scarlet lips formed a cruel smile. "Well, there's no hurry. After all, we have the machine. You'll tell us...eventually. Make it hard on yourself if you want...it's your choice. And don't forget, we can always round up your other four friends, who are silly enough to have stayed in the city. I'm sure your precious...what's his name—André?—would be happy to talk to save you. Don't you think so? Or maybe you might be willing to talk to save him from, say, going through what your friend Eris went through in my Agony Machine. Hmmmm?"

Still smiling, Kathy moved menacingly toward Gaby, huddled in horror on the bed. "Just think about *that*, little sister, while you and I take up where we left off before. Remember?" She removed the weapon from her belt and tossed it nonchalantly into a far corner where it landed with a muffled thud on the thick carpet. "Bet you'd love to get your paws on *that*, wouldn't you?" Kathy taunted. "Now...let's get down to...pleasure...."

Typhon was slowly backing Eris into a corner; although hungry, he had intelligence enough to know his prey could not escape. So he could afford to be patient. The monster's coils seemed to be expanding to fill the whole room, Eris thought. Now they had blocked her access to the only window; although they were on the third floor, she thought a dive out that window might be preferable to this kind of death. But now even that was out. She had recovered from the shock of the snake's speaking to her mentally and had tried to communicate with it in return—maybe she could somehow reason with it (how do you reason with a hungry python?); but that hadn't worked. Either the snake couldn't

346

receive her thoughts or it ignored her. But those icy emerald eyes never left hers as, inch by inch, it drew its powerful coils toward her.

Now it was almost within striking range. An enormous pink maw opened and a reptilian hiss roared out like a jet of steam. Eris jumped back as though shot; the wall slammed into her naked back. She could see the rows of backward-pointing teeth that would grab and hold her as the great coils looped around her and began to exert a relentless pressure from which there could be no escape. She could smell the stench of past carrion (human?) as she stared with horror into its terrible gaping mouth.

Desperate for anything to keep it at bay a few moments longer, Eris picked up the almost empty backpack. Maybe if she could stuff it into that mouth, the snake might choke, or at least be distracted for a while....

As she lifted the pack, something fell out onto the floor with a small plop. She looked down and her heart jumped in her breast like a mad kangaroo. A plastic bag lay there: one of Raymond's ingenious "baggie-potties." That was it! Her one chance! Stooping, she grabbed the bag, whipped it open, and gathering every ounce of courage she had left, stepped forward, pressed the button on the incendiary disposal device and rammed the bag as far down the snake's throat as she could reach!

Totally surprised by this unexpected agression from his prey, Typhon whipped his head back, almost taking part of Eris' arm with it, and slammed his jaws shut. Her arm was covered with blood where needle-sharp teeth had raked it, but she felt nothing but a fierce elation.

"Okay, you scaly sonovabitch," she yelled at him, "you wanted a hot meal—you got it!" Then, shielding her face with her arms, she threw herself into the corner, curling up into as small a ball as possible. She had six seconds....

They seemed interminable. The monster's incoherent babble of confusion and alarm beat at her brain as it frantic-ally tried to dislodge this strange object in its throat—

Then the world erupted in a tremendous blast of light and heat. Eris' back felt as though someone had tossed a bucket of boiling water on it; if she screamed, it was

347

drowned out by the mental scream of the great snake as its head vanished in a white-hot inferno.

Eris turned around to see a fearsome sight: the entire enormous length of the python's body was whipping and jerking in the convulsions of death; where the snake's head had been was only a blackened, smoking skull, nodding and swaying in a macabre death dance, impelled by shocked and twitching muscles that had not yet realized they were dead. As Typhon's huge body spasmed, it smashed against the bed frame, reducing it to kindling, and spraying flaming gobbets of squamous flesh around the room.

Eris watched in alarm as a new danger developed: several of those fiery pieces of snake were igniting the draperies around the window! She realized she couldn't get to the window to put them out, for the python's wildly convulsing coils could still crush her accidently.

Sparks jumped onto the tangle of bedding that now lay near the window. Flames bloomed like deadly orange flowers. Eris' eyes grew wide with panic as the room began to burn.

As Chris, Avram, André, and Raymond reached the edge of the grove of trees, they paused and looked about them cautiously. No one was in sight. Chris signaled for them to move forward—

And brilliant shafts of light suddenly blasted the darkness away! From all around them, a battery of powerful spotlights set into the wall and the front of the house pinpointed them like insect specimens under a microscope.

Dazzled and confused, they started to duck back into the trees, but a harsh voice suddenly grated out, "Freeze!"

The front door to the house was now open, and standing on the steps was a huge black man with eyes like a cat's glowing with emerald malice, holding a .357 Magnum trained unwaveringly on them.

Chris recognized him immediately as the leader of the gang at the Sphinx, the man who had coldly ordered his men to kill Eris and him, then disappeared.

"Okay, now, nice and easy...take off those headbands and toss 'em over here. Cute gadgets. You know, you dudes might as well have brought a fuckin' brass band in here. We been watchin' you ever since you zapped the gate lock. Did you really think you could bust in here and catch us all playin' Trivial Pursuit or somethin'?"

Carefully, the four men eased off their Headlights and tossed them on the grass. Their eyes were beginning to become accustomed to the bright lights. Chris' mind was racing like an engine trying to come up with something to get them out of this.

"That's good," Reaper said, savoring his triumph. "Now we're all gonna go 'round back. We got a nice, comfortable 'guest house' for you to cool your heels in till the boss lady decides what to do with you." He jerked his head to the rear. "Move it!"

Raymond's mind had been racing too. He knew their only chance was a diversion. He glanced down to see Marielle crouched tensely at his feet, tail switching nervously. Muttering "Forgive me, old girl," he suddenly stomped her tail with his boot. Marielle was not equipped with pain receptors, but her reactions were those of any feline: startled by the unexpected attack, she let out an electronic screech that would have raised the hackles on a statue and jumped three feet into the air, then bolted straight toward Reaper and through his legs.

Startled, the big man almost lost his balance as he jumped to one side; for a split second, the gun barrel was off them. Chris and Raymond acted as one—they lunged forward, smashing into Reaper from two sides. Any other man would have gone down, but the killer's reactions were cat-quick: he staggered back, but one arm swept out and batted Chris away like a rag doll. Ray grappled with the gun arm, but Reaper brought up a knee into the agent's groin, and Ray staggered back, groaning and gasping.

Before Chris could get to his feet, Reaper swung the gun around and, coldly and deliberately, fired. A sound of thunder seemed to blot out the world; the three Psi-Spies stared in horror as a large dark hole suddenly appeared in Raymond's chest and he was slapped backward as though hit by a truck. He landed on his back on the grass and did not move.

349

For a moment, everything was frozen, as though preserved under glass; then with an agonized cry, Avram rushed over to the fallen man and knelt beside him. André was close behind. Raymond's chest was now covered with a spreading crimson stain. He opened eyes glazed with pain and shock and whispered weakly, "Av...an old hunter friend...once told me... 'Sometimes you get the bear...and sometimes...the bear gets you'.... So long, pals...take care of...Marielle...."

Just then the robot cat, having circled around and returned to her master to find out what was wrong, appeared at his side. Anxiously, her huge green eyes peered into his dimming ones. He grinned, reached out a hand weakly to stroke her. "Marielle...sorry I stomped you...didn't do either of us much good, did it? Listen...go...in the house...find Eris and Gaby. *Find them!* Understand?"

She put a paw on his blood-soaked chest, staring into his face. His eyes closed then, and his hand fell away from her head into the grass. For a long moment she remained motionless, then with another loud yowl, turned and raced back toward the house, a golden blur.

Reaper turned when he saw the cat go by and snapped off a shot at her, but missed. This jerked Chris out of his horrified immobility. A red glow seemed to shimmer over everything and suddenly he was no longer Christopher Troy, Egyptologist and Psi-Spy—he was...Tiger! As he felt the *chi* of the earth flow up into him, filling him with power, he heard Master Sho Shin's voice come back to him across a great void: *"Christopher, show me what you know of the way of the tiger...you must become the tiger...."* All reasoning, all civilization dropped away like a discarded cloak; hate was a torch burning between the tiger's eyes as he smashed into the huge form of Reaper Drum, lashing out with sledgehammer blows of hands and feet.

The big killer staggered back, caught totally off guard; he had been carefully watching the other two men as they knelt by their fallen comrade. He swung the gun up, but a sharp ridge-hand blow to his wrist sent the weapon spinning off into the night.

Snarling his fury, Reaper stepped back; then, well acquainted with Kung Fu himself, met Chris' attack with his

350

own, blocking punches and kicks and returning them with a surprising speed and agility for a man so large.

But Reaper was at a disadvantage: he was angry and eager to kill, but his was not the fury of the tiger. He had not just seen his friend brutally gunned down before his eyes. The tiger roared his hatred and came at him, all four limbs flashing in a blur of fakes and attacks, a Knife-Point spearing his shoulder painfully, a Hammer Blow slamming the side of his head, splitting the skin. Blood and sweat began to run into Reaper's eyes, making them blur and sting. He brushed aside a Lightning Kick and surged forward with a powerful Dragon Stamp to his opponent's knee, then a Rock-Smash slammed into the tiger's arm. The tiger felt a bone snap, but the pain only fed the fuel of his burning as he whipped a high hook kick to the big man's head, then speared his kidney with the single knuckle of a Buffalo Horn. Reaper grunted and staggered; it was hard to hurt him, but he was slowly being driven back by the skill and fury of the crazed man-animal that was attacking him mercilessly.

Reaper threw all his great power into a lightning Monkey Blow that would have ended the fight had it landed, but a twitch of the tiger's chin kept it from killing. Still the force of it sent the tiger reeling back for a moment, long enough for Reaper to wipe the blood and sweat from his eyes and turn, lunging for the gun he had spotted earlier, glittering in the tall bright grass. He'd had enough and he meant to end it now.

"No!" Avram bellowed in a voice like thunder. His eyes blazed with ebon fires as he saw Reaper go for the gun. Just before his fingers closed around the handle, the big pistol jumped up away from his grasp, soaring high into the air!

Reaper's eyes grew enormous with amazement. "What th' fuck—?" He stared at the Magnum as it hung suspended just out of reach, long barrel gleaming in the brilliant illumination.

Then the tiger charged again; in desperation, Reaper poured all his remaining strength into a leap that carrried him high into the air. His hand closed around the weapon, but the barrel was toward him. In another split second, he would have control of it and would turn it on the tiger hurtling at him like a missile.

"No." This time it was a quiet statement, uttered in a cold, dark voice.

Avram's facial muscles twitched once—

And the trigger jerked back.

There was a sound that seemed to erase all sound forever, a bright flash, and a round black hole appeared between Reaper's startled, frantic eyes, an obscene third eye that could see nothing but the darkness that rushed in to take him down to hell. A crimson fountain of blood and bone burst from where the back of his head had been. Like a great tree, he slowly toppled backward into the grass.

The shock of his opponent's sudden death sent the tiger snarling back into the depths of Chris' mind. He stood there for a moment, dazed, as left-brain reality rushed back over him like a great wave. The stench of cordite hung harshly on the night air. Gradually he began to feel the pain of the terrible beating he had received: his arm was aflame with agony, hanging useless now by his side, his ears singing loudly from the noise of the gunshots, but he managed a broad grin as Avram and André came over to him, putting their arms around his shoulders to support him.

"Nice work, Av," he said weakly. "We're still a good team...." He broke off at the sight of Raymond's sprawled body a few feet away. He started to go over to it, but Avram stopped him.

"No time, Chris. We've got to get inside and find the girls before all hell breaks loose. Those gunshots are bound to bring somebody any second!"

André nodded, scooped up the Magnum and sprinted for the house. In a moment he was inside. But before Avram and Chris could follow him, Avram's warning turned into deadly truth: around the corner of the house came a squad of Arab guards, clad in black fatigues and armed with automatic rifles!

"Oh, shit," said Chris. "This time I think we've bought it, Av...."

* * * * * * *

When the spotlights flared on and the gunshots began, most of the servants and occupants of the house who were still awake crowded to the front windows of the mansion to see what was happening. No one noticed a streak of golden fur that flashed in the front door and up the stairs, sensors scanning for the two entities it knew as Eris Campbell and Gabrielle Bane. After searching several rooms, Marielle reached the third floor. From a bedroom a short way down the hall, she suddenly heard a voice she recognized as Gaby's. It sounded shrill and desperate. She raced to the door, found it open and entered.

She saw a tall blond-haired human female attacking Gaby. Her master had been terminated, but he had ordered her to find both Gaby and Eris. Here was Gaby—clearly in need of assistance, reasoned the cat's computer brain, so....

Kathy's patience with Gaby had worn thin. "I've put up with enough shit from you, you little bitch," she hissed. "You'll tell us what we want to know, but first I'm going to have your ass, like I promised—and your energy."

"No!" screamed Gaby, terrified of this gaunt, evil woman who threatened to violate her both physically and mentally. "Stay away from me!"

Kathy slapped her again, hard, leaving a burning hand-print on Gaby's cheek. Blood trickled from one nostril. "Shut up! I'm going to drain you dry, until you're as weak as a kit—"

Her sentence ended in an ear-shattering scream, as thirty pounds of electronic feline suddenly launched itself at her back, clawing and biting ferociously with titanium-steel fangs and claws. Kathy's face was distorted and ugly with pain and fear as she frantically reached back, trying to dislodge the snarling, spitting monster on her shoulders. Finally she got hold of enough fur, and with a tremendous heave, ripped the cat off her back and hurled her against the wall. As Marielle was torn loose, she slashed out with her tiny sabers, raking huge gouges across the woman's face. Kathy screamed in pain, her eyes blazing with fury. Marielle caromed off the wall, lighting agilely on the headboard of Gaby's bed, her back arched, fur on end. Shrieking curses like a harpy gone mad, Kathy turned and scooped up the alien weapon she had tossed into the corner. Blood streamed down her face in cascades as she raised the weapon and fired. An emerald beam sizzled out and took off Marielle's left paw, blasting a hole in the wall behind her. The cat screeched and leaped to the foot of the bed, then turned to face her assailant again.

"Marielle!" screamed Gaby. "Run! She'll kill you!"

Kathy swung the weapon around to fire again, but blood from her slashed forehead was now running into her eyes. For a moment she was blinded, then she wiped her sleeve across her eyes until she could see again.

Marielle's realization of her danger finally reached critical. This was definitely an enemy to be dealt with. Very well. Her eyes changed from green to a hellish red, and before Kathy could fire again, twin laser beams drilled out of Marielle's orbs and straight into Kathy's. There were two loud pops as the fluid in the woman's eyes instantly exploded into steam. Kathy Bane was dead before she could even scream, her eyes two charred and smoking sockets, her brain a blackened mass of charcoal. As she toppled forward onto the bed, Marielle's eyes changed back to their normal green color, her fur went down, and she began to lick the stump of her left paw, from which several fused wires protruded. The danger was over.

Gaby's eyes were wide with disbelief. "My...God, kitty! I didn't know you could do that! I'm sure glad you're on *our* side!"

Kathy's death seemed to release a great weight from Gaby's soul. She swung into action, picking up the Algolian weapon and motioning the cat to follow her. She wished the cat could speak; maybe André had come too....

As she tiptoed cautiously into the hall, she heard a commotion downstairs: people shouting, running footsteps, gunshots. She thought she smelled smoke, too, but could see nothing unusual. Still keyed to her aura, the Immobilizer floated silently after her, gleaming dully in the dim light.

But Marielle still had work to do: she had been told to locate both Gaby and Eris, so now that she had found one, she bolted down the hallway in search of the other, her missing paw slowing her down only slightly.

Dismayed, Gaby called, "Marielle! Come back!" But it was no use. The cat zipped around the corner and was gone. Gaby felt alone and afraid again, but she told herself that she did at least have a weapon. Cautiously, she began to descend the dark stairs.

Eris' bedroom was now a blazing inferno. She had made her way over to the window, as the python's body had finally stopped convulsing, and was crouched as close to the floor as possible, to avoid suffocation from smoke inhalation. She had managed to save the bedsheets from burning, although the bedspread was a loss, and was frantically fashioning a crude halter and diaper-like loincloth from pieces of one sheet. I don't know why I'm worrying about modesty when I'm about to be barbecued, she wondered. Once she managed to knot the makeshift garments in place (she would have killed for a safety pin!), she felt better; then, working as quickly as possible, began knotting the sheets together in the traditional manner of escaping from a high window. She secured one end firmly to the snake's body (the heaviest thing in the room), and breathing a silent prayer, let herself carefully out of the window and began to rappel down the side of the house like a mountain climber.

When she was about two-thirds of the way down, the fire burned through the sheet and she fell the rest of the distance, landing heavily on the ground. A sharp pain shot through her right ankle, which twisted under her. Cautiously she tested it: it didn't seem to be broken, just badly sprained. The back of her head still ached ferociously, her arm was still bleeding and she could feel blisters already forming on her back from the heat of the exploding baggie-potty. "Boy, am I a mess," she muttered aloud, then, glancing up at the roaring flames now shooting out of the window she had just escaped from, added, "But at least I'm a *live* mess...." Eris began to limp painfully toward the front of the house, where she could see bright lights and hear occasional shots.

"Stop!" The word was a harsh, guttural bleat. Eris whirled around to see a goat-man glaring menacingly at her.

355

On patrol around the grounds, he had no doubt seen the fire...and then her.

Eris suddenly realized that she was too tired and sore to be afraid. She was just disgusted. And angry.

"Look, tin-can-breath," she told the surprised alien, "I've been shot in the head, almost eaten by a snake, half charbroiled, and I've turned my ankle. Now what do I get? Billy Goat Gruff! I'm not having a very good night...and I'm mad as hell!"

This goat-man apparently didn't understand English very well, and he looked puzzled as Eris boldly limped right up to him. She looked him over: he wasn't nearly as big as the one she had seen on the cobracraft; she wondered if goat-men had the same kind of equipment as human men. She decided to find out.

"Hey! Look at that! One of our helicopters!" she cried suddenly, pointing up into the sky. The goat-man's head jerked up in alarm, and Eris slammed the stiffened points of her fingers into his neck with all her strength; then, while he was choking and gasping, brought her knee up with crushing force into his groin. The creature bleated horribly and collapsed, one hand holding his throat, the other his crotch. Then Eris brought the heel of her uninjured foot against his temple in a powerful kick, and he relaxed into unconsciousness.

Gritting her teeth against the pain in her other ankle, she managed a grim smile. "I didn't think you guys knew that trick on your planet...."

Looking at the alien's sprawled body, she realized that his metallic suit would fit her fairly well. "It's gotta be better than this bedsheet bikini I'm wearing," she muttered as she began to strip the uniform from him.

When André burst through the front door of the mansion, holding Reaper's pistol before him, two-handed and stiff-armed, several of Nicasia's servants, who had come to see what was going on, scurried for cover with shrieks of terror. He collared one quivering woman, asking if she had seen an American girl with dark hair, or one with blond hair, but he could get nothing coherent out of her. She babbled tearfully in Arabic, which André couldn't understand. Cursing, he flung her aside, just as a brilliant bolt of green light flashed past his head, missing him by inches and blasting a neat round hole in the hardwood floor behind him.

He dived for cover under a large table as another bolt came even closer. At the top of the stairs was a slim dark-haired girl with a strange beam weapon aimed at him. For a sick, terrible moment in the dim light he thought it was Gaby, but then realized it wasn't. She had him pinned down—and a table was no cover for *that* weapon. Nothing was!

"Sorry, *chérie*," he muttered, taking aim and squeezing off a round, "but in this fight, I'm afraid chivalry is as dead...as you are!"

The bullet struck Tina in the chest, hurling her back against the bannister. It gave way, and with a demonic shriek, another of Nicasia's psychic vampire "daughters" plunged to her death with a loud crash.

Almost before Tina hit the floor, André was racing up the stairs. At the top, more servants screamed and ran. He hurried down the corridor, opening doors, frantically searching for the girls. A large goat-man suddenly rounded the corner of the hallway and came charging toward him, murder blazing in his slit-pupiled eyes. André stopped him cold with one of his last two bullets and kept on running. He *had* to find Gaby—she had to be somewhere in this nightmare labyrinth!

At last he came to a door marked "Private"; it was locked, but a well-placed kick smashed it open. It was an office, empty but with the lights still on—somebody must have just left in haste. A large desk, expensive furniture, filing cabinets...and four video monitors set into the wall above the desk. One of them was on: André could see the front yard where he had just been with the others. The area was still awash with light, and he saw with alarm a semicircle of guards with automatic weapons grouped around Avram and Chris! "Holy shit!" he exclaimed. "They must have shown up just after I left. What can I do from in here?" Frantically he looked around the office, hoping he might at least find the master control for the spotlights. This would seem a logical place for it, he reasoned.

He noticed a keyboard of buttons on one side of the desk and started pressing them. At first nothing happened, but then suddenly a bookcase slid aside, revealing a small alcove in which a large black control box hummed softly.

"That must be it!" he exclaimed with delight, hurrying over to examine it more closely. There were several rows of small green lights glowing on the box; beneath each light was a red button and a word in Arabic. Some of the lights were dark. At one end of the control panel was a large red lever, but it was locked in place. This confirmed his suspicion. That must be the master control switch for the entire light bank. He decided to use his last bullet to blast the lock off. The report was deafening in the enclosed space, but André didn't care—the switch was unlocked! This would give his friends at least a small chance to escape the guards in the sudden darkness. He grabbed the master switch and pulled. The black box seemed to pulse; the humming increased in volume for a second, then stopped. All the green lights went out.

He hurried back over to the monitor to watch the results—and was appalled to see that the lights were still on! He started to curse in French, but then he stopped.

Because what he was seeing was much more effective than darkness...and much more horrible. He had no way of knowing that those Arabic words beneath the tiny glowing lights were the names of men!

Gaby descended the stairs slowly and cautiously, hardly daring to breathe. She could see nothing at the bottom of the stairs—only blackness. She found this very strange: she thought she remembered seeing some light down there before. She shivered—it looked as if she were descending into an inky pool of—

The darkness *moved*? It flowed suddenly toward her, surging up the stairwell in viscous waves. Gaby screamed, tried to turn and run, but the slimy black mass was upon her; she tried to struggle, but it was soon up to her waist, cold as ice and thick as syrup. It smelled like rotten cabbage. Soon she was frantically trying to keep her head above the awful fluid; it was rapidly filling up the entire stairwell? This wasn't possible—yet it was happening! She was going to drown in this horrible stuff! She dropped the weapon in her frantic attempts to tread water—

And suddenly the black liquid was gone! Gaby was dry and sitting on the steps, her eyes huge with horror.

For at the bottom of the stairs, grinning evilly up at her, stood Nicasia and Furca. The dwarf giggled obscenely.

"Very nice, wizard," Nicasia said, hefting the alien weapon she had retrieved from where Gaby had thrown it. "Your illusions do have their uses." Her eyes narrowed into slits of yellow flame as she glared up at Gaby. Pointing the weapon at her, Nicasia said, "All right, child—playtime's over. Apparently this damn house is on fire. We're getting out of here now. You and your friends have caused me a lot of trouble tonight. But you've got the Immobilizer and I've got you. March down these stairs and do exactly what I tell you if you want to stay alive. Understand?"

Billowing tendrils of grayish smoke were beginning to fill the third floor above. Gaby nodded meekly and went down to her stepmother, who had somehow slammed the trap shut on her once again.

Beware of snakes when they are about to die.
—Oriental Proverb

CHAPTER THIRTY-TWO

SACRIFICE PLAY

CAIRO: 20 DECEMBER 2020

Chris and Avram stood like frozen statues in the harsh brilliance, their faces masks of incredulous horror. Facing them moments before had been twelve Arab guards pointing automatic rifles at them, eyes burning with hatred and kill-lust. The leader of the squad had just raised his hand to give the signal to fire, when something incredible had happened.

All of the men, including the leader, had suddenly began to dance—a horrible, grotesque dance of death: their eyes bulged, first with astonishment, then agony; weapons fell with a metallic clatter from suddenly nerveless fingers.

And then the blue fire began. It burst from their eyes and mouths and ears with a horrid hissing sound, consuming screams along with flesh; azure tongues of flame licked greedily out of seared openings in chests and backs and arms, eating the men alive with sickening ferocity, until at last there were only twelve piles of greasy black ash smoldering in the carefully tended grass of Zeinhom Manor's elegant front lawn.

"What in God's name...?" began Avram, when he could speak.

Chris grabbed his arm. "Av! *I've seen this before!* The night this all started...Eris and I were fighting some of Nicasia's thugs at the Sphinx. I followed one of them up to the

360

top of the Pyramid...but before I could capture him, he burned up like these men just did!"

"But how—"

"I don't know, Av—but it's *deliberate!* Some hellish device Nicasia uses to make sure none of her men are ever captured."

"That ice-blooded bitch...but why would she suddenly execute all of her men now—just when they were about to finish us? It doesn't make sense!"

Just then Chris noticed the towering column of smoke billowing up from the mansion. Tongues of yellow flame were raging from the third-story windows. "Av, look! The place is on fire! My God! Eris and Gaby—and André—they're all still in there! Come on—we've gotta get 'em out!"

The two men scooped up two of the automatic rifles, which were still hot to the touch, and started for the front door. As they approached, several groups of terrified servants erupted from the entrance and ran screaming over to the shelter of the trees. Chris and Avram, seeing that there were no soldiers or goat-men among them, waited impatiently until the doorway was clear.

"Chris!" A gloriously familiar voice suddenly rang in Chris' ears like music. He spun around to see Eris limping around the corner of the house toward him.

Shouting her name joyously, he dropped his weapon and ran to her. They held each other tightly, gasping with pain—Chris from his broken arm and Eris from her burned back—but not minding the pain, almost delirious with relief at finding each other alive and safe.

Avram waved at Eris, a wry grin on his dark features. "Well, those two'll be useless for awhile. Guess it's up to me...."

As he turned to plunge through the doorway, from which gray smoke was beginning to coil, suddenly André appeared there, a wet cloth tied around his nose and mouth. Coughing heavily, he reeled out and down the steps and into Avram's arms. Ripping the cloth from his face, André drew in great shuddering gasps of the cool night air.

"André—are you all right?" asked Avram.

"Sure, I'm okay," he replied hoarsely, steadying himself on Avram's shoulder. "But I couldn't find her, Av! I know Gaby's in there...I kept looking until the fire forced me out...."

"You can stop looking, Frenchman," came a silken voice from the doorway. "You can *all* stop looking. I have what you're looking for right here."

The two men turned to see three figures framed in the smoky doorway: Nicasia, Furca...and Gaby! Nicasia was holding the girl close to her body, an arm around her throat. With her other hand, she held an Algolian beam weapon to Gaby's temple. Beside her, the dwarf fidgeted and twitched nervously.

"Gaby!" exclaimed André, joy singing in his voice. He started to run to her, but Nicasia jabbed the weapon painfully into Gaby's soft flesh.

"Stay where you are! All of you! Unless you want to watch her head disappear!" Nicasia's eyes burned yellower and hotter than the flames behind her. "And you—" she spat at Avram, "—drop the rifle!"

Avram let the weapon fall to the grass at his feet. Then Gaby saw Eris. She let out a a strangled cry of astonishment and joy.

"*Eris!* You're not dead! I didn't kill you! Oh, thank God—"

Nicasia tightened her arm against Gaby's throat, cruelly choking off her words, and hissed her to silence. But renewed hope sparkled now in the girl's eyes. Eris smiled at her reassuringly but said nothing.

Slowly, the trio came down the steps and into the yard. Behind them bobbed the Immobilizer, dull and inert as stone.

"Let her go, Nicasia," said André, fighting to control himself. "It's all over—you know it. Surrender and you can save yourself...and your little friend."

Nicasia's smile was ice. "Oh, no, Frenchman, you're wrong. It's not all over. My little friend, as you call him, and I...and *your* little friend...are going to take a trip now. And you won't try to stop us."

Chris and Eris came over to join the others.

362

"Where can you go now, Nicasia?" asked Chris. "This place is lost...and you can't go back to Wolfe Island...."

"Up. We're going up to Kalon 22—the Algolian mothership parked in orbit over Cairo. It's undetectable by your government's crude radar devices and absolutely invulnerable. And since you've disposed of all my available pilots, I'm taking the saucership you so kindly delivered to me. And Gabrielle will be happy to pilot it for me, won't you, dear?"

The girl didn't answer, but Eris did.

"No!"

Nicasia snarled in fury. "*You!* I don't know how you escaped from Typhon.... I should have killed you myself!"

Eris matched the woman's fury with her own. Her eyes were slits of blue steel as she said, "That was just another of many mistakes you've made, Nicasia. And if you hurt that girl, you've made your last one. *Let her go!*"

For a moment, Nicasia's tiger eyes flickered with uncertainty. Then she said, "I need a pilot...and I want the secret of the Immobilizer."

Eris knew instantly what she had to do. "Then you've got the wrong hostage. Gaby's not an experienced pilot—she couldn't take that ship into space. And she doesn't know anything about the Immobilizer. I was taught to fly the ship...and I know the secret of the weapon. I'm the only one who does. Turn her loose and I'll go with you."

"Eris—no!" Chris cried in horror. "You can't...I won't let you—"

Eris whirled on him savagely. Make this good, she told herself. "Shut up, Chris! I'm the leader of this group! It's my decision! The Star Guardians lied to you...they wanted one of us to know how to activate the machine. They told me secretly, mentally." She turned back to Nicasia. "Well, Nicasia, how about it? Let Gaby go and I'll take you up to your ship and show you how to operate the Immobilizer. Deal?"

Nicasia was silent for a moment, considering. You could almost hear wheels turning in that beautiful head. Finally she said, "Why should I believe you? You lied to me once—you said none of you had the secret."

"That was to keep you from torturing Gaby for nothing. She doesn't know it. I do. I'm your only chance of discovering it, Nicasia. You have to trust me."

Chris wanted to scream. He bit down hard on his lip to keep from blurting something out to stop this madness, *anything*.... Yet something told him to shut up and trust Eris. She had been made the leader of the Pentad for a reason. Now her leadership was being put to its most severe test. His love for her told him that he must go along with her now, whatever her plan might be, no matter how terrible the pain....

"Let her go, Nicasia," Eris repeated evenly. "If you take her with you, you've got nothing. I don't imagine your superiors back on Caput Algol would like that decision much. When they find out you let the secret of the Immobilizer slip through your fingers, your name will be snakeshit. Am I right?"

Sulfuric acid boiled in Nicasia's eyes, telling Eris she had struck a nerve. Pressing her advantage, she continued. "You can't afford to take that chance, and you know it. Even if I'm bluffing, you'll be no worse off. You'll still get a safe trip back to your ship and you'll have possession of the weapon. But if I'm telling the truth, you'll have what you want most. You'd be crazy to turn down my offer."

"So you want me to believe that you're willing to trade the Immobilizer—and yourself—for Gabrielle? You'd become a traitor to your own race to save the life of one girl?"

Eris realized that this was the biggest bluff of her life; she had to make it work. Gaby's life was riding on it.

"I wouldn't call it that," she said flatly. "I was hired to do a job—we all were. We're all paid agents. We tried to grab the Immobilizer for our side, but we blew it. Too bad—that's the breaks. Now my allegiance is to my friends. I don't want Gaby tortured and dumped into space when you find out she knows nothing. I'll ferry you upstairs and show you how the machine works. Then I take the ship back to earth. I'm not sacrificing myself for nothing, either."

"Ah..." Nicasia exclaimed knowingly. Eris had struck the right cynical chord with her at last. "So now the real Eris Campbell stands up. All right...I'll do it...but with one difference."

364

"What's that?"

"The spaceship—it's much too interesting to let you have it back. Our scientists will want to study it very closely. But since you've shown some very human concern for your own safety at last, I'll let you return in one of my cobra-crafts."

Chris half expected Eris to bargain further. He knew how she loved the Guardian ship. But instead, she pretended to consider Nicasia's counteroffer for a long moment, then said, "All right. It's a deal."

"Eris..." Gaby moaned, "no...."

Eris began to walk toward Nicasia and Gaby slowly. "It's okay, baby...I'll be all right," she told the tearful girl softly. When she was a few paces from them, she stopped. "Let her go," she said, her eyes boring into Nicasia's.

Abruptly, the woman released Gaby, shoving her toward André. She swung the muzzle of the beam weapon to cover Eris. "That's close enough," she hissed. "Around to the back. Move."

Eris nodded, passing close to the floating Immobilizer, willing it to transfer itself to her aura. It did. Nicasia nodded in satisfaction, motioned with her weapon, and the three started toward the rear of the house.

Suddenly Eris stopped. "Wait," she said, turning back to her friends. She kept her face emotionless, though it took every ounce of willpower she possessed, as she went over and hugged each of them silently.

"Don't say anything, darling," she whispered in Chris' ear when she came to him. "Please don't. Just know that I love you."

Then, as she stepped back, a black thought suddenly hit her. "Where's Ray?" she asked, a sick feeling in the pit of her stomach. "Didn't he come with—"

Avram's pointing finger chopped off her query like a knife. "He's over there," he said tightly.

Eris turned slowly and saw Raymond's bloodsoaked body sprawled near the trees. With a choked cry she ran over and knelt beside him, head bowed. Just barely, she battled back a hot cascade of tears. She couldn't afford to show any weakness now—not with Nicasia watching her like a hawk.

365

She would mourn for her friend later. *That's another one we owe you, Nicasia*, she thought grimly.

"Okay," she said, her voice like stone. "Let's go."

Nicasia looked back over her shoulder, eyes alight with triumph and malice. "Good-bye, Gaby. What a lucky little girl you are...."

"Eris...." Chris' cry was like that of a man being strangled . He wanted to run to her, grab her, hold her like André was holding Gaby now....

"No, Chris," said Avram softly, his hand firm on Chris' good arm. "Don't make her look back...she might break. We've got to trust her in this...."

Her back stiff as steel, Eris marched around the corner of the house with her captors and was gone. She wasn't limping now, Chris noticed. He also noticed that Nicasia hadn't spared even one backward glance at the body of her dead lieutenant, Reaper Drum....

A great emptiness rushed in upon the four friends then. They could hear the low babbling of the frightened servants in the distance, the sibilance of the wind in the trees, Gaby's quiet sobbing. The crackle of flames was becoming a dull roar, and they were beginning to feel the heat devouring the mansion.

Slowly, like a man beginning to die, Chris sank to his knees in the grass, his face buried in his hands. The pain of his physical wounds was forgotten in the agony that gripped his heart and mind. Dear God, he prayed with silent fervor...please...let her find some way to come safely back to me....

Behind him, the grim citadel that was Zeinhom Manor blazed fiercely, sending a huge pillar of orange and yellow flame high into the night sky, like a funeral pyre for brave warriors lost in battle.

It requires more courage to suffer than to die.
—Napoléon Bonaparte

CHAPTER THIRTY-THREE

KALON 22

ABOARD THE MOTHERSHIP: 20-21 DECEMBER 2020

As she sent the sleek starship of the Star Guardians slicing up into the thinning air over Cairo, Eris was well aware that this was probably her last flight, the last time she would ever take the controls of an aircraft and soar high above the mundane earth into the wide, wonderful sky she loved so much. At least, she thought, I'm flying the ultimate flying machine on this ultimate flight—right through the sky I've always known and into empty space. No, not empty, she corrected herself, for somewhere up ahead, orbiting invisibly like a great alien sword above the neck of the world, was Kalon 22—Nicasia's Algolian mothership.

Below her rounded the glorious blue and white curve of the planet she might never see again; ahead in the deep blackness glittered myriad worlds and suns, including the one from which Nicasia had exiled herself so long ago.

She was aware of the grim presences of Nicasia and Furca beside her as these thoughts raced and tumbled through her head; she was grateful that they said nothing, merely peered anxiously ahead through the transparent viewing area. She was also aware of the beam weapon Nicasia kept pointed unwaveringly at her head.

She considered a drastic alternative: it would be so easy to activate the teleportation drive, visualize the heart of the sun, and hurl them all into instantaneous incandescence, a

367

painless pyre for herself, the Algolian Queen, the dwarf...and the damned hovering Immobilizer, putting it forever beyond the reach of any power. Surely that would be better than what awaited her on board the Algolian ship. When Nicasia discovered that she knew nothing about activating the weapon after all, her fury would be monstrous. At best, Eris might be able to manage a quick death. At worst, well, she had already experienced what this crew was capable of....

She shuddered, her blood suddenly cold, but she shrugged it off. No, she knew she had to go through with this...to face her greatest fear instead of running from it to a quick, fiery oblivion. It was time to stop running. She had done too much running away in her life: from her parents, from other people, especially men, from the earth itself into the welcoming emptiness of the blue sky, from a bad marriage going worse, ignoring the signs until it exploded in fire and death. Then running away again, to Egypt, into the past lives her psychic talent unfolded for her, to the PIA, to excitement and adventure, to anything but responsibility and reality. And running away from Chris, from his love, for so long....

Well, this time she wasn't running. Whatever might happen to her now, at least she knew that her sacrifice would mean something. Nicasia wouldn't have a working weapon and she wouldn't have Gaby any longer. That's worth whatever the cost, she assured herself.

Nicasia nudged Eris with the weapon, bringing her thoughts back to the present. "Does this ship have anything as old-fashioned as a communicator?"

Eris nodded, pointed to a device on the control board and explained its workings to Nicasia, who soon contacted her ship. She spoke in an alien language of clicks and hisses and other horrid sounds that Eris was astonished to hear come from human vocal cords. Then she was chilled to the core by the response from the alien ship: hearing the Algolian tongue spoken by a native, she was suddenly aware of how crude Nicasia's attempt to reproduce it was. Probably embarrasses her, she thought with a trace of amusement. But the being seemed to understand Nicasia and recognize her authority. Eris realized then that the goat-men were not the real Algolians at all, as she had supposed. They were probably just a captured slave-race, used as pilots and soldiers by their Algolian overlords. No, whatever spoke that language was something quite different...and far worse. Something she would shortly meet....

"We're approaching Kalon 22 now," Nicasia informed her. "Veer six degrees to starboard and hold steady. I've made sure they won't open fire on us when they see a strange craft approaching. They'll be expecting us—the docking bay will be open."

"This may seem like a silly question, Nicasia," said Eris, peering anxiously ahead into the apparently empty blackness, "but how am I supposed to dock with a ship I can't see?"

Nicasia smirked proudly. "You'll see it, don't worry. We're due to cross the perimeter of the light-absorption field in approximately thirty seconds."

Now Eris could make out a slight shimmering against the steady background of crystal-bright stars, a section of space, rapidly becoming larger, in which the stars danced and twinkled, as if seen through a dense atmosphere....

And then they were through the field. Eris' eyes widened in shock at what suddenly blinked into view just ahead. A vast dark metallic mountain seemed to fill all of space before her, a looming colossus of jagged angles and twisted vein-like tubular protuberances extending up and back for what looked like a mile or more. The entire tortured mass was studded with tiny red lights like drops of glowing blood—viewing ports, Eris surmised. It resembled some titanic reptilian robot nightmarishly crouching in the high dark, waiting to devour...what? Insect ships like this one, she thought, as she spied the same hellish light spilling from the gaping maw of the docking bay, open and waiting for its next meal—her.

Scraping together every crumb of courage she had left, Eris steered the ship toward that crimson hellgate and deftly piloted it to a smooth landing inside the belly of the immense star beast.

As the huge jaws of the space doors slammed shut behind her and air began to pump into the docking bay, Eris felt her last small shred of hope wither up and blow away in the dark and fearful wind rising in her soul.

When the enormous bay was fully pressurized, she and her captors descended the saucer's glowing light-ramp into Hell. The crimson illumination bathed everything in blood, and the hot steamy atmosphere struck her like a blow. It was like entering some infernal Turkish bath, and she began to sweat immediately. She noticed several of the ominous co-bracraft parked nearby. Heavy smells of hot oily machinery and strange chemicals and a musky, reptilian odor assaulted her nostrils; for a moment she felt sick. Watch yourself, Queenie, she warned Nicasia silently, I could very easily puke all over your shoes....

And then, looming out of the steam and stench...nightmare! A thing that resembled a cross between an eight-foothigh humanoid snake and a baby tyrannosaur stalked up to them, accompanied by several armed goat-men, bowed to Nicasia and began to speak in an abominable parody of English. It clicked and hissed sibilantly, as if chewing its speech like live food, but managed to make itself understood. Obviously, this was what Nicasia had been in communication with previously—here was Eris' first view of the real enemy of earth: a true native of Algol!

"K'velcome aboard, h'Your Majesssssty," the creature said torturously. "K've h'rejoice in h'your sssafe h'return to usss. K've h'your k'ommand avait."

"Thank you, *Kortrak*," Nicasia responded, nodding regally to the swaying monster. Turning to Eris, she said, almost courteously, "This is *Kortrak* Shess'hess, my Science Officer and commander of this ship in my absence. The term 'kortrak' is an Algolian rank approximating that of captain in your navy. He will be most interested in the machine you've brought us, won't you, *Kortrak*?"

Grotesquely, the creature bowed again. "H'yessss, h'Your Majessssty."

She then discussed a few things with him in their native language, and as they did so, Eris was able to observe the creature more closely. It did indeed resemble a small carnivorous dinosaur, with a scaly snake-like skin of mottled gray and black and a belly of obscenely white plates that

370

glowed in the gory light as though burning from within. It stood more erect than a dinosaur, however, and its powerful strong-thighed legs were close to human. Its arms were also man-like and muscular, with five scaly, black-clawed fingers and an opposable thumb. Its head had the blunt snout of a great snake, but when it spoke she could see a mouthful of dagger-sharp teeth like a tyrannosaur's, plus two long venomous fangs like those of a pit viper. It had the flickering black forked tongue of a snake, but it was the eyes that sent chills deep into Eris' spine. They were Nicasia's eyes, except for the slit pupils, hot, glowing pits of boiling sulfur without the slightest trace of mercy or humanity in them. Behind the creature, a long powerful tail like that of a cat twitched constantly. Its uniform, if such it was, consisted of various pieces of metal armor, bristling with spikes and studs: a helmet-like crest, a chest piece, wristlets and armlets, a skirt-like piece about the loins, and heavy metal boots. Around its tail it wore a band of murderous six-inch steel spikes.

Looking at this monster, it was inconceivable to Eris that Nicasia, as ruthless and evil as she was, could ever have been one of these things, that such a reptilian abomination could have been surgically reduced and altered into the beautiful human body she saw before her. For a moment she almost felt sorry for her adversary....

Then the alien conversation was over, and Eris was dismissed and taken to a cell by the goat-men guards. The Immobilizer bobbed along behind her like a metallic balloon on an invisible string. The cell was small but not uncomfortable, except for the all-pervading heat and humidity. The lighting was more normal in this part of the ship, which was a help, and there was a bunk much larger than human size upon which Eris sank gratefully. She wouldn't have cared if it had been concrete, as she closed her eyes and tried to pull herself back together.

But her thoughts swirled away into exhausted oblivion and she sank into deep, dreamless sleep. She awoke in momentary confusion, forgetting where she was, then all that had happened rushed back into her brain like an avalanche. She groaned, looked at her ringwatch: she had been asleep for six hours. She felt awful—her head and burned back

371

ached and her arm and ankle throbbed dully. She was drenched with sweat and stank of goat. Her hair hung in stringy tangles about her shoulders, but she didn't care. She couldn't recall how long it had been since she had eaten, but her stomach was telling her it was too long.

Looking at the innocuous metal globe floating in the corner of the cell, she said, "Well, Mobe, looks like they're in no hurry for us. That's great, but I wonder what you have to do to get something to eat around here. Most of the some-things I've seen look like they'd rather eat *you*."

She wanted to discard the uncomfortable metallic uni-form she had taken from the goat-man back at Zeinhom, but she felt too vulnerable in her makeshift bedsheet undies, so she settled for unsnapping the smelly garment as far down the front as she could decently. She kept the boots on also, as they seemed to give some support to her injured ankle, al-though they had been made for hoofs and not for human feet.

She went to the small steel grill that served as a window and looked out. She spotted a goat-man guard at the end of a long metal corridor and yelled at him. "Hey, hairball, come over here, will you?"

The creature turned and looked at her quizzically.

"Yeah, *you!*" She beckoned to him with a hand painfully squeezed between the grill. "Come here!"

The goat-man looked undecided for a moment, then clumped down the corridor to Eris' cell. Looking angry, he bleated at her, "Wha-a-a-at?"

"What? *Food*, is what. I need something to eat, get it?" She chomped her jaws together to illustrate. "And some wa-ter."

The goat-man nodded, then turned and went noisily off down the corridor. "I think he got it," she said, returning to the bunk. "I just hope they have some human-type food aboard this tub somewhere. Maybe Nicasia has a private pantry in the galley. Although even if they bring me a tin can or a live hamster, I'll probably eat it...."

In a little while that seemed like a long while, the goat-man returned with a bowl of something that looked like vegetable stew and a container of tepid water. She wolfed down the food, which tasted a bit strange but not bad. Then she drank the water. Afterward she felt much better.

She slept again, and this time was awakened by the sound of her cell door opening. Nicasia entered, flanked by a goat-man with drawn weapon. She was now dressed in a uniform similar to the ones worn by the goat-men, only a glittering gold in color, the rearing cobra insignia on her breast beautifully crafted from rubies and sapphires.

"Enough freeloading, Eris," she said sternly. "It's time for us to have a little talk—about that." She pointed a scarlet fingernail at the floating Immobilizer. "Follow me."

Eris and the globe followed Nicasia down the corridor, the guard bringing up the rear, through a labyrinth of passageways and compartments in which she saw other goatmen and Algolians working at bizarre machines that hummed and hissed and glowed with multicolored lights.

At length they came to a large sterile-looking room filled with strange and sinister instruments; some looked as though they were used for research and experimentation but others looked ominously like torture devices. Illuminated by a cold, harsh light, this was obviously some kind of laboratory. Science Officer Shess'hess and Furca were waiting for them.

"Sit down, Eris," Nicasia said, indicating a metal chair at a long metal table. She sat, and Nicasia sat down opposite her and looked her coldly in the eye.

"Now, what can you tell us about the Immobilizer?"

The snake-creature remained standing, swaying from side to side in eagerness, and Eris could feel his ophidian eyes burning into her like cold lasers. Furca prowled around the room, examining the alien instruments with great interest.

"Well..." Eris began, "the Star Guardians told me that because it's such a devastating weapon, there are certain safeguards against setting it off accidentally. They have to be carefully disengaged before you can activate it."

The Science Officer's eyes glowed brighter with interest. "Sssince it k'annot be touched, thessse sssafeguardsss mussst vocal be, h'yessss?"

373

"Ah, yeah, that's right," Eris agreed, her mind working quickly. "You have to talk to it...a series of code words. Let's see...what was the first one? Oh, yeah...."

She turned and faced the implacable metal sphere, saying the first thing that popped into her mind, a line of alien dialogue from an old science-fiction movie she had seen many years ago: "Klaatu barada nikto!"

Eris was watching the Immobilizer, so she never saw the blow coming. Agony suddenly lanced through her skull and she pitched forward onto the hard metal floor. Shaking her head to clear it of dancing spots of light, she turned in surprise to see Nicasia on her feet, rubbing her fist, her face flushed with fury.

"Don't try any bullshit with *me*, girl!" she shouted. "And don't underestimate me—I spent years studying the customs of your pathetic little planet and I have total recall of everything I studied. *Everything*, Eris...and that includes all the thousands of inane TV shows and films I forced myself to watch to familiarize myself with your culture so thoroughly that I could pass for one of you. I remember every line of dialogue in every one of those stupid films—and I remember the one you just used! From *The Day the Earth Stood Still!*"

Eris got unsteadily to her feet and collapsed into her chair, fighting back pain and nausea. She forced herself to grin at the furious woman. "Well, hell, no wonder you're so mean. I'd be mean too if I'd had to go through all that. But I'll bet you're a killer at trivia parties."

Nicasia fought back her rage, forcing calm upon herself, and leaned across the table. Only her eyes still betrayed her feelings, demonic furnaces of hate that threatened to engulf Eris in citrine fire.

"Listen to me, Eris," she said in a tight, controlled tone. "I don't have any more time for games. I accepted your offer. I let Gabrielle go. I've allowed you to rest and eat and become adjusted to the climate aboard this ship. Now it's time for you to fulfill your part of our bargain. It won't do you any good to try to stall. You'd better tell us what we want to know, and *right now*. I intend to keep my promise to let you go if you do, but if you try to back out...."

She left the rest unsaid, and a chill swept through Eris despite her attempts at bravado and despite the tropical atmosphere which was rapidly sapping her remaining energy. Somehow, she had to get out of this laboratory. Letting her shoulders slump in apparent defeat, she said in a weary voice, "Okay, Nicasia, you win. I'll tell you how to activate this thing."

"That's more like it!" Nicasia exclaimed in triumph. "Now you're being smart." She turned to the Algolian Science Officer. "*Kortrak*, I want you to record what she says."

The reptilian monster bowed and went over to a corner of the lab to look for a recording device. As he did so, Eris said, "Look, Nicasia, I know you expect me to sit here and just rattle off the instructions like a recipe for baking a cake, but I can't do that. I need to get out of here—this place gives me the creeps, and so does having rat-breath and the mystery midget stare at me like I'm some kind of a specimen."

Nicasia's eyes narrowed. "What do you mean?"

"I mean the Star Guardians imprinted the information in my subconscious, with instructions on how to retreive it if and when I needed it. I have to be able to meditate for awhile, concentrate on bringing it up into my conscious mind. Let me go back to my cell where I can do that, and I promise I'll have it for you in a few hours. How about it?"

"I don't know," Nicasia said with a frown. "It makes a certain amount of sense, but you might just be stalling again."

"Oh, come on, Queenie, for God's sake—you've got me here like a rat in a trap. What's a couple more hours now?"

Nicasia turned to the dragon-like Algolian, who had returned with a small recorder of some kind. "What do you think, *Kortrak*? Shall I give her a few hours alone in her cell to bring up the information from her subconscious mind?"

The black forked tongue danced and a mouthful of knives glittered in the cold light of the hot room. Eris could swear the thing was grinning!

"H'yessss, Majesssty. It k'annot matter a ssshort time more. But if ssshe fail to do ssso, I have sssseveral eksssperimentsss I have been vanting to perform upon humanssss...."

"I'll just bet you do, scaly," Eris muttered. As she stood up, her knees felt like vanilla pudding.

"All right, then," Nicasia said, "two hours. No more." Turning to the waiting goat-man guard, she snapped, "Take her back to her cell."

If you don't believe in miracles, you're not a realist these days.

—Anwar as-Sadat

CHAPTER THIRTY-FOUR

THE IMMOBILIZER

ABOARD THE MOTHERSHIP: 21 DECEMBER 2020

Alone at last in her cell, Eris buried her face in her hands and fought desperately to keep from plunging into the black abyss of fear and despair that yawned beneath her. She was really up against it now. She couldn't stall Nicasia any longer. She had only two hours before she would have to confess her deception. Then....

Horror surged through her like a tide of sewage at the thought of being a laboratory animal in the hands of that Algolian nightmare. She could still hear the chilling hiss of his last speech, the way he said "ek-sssperimentssss"....

But there was still one tiny thread of hope. The Star Guardians. She remembered what Yod had told them before they parted: *"If you should need us, think of us intently, visualize us in your mind, and we will contact you."*

Well, she sure as all hell needed them now! More desperately than she could ever have imagined back there in the Ruby Pyramid.

Summoning all her remaining powers of concentration, Eris breathed deeply of the foul, humid air, closing her eyes and focusing her mind intensely to beam a mental message of help through her Mentacom Medallion out across infinity to her far-traveling friends ....

Oh, Star Guardians...it didn't take us long to screw everything up on our own. One of us is dead and Nicasia's got the Immobilizer after all...and me. We need you now...I need you, Yod. Please help me, somehow...if you can....

It seemed as though she called for hours, pouring all her misery and fear out into the universe in a silent plea, holding the image of the Star Guardians vividly in her mind.

And then, suddenly, a familiar voice seemed to fill her consciousness.

"We have heard your call, Eris Campbell. I have come to help you, as I promised."

Eris' eyes snapped open in wild joy. Standing before her was Yod—or rather, his holographic image—but looking as real as the metal walls of her cell. He was wearing the white robes she had seen him in aboard his own ship, and he had reduced his height in order to fit inside this confined space.

"Oh, Yod, thank God you're here! Thank you for coming! I didn't know whether—"

His great violet eyes were luminous with compassion and sadness as he held up a long-fingered hand.

"My time is short, Eris. Tell me what has occurred since we parted, and how you come to be a prisoner aboard this dark ship."

As quickly as she could, Eris told him all that had happened and described the desperate situation she was now in.

"Can you teleport me out of here or something?" she asked hopefully.

"Alas, that I cannot do. As I said previously, we cannot interfere directly with the events of your world. Indeed, we may already have overstepped our bounds in doing what we have done."

Eris' face seemed to come apart; her shoulders slumped. "Oh," she said wearily. "Well, I wouldn't want you guys to get in trouble back home on my account...."

"I'm sorry, Eris. These laws were made by our superiors, beings who do not even occupy physical bodies. They were made to be in accord with the Law of the One, Who granted free will to all Its children. We may assist the beings on various worlds to begin their evolutionary journeys, but

378

only with their permission, and after that, we are forbidden to meddle further in their destinies."

"I understand...."

A smile brightened the Star Guardian's sober countenance then. "However...in your ancient Hebrew language, which came from ours, my name means 'open hand.' I would not be living up to that name if I turned my back on you now, at your time of greatest need, would I?"

New hope began to flow back into Eris' heart at his words. "What do you mean? Can you help me after all?"

"You have taken a grave and noble risk, Eris, to save the life of one dear to you. Can I do less? Yes, I will help you, as I promised."

Eris wanted to shout with joy and clap her hands like a little girl, but she was afraid of attracting the attention of the guard. So she restrained herself and asked, "How?"

"By allowing you to give Nicasia Bane exactly what she wants. I am going to give you several phrases in the language of the Ilu. When the time is right, you must repeat them exactly as I say them to you. These are voice-code phrases which will activate the Immobilizer."

"Well, I'll be darned," Eris exclaimed in surprise. "So Nicasia's pet dragon was right—it *does* obey vocal codes!"

"Yes. Now listen to me carefully, Eris...."

For the next half hour, Eris concentrated all her remaining energy on learning what the Star Guardian taught her. She knew that her life and the lives of billions of people on the planet below depended on what she did next. It was an awesome responsibility. There was still a grave risk to herself, she realized, but now there was at least a slim chance where before there had been none. She was determined to take it.

After she had thanked Yod and he had wished her the blessings of the One and disappeared, she prayed a long time for the strength to do what she had to do.

Nicasia returned precisely at the end of two hours, accompanied by the ubiquitous goat-guard. "Time's up. Are you ready to tell us what we want to know?"

Eris looked into those hot tiger eyes and smiled grimly. "Yes, Nicasia, I am."

Back in the sterile glare of the laboratory, the Immobilizer floating silently behind her, Eris again faced her three adversaries. The Science Officer's metal-spiked tail was twitching with anticipation. Furca was watching her closely this time, his small eyes shining with malice. He was thinking about what he would do with her after she gave them the information and after the Science Officer was through "examining" her....

"Well?" Nicasia snapped, hands on hips. "Let's have it, Eris. No more stalling. Your time has run out."

"Okay, Nicasia. Watch carefully." Eris took a deep breath, squared her shoulders and walked over to the impassive metal globe. Her heart was pounding in her throat with such ferocity that she was sure they could hear it.

For a moment she examined the sphere closely, then she saw what she was looking for. A small red dot on the underside of its surface. As Yod had instructed her, she placed her hand beneath the globe, as close as possible before it began to move away from her. Slowly she raised her hand, and the machine rose also, until it was hovering about seven feet off the floor. Then she stepped under it, the red dot directly over her head.

"What are you doing?" Nicasia snapped impatiently. "Playing basketball with it? Come on!"

Eris smiled. Calm had suddenly descended upon her like a sweet benediction. "Patience, Queenie. This is Phase One. Now as for Phase Two, you—

"Stop!" a harsh, high voice suddenly screeched. Shocked, Eris saw that Furca had jumped up on the table, having obtained a beam weapon from somewhere, which he was now pointing at her with both hands.

"You fools!" he squawked. "Don't you see what she's doing? She's going to activate that thing and kill us all!"

"Don't be stupid, Furca," Nicasia said angrily. "She can't do that without killing herself too. Now put down that gun and get down off that table."

Eris froze. The next moment could spell death. Everything depended on Nicasia's regal pride and unwillingness to believe what the dwarf had somehow guessed. Eris smiled reassuringly.

"That's right, Furca. I'm sure as hell not up for a kamikaze number now, after all I've been through. So—"

"She's lying! I know it!" screamed Furca, ignoring Nicasia's orders. He jerked the trigger and a bolt of emerald death hissed out at Eris.

But she had been watching the dwarf closely: she saw his small knuckles whiten as he strained to press the trigger, and her PSI-QUARK training saved her once again. Lightning reflexes threw her to the floor a split second before the beam sizzled over her head. Then she took another deep breath and, loudly and distinctly, spoke a series of words in a language older than earth:

"Khon-tu-sar! Zu salah xet cha'aru ab lomech zo naharah!"

The furious dwarf was aiming for another shot. This had better work, Eris told herself.

A bolt of azure lightning suddenly erupted from the bottom of the Immobilizer and struck Eris, bathing her in a crackling aura of blue sparks and writhing electricities. She felt a tingling throughout her body as she slowly got to her feet in wonder. Nicasia, Furca and Shess'hess were staring at her in shocked disbelief. She saw them now through a shimmering curtain of blue force—an energy vortex that now completely surrounded her in an ovoid cocoon of light.

The dwarf danced on the table in a frenzy of fear and hate, screaming incoherently now. He fired again, but this time the green beam struck the energy cocoon and was absorbed harmlessly in a spray of blue and green sparks.

"Stop him!" Nicasia shrieked at the Science Officer, who was stunned by the rapid sequence of events. "If he kills her, we'll never be able to use the machine!"

The reptilian monster turned and with a quick swat of one arm sent Furca flying off the table and skidding across the metal floor like a tenpin. But somehow he managed to hold onto his weapon. He scrambled to his feet, still gibbering insanely, and again aimed at Eris inside the blue energy egg. He got off one more futile shot before Shess'hess, moving with surprising speed, reached him and slammed his

381

metal-spiked tail into him with crushing force. There was a sickening crunch of bone and a bright spray of blood as the little man hurtled through the air and smashed with tremendous force against the laboratory wall. He hit the floor with a sodden thump, leaving a crimson smear on the wall, and did not move.

Nicasia was furious. "Goddammit, I didn't mean for you to kill him! Have you all gone insane? What's she done with that thing? You're the scientist here—what's that blue energy around her?"

Without a backward glance at the dead dwarf, the Algolian stalked over to Eris and reached out a claw to touch the blue vortex. A small spark jumped to his claw, but he felt nothing. Then he tried to put his hand through it, but the energy was as solid as steel. Puzzled, he swung his scaly fist hard against it, with no result.

Turning back to Nicasia, he said, "Sssseemsss to be sssome k'ind of protective forssse field."

Nicasia's eyes widened in alarm. "Protective force field? To protect her from what? From us? From...."

Eris couldn't restrain a broad grin as Nicasia suddenly got it. An unaccustomed look of fear twisted her beautiful features into a harpy mask.

"*From the effects of the Immobilizer!* Of course...that's the only way it can be safely activated! Furca was right! Stop her, you fool! Do something!"

But for the first time in his life, neither his prowess as a scientist or as a warrior could help Science Officer Shess'hess of the Royal Algolian Spacefleet. He realized then what was going to happen when he saw Eris begin to speak.

Alien syllables again poured out of her throat, spoken exactly as Yod had taught them to her: "*Khon-tu-sar! Zu salah n'gharu seb nakhru au zokh dalethis shim hetru....*"

Nicasia stood rooted in horror as Eris continued to recite the code words. The Algolian Queen wanted to run, to scream. Powerless for the first time in her long, long life, she could not accept a situation she could not control. She snatched a weapon from the cowering goat-man guard and fired—not at Eris, safe in her blue cocoon—but at the Immobilizer itself. But the beam merely glanced harmlessly off the invisible field around the machine and burned a round hole in the ceiling.

Then, as if in retaliation for Nicasia's shot, but actually in response to Eris' completion of its vocal activation code, the Immobilizer began to glow. For the first time since its centuries-long interment deep beneath the earth, it lost its dull metallic sheen and began to gleam with a frigid white light. Brighter and brighter it shone, until they could no longer look directly at it. It resembled a tiny cold sun silently bathing the laboratory in white fire.

"Okay, Queenie," Eris exclaimed, "you wanted it—you got it! I kept my part of the bargain too! Welcome to Phase Three!"

Then she fell silent as she began to observe the effects of the awesome power she had unleashed. The steamy enervating heat that had permeated the ship was suddenly gone; the temperature was dropping rapidly. In merely seconds, it had become drastically colder in the laboratory. Eris knew that the same phenomenon was occurring throughout Kalon 22 and would eventually extend out into space for a hundred-mile radius. Now she understood what Yod had meant when he explained to her the effects of the Immobilizer's terrible influence. The machine emitted radiation that gradually nullified the movement of all matter at the molecular and atomic levels. And as that normally constant motion slowed down to total immobility, all heat would be lost, until the affected area was reduced to the lowest possible temperature: absolute zero! Scientists had come very close to creating this ultimate frigidity, but no one on earth had ever experienced the *total* lack of molecular motion—until now! And certainly not over a wide area!

Now frost was forming on the walls of the lab and on the instruments. Shess'hess, because of his cold reptilian blood, was affected rapidly. He staggered drunkenly to the door, but collapsed in a torpid heap before he could reach it. Eris watched in fascination as silver rime began to form on his dark scales.

"Turn it off, Eris!" screamed Nicasia, her breath puffing out in a cloud of vapor.

383

Eris shrugged. "Sorry, Queenie, I can't. This gadget doesn't know 'off.' I'm afraid you and your goats and snakes are in for a rough winter."

This was true: Yod had told her that the machine would operate continuously for a period of ten hours, then shut itself off automatically. There was no way to halt its effect before then. By that time Kalon 22 would be an orbiting iceberg.

Nicasia's face was aflame with rage and terror as she hurled a curse at Eris, then turned and ran from the room into the clouds of icy vapor that were already forming in the air.

Eris looked up at the Immobilizer, silently blazing above her. The blue energy cocoon protected her from the molecular slowdown, but she could feel some of the outside cold seeping through to her. Eventually it would become to cold for her to survive here, so what now? She had to find some way to get off this ship before it disintegrated around her and left her floating in space.

She took a tentative step forward; the energy shield went with her. Good—apparently she could move away from the Immobilizer now without losing its protection. And now that the machine had been activated, it no longer followed her around.

Nicasia's goat-men had long since fled in terror from the frigid room, so Eris headed unchallenged down the corridor leading from the laboratory, trying to recall the way they had brought her from the docking bay to her cell and then here. As she ran, she heard alarm systems clanging and hooting throughout the ship. Dozens of terrified goat-men were running through the rapidly freezing ship, trying to fight off the numbing life-sapping cold that came from *within* them, without the slightest knowledge of what was happening. In their panic, none of them paid her the slightest attention. She also saw quite a number of Algolians, the first to feel the effects of the terrible cold, sprawled about the corridors.

She stopped to pick up a weapon from one of them and was surprised that she was able to do so. Apparently she could bring objects into the energy cocoon, but nothing from without could touch her! Neat arrangement, she thought. But the weapon's metal handle was so cold she couldn't hold it;

384

it burned like fire, so she wrapped a piece of cloth around it and continued on her way.

Eventually she found the area she was seeking. By now the air was so thick with vapor she could hardly see her way, but she could make out the control room for the docking bay.

A lone goat-man was still at his post, shivering uncontrollably and stamping his hoofs to keep warm as all warmth rapidly fled from his body. Ice had formed on most of the controls in the room, and Eris could only hope that the sub-zero temperature hadn't affected them yet.

A large viewscreen was still working and her heart leaped into her throat as she saw the Star Guardian spaceship parked where she had left it; only now it was covered with a white coat of ice.

The operator's slit-pupiled eyes bulged in surprise at the sudden appearance of a human female enclosed in a shimmering oval of blue energy and threatening him with a weapon.

"Open the air-lock, horn-head," she ordered. "Now!"

The creature shook his head groggily. Maybe he doesn't understand me, Eris thought. Now snow was starting to fall—the very atmosphere in the ship was beginning to freeze! Eris could hear ominous creaks and groans from the structure of the ship itself; she knew that at absolute zero, the strongest metal would be as brittle as glass. She had no time to lose!

Impatiently she jabbed the weapon at the goat-man, pointing to the large inner doors. "Open!"

But the creature's eyes suddenly glazed over and he crumpled to the floor in a shuddering heap.

"Oh, great!" Eris exclaimed in dismay. She looked at the complex control panel before her. All labels were in the Algolian language. "Guess I'll just have to do it myself."

She began to push buttons and throw switches, often pausing to chip ice from them first, hoping to hit the one that would open the inner air-lock doors. If she couldn't gain access to the docking bay, she would be trapped on board the rapidly dying ship with all the others.

Nothing was working. Her hands were becoming numb now; it couldn't be long till frostbite set in. Either the cold had already jammed the controls, or she just couldn't find the right switch—either way, she had only minutes left.

A violent tremor shuddered through the ship. Snow was swirling around her now like a small blizzard. She could see snow falling inside the docking bay also, so she knew the area was pressurized. Desperate now, she ran over to the inner doors and blasted them with the beam weapon, pouring sizzling bolts of emerald energy into them until she had made a hole large enough to crawl through.

Hoping the Immobilizer would obey her mental command, she released it and quickly ran on feet she could no longer feel across the icy floor toward the saucership. Snow surged around her as she ran, blinding her, but she knew where the ship was located from looking at the viewscreen. Then the rounded mass loomed out of the whiteness, and she was there. She had a momentary fear that the cold might have affected the hatch, but as she came closer, it opened and the glowing light-ramp extended itself to her like a welcoming hand.

Inside, she spent a few moments rubbing sensation into her nerveless fingers; then she ran to the control console and quickly energized the electromagnetic drive units.

"Hot damn! I made it!" she exclaimed with a grin, as the ship immediately purred into life. "Glad you guys didn't forget to put anti-freeze in the radiator."

She noticed that the blue energy cocoon was gone now; either something in the ship nullified it, or it dissipated when she reached a certain distance from the Immobilizer. That was bad, because she might be subject to the machine's effects now, although the saucer seemed to be unaffected. The temperature inside was cold, but not the deadly frigidity of outside.

"Haven't you forgotten something?" a hatefully familiar voice suddenly purred over the still-open communicator.

Eris' heart stopped for a second—it felt like a stone in her breast. Nicasia! Still alive? But how? All the atmosphere was solidified by now—there was nothing left to breathe!

Eris flicked on the comscreen, and those familiar golden hellfires blazed out at her—from inside a pressurized space-suit!

386

"Very clever, Queenie," Eris said with a grin. "Snagged yourself a spacesuit while your crew was busy running around turning into snowcones. Well, I wish I could offer you a ride, but—"

"You're not going anywhere, Eris," hissed Nicasia. "I'm in the control room and I've locked the space doors. Your ship's beam can't override the lock. That ship is unarmed, so you can't blast your way out. Nice try, my dear, but I'm afraid you're going to have to stay right here and die with the rest of us. This suit is lined with an Algolian metal that provides protection against any kind of radiation, so the Immobilizer can't harm me. But of course I realize that my oxygen supply is limited; still, knowing that you're trapped here with me will make my death a lot easier to take."

Eris laughed. "Is that so? Well, I'm sorry to spoil your gloat, Queenie, but I've got one more little surprise for you. This baby comes equipped with a custom extra like you wouldn't believe. If you thought my last trick was good, watch this!"

Eris pressed the green panel on the console and the violet ray sprang up to her forehead. Closing her eyes, she visualized a section of empty space about a hundred and fifty miles from the doomed mothership. Black space and diamond-bright stars formed before her. Then, with one last grin at Nicasia's puzzled, angry face, she waved and said, "So long, Nicasia. Have an ice day."

Then she pressed the red panel and the gleaming ice-covered spaceship instantly vanished in a furious whirl and gleam of snow.

I have had a most rare vision. I have had a dream, past the wit of man to say what dream it was.
—William Shakespeare, *A MIDSUMMER-NIGHT'S DREAM, Act IV, Scene 1*

CHAPTER THIRTY-FIVE

DOWN FROM THE STARS

CAIRO: 20-21 DECEMBER 2020

They had stood there a long time, each wrapped in his separate silent thoughts, and watched the dark house burn. Eventually, when they heard sirens, they realized they had better not be caught there by the authorities, so they picked up the body of their fallen comrade and hurried to the rear of the mansion, where Nicasia kept several limousines for her personal use. No one tried to stop them as they loaded Raymond's body into a large black Rolls Royce and drove silently away into the night.

Back at the hotel, they patched up Chris' wounds as best they could, rigging up an improvised splint and sling for his arm. Avram wanted him to go to a hospital and have it set correctly, but Chris refused. He kept pacing the floor like a caged tiger, going over to the window every few minutes and staring up at the black sky. Only when dawn came did he finally sink, exhausted, into bed and sleep.

Nobody felt like eating, but they forced themselves to have some food sent up. André even ordered a bottle of wine for himself and Gaby, since no one else was interested, but it tasted flat and sour to them, despite their joy in being reunited at last. Gaby could not forget what Eris had done for her....

388

Suddenly there was a scratching at the door. Puzzled by the odd sound, Avram went to the door and opened it cautiously. A golden blur shot into the room, accompanied by a joyous yowl of greeting.

"Marielle!" shrieked Gaby, going over and grabbing the slightly scorched bundle of fur and hugging her tightly. Marielle's green diode eyes sparked her pleasure and her electronic purr resonated loudly in the hotel room. Despite the loss of her paw and a few patches of singed hair, the robot feline seemed none the worse for her experiences.

"We're so glad you found us!" Gaby told her happily. "We thought you were another casualty. When you didn't come out of the house...."

"Ray must have included a homing device in her design," said Avram. "Now we have the records of this whole adventure safe and sound. I think the boys back at PSI-QUARK will be able to fix you up with a new paw, old girl."

"Oh, yes, she'll be a wonderful memory of Ray for us," said Gaby sadly. "We'll adopt her, won't we, André?"

The Frenchman smiled. "Of course, *cherie*."

Gaby then told them how Marielle had saved her from Kathy Bane. "She was a real hero! But then she ran off and I couldn't find her."

Avram looked at his watch. "It's six-fifteen. I think the rest of us had better grab some sleep and then we've got some business to take care of. We've got to make arrangements to have Ray's body shipped back to Washington today."

"Yes," agreed André, "and we have the equally sad task of notifying the President of what's happened here. Which of us wants to do that? The one who contacted him was always...."

He trailed off, not even wanting to think about what Eris might be going through. They all wondered if they would ever see her again, but none of them wanted to talk about it.

"I'll do it." Chris stood groggily in the doorway to the bedroom.

"How do you feel?" asked Avram.

"Better—physically. As for the rest...don't ask. I had nightmares the whole time I was asleep. Something about

389

dragons and a thick fog and people running...I don't know...crazy stuff."

Suddenly the sound of a commotion outside the hotel roused the group from their feelings of despondency.

"What the hell's going on out there?" said Avram, going over to the balcony, which overlooked the greenery of Ezbekiya Gardens. What he saw made him stop dead in his tracks. Then a huge grin split his face and he laughed like a maniac.

"What is it?" Chris cried. He and the others hurried to join Avram on the balcony, where they too registered expressions of joy and delight.

Below, in the lush verdure of the garden, stood a bedraggled Eris, hands on hips, still dressed in the borrowed goat-man uniform. Behind her the great silver bulk of the saucership gleamed in the morning light, hovering about eight feet above the carefully manicured lawn. A great crowd of irate and awestruck citizens had gathered to witness this bizarre landing, which had inadvertently taken out several large trees. Eris' coordination had understandably not been at its peak this morning. A huge snarly traffic jam was backing up blaring cars, trucks and buses for blocks.

When she saw her friends peering down at her from the hotel balcony, Eris cupped her hands to her mouth and yelled, "Hey, you bums! You better come down here and rescue me before I get lynched! Or at least one helluva parking ticket!"

Later, after a luxurious hot shower that was better than any shower she had ever had before, after a large, satisfying meal and a hefty slug of André's wine, Eris told her friends all that had happened to her.

"My God, honey," Chris said admiringly, his good arm tightly around her shoulders. "You're incredible. You outwitted the old viper after all. Do you really think she's dead?"

"She must be, Chris. The last thing I saw before I headed back to earth was that ice-covered Algolian mothership cracking apart: great fissures in the hull spewing clouds of snow out into space. God, what a sight! I had to make sure

390

I was far enough away, but I could see it all through the magnification on my viewscreen. I don't see how she could have survived that. She didn't know how to pilot those co-braships, even if she could have reached one in time."

Avram nodded solemnly. "She's gone, and I don't think Algol will try us again, after losing their Queen...but I can't help regretting the loss of that damned machine."

"What'll happen to it, Av?" asked Gaby.

"It'll stay inside that frozen tomb until the orbit decays and the whole mass falls to earth. Most of it will burn up completely when it hits the atmosphere."

"Do you think the Immobilizer will burn up with it?" asked André.

"I don't know," Avram replied thoughtfully. "I really don't...but I wish I did."

"Well, that gadget is better off ashes, if you ask me, said Eris. "It did what it was supposed to do...boy, did it ever!" She shivered at the memory, even in the warmth of Chris's embrace.

Curled up at her feet, Marielle purred contentedly.

I had a dream, which was
not all a dream.
　　　　　—Lord Byron, DARKNESS

EPILOGUE

GIZA PLATEAU: CHRISTMAS DAY 2020

Eris stood again before the colossal stone Guardian of the desert. The fierce noonday sun once more hurled its white fire down upon her, as it had that distant day before the cataclysm that had begun the whole mad adventure. It seemed centuries ago that the Sphinx had spoken in her mind, silently and awesomely, to warn her....

Even now, the whole thing seemed a dream, an impossible black nightmare from which she had at last thankfully awakened. And yet, yesterday she had again begun to feel the nagging summons, that familiar psychic tickle deep inside her mind, the call she had felt before. Did the Sphinx wish to speak to her again? She knew she could not leave Egypt without making an attempt to find out.

Closing her eyes, Eris began to concentrate, focusing her senses inward, probing deep into her mind, reaching for contact with whoever, *whatever*, might be calling to her....

After long anxious moments of silence, the familiar distant whispering began, a hollow, inhuman voice centuries removed, yet coming rapidly closer. Although weaker than before, the stony sibilances and harsh gutturals of the ancient Egyptians once again filled Eris' mind, and once again she understood them.

Hail, Daughter of Time!

392

There was a triumphant note in the ageless greeting this time, where before Eris could discern only feelings of alarm and distress.

Well hast thou done, and thy companions with thee, against the evil that threatened from the star that blinks. Vanquished thou hast the Daughter of Set and her minions, and no further danger from those who sent her do I foresee.

Eris felt a new note enter the ancient voice now.

Thanks to thee and thy companions in Light, my task is finished. The treasures and records I was sent to guard against the day when thy people miqht be ready for their revelation now art unearthed. The Pact consumated is. My spirit, willingly confined to stone by the star gods ere ancient Khem was, may now quit this crumbling shell and be free once more. Even now, thou canst see how this poor body of stone is daily devoured by scouring winds and by waters from below. Soon will it be gone, no more than the sand that hath so often covered it.

The Sphinx's hollow voice paused. Eris, saddened by its words, silently asked,

Do you mean that your task all these centuries was to guard the Ruby Pyramid and its contents, and now that we've rediscovered them, your...life is over? Are you dying?

She knew that what the Sphinx said about itself was true: because of the Aswan Dam, underground crystallized sea water was steadily eating away the stone of the great head and body like a cancer, as it had been for decades now. Great chunks of the flanks and chin were already gone, and on a windy day you could hear small bits of stone like potato chips flying off with a terrible crackling, hissing sound...the sound of the dying of the oldest monument in the world.

But there was an overtone of amusement in the Sphinx's mental reply:

Dying? Knowest thee not there is no death? Only transformation...movement onward...freedom. From this murky plane go I now to other tasks. Even as thee and thine, my spirit now outgroweth this stony shell, the chrysalis openeth, and I fly to new horizons. Again may I be nameless and unfettered and free to roam the stars. No longer is needed the Guardian.

Scalding tears seared her tightly closed lids as Eris understood. The Sphinx had served its long commitment faithfully as Keeper of the Secrets and now, its task done, its reward was not death but new life...elsewhere, beyond the illusory boundaries of time and space. The world would never know the difference, would not feel that the essence of its mystery had departed from the familiar stone carcass...but she would know. Now the Sphinx would become just another ancient monument, eroded by wind and water until it finally crumbled away forever. But joy mixed with the sadness in Eris' heart—joy for the release of its spirit, sadness for the emptiness of its body. She would feel that emptiness...she would know.

Now draws nigh the time for me to bid thee farewell, my daughter. The great voice, eager now, broke into Eris' thoughts. *I thank thee again for thy service to me and to thy people. Well do I wish thee in the struggles that lie before thee. Now do I grant thee that sight which no mortal eye hath ever seen: thou shalt see me rise and depart this shell and go to the horizons of the sun as riseth the Phoenix from the flame. Farewell, Daughter of the Ages—I salute thee!*

A great humming began in Eris' head then, as if enormous reservoirs of power were being opened. Her skin began to itch and tingle. She opened her eyes in alarm...this was no longer an inward, psychic experience; something was happening physically, here, now. Awestruck, she watched as great snapping, writhing serpents of electricity began to arc from the head of the Sphinx to its paws and to the sand and stones nearby, rippling down its back in blue-white ropes of raw power. The entire monument began to glow from within, as if a strong white light were growing steadily brighter inside the stone. Now a nimbus of white sparks danced around the body from paws to flanks.

Eris moved back a few yards, although she instinctively knew she was in no real danger. The humming and crackling grew more intense, as if a great dynamo were reaching peak capacity. The acrid bite of ozone seared the hot air. The Sphinx was glowing white hot now, vicious lightnings snapping all around it. Eris was startled by a slight shock to her hand as her digital ringwatch and wrist computer suddenly exploded with loud pops and tiny flashes of blue sparks.

Then a blinding explosion of pure white light erupted out of the Sphinx with a hissing, rumbling roar, hurling gitantic chunks of stone high into the air. The back of the monument seemed to open up and spew out an enormous ball of roiling blue-white fire which rapidly spread out and began to form itself into...what?

Eris gasped in wonder, for through the stars and sparkles that danced before her dazzled eyes, she could see the canescent glow spreading and spreading across the cobalt sky, forming...great *wings*, a roughly avian figure of great power and splendor. It towered hundreds of feet into the air now, looming over its disintegrating body like some incredible jinn freed from a bottle, changing like a cloud, now vaguely human, now almost angelic in appearance, then once more a huge bird, and finally a great white lion rampant against the heavens.

A sense of great peace and joy seemed to radiate from the awesome figure: Eris could feel it pouring like sweet water over her, over the desert and all the land around....

Then, suddenly, like a light winking out, it was gone, and a thunderous rumble that ended in a loud *crack!* rolled away across the desert as air rushed in to fill the void that had been occupied by...something else.

Stunned and dazzled, Eris shook her head to clear it. Her eyes were watering and there was a high thin ringing in her ears. Her skin still tingled. As she brushed stone dust from her blouse, she looked around. Had others seen this too? she wondered, or was this just her own private *son et lumière* show?

She could see no one. As she turned back to what had been the Sphinx, her breath stuck in her throat like a piece of meat. The great stone sentinel that had stood so faithfully for so many centuries was now reduced to rubble. A huge cloud of ochre dust towered above it like a triumphant banner. Its gigantic battered head had split into two sections and now rested between its ruined paws. One stone eye peered blankly at the sun, the other gazed toward Cairo.

As Eris turned away from the jumble of stone that littered the sands, she smiled wryly as she imagined relating the incident to the Minister of Antiquities. The poor man would probably suffer a coronary when he discovered that one of Egypt's prized tourist attractions was now only a pile of gravel. How would he explain that to his people and to a shocked world? Frankly, she had no idea.

Brushing tears of happiness and sorrow from her eyes, Eris turned toward Cairo, deeply grateful for the honor of being allowed to witness the awesome metamorphosis of the Guardian of the Desert. It was a thing that would be with her always.

She looked back once more, first at the crumbled remnants of a legend, then into the bright sky.

Godspeed, she whispered.